Abigail Bosanko has made a living in various ways, not all of them lazy. Before taking up writing, her favourite job was whisky-tasting tutor for the Scotch Malt Whisky Society, where she still occasionally works. She lives with her husband in Edinburgh. Her second novel, *A Nice Girl Like Me*, is also published by Time Warner Paperbacks. For more information about the author visit www.abigailbosanko.co.uk

Praise for *Lazy Ways to Make a Living*

'Exquisitely realised middle-class fantasy which is just grounded in enough reality to keep it readable . . . *Lazy Ways to Make a Living* is a rare treat' *Sunday Times*

'A sheer, unalloyed delight' *Scotland on Sunday*

'A quirky read' *U Magazine*

Also by the same author

A Nice Girl Like Me

Lazy Ways to Make a Living

Abigail Bosanko

timewarner
paperbacks

To Peter

Keep this

A *Time Warner* Paperback

First published in Great Britain as a paperback original by
Time Warner Paperbacks in 2002

The author gratefully acknowledges permission to quote from the following:
'The Cat That Walked by Himself' and 'If' by Rudyard Kipling by kind permission of A. P.
Watt Ltd on behalf of The National Trust for Places of Historical Interest or Natural Beauty.
The Dictionary of Subjects and Symbols in Art by James Hall by kind permission of John Murray
(Publishers) Ltd. Extracts from *The Right Way to Play Chess* by D. B. Pritchard reproduced by
kind permission of Elliot Right Way Books. Lyrics from 'Greetings To The New Brunette'
by Billy Bragg used by kind permission of BMG Publishing, © Billy Bragg 1986.

A CIP catalogue record for this book
is available from the British Library.

ISBN 0 7515 3702 0

Typeset in Bembo by M Rules
Printed and bound in Great Britain
by Bookmarque Ltd, Croydon, Surrey

Time Warner Paperbacks
An imprint of
Time Warner Book Group UK
Brettenham House
Lancaster Place
London WC2E 7EN

www.twbg.co.uk

Acknowledgements

My husband, Peter, for his patience, inspiration, friendship and support and for the annoying way he would come into my room, hang about behind my chair, and say, 'Have you written anything funny yet?' And for telling me to rewrite the first draft of 'The Opening' because it was blindingly obvious that the hero couldn't possibly be gay.

My parents for presenting me with a new computer when the old one packed up at Chapter 6 and for being impressively unfazed when I told them the second draft of 'The Opening' had been rejected for being too erotic.

My friend Steve Jones for being on-call chess advisor and for the loan of his books and chess computer and for not laughing (too much) at all my chess questions.

My friend Brenda Hudson for her kindness, encouragement, good humour and hugely enjoyable company.

My friend Annabel Meikle, to whom I confided my painful secret that my novel had been rejected on the grounds of eroticism and political incorrectness. Thrilled for me, Annabel told everyone about it. One of the people she told was Fiona McCay, who then told her sister, Roz Kidd, who told the literary agent Eugenie Furniss, who eventually picked the third draft of my novel off her green velvet Soho agent's sofa and phoned me up to tell me she loved it. Eugenie shone the cool white light of her opinion on my beginner's novel and made my luck work.

My editors at Time Warner Books: Tara Lawrence, for the magic bit of turning my late-night scribblings into a published book, and Joanne Coen, who freed the manuscript from my delusions of accuracy and impressed me no end with her good advice. And to my designer, Debbie Clement, for the cover, which I love.

Indisputably, the best two-player game in the world

The Right Way to Play Chess by D. B. Pritchard

Have you ever seen *The Thomas Crown Affair*? Faye Dunaway (sugar pink lips, fabulous nails, playing Black) utterly destroys Steve McQueen (blue eyes, playing White). It's a dazzling performance. A spectacularly effective annihilation of a man's defences. Steve just falls apart. It's a wonderful moment when she says, 'Check.' He's lost and he knows it; he goes to her side of the board, lifts her to her feet and says, 'Let's play something else.' And then they kiss.

I remember that kiss best of all, sitting in the dark in the Odeon. It was a kiss that lasted as long as the toffee I sucked all the way through it. It was a kiss as spinning as my adolescent dreams. That film made me get out the chess set I'd abandoned three years earlier. It made me search throughout East Anglia for a blue-eyed boy suffering from wealth-ennui. I never found one, but my chess and my nails were outstanding for a thirteen-year-old.

Preparing for
the Game

It is surprising that many who have a real desire to learn chess give up the study of the game in the face of disappointing experiences . . . Our task, therefore, is clear. We must seek to remove the difficulties, and to convince the reader that there is such a thing as 'chess made easy'

The Right Way to Play Chess by D. B. Pritchard

Chapter I

There are some areas in life where one can, without shame, simply own up to not having the knack – mental arithmetic, for example, or gardening. 'Can't add up to save my life.' 'Wouldn't know a pelargonium if it hit me in the face.' But one may not say: 'Sex? Never got the hang of it!'

Given the choice between a reputation for financial or sexual incompetence, most people would rather live with an overdraft. As far as I was concerned, Profligacy and Celibacy followed me around, chastely, hand in hand – although I sometimes wondered if the two might have a deeper, guiltier connection . . .

Draped across the sofa, my sister Helen, a gifted geneticist, shared with me her discoveries on human sexual fulfilment. 'It's down to compatibility,' she declared, crossing her long, tanned legs. 'Sexual compatibility is a happy coincidence. It's serendipity. It's meeting the person who turns you on and realising the feeling is mutual.'

Simple as that.

But then she reckoned she was good at it herself, got the hang of it straightaway (a very positive first-time experience on the Côte d'Azur).

'A happy coincidence?' I wept, exhausted by twelve hours on the overnight bus. 'I thought it was all supposed to be about give and take!'

Serendipity and reciprocity.

My ex-boyfriend had had a 'my turn, your turn' approach. He had been very assiduous about it and yet during our parting row he had confessed that I did nothing for him. He certainly never did anything for me. That, too, is reciprocity. He used to say 'I'm coming' and say it with all the passion of a man summoned to collect his dry-cleaning. It was always a relief to get him off my chest, like owning up to guilt. When it was my turn, I used to stare at the ceiling feeling sorry for myself, then curl up in the recovery position for a silent cry.

'Now, Rose,' said my other sister, glancing up from her work. 'You mustn't let one bad experience put you off.' Catherine smoothed her sleek, dark hair and made a brief note in the margin of her company's cash flow forecast. I knew that tomorrow, Paul in Finance would be awestruck by the ingenuity of his employer's accounting adjustment.

'It's not just one, Catherine. It's everyone I've ever slept with.'

'How many's that?' asked Helen, quite interested.

'My complete romantic history.'

'How many?'

'Pointless asking,' said Catherine. 'She can't add up to save her life. She can't count past three, can you, Rose?'

'How many?'

'Three.'

Catherine turned a few more pages, speed-skimming. I ignored her. 'All three of them met by chance at a special vodka promotion.' I shut my eyes and sank back on the sofa next to Helen. 'They discussed my sexual ineptitude.'

'No!'

'Puerile slander,' said Catherine, briskly.

'It's not slander if it's true,' I choked. 'Is it, Helen?' Helen's big blue eyes opened wide and her long lashes radiated surprise.

'And they laughed about me so much, they thought their reminiscences deserved a wider audience. Oh Helen!' I cried. 'They wrote this horrible little sketch about me and they did it on the stage!'

'They didn't!'

'They did!' I cried. 'At the end of term party. Oh God! Oh yes, they did. They didn't know I was there. I wasn't supposed to be there. I'd told everyone I couldn't go because I had to give a lecture.'

'What on?' asked Catherine.

'"The Dynamism of the Diphthong in 'Phwoar!'" It's one of the new words in the Oxford English Dictionary, defined as "appreciation of the opposite sex by the inarticulate".'

'I see.'

'Forget about that,' said Helen, impatiently. 'What about the sketch?'

'I got there late. I didn't realise it was me the audience was laughing at. For a while, I was laughing too. Then somebody shouted: "There she is!" and I turned round to see where she was and one of my students asked if I'd directed it and then someone on the stage shouted that I'd only inspired it. I was a muse.'

'What did you do?'

'I felt sick. People I see every day in the department. My own students!'

Helen leaned closer, all sympathy and curiosity. 'What did they say made you inept?'

'I don't want to talk about it any more.'

'It's always better to talk about it.'

I hesitated, fiddling nervously with my beads, twisting them round and round my fingers. 'Leave that alone,' she said. 'Now, what did they say?'

I decided to tell her.

'They said research had proved I was frigid, but wasn't it hilarious how I could be insatiably mad for it at times? They said I was boring, yet wasn't it weird how alarming I could be with those funny things I suggested? They said are we sure she's normal? And they said isn't it bizarre the way she laughs out loud when she should be moaning in ecstasy?'

'Laughter is spontaneous,' said Catherine.

Like revulsion, I thought, miserably.

'What they did was in poor taste,' she went on. 'It must have been deeply embarrassing for you, but it was only a joke.'

'Next day, everyone was saying it was Art!'

'They'd just had a lot to drink.'

'In vodka veritas. The truth is: *I do it wrong.*'

'But Rose,' said Helen, confused, 'what about that subscription to *Cosmopolitan* I bought you?'

'It expired.'

It had been an angry expiry. I had fled from the party and run up the seventy-two steps to my little study at White Tower College. There, I had written a letter of complaint to the editor of *Cosmopolitan*:

> . . . *the trouble is, dear* Cosmo, *my sexual credibility has been shattered and I believe you're partly to blame. You have decreased my inhibitions and raised my expectations. Are you insured against this sort of thing? In my romantic relationships I have hitherto used both my common sense and my imagination, but I think it should be stated in a future issue that if you do whatever you like in bed, you run the risk that no one will know what to do with you. I feel I have no option now but to take control of my sense of abandon. Please refund my remaining subscription; I intend to take the* Literary Review.
> *Yours sincerely*
> *Rose Budleigh Ph.D.*

Helen was thinking. You would never have known it to look at her. She wriggled in her seat, tossed her blonde curls, pouted and said, 'I'm dying to know, Rose, who were the boyfriends?'

'There was Graham—'

'But Graham is gay!'

'He only decided that at the end of our relationship.'

'That's a difficult one for you,' said Catherine, 'but you must conduct yourself with poise and dignity.'

'I don't have your poise.'

Catherine was so poised she could wear a linen trouser suit without it creasing (she was doing it now). 'Graham's input on your supposed ineptitude should be regarded as irrelevant.' She sipped from her teacup neatly, leaving no trace of lipstick round the rim. 'Discount him.'

'But I can't discount Mark.'

'The one you broke up with last week?'

'Yes.'

'Isn't he the one who said you were kinky?'

'Yes,' I cringed.

'Football-mad Mark?'

'Yes. He's a real man.'

'Season-ticket Mark?'

'Yes. Slept with it under his pillow.'

'Mark who used to shout out all the answers to *A Question of Sport*?'

'Yes. And he got them all right, too. Every single one. Amazing memory!'

She eyed me, coolly. 'He's a total wanker, Rose.'

I caught my breath, shocked.

'Who else?' asked Helen.

'I bet I know who else,' said Catherine, replacing her cup soundlessly in the saucer. 'Dimitri from the Chess Club.'

I nodded, guiltily.

Helen was exasperated. 'But he looks just like a little pink pig!'

'You've met?'

'What on earth made you go out with him?'

'He has this fatal way with compromising pawn structures – just aroused my curiosity.'

'You're hopeless, Rose.'

'I always won!'

'I wish you'd give up the chess. It's such a liability.'

'I can't help it. It's just the way I am.'

'Why didn't you join the Backgammon Bacchanalian Society or something like that? Bound to be lots of nice people there.'

'I thought he was sweet.'

'Sweet?' said Helen, disgusted. 'You don't want sweetness! You want strength, tenderness and firm, masculine beauty. You want bravery and passion. You want intelligence, charm, wit and—'

'That'll do, honestly.'

'—and you want sensuality.'

'Do I?'

'Oh, yes!'

Helen believed in the quest for perfection. She worked in the field of genetic engineering – literally in the field since her specialism was open-air experimentation at top-secret locations. She was quite earthy, Helen. She liked to be at one with Nature – modified.

'You must persevere on the sensuality,' she went on. 'Take that as your starting point. You've just been unlucky. Your only problem is that you choose badly and you're very consistent about it. It's as if you're programmed to pick unsuitable partners.'

'Never mind, Rose,' said Catherine. 'Why don't you try the Russian edition of *Cosmopolitan*? Similar articles but in lovely Cyrillic script. Chess puzzles too. That's more you, isn't it?' She smiled, knowingly.

I had, in the past, confessed things to Catherine – confessions I had later regretted. Out of the corner of my eye I could see that despite her poise she was trying not to giggle.

I fidgeted with my necklace; warm amber beads, all the little mysteries trapped inside, slipping through my fingers. 'You'll get over it,' she went on. 'Stay a few days here in Edinburgh, cheer yourself up. You'll soon be ready to face them all again.'

She returned to her reading. A few seconds' hiatus while I screwed up my courage almost as effectively as I had my career. 'I can't go back; I've resigned my post.'

Helen's glossy mouth rounded into a big 'O'. 'Ooh, Rose!' she exclaimed. 'You haven't!'

Catherine pressed her lips into a firm line and set aside Cybersecurity's accounts. 'You've done what?'

'Resigned. End of term. Seemed like a good time to go.' I tried to look her in the eye and failed. 'I can't face them, Catherine.'

She sat composed, thinking. 'You've resigned because of this . . . this minor embarrassment?'

'It's not a minor matter,' said Helen, being supportive.

'But Rose, you enjoy your work! You even claim to have a sense of vocation; at least, that's always been your excuse for having a low-paid job.' I looked at the floor, miserably. Catherine didn't have a low-paid job. Experts formed an agitated queue to beg for her expensive advice. 'Can't you explain that you resigned in the heat of the moment, at a time of personal crisis?'

'No.'

'Won't they take you back?'

'No. The Dean won't forgive my campaign for the use of the imperative in the department's mission statement. He wanted the subjunctive and nothing ever got done. It's too late to go back now, Catherine. I've got to make a new start. I've come to ask a favour.'

'Well, heaven forbid that one should throw oneself on the mercy of one's sisters!'

'As if !'

We sat together: Catherine-the-Clever-One, Helen-the-Pretty-One, and me. I waited for their merciful offer of a place to stay.

Their flat was certainly spacious enough. Serene white walls, long Georgian windows, shelves devoid of anything but pacified space. It was a calming sort of place, the kind of decor that could never unwarrantedly force itself on a cohabitee; instead, one was soothed into submission. My sisters sat tidily on the white sofa, like two well-dressed installations, and stared with distaste at the spot where I had thrown my two holdalls full of clutter.

'We'd get on all right, wouldn't we?' I heard a little voice say. 'You'd certainly make a difference to the place.'

'Oh, come on! A minimalist can't have everything! And it's great to be home in Edinburgh,' I burbled. 'Wish I'd come back years ago, like you. You enjoyed going to university here, didn't you, Helen?'

Edinburgh, where no one but my sisters knew me. Edinburgh, where my only public embarrassment had been to wet my knickers in the sand-pit at Sciennes Primary School when I was four. After twenty-four years in England I had come home – ignominiously, with no money and the wrong accent.

'How are you going to find a job?' asked Catherine. 'There can't be many openings for an unemployed lexicographer.'

'I'll be fine. Haven't you heard about the New Scots Dictionary for the New Scottish Parliament?' I cheered up just thinking about it.

'They're having a specially commissioned dictionary *as well*?'

'Oh yes. It's a huge project. Massive investment – but necessary, I think. It's a lexicographer's dream job and they're bound to want me on the staff. I've been in touch with the man in charge of the project and he said that they're very busy doing "F" all through August and are consequently fully staffed, but they'll definitely be recruiting again and maybe I could get involved with some interesting work on "O".'

'"O"?'

'I have my fingers crossed.'

At that moment, the fiddling with the amber beads became quite agitated and I heard the familiar 'ping' of a necklace snapping. The beads bounced on to the floorboards and rolled off in all directions. Being deliberately cool and organised, I started picking them up. 'You won't notice I'm here,' I called airily from behind the sofa. 'I'm going to be working long hours. I've got a massive overdraft to clear. I'll sign up with an agency, do some temping or whatever.' I crawled round the side of the sofa. 'Watch the bamboo!' called Helen.

'What bamboo?' A bunch of twigs slapped me across the face. It didn't look like bamboo to me. It had leaves on and everything. The leaves were sharp. I rubbed my cheek. Catherine handed me an amber bead. Her face was a mixture of pity and irritation. She often looked at me like that. 'So can I stay?' I sat up on my heels, hopefully.

'A week, but not any longer.'

'What?'

Helen mouthed a little, pained 'sorry' at me, then disappeared into the kitchen saying she'd make us all some more tea.

'The thing is, Rose,' said Catherine, 'I've always helped you out in the past, but . . .' I stared at her, dumbfounded. 'You can't just turn up and expect . . .'

'But you're my sister. I'd help you.'

'And I'm not going to lend you any money.'

'I've never asked you for any money. I hate loans.'

'I'm not going to give you any money either. I'm not going to provide the soft, easy landing you've come to expect.'

'Don't be so patronising!'

'It seems to me you've always quite enjoyed patronage, Rose, but it's time you looked after yourself. You've never even lived in a proper house! You've either stayed with Mum and Dad or in some glorified hall of residence! It's about time you lived in the real world.'

'But that was my real world,' I said, pathetically.

'Well it's not any more, is it?'

There was an awkward silence. I could feel a nasty ache around my vocal cords and didn't trust myself to speak. 'You can stay a week, but you'll have to sleep on the floor – tidily – over there behind the white shelf unit.'

'On the floor?'

'We don't have the spare bedroom any more; we knocked the wall down. Didn't you notice the place looks bigger? It shouldn't take you long to find somewhere else. It's for the best,' she concluded. 'Best for you, that is.'

'Don't be ridiculous! How is it best for me?'

'You have to learn to stand on your own two feet. How could you resign from your job like that? You live in a dream world! You have to face the consequences.'

'This is the only time I've ever asked you for a favour.'

'I know,' she replied. 'It's not your style to ask. Usually, you just inspire acts of charity.'

I bit my lip. Catherine sighed and said she'd go and see what was taking Helen so long.

Left alone to face the consequences of my actions, I couldn't bear to look. Perhaps I shouldn't have resigned so hastily. I had no contingency plan if the research post at Dictionary House failed to materialise. The prospect of a job in the real world outside academe did not attract me at all. I liked working in the kind of rarefied environment where I could spend years rootling through the correspondence of previous centuries in order to explain the development of the semi-colon in this one. I never earned much as an academic, but I enjoyed the life; it was me. Reality very rarely impinged. I had been happy in my round of libraries, tutorials and long vacations. And I'd been good at it! How could I have thrown it all away? Perhaps all I had really wanted was a change of scene. A different library, a new set of old books.

Feeling lost, I reached for the novel in my bag (comfort reading). I had been reading it at six-thirty that morning, in a café by the bus station, thinking it best not to surprise my sisters too early on a Saturday. Tea and toast and Charlotte Brontë were all I needed to retreat into a soothingly fictional world. I opened the book and found my place again: 'An age seemed to have elapsed since the day which brought me first to Lowood, and I had never quitted it since.' The cover felt sticky; I must have got some jam on *Jane Eyre*. It was sticking to my fingers. '. . . such was all I knew of existence. And now I felt it was not enough.'

'We'll lend you the money for your first month's rent,' said Catherine, returning with the teapot.

'No, don't even think about it,' I said, putting away the book. 'It's not as if I need a big place.'

I looked at the bags at my feet. When I had packed them in Cambridge, I had been very surprised that all my possessions fitted into two big holdalls. Since I was permanently in debt, I had always thought I must have acquired a lot of things. On the bus to Edinburgh, I had spent the whole of Yorkshire working out where my money had gone. (If you've ever done that bus journey, you will know that Yorkshire, in particular, goes on for a very long time.) I had whiled away the hours by remembering 'you only live once' holidays and 'as much as that?' antiquarian books. I thought of 'so much for so little' silk lingerie and 'what the hell?' bottles of wine.

No regrets; only debts.

I consoled myself with the thought that some of those things had turned out to be very practical: silk underwear packs very well and collectable books are an investment. When The National Westminster Bank suggested I sell my valuable books in order to bring my overdraft back from the realms of fantasy, I had reluctantly agreed. I missed my books, but at least I still had my knickers. Nat West didn't know about those.

'I'll find a flat and clear my debts,' I told my sisters confidently. 'By the time the Dictionary is ready for me, I'll be settled and solvent and . . .'

'Why don't you try to find a proper job, Rose?' said Helen, arriving with the Recruitment section from *The Scotsman*. 'Why not re-train? Make yourself more marketable. Think of all the skills you have.'

'Dead languages,' suggested Catherine. 'A detailed knowledge of eighteenth-century slang.'

'You've forgotten my expertise in Medieval Latin shorthand.'

'Why not build a new career?' asked Helen.

'I like being a lexicographer.'

'So how much does a lexicographer make these days?' asked Catherine.

'Not as much as a software geek, I should think.' (Geek, I thought – well established as a word by now.) 'How much do you get for all your computer geekery?' (Is that a new word?) As far as I could work out, Catherine made a living by playing computer games. 'How's *My Little Princess's Power Ponies* coming on?'

'It's just a sideline,' she said, defensively. 'Secure systems, that's our priority. People invest in security. Games and entertainment – simply a useful money-spinner. As soon as we find a friendly buyer for *GirlSoft*, we'll sell out quick. Rose, I know what! You could work for me. Be a game tester.'

'No, thank you.' Not after all she'd just said about patronage and so on.

'It would be a real job, I promise. We're expanding fast.'

I had no doubt whatsoever that Catherine would one day be rich. I would never be rich, but at least I would know the meaning of the word. (Interesting links with the Celtic 'rix' and the Latin 'rex', both meaning 'king'.) My big sister had decided to be rich; therefore, it would happen. I had always had complete faith in her abilities; she was officially a genius – there had been a formal declaration of it by Edinburgh Education Board when she was only three. She had floored their educational psychologist with a piece of sophistry over whether her infant ability should be classified as 'gifted' or simply 'precocious'. She had graduated, aged twelve, having read Computer Science and Maths, plus a study of Chaos Theory and Random Distribution (somehow the extra subjects just slotted into her timetable). After that she'd done Pure Unsullied Maths and Sordid Financial Services Computing, and got all sorts of awards, scholarships, doctorates and sponsorships, but she stopped putting all the letters after her name when she decided it made her company stationery look vulgar. She admitted it all came easily to her. Sometimes she asked to play me at chess, just so she could remember how much she hated defeat. Didn't want to lose that competitive edge, you see. (The first time I beat Catherine, she was seven and I was six. She had sulked for days over her A level Maths revision.)

'I'll find my own job, thank you,' I said, getting up. 'I'll find a job this morning and this afternoon I'll find a nice flat.'

They both looked a bit conscience-stricken. 'You know you can stay until you find somewhere else,' Catherine protested. 'Don't keep rushing into things, Rose.'

'Why can't Rose stay here?' whined Helen. 'I always wanted her to stay. It was just you who said she shouldn't.'

'We agreed!' snapped Catherine. 'She can stay until she gets somewhere else. Rose, stop being so bloody-minded.'

'I'll do what I like!'

Sometimes, with sisters, your behaviour can really regress.

As we said our sulky goodbyes, the buzzer sounded on the front door. It was a whole gang of friends to see Helen – Andrew, Jonathan, Chris, Paul, Steve and Joe. They said they'd been having a drink at the pub round the corner, conversation had turned to Helen and it wasn't very long before they decided to see their pints off and call round – just on the off-chance she might be in. I suppose that sort of thing happened all the time to Helen-the-Pretty-One. She kissed each and every one, face sunny with smiles, and led them into the living room. I felt a sudden overwhelming relief that I wasn't going to be sharing a flat with her.

'I'm leaving straightaway,' I told Catherine.

She nodded, understandingly. I was halfway out the door when I remembered I might need my purse and my A–Z of Edinburgh. I'd left them behind the white shelf unit. When I walked into the living room, I found Helen surrounded. Everyone was laughing at something she'd just said. They turned to look at me. There were some irrepressible broad grins. I wished I hadn't told her my dark secret about being sexually incompetent. 'I'm just leaving!' I said brightly, heading for the door.

'Come back!' called Helen. 'I'll introduce you. This is Rose, my other sister.'

'I have to go.'

A great big 'Ah!' from the assembled crowd. 'Don't go!'

'I've really got to go.'

Helen followed me along the hall to the door. Behind us, I could hear loud, male laughter. 'I think I could fix you up with someone,' she smiled.

'Please don't.'

'But you mustn't give up, Rose. With a bit of luck you'll meet the right man, fall in love and have gorgeous, prolonged, repetitive, sensual sex!'

I opened the door quickly and stepped outside. 'Bye-bye, little sister,' I said, just to annoy her.

'Bye-bye, Rosie-Posie,' she coo-ed. (Hate that!) 'We'll go out tomorrow and do some flat-hunting together.'

She shut the door. I stared at it blankly, then, full of shame, started to cry.

Chapter 2

My Job Seeker's Advisor told me I should expect to change career five times in my working life and flexibility was the key. I thought about the dilettante hours spent in research and I certainly didn't want to give it up. Being a professional academic had always seemed a good idea to me – long holidays, flexible hours and being paid to read books. Five years ago, when I told my parents my career choice, they hadn't been so sure. My father, a world expert on tenth-century Byzantium, said that throughout human history many disasters had started off disguised as good ideas at the time and that I would never earn any money and had I considered the consequences of that? My mother, a respected philosopher and feminist theologian, said that if one had a sense of vocation it might, arguably, be right to follow it and that I shouldn't let my father put me off.

'What if you've got a sense of vocation?' I asked my Job Seeker's Advisor.

'You want to be a nun?'

I offered to do some bar work in the meantime.

'You'd earn more doing tele-sales,' he advised.

'Okay then. Sign me up for that.'

'That's three nights a week.'

'Nights?'

'Is that a problem? I thought you were available for work any time, any place, anywhere – or is that against your vocation?'

As long as I ignored my sense of vocation, my Job Seeker's Advisor was able to help me. He put my name forward for the tele-sales job and asked if I would consider work as a part-time cleaner. 'Cleaning?'

'And I can get you on the early shift at Scot Burger.' He looked satisfied.

'But,' I said, giving it one last try, 'I have a degree in Medieval Literature. What I'm really looking for is a research post.'

'Could you do some market research, maybe? It's outdoor work, but the pay isn't bad.'

'But I'm a lexicographer.'

'You're a what?'

'It's to do with making dictionaries, defining words, research-ing their origins.'

'Filing and such like?'

'Filing is involved, yes, but . . .'

'Sign up with a temp agency. That's the best way to get office work.'

'But I want a—'

'A proper job. I know. Now, here's the number of the tele-sales recruitment helpline and here's the number of Market Research International. MRI are looking for someone who can speak English and stand about for hours with a clipboard. Could you do that? I can't help you any more than that, hen, sorry. You might have a degree in Medieval Literature, you might even have a sense of vocation, but right now tele-sales is your best option. That or the convent.'

I was determined that I would not be unemployed when I next saw Catherine, so I signed up for the four part-time jobs my advisor had suggested. That afternoon, I also found a room in a flat. When I went back to my sisters' place, I was feeling almost smug.

Helen was out having fun, but Catherine was waiting for me, passing the time by trying to hack into a client's computer system, testing out the security.

'I've got a cosy little place in a shared flat just off Easter Road.'

'Box room?' she asked, eyes on the screen.

'It's not that small.'

'Does it have a window?'

'Well, no, but . . .'

'Box room.' She did a triumphant little tap at the keyboard, sat back and admired her criminally good handiwork. 'You're sure you won't stay just one night?'

'No, got to be up very early tomorrow. Pre-dawn shift at Scot Burger. All those Scot Breakfasts to fry.'

She wrinkled her nose, but held back from a full expression of distaste.

'I'm only on morning shifts for a week.'

'Drop by tomorrow afternoon?' she offered. 'I'll be working from home then.'

'That might just be possible. I'll check my engagements . . .' I scrabbled around in my pockets for the list of jobs. 'At four o'clock, I'm cleaning the flat above you. Number six. It says: "Number six. Kitchen: floor and bench tops; living room: horizontal surfaces only; bathroom: whole lot; bedroom 1: hoover floor; bedroom 2: hoover floor, polish mirrors; study: don't touch the desk."'

'That's us,' said Catherine. 'Not number six.'

'It's not, is it?' I laughed. 'What a horrible coincidence.'

She looked at the scribbled note. 'Yes, that's a five, not a six. So you're the cleaner, now? I don't believe it. Bloody Cinderella!'

'You'd better tidy up before I come. Tomorrow I can spare you thirty minutes before I have to leave for my next new job doing market research on Princes Street.'

17

'Three jobs, Rose?'

'Four. I'm going to start a tele-sales night shift in Livingston, too.'

I had almost turned down the tele-sales job. It seemed too far to travel in the middle of the night, but the hourly rate was the highest on offer at the Job Centre and I had forced myself to remember the harsh reality of my overdraft. 'They said I had a lovely telephone voice.'

'And when are you going to sleep?'

'On the bus.'

'Oh, Rose!' she said, exasperated.

'What else am I supposed to do? I've got to earn some money. I've got all this debt! I'm sick of letters from the loans manager, the debt restructuring manager! I've got no credit any more. I've got to earn some cash.'

I went to pick up my bags. She sighed, leaned elegantly back in her chair and watched me. A gentle summer breeze lifted the muslin blinds at the windows. I couldn't remember Edinburgh ever having been so hot. It gave me a headache.

'I'm looking for a personal assistant,' said Catherine, coolly. 'Someone intelligent; touch-typing, good telephone manner.'

'Try the Job Centre.'

'Must look smart – say, someone who wore her sister's designer cast-offs.'

'Only the good ones. And my underwear has always been my own.'

I slung my rucksack across last season's well-cut jacket.

'What's your new address?' she asked, opening her personal organiser. I told her. 'Basement,' she noted, 'never mind. Phone number?'

'There isn't one.'

'Don't worry. I've got your mobile.'

'Cut off.'

'Oh, Rose, you're completely feckless! Here, let me pay the reconnection charge.'

'No.'

'How are we supposed to get in touch with you?'

'I'll be round tomorrow to dust your white shelf units.'

Weighed down, I tried a haughty high-heeled stalk in the direction of the door. I nearly made it, but tripped over something. You've got to be really unlucky to trip over something in a minimalist interior. She helped me up, concerned about the skid mark on the parquet, and we gathered together the bits and pieces that had tumbled on to the floor with me.

'Will you be all right?' she asked. 'All by yourself?'

'I won't be by myself. It's a shared flat, remember?'

'What are they like?'

'I don't know. I only met the landlady.' My arms full, I elbowed the front door open and squeezed through the gap. 'See you tomorrow, Catherine. Four o'clock.'

'Here's the spare key,' she said suddenly, dropping it into my pocket. 'In case I'm late.'

'You're never late.'

'In case I'm late,' she repeated.

The jobs were no better and no worse than I had expected, but the basement flat was a disaster. My three very sociable flatmates had a lot of friends to stay (from Australia mostly) and I never knew, when I got back from tele-sales at dawn, who would be sleeping in my bed. And you can't really crash out on the living room floor if you work night shift, not when other people want to watch surfing from Sydney on cable, so it wasn't long before I packed my bags and moved on.

I became a kind of serial flatmate, addicted to answering small ads in an attempt to find somewhere I hoped would be nicer, cleaner, warmer – somewhere where I wouldn't have the windowless boxroom or the sofa-bed. I told myself it didn't really matter where I lived because I was nearly always out at work, but I was also trying to escape increasingly bizarre flatmates; it never occurred to me that I might be a bizarre flatmate myself – I thought everybody declaimed poetry in the shower and dried their silk knickers on the back of the TV.

I felt very sorry for myself. I felt as though life had nothing more to offer me than half a shelf in someone else's foetid fridge. I yearned for a well-stocked, shiny new fridge to call my own. However, I put on a stoical front, even though stoicism was not a quality I wished to cultivate. Stoicism is what happens to optimists when they have to steel themselves to look on the bright side. It wasn't really me.

My world became a horrible blur of hard work and nasty smells. Early morning bleach and cleaning smells, afternoon frying burger smells or market research exhaust fumes. Night shifts were sleepless but not smelly because the tele-sales in Livingston was air-conditioned. Now and then I got office jobs doing filing or word processing. And despite all my efforts, all my jobs, I wasn't reducing my debt as much as I had hoped. Interest is so tedious, isn't it? Nat West was not impressed with my resignation from what Catherine had called 'a proper, low-paid job'. And as if that weren't bad enough, I became Scot Burger Employee of the Month, Tele-sales Top Executive Helpliner and I was given a mixed bag of free samples from Market Research International. (The cleaning agency didn't have an incentive awards scheme.)

'How do you do it?' Helen asked, after my third consecutive week of burger glory.

'I don't know,' I replied, bewildered. I couldn't help feeling it was a bit of a comedown for someone with a Ph.D.

'Why do you do it?' asked Catherine, more pointedly.

But I was just biding my time, waiting for the promised call from The New Scots Dictionary (Parliamentary Inaugural Special Edition), and at last, six weeks after I'd arrived in Edinburgh, the call came. I was summoned to an interview with the famously erudite Professor Mungo Mackenzie. Catherine suggested I take her laptop and give him a multi-media presentation, but I told her I didn't think that would be appropriate.

Helen offered to lend me her red tartan mini kilt and kitten heels but, sensibly, I declined. I was confident the professor would offer me a job simply because I deserved it. My work was known in lexicographical circles. My most recent paper had been successful enough to cause an academic backlash. I was intelligent, enthusiastic and *right*.

In my neat and eager navy blue suit I sat before Professor Mackenzie in his study at Edinburgh University, watching while he turned the pages of the article I had been asked to write especially for the occasion. It was intended to show my range and potential as a lexicographer of the Scots language. I had included a comparison of the meanings of 'skite' and 'skit', a survey of spelling on 'drookit/droukit', a bit on 'braw', and a thorough exploration of 'rubbage' (the latter, an eighteenth-century noun and an interesting hybrid of 'garbage' and 'rubbish', is still used in the Shetland Islands and parts of Kirkcudbrightshire [pronounced Kur-Coo-Bri-shire for non-Scots readers]).

Books lined the room. Mungo Mackenzie had one of the most precious antiquarian collections in the world. I had read books about his books. And here I was, surrounded by them. Dark oak shelves with roman numerals in gold heading each case. Wall to wall words. The letters of the alphabet, arranged in almost infinite variety. How many ways can you arrange the letters of the alphabet in pronounceable words? I must ask Catherine, I thought. It was the kind of maths she liked: esoteric, theoretical and with a very slim chance of an answer. She would need my linguistic knowledge to help her, though. The alphabet used to include the letters 'thorn' and 'yog', but they both disappeared in the Middle Ages. I had read Professor Mackenzie's discussion of how 'yog' had been supplanted by 'y', and his thesis on the mystery of why 'thorn' had ceased to exist. Thorn stood for 'th' and you'd have thought that a letter for 'th' would be useful, wouldn't you? But it just vanished from the alphabet.

The great mind who had written so masterfully on *The Obsolescence of Th* was now reading my own work. So far he had made no comment. Just the quietly fateful sound of pages turning, from earnest beginning to inevitable end. I had been so sure he would jump at the chance to take on a bright, young Cambridge lexicographer, but he was frowning.

I should have put more effort into my submission, I told myself. I wished I had spent more time on it! Especially when I considered, nervously, what I knew of Mungo Mackenzie's reputation. It was he who had fought for the New Scots Dictionary, he who had loftily demanded and received funding from the new Parliament. He had that patrician air which still commanded respect in some Edinburgh circles. (He commanded it very successfully among the new MSPs, anyway. At a special debate, he had eloquently stated his case in Gaelic and in English, but it was at the Jolly Judge afterwards, in very plain Lowland Scots, that he had actually sealed the deal.) Mackenzie was feared for his mordant wit. He had a talent for criticism, especially of young, professional academics whom he felt had silly ideas above their station and beyond their abilities.

At last, he raised his eyes and fixed me with a cool look through steel-rimmed spectacles. I shivered. The room was slightly chilly – the right temperature for rare books and probably the temperature of Mungo Mackenzie's blood. 'Thank you for your rubbage, Dr Budleigh,' he began. 'A definitive work, I think.' I tried not to squirm. 'As for the rest . . .' He lifted the flimsy pages. 'To what extent is your knowledge of Scots influenced by your reading of *Oor Wullie* annuals?'

'My Scottish granny sent one every Christmas – alternating with *The Broons* of course – and my mother has some fine early editions.'

'I rather assumed you were the proud owner of a complete set.'

He interrogated me briefly about my understanding of the word 'scunner', then suggested I spend time in the more diligent pursuit of my chosen subject. 'Come back in the spring. We might be able to offer you . . . some other little project.'

Outside, I disposed of my rubbage carefully. Keep Scotland Tidy. Then I walked miserably back to my latest box room, lay on the bed and wept.

Catherine called me up on the mobile phone she'd given me for the day. 'How did it go?' she asked. I told her. 'Oh, poor Rose! What are you going to do now?'

'I don't know.'

'What are you doing right now this minute?'

'Lying down.'

'Don't stay in bed. Bad idea.'

'I suppose so.'

I went to John Lewis. There, in the window, was a beautiful red silk scarf, blazing defiance in a display full of grey. After having been frugal for such a long time, the urge to be profligate became too much for me. The silk slipped through my fingers, like cash. At the counter, the assistant asked, 'How are you going to pay for this?' Overwhelmed by guilt, I stammered, 'I don't know . . . I just don't know.'

'Cash or account?'

An hour later, I was standing on Princes Street, in dreich November weather, doing a market research survey. The clock of the Balmoral Hotel hung low in the sky like a pale winter sun, beaming the time all the way down to Boots the Chemist. The survey this time was on pain-killers: paracetamol versus aspirin. Three hours later I had earned twenty-one pounds, cash in hand.

Spent it on a good bottle of wine.

I went round to my sisters' so I could drink it in the bath, by candlelight.

'You're hopeless, Rose!'

At the bottom of the bottle, I arrived at the decision that I couldn't leave Edinburgh because that would be too much like

23

losing. I had to stay until something else came up. I would stick it out until the middle of March and then I could leave knowing I'd given it my best shot. What I really ought to do was try to write a decent piece for Mackenzie and persuade him to give me another chance. How could I have blown it so badly with that 'rubbage' dissertation? What on earth was I supposed to do now? Here I was, drunk and stupid in my sisters' bath-tub, when I should have been celebrating my return to a proper low-paid job as a lexicographer. How often did lexicography jobs come up? Very rarely. What if I never got work as a lexicographer again? Perhaps I should face the brutal facts and re-train for a different career. Perhaps I should go and work for Cybersecurity, but being my big sister's PA was too humiliating a prospect. There had to be something else.

'How much longer are you going to be in there?' called Helen.

I had to stay. There was nowhere else to go. No better ideas. No money. I lay down and went under. What to do? What to do? Perhaps I should learn Pitman shorthand? I came up for air. Perhaps I should put a message in this bottle by the side of the bath and watch it float about in the water. I wrote 'HELP!' in blue eyeliner on a sheet of toilet roll and stuffed it down the neck of the bottle. Couldn't find the cork. The bottle bobbed up and down then sank.

'Rose! It's Catherine.'

I suppose that, apart from my career problems, I was glad I'd come back to Edinburgh.

'Rose, it's not the end of the world. Please get out of the bathroom.'

Edinburgh always looks good – some sustaining architectural loveliness and scenic beauty to keep my spirits up. I needed that panoramic sense of perspective. I needed dense city, green hills, broad sea and big sky, and all at the same time. I needed the view from the top of Arthur's Seat and the great northern vistas between Georgian terraces in the New Town, the width of the streets filled by seascape and landscape. The bigger picture kept me going when I got depressed by minutiae.

'Rose, please!'

I pulled the plug.

The next day, my sisters asked me very nicely if I would like to move in with them. They said they'd talked it over and it wouldn't be an act of charity – it wouldn't be doing me a favour at all. 'We'd pay you to be a cook-housekeeper,' said Catherine. 'You already do the cleaning and,' she wheedled, 'you're a very good cook.'

'Do you think so?' I asked, pleased.

'You know you are.' She turned to Helen. 'Wouldn't it be lovely if Rose had the tea ready when we came home from work?'

'Yes,' said Helen. 'And she could do all the ironing as well.'

'What d'you think, Rose? Sunday could be your day off.'

'My day off?'

'We'd have to do it properly or not at all.'

'I don't think I want the job.'

I stayed with them over Christmas and Hogmanay. Mum and Dad came for a visit and said how they missed me in Cambridge and asked if I felt any better for the change of scene. They knew, of course, the real reason I had left. Someone would have told them about my public humiliation at the end of term party – academics are a gossipy lot. Wisely, Mum and Dad didn't question me too closely. They concentrated, instead, on telling me about Mungo Mackenzie. My mother had met him only the week before at a Lexicography Luncheon. 'He does like you,' she said, 'but he's looking for certain criteria in a candidate.'

'Like ability.'

'You *are* able and Mungo knows it, but you didn't give him your best work and he's not interested in second best. You know his reputation. You've got some distance to make up.' Mum waved her arms to indicate the sheer distance I had yet to make up; it was demonstrably long. The gold bangles on her left arm clinked wildly (memento from a lover in Kerala). Her right arm silver bangles (Carnaby Street, 1968) didn't move much because she was holding a coffee cup, but she had made her point. 'Do your research properly and try again.'

Dad said he was glad Catherine was looking after me. Mum asked if I would keep an eye on Helen.

Over the holidays, The Clever One and The Pretty One insisted on including me in their busy social life (no tele-sales on Friday night), but I wasn't a great deal of fun. They seemed to have a lot of dazzlingly successful friends and I dreaded the 'What do you do?' question. For a little while I was quite good at brazening it out: 'I'm a cleaner, but I read a lot.' However, it wasn't long before I lost my nerve. I stopped joining in at parties. I retreated to the kitchen and washed glasses.

It wasn't just my career that was worrying me. It was that other, unmentionable thing that I couldn't possibly talk about, no matter how many double-strength margarita cocktails Helen mixed for me. The subject was an absolute minefield, surrounded by 'Keep Out' signs, but if you'd flown over it in a helicopter you would have seen the letters S-E-X clearly visible. There was no way I was going to talk about it again. Helen, being crudely practical, said I'd just got to get back on the horse. She arranged blind dates, only telling me about them at the last minute. Of course, I always refused to go and she had to go in my place. Catherine, on the other hand, had a different approach: she favoured the old-fashioned, chaperoned introduction. I would turn up to clean the flat and she would be sitting there with a male friend who was supposedly dying to meet me. It could all be very awkward.

Eventually my sisters lost patience and gave up. I was relieved; it meant I was allowed to lead a life of maidenly retreat. Helen had one last attempt to fix me up, in honour of her birthday at the end of January, but her efforts were wasted. 'He came highly recommended,' she complained after her party. 'And he really, really liked you!'

Despite the social embarrassment of a poor, celibate sister baking filo pastry parcels in the kitchen, Helen had enjoyed her birthday. Catherine and I had given her a framed copy of her favourite painting, Botticelli's *Birth of Venus*, and hung it in her bedroom as a surprise. And at the party she had met someone whom she now proclaimed to be the most perfect man on earth. His name was Gordon and he was some kind of travel writer. He got to go on free trips abroad to test out the bedrooms in luxury hotels.

'Don't you think he's a catch?' asked Helen now. She was stretched out lazily on the sofa like a satisfied cat. Gordon was in the shower. It was the morning after the morning after, and he was still around. I, too, had stayed till Sunday, but in a very minimal way, behind the white shelf unit.

'Does he play chess?' I asked.

Helen yawned. ''Course not!'

Beside us, Catherine sat playing with a new bit of software on her laptop. One ear was tuned to our conversation while the other was listening to a 'Brush up Your Mandarin' language course. Between jabbers of Mandarin, she offered her educated guesses about Gordon.

'Gordon isn't brainy,' said Catherine, disappointed. 'He knows nothing about Chaos Theory and, in my opinion, that's essential to any relationship.'

'He's boring,' I said, sulkily.

'He most certainly is not,' said Helen. 'You're just jealous.'

'Rubbage!'

'Leave Rose alone. She's still upset about the Dictionary job.'

'Why did you have to bring that up again?' I moaned.

'But Rose, it's ages ago now.'

'They're never going to offer me anything. My pronunciation is terrible. My Gaelic is non-existent.'

'Never mind,' said Helen, sweetly. 'It's never too late to learn.'

I ignored her and picked up another section of the newspaper. Sunday was the only time I was allowed to be untidy and I made the most of it, surrounding myself with piles of newsprint. In one of the colour supplements there was a picture of a painting that had just sold for a million dollars. An anonymous buyer. I heard myself make a sort of 'hrumph!' noise. The painting was an abstract in blue. A few swipes and swirls with a fat brush. A mess of paint and worth a million. The computer hummed; Catherine tapped busily. 'Have you seen this?' I asked. No one took any notice. A few deep sighs from Helen, a few more gobbets of Mandarin from Catherine. I stared hard at the picture and caught my breath. It was actually figurative and erotic. Two figures. It was the sort of thing that made you want to look at it sideways to work out what was going on. I tried.

'Sir Walter Scott said playing chess was a sad waste of brains,' said Catherine.

'He loved it, though!' I murmured, still staring at the picture.

'He said that in the time it took to learn all the possible per-mutations of a few openings, you could learn a new language.'

'I'm going to see Gordon,' said Helen.

As she drifted out of the room, Catherine unplugged her Mandarin tape and dropped a different CD into her machine. 'Pull the blinds down, would you, Rose? I want to take a look at my presentation for the bank tomorrow. It's my business develop-ment plan.' She opened an invisible cupboard door, switched on a projector and there, on the bare, white wall of the living room, was the edifice of Catherine's finances, in all its baroque flamboy-ance. She seemed pleased with what she saw. 'I'll give you shares when we go public,' she said. 'Maybe for Christmas next year.'

'Can I not have a book token like last year?'

She ignored this. 'What was wrong with Helen's cast-off the other night? Didn't you like him?'

'Nothing wrong with him, it's just . . .'

'Are you going to be celibate for ever?'

'Very likely.'

Catherine made a funny snorting noise – quite undignified for her.

'I'm deadly serious,' I protested.

'Listen, Rose, I'll tell you a secret.' She leaned closer, and so did I. (It was ages since she'd told me a secret.) 'If I ever meet a man cleverer than me . . .'

'Long odds, I should think.'

'And much more brilliant and better at everything than me . . .'

'You'd marry him and have his babies?'

'Maybe.'

I groaned, disappointed. 'And you're supposed to be the clever one!'

'That doesn't stop me hoping I'll meet him,' she said, sounding surprisingly wistful. 'Mr Q.E.D. Right.'

'Why does he have to be better and cleverer?' I asked. 'What about equally clever? What about sexual equality?'

'If he was cleverer than me I wouldn't get bored. I like a challenge.'

But a man cleverer than Catherine was yet to be found. Most of them failed her first test of cleverness and were unable to prove Fermat's Theorem – even when given the answerbook. Or, if they could do that, they didn't know how to cheat at poker. ('It's brilliant, Rose! Sleight of hand and a willing accomplice!') She had had quite a lot of success at fleecing businessmen in first-class lounges, but had yet to meet her match. Frustratingly, until she met the hero who could dazzle her with a deftly cut pack or a surprisingly discovered ace of hearts, she had to make do with inferior accomplices.

'So what else are you doing wrong this year?' I asked. 'Apart from cheating at cards?' (Catherine was so right all the time about just about everything that each year she chose a different area in which to be deliberately and recklessly wrong.) I realised that I didn't often see her look embarrassed. 'This year it's sexual politics,' she said, almost blushing. 'What do you think?'

'A risky area for incorrectness,' I replied. 'Not boring, though.'

I got sacked from the cleaning job for dusting vertical surfaces. 'We're only contracted to do horizontal surfaces,' I was told. 'You've had two warnings.' After that, I cleaned only for certain favoured clients (Catherine and Helen) and in my brief spare time between other jobs, I read. Reading has to be the easiest method of escape.

And at home, in a better flat with now familiarly bizarre flat-mates, I borrowed novels with snappy, trippy modern covers and began work on a new project I intended to submit to Professor Mackenzie. Until it was finished, there wasn't much else I could do but keep on trying to make a living. More months of burger-selling, tele-sales and standing around on Princes Street doing market research. By March, I was just plain weary with not having any money. I was tired of looking in shop windows at things I couldn't afford, bored with baked pota-toes. Debt is such a drag.

'Met anyone nice yet?' asked Helen, calling in at Scot Burger. Soon she would be going away with Gorgeous Gordon for a whole month of luxury hotel-testing in France.

'No. Have a good trip.'

'I will.'

'Helen . . . Helen, do you love him?' She smiled a little smile. 'Do you think you might be in love with him?'

She put her head on one side, stuck her finger in her mouth and thought about it. 'He's totally gorgeous and he thinks I'm wonderful. He turns me on.'

'Do you want to stay with him for ever? Could you marry him?'

'You're such a hopeless romantic, Rose!'

'Aren't you?'

She gave me a condescending look. 'I'm a scientist,' she said, very reasonably. 'Gordon is as near to perfection as you can get. His only flaw is that he's obsessed with football, but it's very hard to find a man these days who isn't. I'm having to compromise on that one. I've actually agreed to go and see Paris St Germain while we're away. He said I ought to take an interest in the things that mean a lot to him and I said there was no way I was going to see Dunfermline Athletic.'

'But he takes an interest in your work, doesn't he?'

'He tries. I suppose, yes, he's quite interested.'

'Not many people are really interested in genetically modified potatoes, Helen.'

'Oh, I don't know. There are marked similarities with Dunfermline Athletic.'

'Did you say that to Gordon?'

'Wouldn't want to hurt his feelings – maybe I love him. Now get my french fries, Rose. Put them in this, would you?' She handed me a zip-up plastic bag. 'I want to run some tests.'

'What sort of tests?'

'Just hurry up.' (I was being slow for a Fast Track Burger Executive.)

After my shift, I walked up through Holyrood Park to get the burger smell out of my hair and clothes. I took the path up Salisbury Crags and when I saw a plane flying overhead, I thought of Helen and Gordon jetting off to Paris together. 'He turns me on,' she had said.

I couldn't help being bothered by the fact that sex seemed to be everywhere, shouting from the newspapers, steaming out from the television, whimpering along the radio waves on phone-ins – massive media coverage, like a war. There were first-hand accounts from the walking wounded about how he was a bastard, a deserter and ought to be shot! There were nasty situations and last chances, truces and betrayals. For people like Helen there were triumphs. It was all very upsetting for a bombed-out conscientious objector such as myself.

I marched uphill. Keep going, I thought. I told myself I had achieved my aims: I had repelled all advances and diplomatically avoided any fraternisation with the enemy. I was celibate and sto-ical. Celibacy is liberation of a kind. I stood cleanly at the top of the cliffs. The moral high ground is a reassuringly unassailable position. No chance of a damaging encounter; no risk of a dangerous liaison. I surveyed the horizon. No chance, either, of someone totally gorgeous thinking I was wonderful.

'Maybe you're in this city, now,' I whispered to no one. 'The one who would think I was wonderful. The one who would turn me on. Love me. It's just luck, it's just serendipity. What if we met?' I stared into the distance. 'When am I going to meet you?'

When?

The Opening

The King's Gambit provides a good example of speedy
development of the pieces; play is often wild with
both sides in peril of a sudden collapse. It is on this
razor-blade margin between success and failure that
the appeal of the opening rests.
Here is a typical skirmish

The Right Way to Play Chess by D. B. Pritchard

Chapter 3

Friday, 13th March.

Standing in the rain on Princes Street, I heard the gun being fired at Edinburgh Castle. One o'clock. I was due a break. It was bitterly cold and windy, the kind of day when Market Research International's field executives failed to reach their targets. Despite layers of clothing, thermal socks and Helen's fleece-lined wellies, I was wet, shivering and miserable. My red umbrella blew inside-out and I struggled to keep a grip.

Perhaps it was because of the hazardous umbrella, but potential respondents had been scurrying past me all morning. The toothpaste survey was proving to be a tough one. Who wants to be stopped on the street and probed on the subject of dental hygiene? Even for the free gift of a toothbrush? I paced up and down my pitch, gripping my clipboard with numb fingers. If only one more person would stop and answer my questions then I could complete my quota of respondents and take a break.

Feeling desperate, I begged passers-by: 'Scuse me, would you mind answering two brief questions?'; 'Scuse me, but have you got a moment?'; 'If you're not in too much of a hurry, could you . . .?' I had never before filled so many hours with so many unanswered questions. Never. Not even during my occasional temp job as a filing clerk at Edinburgh University's Department of Parapsychology.

Now and then I got a muttered 'Sorry, hen,' and a look of pity. And then, like the answer to a prayer, a tall and handsome man appeared before me, carrying a smart black umbrella which seemed to resist the wind as well as the rain. He wore a beautiful black cashmere overcoat and the hand clasping the umbrella was encased in a soft leather glove. I didn't have to say to him, as I had been saying to people all morning, 'Scuse me! Have you got a minute?' He made the first move. He smiled warmly. It was the first bit of warmth I had experienced in forty-eight hours. His mouth was quite sensuous. Surprisingly blue eyes.

'Rose?' he asked, taking me in from head to wellies. I didn't recognise him. 'It is Rose, isn't it?'

'Yes.'

He was obviously delighted. Who was he? He had the kind of heroic appearance I ought to remember, but I couldn't. And he knew my name! I hoped I would remember his quickly and so save myself the embarrassment of asking.

'Rose Budleigh,' he repeated, slowly. There was a bit of amazement there too. Easy to read, I thought. Not a poker player. Together we stood under his umbrella and waited for the amazement to pass. Even then there was still all that delight to contend with. 'Do you still play chess?' he asked.

'What?'

'Do you still play chess?' he said, carefully.

'Yes.'

'What are you doing this for, then?'

'It's my job.'

He just laughed. 'Bloody awful job!' Although I heartily agreed with him, I felt offended.

'It's still a job!' I said, huffily. He looked at me as if I were mad.

'So, what's the survey?'

I had to force myself to remember, even though I'd been staring at it on my clipboard for days. Putting on my most professionally detached voice, I asked him if he used toothpaste.

'Yes.'

'Do you use any of the above brands of toothpaste?' I showed him the list.

'Yes. Do you want to know which ones?'

'No, that's part of the slightly more detailed questionnaire. That's the bit you get to do inside. It wouldn't take long.' I stamped my wellies and shivered. 'You get a free gift,' I tempted. 'And there's coffee.'

'Will it be you asking the questions?'

'Will I do?' I gave him what I hoped was my winning smile. He responded with a dazzlingly confident, winning smile of his own.

'You look freezing, poor thing! Let's go in. I'll answer the more detailed questionnaire.'

Market Research International had hired a room nearby for the purpose of conducting interviews with the people we managed to lure off the streets. There were half a dozen small tables with plastic chairs, none of them occupied, and by a wall there was a coffee machine and a stack of plastic cups. My supervisor, Mavis, sat beside a hissing gas fire, staring at a wordsearch in a puzzle magazine. Mavis had spent twenty years standing outside in all weathers with her clipboard and promotion indoors had seen her greatest ambition realised. Her face was as leathery as a highland crofter's and her sense of humour had suffered an eviction. The thought that twenty years of market research might turn me into Mavis was more than I could bear. She nodded grudgingly when I came in with my capture and I watched her put another notch against my name on an Appraisal Form. 'Rose!' she barked. 'Don't forget this time!' She pointed to the tubes of toothpaste arranged before her.

'Right,' I said, gathering them up.

'And the profile questionnaire.'

'Yes.'

'Coffee.'

'I'll get him one.'

'For me!'

'Oh!'

'Hurry up!'

'But I'm looking for the free gift. Where's the multi-tuft toothbrush?'

'Not yet. Do you think we *give* them away?'

I ushered my respondent to a table by the window with a view of the castle. Edinburgh Castle is a real citadel, rising impressively out of its black rock. On a wintry day it's even more bleakly menacing than usual. I remembered that Muriel Spark said its sheer presence at the heart of the city had made her contemplate the existence of God. I didn't think the sight would inspire my respondent to higher thoughts, I just thought it might be more uplifting than having to look at the room's interior. However, he sat with his back to the window; he looked at me and kept his thoughts to himself.

Pathetic though it may be to admit, I had already begun to fantasise about marrying this well-dressed stranger who knew my name, and despite the fact that we had to have a less than romantic conversation I thought things were going rather well. I was already rehearsing a 'Darling, do you remember how we met?' story which I imagined telling our dinner guests for years to come.

He removed his overcoat, slapped his gloves on the table and sprawled on the plastic chair, taking up as much space as possible. 'Mind if I smoke?' he asked.

'No problem,' I said. 'Smoking's allowed.' I took off my ski jacket, microfibre thermal waistcoat and last season's chunky cable-knit. Underneath all that was a very old, but cosy, pink lambswool cardigan with pearl buttons and holes at the elbows. 'I remember that,' he laughed, lighting a cigarette. 'How wonderful you've still got it!'

How rude! I thought, feeling unnerved, and I put the chunky cable-knit back on. He smiled to himself. He knew I couldn't remember where we'd met before and he was enjoying keeping me in suspense. I gave him a questionnaire and asked him to tick the relevant boxes while I fetched the coffee. I silently hoped he'd write his name on it too. At the coffee machine, I raced through mental photofits trying to identify him: someone I had met on holiday? Someone I knew at school? The pink cardigan was . . . a present for my sixteenth birthday. Good grief! It was twelve years old! How had it survived? I really ought to throw it out.

I looked across at Mavis to see her mouthing the words 'No Smoking'. Petty power suited her; she excelled at the spontaneous diktat. With a crooked finger, my supervisor beckoned me across.

'But I told him it wasn't a problem,' I said in a low voice.

'Then tell him you made a mistake!' she hissed.

No choice in the matter. Her nails were already scratching at a Field Executive Performance Related Pay Sheet. I would have to ask him, politely, to put his cigarette out, which was a shame because it would spoil my after-dinner story. (Can't lie, can't even exaggerate.) I returned to my intended with his coffee, took away the toothpaste questionnaire and glanced at the 'Your Name' box. He'd opted for anonymity. I gave him the next form.

'What's this one for?' he asked.

'Just a simple little form.'

'The last one?' He sipped his coffee and grimaced.

Truthfully, once a market researcher has a respondent in the confines of an interview room, she won't easily let him go. That free gift has to be sweated for. After the customer profile sheet there were at least a hundred other questions to be answered and many, many boxes to be ticked.

'It isn't quite the last form, no.'

'How long will this take?'

'Won't you do just this one? It's very, very short.'

'What's it for?'

'I think it's designed to enable our client to place you in the appropriate socio-economic group.'

'It'll be AB one,' he said, helpfully. 'Here, let me write it across the top.' He took the form and began to fill it in, rapidly working his way through the questions. I was an expert by now at reading upside down and extremely interested to see which boxes he ticked.

He was British, aged 30–40, single (Yes!) and 'Professional' by occupation. He read every single broadsheet newspaper, every single day, plus a few tabloids. 'How do you get through them all?' I asked, forgetting I wasn't supposed to be looking.

'I have to have really, really long lunch hours.'

In Section B he came to 'Holidays In The Past Year' and at last got down to work. *Cuba, Mexico, Argentina* (strong, clear handwriting travelling confidently across the page), *U.S.A., Madagascar, Zanzibar* and then he ran out of space.

'Write on the back,' I suggested. 'You haven't mentioned any European trips yet.'

'I don't think I'll bother,' he said. 'You can't count long week-ends on the continent.'

A few more seemingly random ticks through 'Magazines and Periodicals' and he had reached the end of the form, where there lurked: 'What is your annual income?' A range of bands were listed, starting from £5,000–10,000 and going up in incre-ments to a heady '£200,000 or more'. He glanced up to catch me watching again and neatly circled 'or more'.

Mavis announced loudly: 'There is a no smoking rule!' I had forgotten all about her, but there she was, watching us like a harpy. He leaned across the table and asked, 'Do *you* mind if I smoke, Rose?' I shook my head, enthralled at meeting someone who earned so much. I wondered what he did. He was older than me so I supposed he'd had more time to get rich. He offered me one of his cigarettes. I hadn't smoked for six months but I took one anyway because I wanted him to light it for me.

His face was very close to mine; I could see the smooth texture of his skin and the dark lashes against his cheek.

I suppose it was going a bit far. Mavis made some nasty cawing noises and tore up my Performance Related Pay Sheet. Then a prolonged bout of bronchial unpleasantness: cough, cough, wheeze, wheeze, hack, hack.

My fiancé heaved a sigh, got to his feet and strolled up to her desk. 'I'd hate my cigarette smoke to bother you,' he said. 'Perhaps you'd like some fresh air?'

'I've had enough bloody fresh air!'

'Five minutes,' he said. 'Please.'

She gave a very gothic cackle. Unfazed, he produced a twenty-pound note and placed it on her wordsearch puzzle. A nasty silence. Rash move, I thought. Naive, insulting, stupid. Mavis would shred him like a Staff Bonus Form. And so I watched, open-mouthed, when she tucked the money up her sleeve and left the room.

Returning to his seat, my hero blew a triumphant little smoke ring in the air. 'Now, Rose,' he said, happily, 'let's set all this questionnaire rubbish to one side, shall we?'

I still hadn't worked out how he knew me and I was leaving it a bit late to ask. The longer it went on, the more awkward it became. I tapped my biro furiously on to the palm of my hand, willing myself to remember. He smiled lazily and leaned back in his seat. What was he going to say now? I was breathing in a peculiarly shallow way ('bated breath', I believe) when he finally asked, 'So, what have you been doing since you beat me in that tournament?'

'What tournament?'

'Chess tournament. Surely you remember now?' I shook my head. He looked offended, sat up straight again. 'It was here, in Edinburgh. I came home specially for it. You said you'd travelled from Cambridge. You were White, went for King's Gambit, which kind of surprised me – bit reckless, bit daring but kind of appealingly direct – and I thought: might as well go along with it, see what she does after castling. Then there was all this devastating positional play and I couldn't help being impressed by the way you just breezed along – cracking pace – wonderful sang-froid!' He spoke quickly, increasingly animated. 'I didn't think for a moment you'd be able to keep it up! And sure enough, you didn't. Just collapsed. You'd been playing beautifully, then got a bit overconfident and went in for some fairly idiosyncratic variations. We got into all this Muzio nightmare stuff – horribly complicated. You came very unstuck, I closed in on you, set about all the major fate-sealing moves and it looked like you were done for!' He paused for breath. I was on the edge of my plastic seat, hanging on to his every word. 'And do you remember what happened then?'

I couldn't, but it sounded like I used to be really exciting. Still tapping like mad with my pen, lots of inky splotches now – bad habit, couldn't stop.

'I thought I was about to finish you off and you began to play this blinder of an endgame. The most alarming kind of speculative sacrifices. Had to be desperate to do it, really, but you kept your objective in sight and pressed on regardless. All very tricky and tactical and risky. I was amazed at your nerve! And you turned it around and beat me! Never forgotten it! Gave up tournaments after that.' He paused, as though still shattered by the experience. 'You don't remember, do you?' he said, disappointed. 'I suppose it was a long time ago – you were very young, sixteen I think, but Rose, you were bloody good!'

'Thank you,' was all I could say.

He looked at his watch. 'I have to go,' he said, reluctantly. 'I really must go. I wish we'd bumped into each other yesterday, nothing urgent on then. Work's such a bore, isn't it?' I nodded. 'It's been wonderful seeing you again.'

'Thank you for doing the questions. Nice to get out of the rain for a bit. I didn't know I'd made such an impression with the chess.'

'You did.' And then he added, quietly: 'Are you happy, Rose?

Are you well?' I nodded, confused. 'You've grown into such an attractive woman – despite the wellies.' He watched for my reaction.

I still didn't know his name, but I did know he earned two hundred thousand pounds a year or more. He was arrogant and conceited; he was handsome, clever and very, very rich. No contest.

I must remember him! Tap, tap, tap went my pen. I ought to be able to remember. We were sitting a table's width apart. Who was he? I looked directly into his eyes and he held my gaze. Then, with a sudden burst of clarity, I knew who he was. I remembered his expression as he took his seat across the board. A sort of patronising pleasure. The eyes, the mouth, the easy charm, the self-assurance. I could recall his incredulity when he began to lose in the endgame. His utter disarray. Older than me, more experienced than me, defeated by me. Very satisfying. 'I remember now!' I said, waving my pen. 'James Cameron! I mean, Jamie – you're Jamie Cameron, aren't you?'

Smiling, he leaned forward, removed the pen from my agitated fingers and touched my hand. The shock of touch. 'Still fidgeting,' he said. I heard the fondness in his voice. 'What a mess!' He turned my palm upwards. Ink smudges. 'Look,' he said, tenderly, 'just the same.' There was a pause, a moment of suspense, a breath taken at the same time. Recognition or love at first sight, difficult to define it. You, I thought. You.

He held my inky hand in his. 'Meet me tonight for dinner?'

'Yes.'

Chapter 4

He arrived at the flat early and I wasn't ready. This was because Mavis had kept me back after work to give me a verbal warning. When I reminded her that she had accepted a bribe to leave her post, I got a verbal threat. Subdued, I promised never to allow anyone to smoke in the interview room again. The immediate consequence of all this was that I was late. Lateness is bad in chess. Getting ahead of your opponent is called gaining a tempo and it gives you a clear advantage.

After the wellies and cardigan I had wanted to appear as glamorous as possible. My new dress and shoes were reassuringly black and strappy and I had planned to saunter straight out to the taxi as soon as I saw Jamie arrive. Instead, I had to open the door wearing an anorak I'd grabbed off the coat-hook in the hall.

'Hello, Rose,' he smiled. 'What a beautiful anorak.'

'I'll be ready in five minutes.'

He looked just as handsome as the picture I had been cherishing in my mind all afternoon (my romantic daydreams had grown increasingly soft-focused so it was almost surprising he didn't disappoint).

I hadn't wanted him to see where I lived. Although I had a room of my own this time, with a window (and psychedelic curtains), the window had bars and the view outside was of the tenement's rubbish piling up on the basement steps. I took him into the living room which was still suffering from a party held the weekend before. Someone had started to tidy up, but hadn't been able to see it through. Bottles and cans burst from a split bin-liner and newspapers were dotted around the floor absorbing the wet patches on the carpet. The smell of stale beer and cigarettes blended atmospherically with the all-pervasive damp.

'How was the party?' asked Jamie.

'Missed it. I was doing tele-sales in Livingston.'

'Shall I wait in the kitchen?'

'No. You wouldn't like the kitchen.'

He stood there in his immaculate clothes, looking completely out of place. It reminded me of the time I dropped my favourite gold earring down the toilet.

One of my flatmates appeared (at least I think he was one of my flatmates, I vaguely remembered having seen him before). He ignored us both, swept a pile of takeaway cartons off the sofa and settled down to watch *Coronation Street*.

I ran to my room, wriggled into the dress, took my new shoes out of their box and kissed the soles (superstitious). 'Walk me to luck!' I whispered. (Can't put new shoes on without going through this little ritual.) Moments later we were climbing the basement steps, past the barred window of my room, and I was privately hoping I'd never see those psychedelic curtains again.

We went to a place up by the castle. He led me along a dimly lit medieval close, through a low doorway and down a flight of stone steps. I could feel the warmth rising to meet us as we descended. There was trailing ivy, dark tapestries and, above us, the panelled ceiling was painted with figures from the Tarot. The base of a stone tower curved into the room.

A waiter led us between busy tables and the gothic gloom disappeared in a golden glow: fat cherubs clutching candles, bronze vases on stone pillars, gold leaf amongst the greenery, bright glasses, shining cutlery. Concealed among the cupids were a few gargoyles. We stopped at a perfect, quiet corner table and a gilt chair was pulled out for me to sit down on. Glancing at the ceiling, I saw that I was about to dine beneath the skeletal figure of Death. 'Can we move?' I asked.

'I'll swap places with you,' said Jamie, all amiable.

'No, I couldn't have that on my conscience.'

The waiter shrugged and took us to a smaller, wobbly table, bang in the middle of the room, presided over by a pot of gold and a flower arrangement. He presented the menus, flapped the napkins and left. I didn't recognise the figure on the ceiling but she was dancing.

Jamie was nonplussed. 'I especially asked for that table,' he said, leaning on the new one and making it see-saw. 'I put a lot of effort into finding the best table.'

'A lot of effort? Very, very long lunch hours?'

'Hours of selfless corporate entertaining.'

'I'm happier sitting here, honestly. I'm just a bit superstitious.'

'So would you rather have gone out tomorrow night? The fourteenth?'

'I'll take a risk.'

A different waiter arrived with a bit of bent cardboard and stuffed it under one of the table legs. 'It might not work,' he warned. 'It's an uneven floor, rather than an uneven table.' He stood up again. 'Flagstones,' he said. 'Know what I mean?'

Around us, the room hummed with quiet, early evening voices. The couple at the next table spoke intensely and held hands. Jamie looked at the menu and I looked at him. I felt a kind of desperate desire to love him, or maybe it was just a desperate desire.

Whisky first, to whet the appetite and steady the nerves. It was a good Lowland malt and, as my mother had taught me, I tried it neat, added a splash of water and sipped it slowly.

'I can't decide,' said Jamie, looking at the menu. 'Should I have sirloin with fresh horseradish, mushrooms and chips or . . . I'm swithering . . .'

'A useful Scots word. I use it all the time now.'

'Or . . . breast of Gressingham duck with roast peach and elderflower?'

'I'm having the duck.'

'Then I'll have the other one.'

After that, the starters just fell into place. He opted for lobster with a new potato and dill remoulade and I went for whisky cured salmon with capers and citrus sauce. 'Now, to drink . . .' More moments of silent prayer over the wine list – it was about the size of a Gutenberg Bible. 'This is one of the reasons I come here,' he confided. 'I just like to look at it.' He offered to choose for both of us and since it seemed to make him happy, I let him. Once our order was safely in the hands of the waiter, I made another tentative start at conversation. 'Thank you for bringing me here,' I said.

'My pleasure. Tell me how you ended up on Princes Street with your clipboard.'

'It's not my main career. It's just to tide me over until something comes up at the New Scots Dictionary. I'm really a lexicographer.'

'A what?'

I defined it for him.

I explained the only reason I was doing market research, cleaning, tele-sales and burger-filling was to fend off my bank. I told the truth and didn't pretend it was any better than it actually was because I had this vague idea that he might feel protective towards me. His face showed gratifying concern.

'And they're making you pay up. How could they? That's so unfair, isn't it?'

'Yes,' I said, warming to him even more. 'They recommended I sell my collection of rare books because it was the only thing I had of any value. I lost a lovely edition of *Jane Eyre* and a badly printed, illegally copied eighteenth-century selection of letters from *Les Liaisons Dangereuses*.'

'What a shame!'

'I don't think much of Nat West.'

'If it's any consolation, Rose, they're probably ripe for a hostile takeover. Serve them right!'

The nice mouth rounded into a smile. I imagined what it would be like to kiss those lips and to put my arms around him. I liked his shape; it was a well proportioned, desirable, masculine shape.

'So, when do you start your job at the Dictionary?' he asked, stabbing at the lobster that had just arrived.

'I don't know. I'm going to submit a new thesis and if they like it I'll start straightaway.'

'And what if they don't like it?'

'I'm going to London.'

'Are you?' He looked up sharply. 'Well, that's a disappointment! What are you going to do in London anyway? Live in another stoury flat? Do other grotty jobs?'

'No,' I said, offended. 'I'm going to get a much nicer flat and—'

'—do other grotty jobs!'

'There are lots of things I could do!'

'What are your alternatives, then?' he asked, crisply. It was rather as if he had snapped his fingers and demanded: 'Rose! What's nine times eight?' I ought to have known the answer. I realised I was winding my hair nervously round and round my finger. I stopped, annoyed at myself. He put down his knife and fork. 'You mustn't go to London.'

'Why not? Give me one good reason.'

'I'd miss you.'

'You don't know me well enough to miss me.'

'I've been missing you for years.' I think he meant it to come out as a joke, but he didn't say it with the right kind of insouciance. 'I never dreamt we would run into each other again, and . . .' he watched while I tried to smooth my hair, '. . . here we are.' Then he reached across and put a few strands back into place – the sort of ordinary, intimate thing that only someone who was very close would be permitted to do. I tried to remember Catherine's poise. 'You fidget all the time,' he said, quietly. 'All the time.'

'No, I don't!'

'All right,' he laughed. 'You never fidget. Anything you say, Rose.' He looked at me earnestly. 'Please don't go to London.'

'I've already made up my mind.'

'But what will you do? Scot Burger again?'

'There's a very nice branch in Bloomsbury.'

'Be serious, Rose.'

'I am being serious!'

Disbelief. He cast his eyes up to the ceiling, and by this small gesture I felt wounded. We ate the rest of the first course in silence. I was annoyed at his rudeness, but really I wanted the evening to last. You see, the food was pretty good and there was no way I was leaving without seeing the dessert menu. I was just thinking to myself that he wasn't all that wonderful and that I was quite looking forward to selling advertising space on *Time Out* when he said with great sincerity: 'I'm sorry, Rose. I shouldn't have said anything, it's none of my business which branch of Scot Burger you want to work in.' I reached for my glass, took a thoughtful sip of wine. 'Forgive me?' he asked.

I thought about how rich he was. How desirable. 'You're forgiven,' I said.

I was easily won.

The sensuality of the room wrapped its arms around me where my dining companion had not and I was lulled into a state of dreamy satisfaction. I think the part of my brain controlling perception of reality must have shut down – but then it was a very underdeveloped part of my brain anyway. Use it or lose it, as they say.

Over the main course he had a lot of questions. He was as surprised at my poverty as I was at his wealth. 'How can someone so highly intelligent have earned so little?'

'But I've earned a Ph.D.' (The most useful thing about it was that it enabled me to say that.) 'I have a doctorate.'

'I meant,' said Jamie, bent on making himself clear, 'achieved so little financially. I don't doubt your academic achievement – all that highly esoteric lexicography. But let's be frank, Rose, what's the point of spending your life looking up the origins of words?'

'It's important.'

Baffled look on his face.

'There is no one else in the world with my particular knowledge of Anglo-Norman etymological sources.'

'How is that important?'

I hadn't really run up against this line of questioning before. I tried to take him through it slowly: 'Our linguistic heritage is a part of our cultural identity.'

'You've lost me.'

'It's vital to our understanding of the way we express ourselves.'

'Is it? I've always managed.'

He was obviously only pretending to be stupid. 'The study of language is vital to society,' I said, getting impatient with him. 'It's essential to civilisation.' His mouth began to twitch at the corners.

'As important as that? Gosh!'

'What do you mean, "Gosh!" It's more important than your job!' I spluttered. 'It's more interesting than bloody banking!'

'I completely agree with you. And it's not bloody banking I do, it's bloody investment—'

'My work is about true meaning. Truth! People care about the source, the origins of their language!'

'Oh, Rose,' he laughed, giving up. 'Nobody gives a fuck.'

Some lexicographers can happily talk for hours about this most flagrantly versatile of words, but it was clear that in Jamie Cameron I was dealing with a philistine, so I merely summarised: 'The first recorded use of that word was in 1503, in a work by the Scottish poet William Dunbar.'

'A first for Scotland! Makes you proud.'

'Actually, the second and third citations are also Scottish in origin.'

'Every place on the podium! Tell me something else good.'

Since we'd only just met, I decided to steer clear of further obscenity. (Save it for later.) Instead, I opted for: 'Did you know that English has more verbs than French and German put together? Anything they can do – we can do, enact, perpetrate, perform, commit, conduct and activate.'

'Really? Would you do something for me?'

The time passed so quickly as we ate and drank and talked together. I told him a few colourful eighteenth-century insults and mentioned the South Sea Bubble (which was all I knew of investment). He told me there were Bubbles all the time – something very similar happened in Rumania quite recently – and we agreed that it was all a very bad idea, but okay if you got in at the beginning and out before the end. We talked about how to guess the timing of these things, how much was luck, how much was skill and how much was acquired information. (Ans = 4:2:3.) I said I reckoned you could get away with having half as much skill as everyone else if you had twice as much luck. If you also happened to know the right people, you certainly had an edge. 'Rose,' he said, 'you're such a clever person. Why aren't you rich?'

'You can be clever and poor, you can be stupid and rich. I know loads of highly intelligent people who earn a pittance.'

'But you've spent the past six months working day and night, your only objective being to pay off your overdraft.'

'What is it to you?' I asked, unhappily. 'And anyway, I haven't quite achieved that objective.'

'Well, that makes it all the more futile, doesn't it?' he said. 'How much do you still owe?'

I winced and admitted to credit card and student loans totalling fifteen thousand pounds. He shook his head and sighed; I felt a failure. I waited for his disapproval, his condemnation of my running up such a burden of debt, but he said: 'It's not a lot, relatively speaking, and yet how many more years is it going to take you to pay that off?'

'It may not be a lot to you,' I began, appalled at hearing my voice tremble, 'but to me – to me and the vast majority of the population . . .'

'What's fifteen thousand?' he said, smoothly. 'I'll tell you. It's a week's skiing in Aspen . . .'

'Only a week?' I was being sarcastic.

'Depends how you want to travel; depends where you want to stay. It's, oh . . . about five kilos of white Alba truffles from Valvona and Crolla.'

'I bought an orange there once. It still had leaves on. I took it to Gayfield Square and ate it and the juice ran up my arm. So you bought truffles. There's nothing better than a few shreds of truffle in a nice risotto. I suppose you had truffles in everything for a while, did you?'

'I hate to admit this, but I went skiing and forgot about them. They went off.'

'That's terrible, Jamie.'

'I know. I haven't done it again.'

'How much did you buy?'

'A hundred and eighty pounds' worth of fungus. I ordered over the phone and some nice girl in the office at Valvona and Crolla didn't even get to see the colour of my credit card.'

'Gold?'

'Black.'

'Black?'

'Amex marketing to the wealthy insecure – but you wouldn't understand.' I didn't. 'I bought some very good wine at the same time.' He picked up his glass, looked thoughtful.

'How much was that?'

He whispered something plausibly absurd. I told him he was mad. He replied that he would never live beyond his means. 'Don't take me too seriously, Rose.'

'I don't.'

'I don't hoard money. Life's too short.'

'I wouldn't hoard it either, but enough would be nice.'

'What would you call enough?'

'Enough to cover necessary basics, plus a bit left over to enjoy.'

'Say you had quite a lot of money – more than you needed. What would you do with it?'

This fantasy had whiled away many a long night shift. 'I'd buy an interesting house with character.'

'Assume you've already got that.'

'It has to have a brand new fridge that I don't share with anyone else.'

'Seems a funny thing to be possessive about, but okay.'

'I'd buy lots of clothes instead of wearing my sisters' cast-offs. I'd travel. I'd buy novels by my favourite authors as soon as they came out in hardback. I'd buy nice things to eat and nice things to drink and . . .'

'These are necessary basics, Rose. What about the other things?'

'If I was travelling long distance, I'd go first class. I'd have long-distance trips and lots of shorter breaks and weekends in famous hotels, like The Cipriani in Venice. Last time I went to Venice, I slept on the steps outside the station.'

'Poor thing!'

'It was still good though.'

'You innocent!'

We smiled at each other. 'Anything else?' he asked.

'I'd find a good masseuse. I'd go to a beauty salon and have manicures and pedicures and facials and things like that. I'd always have fresh flowers in the house and chocolates. And I'd get a piano and have lessons.'

'A piano?'

'I've always wanted to learn the piano.'

'Fair enough.'

'I'd buy dozens of glossy magazines and . . . and . . . I'd lunch!'

He smiled at me, like Santa Claus making a mental note.

'What about you?' I asked. 'It must be boring – already having everything.'

'I cope.'

'What more could you possibly want? A platinum cigarette lighter with a discreet diamond on the side?' He showed it to me. 'It's a bit glam, isn't it?'

'Is it?' He looked worried. 'Better get rid of it then.'

'What about a yacht?'

'Had half a catamaran once.'

'Villa in the south of France?'

'Sold it.'

'Fifteenth-century Italian chess set?'

'Bought it in New York.'

Over dessert (chocolate roulade for me, crème brulée for him), he told me how he made a living. If one were to describe what Jamie and his ilk actually did during office hours, 'work' would be hyperbolic. They seemed to operate under the kind of breaks and tea trolleys atmosphere only experienced in Britain during the 1950s. The reason for this was because the firm had to indulge them; these particular employees had sway over the investment of millions and nothing must be allowed to upset them. They were financial riveters, making widgets for the City.

He said he didn't have to make decisions very often, but when he did they were as big as . . . as big as the distance between his outstretched arms and almost as far-reaching. It seemed the power could be God-like – albeit God working on a hunch. I suppose it wasn't just a hunch – when it comes to investment there's no such thing as a free hunch. He worked hard for his bonus, he claimed. And he had made sacrifices.

There was a time, ten years ago, when all he had wanted to do was travel round South America climbing mountains, but after falling down a ravine and spending months in a wheelchair, he had abandoned his dreams of the remoter Patagonian peaks. Stuck in a gale-blasted town near the Paine Massif, he had had nothing to occupy his mind but slow-knitting bones and Spanish conversation lessons. 'Very poor access for the disabled in Puerto Natales,' he said. 'It made me think.'

'About what?'

'Stairs.'

'Stairs?'

'Yes. A big house with stairs. High ceilings, tall windows and four flights of stairs. I made the money and I bought one.'

He sat back. This was clearly the hiatus in his story reserved for my gasp of admiration. I asked why he hadn't just bought a fourth-floor flat.

'Because,' he said, impatiently, 'I had promised myself I'd buy a whole house.'

'Couldn't you have changed your mind?'

'I'd made a *promise*, Rose.' He spoke as though he'd written it with his own blood in setting concrete. 'It was a reason. Motivation. I spent a lot of time working out how I could buy a house. I didn't have much money ten years ago. Think of it as mental physiotherapy.'

'So you got rich. Gosh! Well done, you!' He grinned and stole a spoonful of my chocolate roulade. 'So how did you get from falling into the ravine to arriving at the desperate state you're in now?'

He had fallen into something much worse. He had made a pact with the devil and sold his soul to finance – Dr Faustus MBA.

'How *could* you do an MBA? It's so vulgar!'

'But it was ages ago, Rose. Water under the bridge. And everybody was doing them back then and at least I did it abroad – in the States.' He had planned to earn his house money in five years. 'I was pretty certain I could make it through sheer pragmatic realism and cynical calculation and five's my lucky number.'

Having got the MBA – 'very hard work; nasty' – he went to Seattle for a rest. 'It was lovely there – skiing, sailing, scenery. I mucked about, made some nice friends.' After Seattle he moved to New York and 'got more into the finance thing'. Once he'd got the hang of it, he moved to London and then: 'I had a good idea.'

'A whole one?'

'Half-baked, but still . . .'

'So going to London worked for you, did it?'

'Right place, right time, got lucky.' After that he reckoned he could afford to live off his investments.

'But Jamie, isn't that hoarding?'

'No.'

'Yes, it is.'

'No, it isn't.'

He had come home to Edinburgh (his nice accent still triumphantly intact), taken up a 'harmless job offer' and bought a large Georgian townhouse.

'So you like your job, do you?'

'Not much, it's a bit boring.'

'Why do you do it, then?'

'Golden handcuffs. I'm highly paid to ignore my boredom. Don't be hard on me, Rose. I've negotiated extra holiday instead of some of my bonus. The money doesn't mean that much to me, to be honest.'

'But at least you've got your subscription to *Period Homes* and you can fill your big house with investment furniture and cosy old paintings and little bits of Art. So fulfilling!'

'Big Art – high ceilings, remember – and that particular magazine was not one I ticked on your survey. You'd like my house – it's got character. I do have one old picture, but it's not cosy. It's a portrait of a famous Victorian engineer. An arms dealer. He invented a big gun and had a massive factory on the Clyde. I bought the portrait because the house used to be his.'

'Really?'

'Yes, and after he died, his beautiful young widow ran up massive debts. She was a gambler. Feckless. I found a pack of playing cards in a silver box hidden up a chimney.'

'Honestly?'

'Yes, and the court cards and the aces are wider at one end, but I shouldn't have told you that.'

'Why shouldn't you?'

'Because I could have played you and won.'

'Who lives with you in your big house?'

'No one.'

'All alone?'

'All alone. Well, Irina's there for a few hours most days, pottering around when I'm out. Housekeeping and so on. Don't worry, Rose, she's a hundred and six.'

'I wasn't worried. Isn't she a bit old for the job?'

'I tried having a much younger housekeeper but it didn't work out. The place just fell apart domestically, so I offered Irina the job. Irina's a retired spy,' he added.

'Really? Honestly?'

'They've got to make a living now the Cold War's over.'

'Is she really a retired spy?'

'And concert pianist,' he said, dead-pan, 'but that was just a front.'

'Have you got a piano?'

'Yes. My mother used to play. Irina gave lessons.'

'Are your parents in Edinburgh?'

'They're dead.'

'Oh, I am sorry.'

'It's a long time ago now.'

'Who brought you up?'

'People who were very well paid to do it. I had inherited the earth.'

'You don't strike me as particularly meek.'

'Meek?'

'"And the meek shall inherit the earth",' I explained. 'You know, from the Sermon on the Mount.'

'Ah, yes,' he said, 'and have you heard Getty's version?'

'Getty?'

'John Paul Getty, the billionaire. "And the meek shall inherit the earth – but not the mineral rights thereof."' He drained his glass as near to the dregs as possible.

'Did you really inherit a lot of money?'

'Yes and no.'

'When you woke up at the bottom of the ravine, how did you feel?'

'Electrifyingly alive.'

'Did you have to wait long to be rescued?'

'I dragged myself back to the beaten track.'

'How far?'

'Two miles.'

'I don't believe you!'

'Is that the first thing I've said you don't believe?' he asked, gleefully.

'You'd have sent your Patagonian personal guide for help and started eating the hotel's packed lunch!'

Our dinner was inexorably drawing to the bill, tip and taxi stage. I had a double espresso to get my mind into gear. When the bill came, I read it upside-down and saw that it amounted to six months' worth of early morning office cleaning. It made me wish I had paid more attention to the wine. The thought occurred to me that Jamie would spend more money on eating out than I would earn in my entire lifetime.

'Do you really have absolutely everything you want, Jamie?'

'Not absolutely everything, no,' he replied, getting into his coat. I didn't have a coat. The anorak was back at the flat; I hadn't thought it co-ordinated with my cocktail dress.

'What else could you possibly want?'

He watched me smooth down the creases in my new strappy dress. 'It's not quite the right time to tell you, Rose.'

He was as smug as a jar of caviar and just as rich and sleek.

Chapter 5

We walked to the waiting taxi. 'Rose,' he said, 'you're not very good at spotting lies, are you?' His clear, blue eyes watching my face intently.

'I might miss a few, I suppose. I don't do lies myself.'

He took my right hand in his and said very solemnly, as if making a promise: 'Rose, don't believe me.'

'I'll have to rely on your actions then.'

He laughed, put his arm round me, hugged me. I felt warm and pleased. 'Where would you like to go?' he asked, quietly. 'Home or home with me?'

'Home with you.'

We sat side by side in the back of the cab.

He lived in one of a single row of Georgian houses built with an outlook of Salisbury Crags and Holyrood Park. The cab rumbled over cobbles and stopped halfway down the street. I got out, he paid the driver. A few steps up to a broad front door, his hand resting lightly at the small of my back, and then I passed through the door into a large vestibule. Tarnished old mirrors on the walls. On again through double glass doors to a wide hallway. Black and white floor tiles and then stairs rising up four floors with a wrought iron balustrade. It was very typical of houses in Edinburgh's New Town. (I knew this because of my cleaning career.) The only obvious difference was that this house was warm. Jamie flung his coat over a chair and showed me upstairs to the drawing room.

It was at the front of the house; very large, beautifully proportioned with high ceilings and three tall windows with long reveals. The room was mostly plain but he obviously had eclectic taste for there was a fantastical Venetian glass chandelier, the rarer kind, with coloured as well as clear glass drops, like sweets. (The rarer kind because of the few that were made, so many got smashed in transit over the centuries – all those careless stevedores and mulepackers.)

On one wall hung three striking avant-garde paintings which looked like part of a series – maybe it was the whole series. Between the windows stood two delicate chairs. For more practical sitting down there was a large, asymmetrical modern sofa and two decrepit leather armchairs. These were arranged around a fireplace with high marble surround. The floor was polished at the edges, covered almost completely by a sun-spoilt Turkish rug – a kind of ruined glory. There was an air of refined ravishment about Jamie's house. More or less what you'd hope to find in the house of a rich thirty-to-forty-year-old who could have anything.

He threw some fuel at the grate (peat – an earthy smell, perfect for late-night drawing room whisky drinking) and I sat down in one of the armchairs. Between us was a low table and on it I saw a yellowed piece of paper with the words 'Edinburgh Tournament' printed across the top. It was his record of the moves from our last game – briskly neat at first, a defeated scrawl by the end. Jamie lit a cigarette and poured our drinks. I set up the board. Beautiful old oak and mahogany pieces.

This most cerebral of games always begins with a round of Which Hand Is It In? (also known as sortilege). 'Left hand,' I said. He disclosed a black pawn which was bad news for me because it meant he had the advantage of the first move, playing White. He tried not to look too pleased about it.

When I used to play competitively, I made it a habit to wear nail varnish. I just liked seeing long painted nails poised over the board. Male chess players cannot achieve this psychological advantage. Not the ones I've played anyway. For my evening with Jamie, I had chosen a flame red called 'Revenge'.

The opening I knew he'd choose and we played on. My painted nails accepted the pawn sacrifice and the minutes ticked by. I moved another pawn in what I knew would be an open invitation to trouble and he sat for some time considering how best to reply. I took a good look at him. His dark lashes lowered, his hand resting on his cheek. If I could touch him now, his skin would feel warm under my fingers.

His move, my move. All up to him now. I held my breath and hoped he wouldn't go for it, although part of me hoped he would. His fingers paused for a second over the king, but there was never really any doubt he'd do it. The clock struck midnight and Jamie castled, which meant I had to take his knight. Fortunately, the depth of my own concentration took away any unsettling thoughts of going to bed with him. I sipped my whisky, feeling it evaporate hotly in my mouth. Decided against a cigarette. On the mantelpiece were silver candlesticks support-ing a drift of stiff white cards – invitations to dinners and parties and various soirées.

He moved his queen and captured a pawn, then relaxed in-to the armchair and looked at the board with disconcerting pleasure.

I didn't want to lose. I knew I should probably move my queen too. Is it a good idea or not to exchange queens? I thought hard. I looked at it from different angles. I even sat on the floor to see if the position looked any better from eye-level. It didn't. After considerable mental exertion, I worked out I didn't have the answer. 'I need longer to think about this,' I said, still staring at the board.

'Come back to it later?'

I looked up and oh, the curve of his smile! He certainly didn't come out with a kitsch line like 'Let's play something else', and if he had I would have died of embarrassment. He stood up and held out his hand. I thought, oh dear, this is where he finds out I can't do sex. Pretty good at chess, but sex – still only playing draughts, I'm afraid. But for me to have run away at that point would have been bad manners and cowardice. As gracefully as I could, I levered myself out of the armchair and accepted his hand.

He led me out of the room. On the landing, the moonlight melted palely through the glass cupola on the roof and swooned down four floors to the hall. We walked quickly to the stairs, and on the third step passed a portrait. 'Who's that?' I asked, playing for time.

'That's the arms dealer.'

'The one who died and left a feckless, gambling widow?'

'That's the one.'

'Where's her portrait, then?'

'Not here. She gave it to her lover.'

'Oh!'

'The arms dealer just didn't turn her on – plenty of feck, but obviously no fun at all.'

I can't do this, I thought. I'll be no fun at all. I couldn't move any further. He didn't realise I was petrified because he said happily, 'Come on,' and took my hand again, went up to the next step. My hand and heart stretched out to him, but my body didn't follow.

'Isn't the moonlight lovely?' I tried. 'Friday the thirteenth and a full moon too!' My next comment would have been something panicky about the weather, but very, very fortunately he had already stopped on that one step ahead of me, looking at my washed-clean, non-inky hand in his.

'Oh, Rose!' he said achingly, pressing it to his lips. He returned with my hand and arm and drew the rest of my petrified body towards him. He kissed me. A warm, beautiful kiss that left my lips tingling. It felt like shockingly intimate contact. I stopped feeling as though I'd been turned to stone and instead gave in to the feeling of wanting him. Desire! The mouth I had wanted on mine was full of kisses. Fell slowly, rapturously, on to the stairs, kissing. Sort of got lowered there, his arms around me. Astonishing! All very passionate. He kissed my face and my neck and my shoulders and then straps got slipped off the strappy dress, buttons got undone and everything. And I thought: look how desirable I am! We're going to do it right here, on the stairs. But then he stopped, breathless. 'Oh God!' he cried, took my hand again, helped me up and we made it to the bedroom.

I didn't notice the room itself – just stared with dreadful fascination at the big, dark mahogany bed, the soft, plump, white pillows, the serenely smooth sheets. He said: 'I'll leave you a moment.' In a daze, I dropped my clothes on the floor, pulled back the bedcovers and climbed in. It felt cool and gently yielding. I waited, nervously. What had they all said about me? The words came back and started creeping furtively around the room, ready to jump out and appal me.

He returned. I didn't want him to see me looking anxious and ghastly so I quickly switched the light off. I felt the corner of the bedcover being lifted and he moved close up to me. Tentatively, I reached out a hand and checked down the length of his body. Everything seemed to be there.

Clothed kissing on the stairs was much more my level. Everything was now just a bit too nakedly, horizontally, sexually challenging. He was saying something, but I was too busy keeping my panic under control to take any notice. I told myself it was my own stupid fault I'd ended up in his bed and I'd just have to go through with it. Make a fool of myself. Get it over with.

I told him if he didn't hurry up I was going home. He laughed. 'Now!' I cried. He asked me if I really meant that. I shut my eyes and said 'Yes!' – said it quite a few times, actually. After that, things got desperate. I wondered what to think of to take my mind off it. England? Scotland? Why not Majorca? Had a lovely holiday there last summer. I played football on the beach at Puerto Pollença with my friends – girls versus boys and the girls won. The boys just couldn't believe it, said we'd moved the beach towel goalposts, said it should never have gone to penalties. My ex-boyfriend's favourite line from a song: 'How can you lie there and think of England when you don't even know who's in the team?' We won by one goal. I kept some sand as a souvenir, put it in a jam jar on my desk when I got home. Happy memories. My favourite holiday.

He knew I was pretending, I'm sure of it. I'm so useless at pretending. What must he think of me? Probably that I was a boring, embarrassing waste of time. What a big mistake. What a really bad one-night stand. Good job she'll be gone tomorrow.

Complete and utter and absolute catastrophe.

I curled up, thinking to myself: Well, that's got that over with, then. He hugged me, kissed the back of my neck and said something about 'truly, madly, *briefly*', said we had 'hours and hours and hours now'. I thought: Christ! As many as that! I pretended to be asleep. I ignored all the gentle little caresses and after a while he gave up.

Quite a while later, I edged my way out of bed. Creeping out of the room, I ran down two flights of stairs, in the nude, past the disapproving portrait. I had this urge to laugh hysterically and I had to get as far away from him as possible. I opened doors to bedrooms, doors to sitting rooms and eventually found a bathroom, locked the door, turned the lights on and there was my reflection in a long mirror. My body mocked me and I reached for a towel to cover myself up. The bath towel was thick and soft and warm. I leaned against the towel rail and felt a few degrees warmer. Funny how some little bit of physical comfort can console you.

I stared into space. I wasn't pretty like The Pretty One and I wasn't very clever either. I thought about how celibacy was all right, really; thought how much I wished I was good in bed – whatever that meant; wondered what making love with him would have been like if I had been; felt a bit upset when I remembered how much I had wanted him when we had kissed on the stairs. And the whole difficult experience wasn't over yet because I wasn't the sort of coward to sneak off before morning. At least I could manage to avoid any more sex: not fall asleep in order to get up first. When I faced him in the morning, I would be dignified. I would conduct myself in a manner befitting an invited guest. I hoped he would be polite to me, like a hospitable host. We could have a cup of coffee and part amicably.

But in the meantime, what could I do?

I was in a very big bathroom. It was big enough to contain a sofa and a wardrobe as well as a bath. I opened the right door of the wardrobe and there were towels and bathrobes; I opened the left door and realised it was a fridge. A lot of beer, some wine, some orange juice. I couldn't help but be envious. And then, turning around, I noticed that above the bath there was writing on the wall. I looked closer. Yes, writing on the wall. Some trendy design of wall tile, perhaps? No, it was real writing. It was chess notation. A special waterproof pencil (the kind that divers use) was resting in the soap dish. He must do his thinking in the bath. I wondered if it was cheating to read your opponent's preparatory notes for a game, but I set my misgivings aside. All's fair in Love and War. I read the opening: *1. e4, e5. 2. f4, exf4. 3. Nf3, g5.*

The highly tactical King's Gambit was most popular during the nineteenth century. Nowadays, people avoid it as too risky because it gives White as many problems as Black. It's an extravagant kind of opening, freeing up the board to all manner of possibilities. When I'd first met Jamie in the tournament twelve years ago, I had banked on his being unfamiliar with the King's Gambit. It had rattled me a little when he had been unable to resist the reckless g5 move. After that, there was never any question about our willingness to get into trouble together.

I read on: *4. Bc4, g4* and then he had castled, with the Muzio, which is even more spectacularly risky than the King's Gambit. Material differences don't count as much in the Muzio. It's more a matter of nerve. It's about having the nerve to forgo the reassuring niceties of logic and allowing the intuitive side of the brain to engage with a puzzle of staggering complexity. (Computers flounder at the Muzio because it defies reason, but the move holds a fatal attraction for players who love chess as a kind of art.) I accepted Jamie's sacrifice of a knight and that got him a very nice piece of development. His next and final move before we adjourned had been to use his queen to take my pawn: *6. Qxf 3 . . .* which was where the notes stopped. He hadn't speculated on how I might reply to that. Maybe the bath water had gone cold by then. He had simply written: *Even Chances.*

And now it was my turn again; I was under pressure, doing badly and very short on inspiration. I looked about. There was a broad ledge all the way round the bath and at one end stood an empty bottle of wine, a hipflask (also empty) and a cigar cutter. On the floor were two remote controls. I picked up one, pointed it at a cluttered shelf on the opposite wall and pressed play. A maudlin guitar solo about having a hard road to travel and how his baby don't treat him right. I switched it off. Nothing on the TV either, just a football video: 'Classic Own Goals'. Nothing of interest there. But there was also a stack of water-damaged paperbacks and all of last week's newspapers. I used the diving pencil to do the *Financial Times* crossword, then started browsing through his books: a novel by Graham Greene, a novel by Ernest Hemingway, a disintegrating chess book with dense columns of notation. A hand-written receipt (twenty pesos) was tucked into an analysis of the King's Gambit ('Inadvisable,' I read, 'but under certain circumstances . . .').

Eventually, I had to go back upstairs. The moonlight streamed in through the bedroom window. He didn't move when I lay down beside him. I thought how nice he looked asleep. I closed my eyes. I did like him a lot, didn't I, despite everything? The pillow felt cool and I started twisting my hair again, feeling sad. I could hear him breathing quietly, then the soft sound of sheets slipping as he moved towards me. I was very still. And then he reached across the pillow to where my hand was still caught up in my hair and I felt his fingertips somehow slip between mine and begin to circle, very gently, in the palm of my hand. It made me want to cry.

'Rose?' he whispered.

I couldn't speak; tried and failed. I must remember to breathe, I thought. 'Rose?' I opened my eyes and faced him in the moonlight, lifted his hand to my lips and kissed it.

He seemed to take a deep breath. We both did, actually. Mine was for courage – that moment on the edge of the highest diving board; his sounded more like hope. He traced his fingers over my face, touching my cheek, brushing across my lips. A bit overwhelming to watch his expression while he did that, so I shut my eyes again. He kissed my throat. Warm lips lingering there. I opened my eyes, surprised at how I felt. 'I can feel your pulse racing,' he said. I wanted to make some glib comment, just to prove I wasn't completely clueless, just to pretend that the stupid thing he'd said hadn't turned me on, but I couldn't say a word. Incoherent. I wrapped my arms around him and felt the warmth of his hands moving down over my thighs. 'Warm and soft and beautiful,' he sighed. And that's when I froze. Research has proved she's frigid, I thought. Frigid and boring apart from when she's alarming and mad for it. And those funny things she says and those weird things she does. Isn't it hilarious? Was she like that with you, too? Freeze, froze, frozen.

'What's the matter, Rose?'

'Nothing,' I squeaked.

I couldn't tell him. I couldn't own up. It was too humiliating.

'Rose?'

'Nothing.'

He held me closer, pulled the duvet up over our heads. 'It's dark,' he said, ruffling my hair a bit. 'Tell me.'

'No.'

'Tell me.'

'I can't.'

'Lie to me, then.'

'Lie?'

'Yes. Make something up.'

We were wrapped in the dark together, he kissed my fore-head, held my hand. 'Lie to me,' he repeated. So I told him that, despite the strappy dress and the high heels, despite my doctorate and my former subscription to *Cosmopolitan*, there were some areas where, surprisingly enough, to be perfectly honest, I didn't really have such a very high personal success rating.

He said, 'Such as?'

I stuttered and stammered and fidgeted with the duvet and eventually I blurted out: 'I can't do maths!'

'Maths?'

'I can't do maths!' I cried, amazed at myself. I told him that it was a constant surprise to myself and to everyone else that despite being very good at chess I couldn't do maths. It was just a mental block. I had never really got the hang of it. I had a record of terrible mistakes, basic errors and exposure to ridicule and if he asked me to do fractions I'd panic. I was fraught with anxiety. 'I can't do maths, I can't do maths.' All my fears seizing me at once. Incredible! And in fact, he said:

'That's incredible. I don't believe you.'

'It's true!'

'But maths is such a doddle.'

'I've never thought so.'

'I'd never have guessed.'

'Percentages! Oh God, percentages!'

'Piece of cake.'

'And algebra!'

'You're just trying to turn me on.'

'I'm not.'

'Well, you have.'

I could tell by his voice that he was smiling. I began to feel better and even mentioned geometry. I told him that if he'd met my sister they'd probably be doing quadratic equations by now, but he'd met me – so no such luck. He said: 'I think you should use the real words, Rose.'

After that, he wouldn't let me use a metaphor again (even though he said it had been nice). We talked real words in the dark together and I felt myself unwrapping with the relief of it all. Unwrapped and enraptured. We talked beauty and obscenity. We defined it. And he gave me so much exquisite attention and so much praise that soon I was convinced I was the most wonderful thing that had ever happened to him. We made love all night, and some time in the early hours of the morning, sleepy and exhaustively happy, I thought to myself how a little bit of praise can go a long way. A little bit of praise can wrap its arms around me and go as far as it likes, whenever it feels like it.

Chapter 6

I started seeing a lot of him. Our meetings tended not to be pre-arranged; he just turned up. Mid-morning, Jamie would come in to Scot Burger and buy a Scotia-Cola. At lunchtime he would offer to respond to whatever market research survey I had on my clipboard. In this way he provided AB1 data on the wholesome-ness of Organic Oatmeal Soap ('fairly wholesome'), the scariness of Vampire Bubble Blood Bath ('very scary'), and the sexiness of Glamorama Body Spray ('about as sexy as being downwind of a cheese pasty').

He gave me a lift to my night shifts at the call centre in Livingston, but what was really surprising to both of us was that he would return at two a.m. to pick me up. I repaid his kindness by falling asleep in the car on the way home. He knew I would fall asleep so he asked me the important question straightaway:

'Where do you want to go?'

'Home with you.'

After a week of this I was completely exhausted. At Scot Burger, I got a reprimand for persistent day-dreaming. At the call centre, I fell asleep and got marched around the car park by the supervisor and given two Pro-Plus tablets. That night, Jamie didn't appear to pick me up and I realised, wide-awake and agitated, that I had been depending on it.

The next day, when he strolled up to me on Princes Street, I demanded to know where he had been at two a.m.

'I was asleep.'

'But you didn't come and get me,' I said, fretfully. 'I know we never actually arrange it, but . . .'

He put his arms around me. 'I wish you didn't work all the time, Rose.' I gave in to the hug. 'You smell nice again,' he said, happily. 'I couldn't stand that Glamorama stuff.'

'I'm tired!' I whinged. 'I want to go home to my own flat. I've got three free hours before I have to leave to do tele-sales and I want to go to sleep.'

'Not doing your sisters' cleaning, then?'

'Not on Tuesdays.'

'Take your clipboard back to Scary Mavis. I'll walk home with you. I've finished at the office for today.'

'Lucky you!'

'I'm working from home. Got to do some sums for a meeting.'

We walked along Princes Street together, his hand holding firmly on to mine. (He had noticed straightaway that I tended not to pay attention at crossroads. Unlike me, he always looked both ways, never wandered dreamily out and there was no danger he'd ever get run over.) 'My friend Claudine met her husband on a train,' I said, à propos of nothing at all.

'Did she?'

'They were both going from Dijon to Paris on a high-speed train. He was an American tourist. Have you ever been on a TGV? It's quite interesting, travelling at two hundred and twenty-five miles an hour at ground level. The scenery goes by so fast – except if you're looking at the horizon of course, but even then it's fast, relatively speaking. The journey took ninety minutes and they fell in love.'

We walked on, through the crowds, past the beggars and the shoppers and the tourists, past the party of French teenagers with their identical mini-rucksacks, hanging around outside Scot Burger.

'Claudine used to be a librarian at the Sorbonne. She found me this twelfth-century manuscript with the earliest recorded use of the verb "dalier". I got a grant to write about it. Took me months and months. Jamie . . .'

'Hm?'

'They spent a week not going out together in Paris.'

'Nice holiday.'

'At the end of the week he asked her to marry him and she said yes. And then he confessed that he had just inherited a hundred million dollars' worth of Californian real estate and he hoped she wouldn't hold that against him.'

'She didn't, I suppose.'

I thought about Claudine who had never bothered to work again. She had become a pool-side reader. At the age of twenty-six, Fortune had smiled most munificently upon her. *Voilà!* She was made.

I felt a sharp tug on my arm. 'Rose!' he shouted, pulling me back. 'Didn't you see the bus?'

'What bus?' I vaguely remembered seeing a colour and feeling hot air rushing past my face. Looking around, I realised we were standing on an island in the middle of the road. 'Was it a Lothian Regional Transport bus?' I asked. 'Maroon?'

'How have you survived this long?'

'Missed me by a mile.'

We reached the other side, him repeating to himself, awestruck: 'I've just saved your life. I've just saved your life.'

Hours later, staring at the psychedelic curtains, he said: 'Don't go to work. Don't go to Livingston.'

'Why not?' I asked, looking for my clothes.

'Because I can't give you a lift as I've got to do some corporate schmoozing at Scottish Accidental and I'm worried about you crossing the road.'

'I have to go. Tele-sales is my best-paid job.'

'I don't see you often enough. I never see you for long enough. Tell them you can't go in.'

'I can't do that.'

'I'll tell them. What's their number?'

'Why bother? I can't be with you if you're schmoozing, can I?'

He looked at me standing there, clothes in my arms, and seemed to make something of a snap decision. I listened while he phoned Scottish Accidental and claimed a personal injury which prevented his attendance at their meeting with General Liability. After that, he sounded very sincere explaining to Tell-Tales Tele-sales that Rose Budleigh couldn't come to work this evening because she had had an accident.

I felt guilty about it, but he was very consoling.

The alarm woke me at 5.20 a.m. I only had ten minutes before leaving the flat. My early mornings were the worst time of my day, so I always tried to keep them as brief as possible.

'I have to go,' I said, kneeling by the bed.

'Right now?'

'In a couple of minutes. I'm nearly ready. Where's my pink cardigan with the holes in the elbows?'

'Where you left it.'

'Where's that?'

'My house. It's lying on the sofa in the nice warm bathroom.'

'Will I see you this lunchtime?'

He shut his eyes, winced. 'Might be working my lunch hour.'

'Surely not?'

'Scottish Accidental. I'm scunnered. They'll want an explanation. Personal injury! Christ!'

'I thought it was just a bit of schmoozing you missed.'

He looked at me helplessly. 'Sometimes I wish we hadn't met again. Hard to keep you in perspective.' I kissed him goodbye. 'Maybe I'll just keep you.'

Chapter 7

'Where have you been?' asked Catherine. 'You've missed three weeks' cleaning. The living room's a mess.'

'There's a single empty coffee cup on the floor.'

'And the kitchen's positively stoury.'

'As bad as that? I'd better go and see.'

The kitchen looked like an operating theatre: white tiles and stainless steel. 'What have you been up to?' asked Catherine. 'I've missed our little chats. I always block time off specially.' She put the kettle on, got two mugs out. 'I won't be seeing you for a while. I'm leaving tomorrow for London. I've got quite a big contract on. Helen's away for a few weeks. She's all those on-site experiments coming up. She's going to be spending next month in a muddy field near Banff, looking for the potato that will save the world. She's daft, Helen.'

It should not be assumed from this that Helen was a member of some bizarre potato-centric cult. She was indeed daft, but in the Budleigh tradition she still had a high IQ. When it came to research into genetically modified potatoes, Helen Budleigh led the world's elite. She had created a potato that was immune to all forms of blight, resistant even to the deadly Colorado Beetle. Potato perfection. The potato to save the world.

'How's she's getting on?'

'Very well. There has been a secret consumer test held at Scot Burger. All the results went back to the US for analysis and the vice president for French Fries has decided that the Budleigh Beauty makes the best chips. They're talking about a deal with Bio-Caledonian.'

'Helen's going to be rich!'

'Possibly. The only trouble is, there are all these non-potato people getting involved now – marketing and PR – and they've decided that the best presentational angle for the Budleigh Beauty is not, repeat not, the fact that it is genetically modified.'

'Poor Helen! And she's spent years on her genetic tractor digging for the right DNA.'

'Too much public hostility to genetically modified food. They need a different angle now – something fun and tabloidy. They want to focus on the fact that the potato is almost a perfect oblong.'

'Of course. Ideal for chips.'

'And they think Scotland is the place to launch. But they don't like the name Budleigh Beauty so it's going to be renamed the Braveheart Potato. The idea is that it will rival the King Edward. Helen's distraught.'

Catherine held back from a smirk and for a few seconds we were united in a kind of sibling schadenfreude – happens all the time in families with three children.

'Oh, poor Helen!' I said, feeling bad. 'I must go to Banff and see her.'

'You can tell her what you've been up to,' said Catherine, slyly.

'I don't think so.'

'What have you been up to?'

'Just busy.' I opened the fridge so I wouldn't have to face her and reached inside for the milk:

'Busy doing something nice?' she asked, seeing my smile reflected in the stainless steel door.

'Yes,' I admitted.

'With whom?'

I dropped the milk and created a diversion.

'Oh, Rose, look at the mess!'

'Sorry.' I started mopping the floor. I didn't want to tell her about Jamie because I didn't want to face the interrogation. And I was very pleased to hear that Helen was stuck in a muddy field in Banffshire, because if Jamie saw her he would realise that I was a pale shadow trailing in her golden wake. I had been deserted for the Pretty One before.

'What's his name?' asked Catherine as I wrung out the floor cloth. I decided she couldn't discover much about him if I only gave away his first name.

'James.'

'A sound, Scottish name – all those Scottish kings called James. James who?'

'Not telling.'

'Why not?'

'Because you'd only find out exactly what his bank balance is and what he spends on his credit card and where he buys his socks.'

'No, I wouldn't.'

'You would, Catherine, and I don't want you to know.'

I wiped the slate floor clean. 'You've missed a bit,' she pointed, 'over there. Is he clever?'

'Sometimes,' I replied, cautiously.

At its worst, Jamie's cleverness manifested itself in an 'I've finished off the Supreme Challenge Prize cryptic crossword for you' sort of way. He always seemed to know a bit more. Perhaps it was just because he was older than me – widely travelled, seen a few more exotic crosswords. The things I knew about that Jamie didn't – medieval literature, low-paid jobs, dictionaries and old-fashioned roses – weren't always of great interest to him. However, there were a few things he knew about that I decided I wanted to know too. For example: 'Why all this fuss about wine, then? Why's that vintage not as good as this one?' Answer: usually to do with the weather: 'It rained,' he would say with affected grief, 'just at the wrong time.' I asked if he would explain how to read the *FT* share index. He said it was dead simple, that anyone with half a brain could understand it. He told me to pick a pretend portfolio and see what happened. It wasn't long before mine was out-performing his by a mile. He said it didn't surprise him in the least. I thought investment was like Fantasy Football – only it was Fantasy Finances. I'd been playing Fantasy Finances for years so it came very easily to me. However, I hadn't expected to meet with such success when pitted against a professional. It made me wonder what on earth he was paid to do at work.

'Haven't they got a computer that can do your job?' I asked.

'Yes.'

'Can it do it better than you?'

'Pretty often.'

'How have you still got a job, then? Why do they pay you so much?'

'They don't want to take a risk.'

I was amazed. 'Jamie, how clever do you think you are?'

'Clever enough,' he said, cagily.

'Only, there are things you've told me that prove you can rise to stupidity on occasion.'

'It wasn't all stupidity,' he protested. 'It was curiosity. That's what intelligence is about – and memory. Remembering vital details, like the name of your hotel and that kind of thing.'

'Or remembering: "I swear that I shall never mix champagne and vodka again as long as I live."'

'Blocked that one out.'

Some people are very curious but can't remember next day what they've found out or why. Some people have very good memories but the sports statistics they store up are of no curiosity to their girlfriends. He couldn't help the sports statistics: he was a man.

However . . .

His CD collection consisted of almost everything I had, plus everything I might have had given the money and a ten-year head start. In particular, he knew a lot more about classical music. Must be age. I told him I'd been to the Usher Hall to hear Shostakovich's Second Symphony (huge orchestra required, masses of trumpets and horns, all blasting away – exhilarating and very rarely performed). The bass and soprano parts were played by a trombone and a clarinet. I was telling Jamie all about it when he said: 'I remember going to a performance of the Second Symphony like that in New York. Did you like the daring trombone solo? Kind of defying the orchestra?'

'Yes, best bit.'

'Thought so.'

I loved being with him. He was generous and kind and handsome and funny. I wanted to be with him all the time and we were together as often as my four jobs would allow.

In my reading of romantic novels, I have always found it frustrating that you never really know exactly what's going on between the hero and heroine. All you know is that they are besotted with each other. The rest is modestly blurred. There might be dots at the end of the sentence like this: 'He unfastened the last three buttons on my flimsy chiffon blouse, Ping! Ping! Ping!, and bent to kiss me as I lay on the chaise longue . . .' (dot dot dot). And the dots don't really tell you anything, do they? Unless, like me, you are an expert in Morse Code, in which case they might tell you the first letter of what is going on. Which is 'S', of course. (Learnt Morse Code when I was a Girl Guide – got a badge for it.) 'Then he undid both buttons on my unwrap-over skirt –

Ping! Ping! – and sighed with desire when he realised I was wearing nothing else.'

Dot dot dot.

Dot.

Dash dot dot dash.

When the Budleigh sisters were Girl Guides, we used to think it was hilarious to tap out the above word at the family dinner table, knowing no one realised what we were doing. Every week we had Sunday lunch at our Cambridge Granny's with our relatives in all their trimmings, and this was the best time for secret Morse defiance. We did one letter each. 'I'll start,' Catherine would hiss in my ear, 'we're doing SEX – tell Helen.' Catherine would do 'S' on her place mat, I would do 'E' on the gravy boat and Helen, raring to go, would do 'X' on the spot.

I was reminded of this little family joke one night when Jamie and I were at the Café Royal, not far from his house. I'd never been there before and he thought I'd like it. It's quite small, the Café Royal in Edinburgh. Dark wooden panelling, Victorian mirrors and stained glass, smoke drifting in from the bar – all pleasantly louche. We were finishing off some oysters. (He had asked for them unopened so he could show off. Jamie had spent years successfully avoiding life's sharp edges which was probably why he was so good at oyster-shucking. It's one of those slightly esoteric skills, like Morse code or blindfold chess – there might come a time when you'll be glad you learnt how to do it.) The scene seemed perfect and I couldn't resist tapping out the wicked word on my glass of champagne. If my sisters could see me now! I thought. I moved on to drumming it on the tablecloth when suddenly he clamped his hand over mine and said, 'Shall we just go home now, then?'

Home was five minutes' walk away. I got my coat.

'Only my sisters would have picked up on that,' I told him as we set off briskly up Waterloo Place. 'So you know Morse Code, then?'

'No, just S-O-S.'

'How did you know E and X?'

'You never drum your fingers – that's never been a habit, even when you used to fidget all the time. Plus you were tapping in a pattern. "E" had to be a dot, didn't it? "X" had to be something long because it's not a commonly used letter. But mostly it was the smile on your face. And doing something like that is exactly your kind of whimsical silliness.'

'Is it?' I said, embarrassed.

'Yes, and I wasn't the only person who noticed. The elderly couple at the next table were having a discreet little laugh at us.'

'I don't believe you!'

'Believe me, Rose. She's an expert and he gives lectures. I went to hear him at the Royal Museum last year and I know they met at Bletchley Park during the War. You ought to be aware, Rose, that Edinburgh has more than its fair share of retired cryptanalysts. You never know who might be tuning in. You really must be more careful.' He kissed me. 'But it's all right, because I think you're lovely.' I was very impressed by this bit of deduction. A successful piece of seduction deduction. 'The trouble is, Rose,' he whispered in my ear, 'you're very easy to read.'

'Am I?' I said, disappointed.

I tried to keep up. We rounded the corner by St Andrew's House and all the flags were flying, brave and optimistic.

'Jamie, don't we get on well?' I said, impatient to be home. 'Do you think it's all down to reciprocity and serendipity?'

'Down to what?'

'Reciprocity and serendipity.'

He gave me an indulgent look. 'What's wrong with give and take and a bit of good luck? And anyway,' he smiled happily to himself, 'love is just a happy coincidence.'

'I wasn't talking about love.'

'Weren't you?' he said, quickly. 'Neither was I.'

'So,' I panted, hurrying along, 'give and take's got nothing to do with it.'

He stopped suddenly and turned to look at me. 'Sex is selfish,' he said, very deliberately. 'Mutually, agreeably selfish.' He was disarmingly direct. But then, it was Jamie's proud boast that he could never claim to be misunderstood. The fact that he enjoyed making love with me as much as I did with him was simply a lucky coincidence

So far, so lucky.

Chapter 8

On my next free Friday night, Jamie tried to prove he wasn't a philistine by taking me out to the theatre. 'I've bought tickets for some weird play you've never heard of on at The Traverse – you'd like that, wouldn't you? I'd do it for you, Rose. It only lasts an hour and then we can go home.'

The play was a dark musical comedy called *I Did It My Way*. It revolved (quite literally) around a man lying on his death bed and his thoughts during that final hour. 'Regrets, I've had a few . . .' – failed relationships, drink, drugs and bad decisions – but mostly it seemed he regretted the things he hadn't done, especially with a girl called Delilah (cue for another song). I thought the play was great fun, but Jamie was very quiet afterwards.

We got home and had penne puttanesca for supper, but not much conversation. 'Game of blitz?' I suggested.

'Okay.'

He waged a blitzkrieg of chess, beating me so comprehensively I was actually accused of not trying. 'Another game?' I offered, keen for some pay-back. 'Best of three?'

'No. I think I'll run a bath. See you in an hour or so.'

He disappeared and I was left alone, frustrated. I analysed the chess and realised how stupid I'd been. Why is it that a reasonably good player can make such unreasonably bad mistakes? Mistakes which Jamie had exploited with swift precision. I must be losing my touch, I thought, and vowed to stage a comeback just as soon as he got out the bath. I would redefine my strategy and sort out my timing.

Planning several hours ahead, I whipped up some meringues, and while I was waiting for them to cook, I read the paperback he had brought home from a business conference. It was called *The Bored Executive's Handbook: Feel the Apathy and Do It Anyway*. He had drawn cartoons in the margins and doodled over the diagrams. I thought: maybe I should go and see how he is now; he's had long enough. (It takes fifty minutes to cook meringues.) I turned off the oven, tucked the day's newspapers under my arm and headed upstairs.

At the bathroom door, I heard the final notes of Brahms' 'German Requiem'.

'Hello,' called a morose voice.

I went in. He was watching football with the sound off. 'What's this?'

'Peru,' he said, bitterly, '1978.'

'Why do you torment yourself like this?'

He shook his head and sank further down in the bath, blue eyes tragic as he stared at the screen. I sat on the floor beside him. 'Do you want some other music on, now?' He nodded.

In these circumstances, you have to be sensitive. You can't just slap on 'Summer Hits Ibiza' and expect it to do the trick. Plus, Scotland were still on the pitch. I found the right music, then settled myself on to the rug with the newspapers and my notebook. Jamie pulled himself together enough to ask what was playing. 'Is this one of yours?'

I nodded and passed him a sweet. I was quite content, sucking a soor plum and making notes on slangy catchwords for my new thesis. After a minute, he switched off the television.

'Rose . . .'

'Hmm?'

I listened while he talked himself round from melancholy. He began with the Munros he'd climbed last winter and how beautiful the view was from the top of Suilven – which wasn't a Munro but was still his favourite mountain in Scotland. Then he started on the problems of Pacific Rim economies and lost my attention. He captured it again with: 'Don't you think that a Graham Greene novel is always about struggling with your conscience?' Finally he reached for the hipflask and began on the qualities of his ideal marriage partner. Maybe I was just imagining it, but I couldn't help thinking she sounded a lot like me.

He got out of the bath to tell me how perfect I was. Eventually, we made it to the bedroom.

To win at speed chess, your responses have to be instinctively right. Hesitation is out of the question. Swithering can be fatal. In the thick of the action, you have to trust your intuition to carry you through.

'You're going to run out of time, Rose. What's the point of that fianchetto move?' He was trying to put me off because all his ideas had led nowhere and he was rapidly losing the centre. It would do him good! I rushed through a few pawn exchanges, then swept up both rooks, a bishop and a knight. I disposed of his queen and he was staggered. His lonely king limped around the board while I demonstrated a little queen-versus-minor-piece endgame. Jamie collapsed face down in the sheets of defeat. I didn't feel sorry for him; there's no room for compassion in chess. I threw on my bathrobe and headed downstairs. The meringues would be softly warm now – a late dessert to enjoy after the theatre, chess, music and sex. All the things I care for in life require a perfect sense of timing.

Very late in the evening, we sat up in the kitchen, drinking coffee and talking. 'Why don't we take a holiday?' he suggested. 'Have a weekend away somewhere?'

'I can't.'

'Can't you take one weekend off work?'

'Scot Burger isn't really like that. And I can't risk losing my tele-sales job. I've already got a black mark against my name for falling asleep and another one for having an accident. And Saturday is the biggest day of the week for market research. They don't do weekends off.'

He looked disappointed. Better change the subject, I thought. I don't want him miserable and boring again. I was about to give him the benefit of my knowledge on the art of fianchettoing when he said: 'Rose, darling.' Then he stopped, took a deep breath. Tried again: 'Darling Rose.'

'You never "darling" me,' I said, carefully. 'What's the matter? I don't like being darlinged.'

Heavy sigh. I waited. 'All right then, you're not a darling, but I think you're . . . well, you're . . . I worry about you, you know.'

'You do? Why?'

'Because you don't look where you're going. You're dreamy.'

'I'm not that bad.'

'You're hopeless, Rose. You don't even know what day it is.'

'Yes, I do.'

'What day is it? You're having to think about it, aren't you?'

'It's different when you work funny shifts.'

'It's Friday.'

'I know it's Friday! How do you think I managed before I met you?'

'Badly. You're a terrible responsibility to me.'

'You're not responsible for me!'

'I care about you. We're responsible for each other.'

'I don't look after you!'

'But you do,' he insisted.

He reached across the table, took my hands in his and stroked the fingers, distractedly. Holding both hands at the same time was always a sign of something momentous. He loved my hands. Loved them! The chess was a foible; hands a passionate fetish. He was gazing at them adoringly now. 'Have you always been like this about your girlfriends' hands?'

'No, only yours. Look how still they are now!' he said, marvelling. 'And they were still even though you had some tricky decisions to make around the fourteenth move. They were perfectly still and composed.'

'Still?' I said, baffled.

'Still and soft and relaxed.' Kiss. Kiss.

He didn't normally talk about it and I didn't ask him to explain himself. A fetish is incomprehensible to the uninitiated – completely esoteric – but if you're going to have any sort of fetish, hands must be the best one. So visible, so responsive, so many things you can do with them. Sometimes, he would raise my hand to his cheek, kiss the palm and then close my fingers around it – a kiss for me to keep. He did it now. It always made my heart turn over.

'Rose, what would you say if . . .?' His voice trailed away.

'What do you want to tell me?'

He laughed, nervously.

'Are you playing some kind of game with me here?'

'That'll do,' he said, beginning to look pleased.

'That'll do?'

'That's probably the best way to approach it.' His expression brightened, just a little.

'What are you talking about?'

'You'll see.'

'Do I get a clue?'

Long pause. He was trying to think of a cryptic one . . .

'No.'

. . . and had failed.

'So when do I find out?'

'Tomorrow.'

He smiled wickedly, seeing himself as some kind of rake, making progress. The walls of Jamie's house positively reeked with rakishness. I suppose it did have character. You got the feeling that there were scores of people who had philandered in the parlour, gambled away their inheritance in the drawing room, rolled drunkenly in the dining room grate, expired syphilitically in the beds where they'd been cuckolded.

The candlelight cast shadows over his face. 'You do mean a lot to me,' he said. And then, seeing my hand in his own, he added very quietly: 'You do *know*, Rose, don't you?' For a moment, he seemed unsure of himself. 'You do know that I . . . only want you to be happy.'

'I am happy.'

'Is there anything you want? Anything you need?'

'No.'

'Nothing at all?'

'Well, maybe a kiss.'

'Have mine,' he said.

Self-interested generosity. Then: 'Close your eyes.' He pressed something round and hard into my hand. 'Little present.'

'It's a sweet. It's a soor plum.'

'Don't eat it, Rose! And don't look yet – just hold on to it.'

I held on to it for ages but it didn't melt.

'Oh!' I exclaimed when I was allowed to look. 'Is it real?'

'Of course it's real.'

'It's lovely! But, oh, what shall I do with it – one pearl?'

'It's a very big pearl,' he said, hurt.

'I mean, I can't wear it or anything. It's got nothing attached to it.'

'That's because it's flawless.'

'Is it matchless, too?'

'I don't think I can run to joined-up ones that size.'

There was a special velvet box to keep it in. Such a pearl is a secret thing to treasure in private. I put his gift on the table. It glowed in the candlelight, a luminous full moon of a pearl. 'Do you like it?' he asked.

'Yes. Yes, I do. Thank you. It's a bit valuable though, isn't it?'

'Please don't say I shouldn't have bothered.'

'I would never say that, but *why* did you bother?'

'I wanted to.'

I wondered how much a very big pearl cost. Bad manners to ask. Any self-respecting rich man's girlfriend would have grabbed it with breathless enthusiasm, but I didn't.

I stared at it; I dwelt on it. Something peculiar was happening to me – an extraordinary physical sensation like joy and fear at the same time. Joy at finding him and fear of losing him, which could be a way of defining love, couldn't it? And falling in love meant gambling everything on a piece of hopeful speculation.

He watched me draw circles in the spilt sugar on the table. Little orbits of sugar round and round the pearl. 'Have you ever done any serious gambling, Jamie?'

'Apart from my day job, you mean? There was a time when I got into poker. Not any more.'

'Did you win much?'

'Being quick at figures helps. Good memory and so on.'

'Why did you stop playing?'

'Robert made me practise and I got bored.'

'Who's Robert?'

'I've known him for years, since we were kids. He mentioned poker just the other night, by way of telling me I was a complete liability.'

'Is he the one you told me about who makes a lot of money but no one really knows how?'

'I said very few people know how.'

'Is he any good at card tricks?'

'Very likely.'

'Is he a genius?'

'People have suggested as much.'

'Can he prove Fermat's Theorem? Because if he can, my sister Catherine would like to marry him.'

'What does she look like?' he asked, reaching for me. 'Like you?'

'A bit like me, only an inch shorter and with straight hair. She's the clever one.'

'Cleverer than you? What about your other sister?'

'She's the pretty one.'

'I don't believe it.'

'Oh, Helen's very pretty.'

'If she's supposed to be the pretty one, what do they call you?'

'I'm just the middle one.'

'The middle one!' he laughed.

'It's not great,' I admitted.

He kissed me. 'We'll have to go and see the statue of *The Three Graces*.'

'Why?'

'Because I've got these long lunch hours to fill.'

'I'll buy you lunch, if you like. I can run to coffee and a doughnut.'

'That's very kind of you.'

'Thank you for the pearl,' I said. 'I'm glad I didn't eat it.'

'Come on, Rose,' he whispered. Mutual intent. Complicity. We made for the bedroom, slipped between the sheets. No conversation need take place, just some self-indulgent, requited love-making.

The next morning, I didn't have to start my Market Research International shift until eleven o'clock. We stood at Jamie's bedroom window and he said: 'If you look down to the bottom of the garden, you can see a lane with a row of mews houses. That one on the end belongs to me.'

He had been very nice to me all morning, and when I wandered downstairs he made me breakfast. Lots of attention to detail – your whim is my command sort of thing. 'What kind of toast would you like?' he asked. 'White? Brown? Sourdough? Thick? Thin? How toasted do you want it? Well-done? Medium? Raw?'

'What do you really want to ask me?'

'Just tell me what you want for breakfast.'

'Thick, sourdough, medium. What's the real question?'

'What kind of coffee would you like?'

'What's on offer?'

I went for a rich, well-balanced, full-bodied blend. Can I really say it was a Fair Trade coffee? Why not? It was. When I agreed to look at his mews house, he seemed grateful.

The weather had turned clear and bright. He led me down the garden path, through the gate and there was the little house, tucked away at the end of the lane. It was very quiet. He opened the front door and we walked down a flagstoned hallway into a kitchen. 'There's a big, shiny, new fridge!' I exclaimed. Upstairs there were two bedrooms and a bathroom, all about as well appointed as any estate agent could wish for.

'Who did you let it out to before?'

'No one. Just bought it.'

We walked round once more; he asked my opinion on the decor. 'Not bad, bit boring.'

'It's not boring!' he said, offended. 'I think it's great!' And then he remembered he was making a pitch: 'How would you have it, then?'

Eventually, we wandered back to the big house.

At the kitchen table, we silently ate more hot buttered toast, both of us thinking hard. 'Did you pay much for it?' I asked, licking my fingers.

'It's an investment.'

'Are you going to let it?'

'You could stay there,' he said. 'If you like.'

'I couldn't afford the rent.'

'You wouldn't have to. Here are the keys.' He put them on the table – all to play for. 'They're yours if you want them.'

'It's free?'

'Yes.'

'I'd still be doing all my jobs, though,' I said, cautiously.

'That's not the idea.'

I watched him, fascinated. 'It isn't?'

'No.' Deep breath. 'I'd support you.'

'You want to keep me?' I laughed.

'Listen, Rose,' he said, sounding all serious. 'Let's be honest about this. You've got four lousy jobs and no money. I never see you. It feels like the only time I get to see you is when I'm watching you sleep. I want to be with you and it would be really good if you were awake at the same time.'

'I object in principle to being kept.'

'I'm sure you do. How about in practice? It's only money, Rose.'

'It's only money,' I repeated, slowly.

'Don't think about it as being kept,' he urged. 'It's not that. Time's much more precious. You're working all these hours and you're never, ever going to clear all your debts and . . .'

'Yes, I will!'

'You won't, Rose. You just won't.'

I played for time by getting another slice of toast and doing a bit of aggressive buttering. It's possible to make a mess of even the simplest thing if you're feeling cornered. Broken toast, crumbs everywhere. He touched my arm and said gently, 'Those jobs of yours – you're wasting your time. Far worse to waste your time than waste your money. Don't you want us to be together?'

'Yes, but . . .'

'Why not be self-*un*employed?'

'I could make a strong moral argument against what you're suggesting,' I said primly. 'What would my sisters think of me?'

'Keep it a secret.'

'I don't have any secrets from them.'

'Why not start?' he said, brightly. 'Let me keep you, and you can keep it a secret.'

'They'd know I couldn't afford to live there.'

'Say you've got a new job house-sitting.'

'I can't do that!'

'Rose, I just want to be with you.'

91

'Do you?' I poked the keys, resentfully. 'Why haven't you asked me to stay with you, here, in this house?'

'Stay wherever you like. Stay with me, but have the mews house as your address.'

'Why does it have to be my address?'

'Because I think things will work better that way.'

'Why can't I just have your address as my address?'

'If you wait until the end of July, I promise you'll understand then. You'll see why I think we should do it this way.'

'What's happening at the end of July?'

'I can't tell you right now. Please trust me.'

When he came out with that, I felt quite cheered. 'That's a very poor line of argument. You'll have to do better than that.'

'Okay. Why not look on the next few months as a holiday?'

'I'd like to take a holiday from my four lousy jobs,' I said, crossly, 'but I can't, because I need the lousy money. But at least it's my own self-supporting, lousy money – my own hard-earned income and . . .'

'Want some of my unearned income, Rose?' he said quickly. 'Want a credit card on my account?' He took my sticky fingers tenderly in his own. 'I mean it,' he said in a low voice. 'I really mean it. I'm not joking. I'm not playing at this.'

I stared at him, withdrew my hand. He watched it go all the way back to my fluttering heart, where it rested, shocked, a few toast crumbs still clinging. I could hear the clock in the hall, tick-tock, the seconds passing.

I couldn't help thinking that this was a very clever move for him to make. I could see his strategy clearly. In a game of chess, the aim is to keep your opponent neatly confined and under your control. He was thinking: I'll keep her exactly where I want her. Trap her in a corner, tempt her with gifts and seize the advantage. Spatial control is very important in chess. The game is a contest for space, time and material. He already had the material advantage. He had money to throw away on things like this. He had plenty of spare time to enjoy it. And now he was offering me a more tempting place to move to. Temptation, temptation. I shouldn't say yes. How much of a better player was I? Could I accept his offer and still win? Yes, no, maybe.

'I really don't know, Jamie.'

He leaned towards me, intently. 'When we met four weeks ago, I don't think I've ever been so attracted to anyone in my life. And it was so strange meeting you by chance like that because I'd never really forgotten you from twelve years earlier. You were so pretty then and now you're absolutely beautiful and I want you very much, and as if that weren't enough you're just exactly the level I want to play at chess.'

'How much of your unearned income?' I blurted out.

'Do you want to be that precise about it?' he asked, only slightly taken aback.

I hesitated; he was brilliant at exploiting hesitation. 'You decide. I'll play you for it,' he said.

'What?'

'I mean, we'll play chess and I'll bet on winning.'

'But I've been winning two games out of three. Odds are you'll lose your money.'

'Yes,' he said, patiently. 'So you can do maths, after all.'

And then I realised that there was a dazzling kind of fuzzy logic to all this. He watched me thinking about it. 'But what if you suddenly improved?' I asked. 'What if you started winning more often. I wouldn't be able to pay up and then—'

'Rose,' he interrupted. 'Rose, it really needn't be a problem.' He smiled knowingly, and I was out-manoeuvred.

I had met my match and it was very unnerving. If I loved him, it made everything more complicated and it made everything possible. I couldn't admit to love because that would be a kind of surrender. Whoever said it first would be giving up valuable material, admitting a vulnerabilty. And I wasn't completely sure yet what he thought of me.

'Jamie, tell me honestly what you think of me.'

'I think you're wonderful,' he said. 'I adore you. What do you think of me?'

'I think you're patronising and arrogant.' His face fell. 'But I'm very, very fond of you.' He looked more hopeful. 'The money's very nice and everything, but it's also a bit of a problem.'

'Think of it as sponsorship. I'll give you an interest-free fifteen thousand to pay off your debts.'

'A loan? You must be joking!'

'But don't pay it back. It's called a golden hello.'

'It's a bare-faced bribe!'

'A sweetener, Rose.'

'Enticement.'

'A gift.'

'How many more financial euphemisms do you know?'

'Quite a few.'

I have to be infatuated, I thought. It's the only explanation. 'It would be an interesting experience to look back on, I suppose,' I said, breezily. 'And it would only be until the end of July. Because after that I wouldn't need you any more.'

'Wouldn't you?' he said, anxiously.

'No, because after that I'd start my real job on the New Scots Dictionary. I'm sure they're going to like my new thesis and until then – well, you'd be a pleasant enough diversion for the holidays, wouldn't you?'

'You'd be my most treasured and beloved hobby.'

'I'd want a proper arrangement,' I began, sounding brisk about it, 'with a July thirty-first expiry date. After that, I won't be kept. But until then, I'd like certain things. I'd like a piano. And lessons. I'd like flowers, chocolates, clothes, accounts at my favourite shops. I'd like subscriptions to Italian *Vogue*, French *Marie-Claire*, Russian *Cosmopolitan*, *The New Yorker* and *Chess Monthly*. Oh, and I must remember to redirect my copy of the *Literary Review*. I'd like manicures, pedicures and other cures, facials, treatments and treats, and . . . and . . .'

'And you'd lunch,' he said. 'I seem to remember.'

I looked up into his face. He had a smile that could light a mile. I offered him my hand to hold. He took the other, too – stared at them, stroked them – all happiness. 'Why are your hands so nice?' he whispered.

'I don't know. Would you stay with me at that mews place or would I stay with you here?'

'Yes.'

'It was an either or kind of question.'

'With you. Anywhere. They're very soft.' Kiss left palm, kiss right palm, turn over, do it again. I got the impression he wasn't really listening. He put my hands together and closed them in his own, shut his eyes, funny little sigh. 'Now go and ring up all your jobs and resign.'

The Middle Game

Very little clear-cut instruction can be given on this phase of the game, but there exists an extensive field of theory. A lot of this theory is based on personal preferences, but certain aims and the means of achieving these aims are endorsed by all authorities. One thing is certain: it never pays to adopt wait-and-see tactics in the middle game

The Right Way to Play Chess by D. B. Pritchard

Chapter 9

I woke very late, got up very slowly and opened the curtains of my new bedroom. Another bright, sunny day. I had no plans, no obligations. I was completely free to do as I liked and it was a cheering thought. I walked downstairs, pushed open the kitchen door and there was the disorder of a decadent night before. Wax had dribbled down the candlesticks and was blobbed about the table, in between bottles and glasses, smears and stains. Underneath the table was carved for posterity the move: '0-0-0!!' – chess notation for castling queenside (brilliantly) and only funny if you're drunk at the time and have an incoherent girlfriend for an opponent. My favourite hangover cure was two ibuprofen, a pot of tea, oatcakes and honey. Jamie favoured deep breaths of pure oxygen and always kept a canister handy for this purpose. That and Irn-Bru (an infallible combination that had taken years of research and development). He had left me a note stuck to the honeypot: 'By the time you read this, it will probably be too late to meet you for lunch, but call me anyway.'

Drinking my tea, I looked at the mail. There was a postcard with his latest chess move on it. We had a correspondence game going too. I know we could have just walked down the garden and delivered the note by hand, but that wasn't the point. The postcards could be interesting, too. This one was a remnant of his holiday in Cuba – a beautiful girl in a string bikini. He had written: 'Kxf3. Having a great time. Wish you were her.' I found the postcard I had bought at the Musée d'Orsay on our trip to Paris and triumphantly wrote: '0-0-0!!' on the back of Courbet's *La Naissance du Monde*.

Now for the rest of the mail and my statement from John Lewis. In the left-hand column I read: Hosiery, Cosmetics, Hosiery, Lingerie, Handbags. I had spent a few hundred pounds. I moved on to the next envelope. I had only to scratch a card to win half a million. I did and found I was a lucky winner. I'd send it off to be entered into the free prize draw. I've always been a compulsive filler-in of competition forms. I can't throw them away – I might win! Which was probably why the marketing companies of the world had my new address long before my immediate family. Today, the junk looked very promising. Best of all was the prize of a holiday in India, courtesy of Bewley's, tea merchants, and all I had to do was complete the tie-breaking sentence: 'Bewley's make the best cup of tea because . . .' I munched my honey and oatcakes, picked up my lucky competition fountain pen and gave the sentence all the consideration my expensive education would allow. The gold-plated nib raced over the dotted line: '. . . it ain't just what they brew, it's the way that they brew it!' It didn't quite scan, but it was good enough to get to the short list and win a hamper.

I read *The Herald* and *The Scotsman*. To help my language studies, I always tackled the Gaelic column. Although at first glance those double consonants can be intimidating, Gaelic sounds much softer than it looks. I had started going to a beginners' class at the university and I never missed a Gaelic soap opera on TV in the afternoon. On one memorable occasion, Jamie 'working from home' had offered to translate. (If you ever get the chance to watch a soap opera in a language you don't understand, with live translation from a dear friend – do so. I could hardly breathe for laughing.) I was very impressed by his ability to speak Gaelic. (But then, most mainland Scots are easily impressed by a bit of Gaelic.) He told me he had spent every school holiday on the Isle of Barra, staying with his Great Aunt Flora, 'and when you're little, it's dead easy to pick up a language – especially if the locals are the only ones who ever take any notice of you'. He said to me: 'Let's go to Barra and you can practise your Gaelic. You go in a little sixteen-seater plane that lands on the beach at low-tide. Scheduled flights from Glasgow according to the phases of the moon.'

I was enchanted.

I folded the newspaper and tried to pronounce the words of the Gaelic column. It was something about love. I knew the word for love was 'gaol' because I'd looked it up fairly early on. 'Love is "gaol",' I had told him. 'That's so appropriate, isn't it? When you're being kept.'

'But you don't pronounce it like that.'

'How do you pronounce it, then?' He had told me and I practised.

Time to get dressed. I opened the wardrobe and lay on the bed. For all my pretensions to being a cultured person and having the time to appreciate the galleries, concerts, museums and theatres of one of the most civilised cities in the world, I seemed to spend an awful lot of my time in shops. And thousands of pounds. (Like an economy coming out of recession, there had been a lot of pent-up demand.) Between clothes shops, I fitted in other kinds of shops. I cruised through the galleries in the New Town picking up paintings. I suppose I could classify that as 'culture' rather than 'shopping' but it would be a close-run thing.

I had clothes for all possible occasions and the shoes to go with them. And the bags, belts and accessories. I had drawers full of fabulous lingerie, layers of silk between layers of tissue paper. My wardrobe and I spent a happy hour together every morning – although it was usually afternoon by then. After trying on three or four different outfits I picked out one in which to spend the next few hours.

My daily routine had to work to a deadline on Thursdays because that was when my piano teacher came to give me my weekly lesson. At first I had hoped Irina, the former communist spy and concert pianist, would be my teacher, but Jamie's house-keeper said she had too many commitments. Instead, she gave me the name of one of her former pupils. Cynthia cycled uphill all the way from Trinity to give me my lesson. (Pupils normally went to her, but she chose to make an exception in my case when I offered to pay double in order to learn on my own piano.) At our first lesson, Cynthia had given me her business card. It was very thick, had a treble clef down one side and looked very smart. She had just had five hundred printed; it had been very expensive but she was proud of them. She said she was enjoying the independence of self-employment. Cynthia seemed keen for me to take exams. There was no reason why I should have agreed, but old habits die hard and I'd been on an examination conveyor belt all my life, either sitting them myself or marking other people's. How could I know I'd learnt a lesson until I'd been tested?

At first I had been a diligent pupil, full of enthusiasm. I had persevered with my scales, playing them over and over again – as Cynthia had instructed. Jamie could play, but he very rarely did. When I was persevering with a tricky right hand arpeggio (E Major: four sharps and three ledger lines), he had walked up behind me, placed his fingers on exactly the right notes and said, 'There! Like that!'

After that, practice had slipped a little. Although I now had all the time in the world, somehow I only got down to it for that crucial half hour immediately before my piano teacher was due to arrive. It was just amazing how much I could cram into those thirty minutes! Today, Cynthia was coming at two o'clock. She would bring a piece for me to sight-read, but I was having trouble just clapping my way through the Grade 1 easy Mozart that I was supposed to have learnt off by heart last week. Cynthia's bicycle bounced along the cobbles in the lane, and when I heard it being manacled to the drainpipe outside my front door I gave up on the Mozart. I hoped that I might be able to delay the sight-reading with the offer of a cappuccino or maybe even a Kir Royale, but to my disappointment Cynthia declined. She didn't seem her usual good-natured self. 'Let's get on with it,' she said. 'I've got to cycle all the way to Morningside after this.' I stumbled through the piece and her face wore an expression of weariness. 'You haven't practised,' she stated flatly.

'I know. I'm sorry. I just haven't had the time. Things have been so hectic this week.'

'Have you learnt those arpeggios? Do B Major.' I did my best. 'Keep your wrists down,' she said. 'Do it again.' She made me repeat it about a dozen times until she was satisfied. Then we moved on to scales: major, minor and chromatic. I offered to have a stab at B minor harmonic since I had run up and down it twice before she came, but she was disappointed.

'If you want to learn the piano, you have to play the piano,' she admonished at the end of our hour. 'You have to practise. Over and over and over again.' I hung my head. 'Do you still want me to enter you for this exam?'

'Yes,' I said humbly. I needed a little rigour in my life.

'Right, I will. Now that's fifty pounds and we'll meet same time next week. Make sure you practise. And get yourself a metronome.' Cynthia gathered up her music ready to leave, then hesitated, tapping out a nervous little six-eight time on the lid of the piano. 'The week after next, I won't be able to give you a lesson,' she said.

'Oh?'

'I'm going into hospital. Got to have my wisdom teeth out. They're impacted.'

'Nasty.' I winced for her. One of my flatmates had had her

103

wisdom teeth out and for two weeks she had sucked Nurofen Soluble through a straw.

'But I'm making the best of it,' said Cynthia, 'and eating a lot of chocolate now, because after the operation I'm expecting to lose at least half a stone.'

'Very sensible.'

'I'll cope,' she said, bravely. 'Although the business will suffer as much as I will. I'll just have to dope myself up on pain-killers and keep going.'

My heart went out to her. Once again, my life seemed a breeze in comparison. Opening my big fridge, I reached for the little floral-patterned box of chocolates I kept in the butter-conditioning compartment. 'Here,' I said, 'take these. Your need is greater than mine.'

'But aren't they the really expensive kind?'

'Eighteen pounds fifty a pound.'

'No – you keep them.'

'No – I'd like you to have them. Please.'

'Well, if you're sure.'

'I am.'

'Great!' said Cynthia, stuffing the box in her pocket and heading for her bike.

Lady Bountiful. One of the best things about having money was giving it away. From Jamie's direct debit I had set up my own to a dozen different causes. They each got twenty pounds a month. It made me feel less guilty.

After my piano lesson, it was time to walk to the Sybaritia Beauty Salon. I was in a happy mood and it was a warm day – blue sky and sunshine. I had known Edinburgh in the winter when I had been cold, poor and stoical, and now it was summer and I was warm, affluent and hedonistic. There isn't much to being a wealthy woman in Edinburgh. I'd got the hang of it straightaway: I knew my way around Jenner's, I could dance the Reel of the 51st Division and I didn't have a proper job.

At the Royal Terrace Hotel there was a red carpet rolled out at the entrance and a few kilted ushers hanging about the door. A short burst of bagpipes inside the hotel. There would be a ceilidh at the wedding. In Scotland, everyone knows how to dance. All Scottish babies are born knowing how to do a basic Strathspey travelling step; when they're ready, it's the first step they take.

A vintage car drew up, white ribbons rippling over the bonnet. The bride stepped out in a crescendo of tulle and her bridegroom darted round from the other side of the car to escort her up the steps. The bride's dress was too frilly for my taste; I would have something more fitted. I wondered if Jamie would wear a kilt. Cameron tartan was red and reliable. It was the likes of the McLeods of Lewis who were unfortunate in their tartan; not many bridegrooms could feel confident in a bold yellow check.

Jamie never mentioned any Cameron relatives. There was the reclusive aunt on the Isle of Barra who studied cloud formations and collected data for the Meteorological Office – 'excellent job for a recluse' – and an uncle in Canada who was a Moose Warden. 'Moose?' I had asked, hoping for more. 'Moose,' said Jamie with finality. He had only two relatives but he had a huge social circle, and at times I found it tedious being a secret. Once our relationship had jumped free of its deadline Jamie could say: 'Why not come with me and meet Jack and Amy/Hamish and Gary/Eddie and Flora/Paul and Mo? They've got a weird flat/talking parrot/Steinway piano/really bizarre sense of humour.' I felt I already knew his friends – their children, their pets and peccadillos – but still I insisted on remaining a secret. My choice; I didn't want to own up to being self-unemployed.

At first Jamie hadn't take me seriously on this point and only a week into our arrangement there was a small but significant crisis:

'It's not any of his business!' I cried. 'Why did you have to tell Robert?'

'I didn't tell him. He guessed. He asked me how much it cost to keep a secret.'

'Blackmail!'

'To keep a secret very comfortably – generous allowance, a few foreign holidays. Rose, he's my oldest friend and he just guessed. But he'll be good, honestly. Soul of discretion, Rob Fraser.'

But I wasn't placated. 'I'll have to leave you now!' I wept.

'Don't leave me, Rose,' he said, hugging me, still smiling.

'Why did you have to tell him?'

'Euphoria.'

'What?'

'But she says she's leaving me now,' he quipped.

It was a difficult moment, but we got over it.

I think my insistence on secrecy curtailed his social life to some extent. He must have turned down a lot of invitations in order to spend so much time with me. When he was out of the country on business ('it's just work, very boring'), I got phone calls saying how much he missed me. He always wanted me to meet him at the airport when he got back, so we could be together again as soon as possible. Apart from his boring business trips abroad, we never spent a night apart. If he had to go to some unavoidable evening do, I waited up for him – rather pathetically passing the time by reading, listening to music, watching videos, drinking alone so as to have consumed approximately the same units of alcohol as he had by the time he came back. And he always did come back. We were always very lovingly reunited.

The girl in the sleeping bag at the Bank of Scotland cashpoint had spotted me and was waving. I gave her the usual fiver and she gave me a Polo mint.

I arrived at Sybaritia for my weekly manicure, pedicure and facial. Having a facial meant I couldn't read the novel I'd brought with me, but then I could always linger over lunch, propping up *Memoirs of a Geisha* against a bottle of wine. It was pleasantly warm in the beauty salon; quiet music and soothing voices in a pink bower of seclusion. I closed my eyes and felt the beautician gently lifting my left hand. In a professional whisper, she told me to imagine it felt very heavy; she would massage it for me with lavender oil and ylang ylang. I was already so relaxed as to be almost asleep. My hand was deliciously heavy when she took it in her own, expertly cradling my arm so that no muscle in my body felt the need to exert itself. Each finger, cuticle, crevice and line of my left hand received her minute attention. The tip of my little finger had never felt so loved. Until I met my lover, no one had ever cared for me in such detail before.

Eventually they had to wake me up, but even then I was still dreaming. I floated out of Sybaritia and sauntered down Thistle Street on my expensively pedicured feet. My new handcream cost as much as I used to earn in three hours with Market Research International. Little ironies like this were never lost on me. And I had noticed that since I got my hands massaged on a regular basis, I had ceased to wring them guiltily.

By five o'clock I didn't really know what to do with myself. I'd been French-manicured, finished reading my book, had my piano lesson, done a bit of light shopping, lunched. I was very inbetween things: between novels, between facials, between bottles of wine. Oh dear, between kisses!

I walked. I walked along Princes Street listening to the buskers playing 'Amazing Grace' on the bagpipes. I read some of the plaques on the park benches. There must be a hundred of them, benches almost arm to arm: International Conference for This, Silver Jubilee for That, Spanish Civil War International Brigade, Trade Unionists and people 'Who Loved This City'. (My favourite was dedicated to the memory of someone 'Who Liked To Sit Down' – so honest.) I got right to the West End, then walked all the way back on the other side, looking in the shop windows, nodding to the regular beggars and doing a bit of alms dealing. I had given quite a bit to charity since I became a kept woman.

When I got home, I was full of good intentions to do a bit of piano practice, but then forgot and had a little lie down instead. I dozed on the bed in a nest of duck-down duvet and thought how much I loved this bed, this house, this life. I thought of how deliciously deluding love could be.

The phone by the bed woke me up. It was Catherine, back sooner than expected from her research trip to the States. 'I'm coming to see you!'

'You've got my address?' I asked cautiously.

'Yes.'

'How?'

'You sent me an e-mail.'

'But I didn't say where I lived.'

'I found out.'

This was bad news. 'You're coming now? Right now?'

'I'm in a taxi, on my way. See you in six minutes.'

This was very bad news indeed.

She arrived punctually, as ever. Tucked under her arm was a copy of *Mainframe Magazine* and I remembered she had been celebrity guest editor for that month's edition. In the hall, her eyes were already focusing beyond my shoulder to my new home's interior.

'Well, this is nice!' she cooed, her gaze moving rapidly over everything. In the kitchen I primed up the espresso machine while she estimated its value.

'How are you doing, Rose? Expensive area.'

'I'm doing some very lucrative temping.'

'What sort of temping?' She didn't mess about. Not for the first time, I wished I had the ability to tell a straight lie because this was definitely the time for it. I decided to have a stab at equivocation.

'I'm working very closely with a senior executive in a major finance house.'

'That sounds rather vague,' said Catherine.

'Actually, it's getting more complicated all the time.'

She gave me a searching look. I could see I was going to have to provide her with more information. I would just have to do it very selectively. She was programmed to Find.

'What sort of temping?' repeated Catherine. 'He isn't putting together a portfolio of medieval manuscripts, is he?'

Inevitably, the barbed comment. But I was inspired. 'He's interested in investing in Art.' (True.) 'Illuminated manuscripts.' She narrowed her eyes. 'So . . . that's what I advise him on.' I would show Jamie a book about *The Hours of St Ethelburga* in order to make this comment true. I'd tell him why; he'd under-stand.

'You do that nine-to-five?'

'Well, no . . .'

'It is very lucrative, then!'

'It's very well paid because not many people have my particu-lar expertise. He offered me the earth to advise him and I accepted. I'm afraid I can't be more specific because it's very secret. Things to do with high finance often are.'

I could tell by her face it wasn't good enough. Variation needed. Sacrifice necessary. I sighed heavily and said: 'Catherine, I have to be honest and say I'm not renting this place, I'm only house-sitting.' She looked curious. 'There's another house around the corner as well.' (Certainly true.) 'I think they're away skiing.' (A possibility.) 'The full service is when the house-sitter actually lives there, but some people don't want that, in which case the house-sitter just goes every day to open and shut the curtains and put the lights on and off.' Catherine put her head on one side; she seemed thoughtful.

'Are there really companies that do house-sitting?'

'Haven't you heard of it before?' (She must have done; she was a genius. There was nothing she didn't know.)

'It's quite a good idea, I suppose.'

'Oh yes, it's great! And you often end up in really nice areas like this because that's the clientele. People who don't want their marble fireplaces ripped out while they're away skiing.' She was falling for it . . . it was working . . . . 'Of course,' I added, 'the only downside is having to walk the dogs. They've got a Giant Poodle around the corner. It gets clipped regularly.' (True: it was a complete topiary of a dog.)

Her guard fell. 'Oh, poor Rose! You're scared of dogs, aren't you?'

'Only giant ones.'

She laughed. 'My poor little sister! I can still remember when that Great Dane chased you into the sea at Brighton.'

'Ah, yes,' I said.

'So you house-sit and give investment advice on medieval manuscripts.'

'Yes.' We both looked hard at each other. 'Good, eh?'

'It'll do, I suppose,' she said. 'Short term.'

In the brief preparation time I had had before she arrived, I had flown about the house removing the most obvious signs that a man stayed there a lot of the time too. Jamie's clothes were stuffed under the bed, together with all other indications of a masculine presence.

Think ahead. Get her out of the house. Take her somewhere else. I put down my coffee. 'Would you like to see the garden? Wonderful views to Holyrood Park and across the Firth of Forth.'

'No, thanks. I'd rather have a guided tour of your house.'

'It's not mine.'

'But you live here and you seem well settled. Everything I've seen so far reflects your taste. It looks like you've made yourself at home. Who lives here when you don't?'

'A single woman, and you're right, we do share similar tastes. I just love her Turbo Magnifico espresso machine, don't you?'

'And how long is she away?'

'It's been about two months now.'

'Enough time for quite a lot of manuscript consultancy . . .' She turned to me, her big sister smile of superiority making me feel shorter, '. . . for which he offered you the earth!' She let out

110

a gale of laughter and I knew I would rather suffer her mockery than her discovery of the truth. 'Come on, Rose, show me around.'

I led her into the sitting room. She admired the multi-CD hi-fi and the large-screen television. (Portable TVs – such an affectation and very prevalent amongst myopic academics.) She liked the sofa and the rug and the pictures I had bought. 'Other people's houses are so fascinating, aren't they? What are the bedrooms like?'

'Very romantic.' My only option now was to brazen it out. On the threshold to the bedroom she paused, her eyes scanning it all, storing everything in her high-density memory.

'Nice bed,' she said, admiringly. 'Well-sprung,' she added, bouncing up and down on it. 'There's a chaise longue. And you've got a lovely old cheval mirror. Nice antique chest of drawers.' It was then that I noticed, on the floor, just sticking out from under the bed, a pair of Jamie's boxer shorts. As casually as I could, I kicked them out of sight. Catherine hadn't noticed. She was too busy opening up the wardrobe. 'I bet you're not supposed to wear her clothes,' she said, 'but I bet you do!' She began to rummage. 'Look at this little pink number!' She held up a dress that was my favourite. 'I bet this would fit you, Rose.'

'It does,' I said, owning up.

'Try it on. No, no, I will, I've just got time.'

Within seconds, my sister was out of her crease-free linen trouser suit and into my favourite dress. I couldn't even say: 'No you can't, it's mine!' She paraded in front of the mirror, checking her appearance from every angle. 'Whaddya think? Suits me, doesn't it?' Then she caught sight of the silk embroidered camisole I had bought in Paris and wanted to try that on too. 'It should have a matching bra,' she said, going over to the chest of drawers. 'What size is she?'

I was faintly shocked. 'Don't try her underwear on, Catherine! How could you? Leave her things alone!' But

Catherine was already rustling amongst the tissue paper in the top drawer, oohing and aahing as she uncovered one slip of lingerie after another. Lace and satin brassières lay strewn across the bed.

'Don't be so goody-goody, Rose. You know you've been through all her things yourself. I'm not going to try her knickers on, for God's sake! Ooh, here we are!' she exclaimed. 'Gorgeous!' Catherine picked up a cobwebby lace bra with silk embroidery and checked the size. 'This bra would fit me,' she said triumphantly, casting off her own, 'if I stuff a pair of socks in each cup!'

I had a colour-coded storage system for all my fabulous lingerie. Top drawer: white and cream shades; second drawer: pink and pastels; third drawer: rather more interesting things like a lovely deep purple velvet bustier, a waist-cinching black satin corset, a leopard-print chiffon slip dress (I could never decide in which drawer to keep the pink leopard-print chiffon slip dress, but that was the only grey area).

Why had Catherine's computer-brain failed to realise that all the clothes and all the lingerie fitted me? A well-fitting dress could be a coincidence, but a bra size is highly specific. Fortunately, she must have assumed that the other drawers contained only socks and tee-shirts because she didn't bother looking any further. Instead, she worked her way through my wardrobe until its entire contents littered the room. I moved to sit unhappily on the bed.

'How's the incorrect sexual politics coming along?' I asked. 'What have you done wrong so far?'

'I spend hours fantasising about being a housewife without a bank account when really I ought to be tracking the NASDAQ.'

'Is that all? That's feeble!'

'I've lost money, Rose. I've lost opportunities to make a few thousand pounds' worth of financial independence. Sexual politics is mostly a matter of economics, you know.'

'It's not a matter of sex, then?'

'Not for a long time,' she muttered.

'How's your accomplice?'

'Disappointing. We parted amicably though.'

Catherine never actually used the words 'boyfriend' or 'partner'. She felt neither quite described her relationships. She always referred to the man in her life as 'my accomplice'.

'Have you heard from Helen?' I asked.

'She's still arguing with the marketing department about potato presentation.'

Catherine bent down by the bed to take off my new stringy-strapped sandals, and as I watched one of the heels hooked up the sleeve of a man's white shirt. She tugged and the rest came out from under the bed, together with the boxer shorts I'd tried to hide earlier She looked at my horrified face and her eyes were full of glee. 'Glee' has always struck me as being a particularly impish kind of emotion. An emotion just holding back from malice. In an instant, she was down on the floor, dragging Jamie's possessions into the light.

'What's all this?' she crowed.

'It's none of your business,' I said as evenly as I could.

'Brilliant! None of my business!' She bent towards me, all her mental faculties concentrated into one laser beam stare. Obviously, I had to look away. 'So!' she said. 'You've hidden all this from me! Why? Lucrative temping! How could you? How dare you be more sexually politically incorrect than me! You're a disgrace, Rose! I don't suppose the Job Centre put you on to this one.'

'Not even on their Last Chance Retraining Programme.' I stood up, hoping to reclaim an inch of superiority. 'I ought to make it clear, Catherine, that I embarked on this with my eyes open.'

'But not all that well-focused, I should think.' She picked up one of the books I'd kicked under the bed. 'That's Helen's!' she exclaimed. 'She's been looking for that.'

'Well, she can have it back.'

Catherine opened the book, turned it sideways, upside down and shook her head. I tried to salvage some pride. 'I'm an academic; I wanted to read around the subject.' She smirked and put the book down. 'I started off with eighteenth-century French erotica and moved on to contemporary sex manuals. I don't know how Helen reads that stuff – all I did was scare myself.'

'Bloody hell! What's this?' she asked, picking up *Cottaging in the Cotswolds*.

'It was the free book! They just sent it anyway. I couldn't stop them. Actually, the books have been a waste of time; I should have just brushed up on my chess.'

Her jaw dropped.

'But Catherine,' I tried, 'this . . . this arrangement. Things will be very different after July – you'll see. And I do like him very, very much and he thinks I'm wonderful and as for being kept – well, it's quite good fun, you know.'

'It's not a career!'

She set her mouth into a disapproving line and I was over-taken by a 'What the hell?' kind of feeling (which I remembered was Robert's explanation of why Jamie would never make a good poker player). 'But it's a gorgeous job!' I cried. 'Soft and feminine as the first bite of a pink marshmallow. It's as effortless as speeding downhill on roller-blades and even more euphoric. And wealth is so easy to get used to! So difficult to turn down! So enjoyable to fling around the boudoir! Yes, Catherine, the pleasures of literally rolling in it. I'm completely at leisure and it's paying like a dream.'

'You've got to leave him,' she said, firmly.

'It's impossible to resign now,' I raced on. 'I am unresistingly locked in, like some highly successful young executive – a golden hello to start and golden handcuffs to stay!'

'You're being a fool,' she said, gravely. 'But while you're doing this foolish thing, you should at least open a Scottish Widowed No Worries savings account for the time when he no longer finds you attractive. Women like you, Rose – kept women – have no long-term career prospects. It is an antiquated career choice, born of ignorance, financial necessity or perverted self-interest. Historically, only a tiny minority have succeeded in marrying their lovers, becoming Queen or taking over the ancestral estates – and they were the elite. Most ended up in Holy Orders or destitute in Calais.'

'Both of which I am determined to avoid.'

There were two loud rings on the doorbell. 'That's my other taxi.'

She changed quickly back into her own clothes, keeping up a running commentary on my bad behaviour. 'What you're doing is not just immoral, Rose, it's amoral!'

'Is that bad?'

Fully dressed, she grabbed her briefcase and made for the front door. There was still one important thing I needed to ask her: 'Catherine, please don't tell Helen. She'll only come over here and make a nuisance of herself.'

On some occasions in the past, Catherine has found buried deep within her a big sister nurture gene which has led her to help me in times of extreme crisis, like the time I thought I was pregnant and was too terrified to do a test (Negative. 'Told you so, Rose!') and the time I was bullied at school and she smacked my tormentor very spectacularly around the head during morning break.

'Say you won't tell Helen!'

'On two conditions . . .'

'Two? It's usually one.'

'Firstly, I want to meet him, and secondly, you have to phone me up tonight and tell me everything.'

'Everything?'

'You could do with some advice, Rose,' she warned. 'I don't think you fully understand the truth of your position.' The taxi driver tooted his horn and Catherine checked her watch. 'I've got to go now or I'll be late.' She hugged me briefly and rushed downstairs. 'Phone me,' she called. 'And remember, I want to know everything!'

I waved my sister goodbye. There was no way I was going to tell Catherine everything. If she had any idea what I hoped I would be doing that night, she could blackmail me for the rest of my life.

Chapter 10

A few days later, Catherine called me up. When the phone rang, I was making my first cappuccino of the day and I was at that crucial stage of keeping the steam spout just on the surface of the milk to froth it up. It wasn't a good time to take a call. I stood there listening to the answerphone, her big sister voice rising above the hiss and bubble. 'Rose, I know you're there.' (She was bluffing with that one.) 'I know you're there and I think we should talk. I've been making some enquiries and I know all about him.'

Worried, I turned off the steamer and picked up the phone. 'What do you mean, you know all about him?'

'I knew you were there!' she gloated.

'I only told you his first name.'

'And I know where you live and what he does for a living and one or two other things. His name is James Cameron.'

'Yes, it is,' I admitted.

'Do you want to know what I've found out?'

'No.'

'You should.'

'Ignorance is very blissful at the moment.'

Catherine made a tutting noise down the phone. 'You're cleverer than that, Rose.' Next, I knew, would come the ultimatum: 'I'll tell you now or not at all.'

'Not at all.'

'That's a rash decision. Are you sure you don't want to think about it?'

'There's nothing to consider.'

'Er, I think . . . um . . . I think there is.'

Catherine rarely used words like 'um' and 'er'. 'There is, er . . . um . . . I think there is . . . something to consider.'

'It's none of your business, Catherine. It has nothing to do with you.' All the frothy bubbles I had made were starting to deflate.

'I . . . er . . . think you should ask him about . . .'

'Don't interfere, Catherine.'

'He's not a poker player,' she said quickly. 'Shame, because he's clever.'

'Chess, he plays chess.'

'I wouldn't play with him.'

'Good.'

'Are you sure you don't want to know about . . .'

'Quite sure.'

'You're in a very poor position, Rose. It's a very ill-advised arrangement you have there and . . .'

'Have you told Helen?'

'I might have mentioned it.'

'Catherine, that's not fair!'

'Considering you didn't phone me up and tell me everything, I think it's reasonable. Anyway, she already knows him. They met at Bio-Caledonian, three months ago when she was trying to attract new investors.'

'And did she?' I asked, stirring my flat coffee. 'Did she attract him?'

'You'll have to ask her.'

★

118

I drove north to Banffshire to see Helen. I knew finding her would be difficult. It always was when she was doing field work. She could be at any number of secret sites dotted around the county. It was a long way to Bio-Caledonian's headquarters and when I got there the receptionist was hardly helpful. 'Of course I can't tell you where she is!'

'Why not?'

'Because she's at a top-secret site!' he explained, excitedly. 'Collecting highly classified information.'

'My name is Rose Budleigh. I'm Helen's sister.'

'Well, I'm Linton and I'd like to help you, I really, really would – only I don't think I can. So sorry.'

'But I'm her sister!'

'Are you, now?' He pursed his lips. 'Well, you might be, I suppose. Same mouth, same cheekbones. Don't you wish you had her hair, though? Now, don't get me wrong, yours is very nice – very brown. Nice brown! It goes with your eyes. You've got lovely big brown eyes like chocolate buttons. Do you dye your eyelashes or are they naturally like that?'

'Can I speak to her, please?'

'But sweetheart, you could be a potato saboteur for all I know!'

'I need to speak to her. It's important.'

'We-ell . . .' The receptionist gave me a sideways look. 'What's that nail varnish you're wearing?' he asked suddenly. 'Oh, it's just gorgeous! So pink!'

'It's called "Dolly Daydream".'

'Sweet!'

Eventually, Linton offered to try to contact Helen for me. He put on his receptionist's head-set, smoothed his hair. 'It might take a wee while!' he warned. 'She does get about!'

'I'll wait.'

He gestured towards a black leather sofa.

I sat and watched Linton chat into his mouthpiece and file his nails. He spoke to five people before he found someone who could tell him where Helen might be. It took a long time because he liked to talk. He had a word for everybody (usually about somebody else).

On the coffee table beside me lay some company brochures. A neat fan of glossy covers. There was the company logo: a happy, anthropomorphic potato with long, curly eyelashes, blue potato eyes and a cupid's bow pout. The Budleigh Beauty — soon to be renamed the Braveheart Potato and given an anthropomorphic sex change.

'Won't be long now!' sang Linton between fruity chunks of gossip. 'We're getting warmer!'

I picked up the Annual Report: *Cashing In Our Chips*. It was full of bold predictions: soaring bar graphs and crescendo-reaching exponential curves. At the back was a photograph of Dr Helen Budleigh, luscious lips puckered up to kiss a potato. Mwah!

I waited. People came and went. And then Linton found her. 'Helen, darling! At last! How *are* you? Is it cold out there? Brrrrr! You're so hard to get hold of! I've been trying for ages and ages and ages! Now, guess who's sitting on Linton's leather sofa?' He waved me over. 'She says she's your sister. Come all the way from Edinburgh to see you!'

'Can I speak to her?'

'Just a sec . . .'

Linton listened, giggling. 'All right, I'll ask her.' He turned to me. 'Rose, we don't know that you really are Helen's sister, so . . .'

'I'll speak to her.'

'As an extra security measure, can you answer the following question—'

'She always does this!' (It's terrible having a relative who works in a high-security environment.)

'Temper, temper! Now, what is Helen Budleigh's middle name?'

'Verity.'

120

This was the correct answer, but I could tell he wasn't satisfied. 'But Helen,' he was saying into his mouthpiece, 'she could have found that out on the website.' He listened for further instructions. 'What did you say, sweetie? No! Really? You've never told me that before! Now, Rose,' he said, turning to me. 'What was the name of the little town on the Côte d'Azur where Helen—'

'St Tropez,' I said quickly.

'St Tropez! I never knew! Promise me, Helen, you'll tell me all about it!'

'Tell her to hurry up!'

'And finally, she says if you really are Rose Budleigh, your most embarrassing moment involved an end of term party when . . .'

'Give me the headset!' I said, crossly. He handed it over, giggling helplessly. 'Helen, where are you?' I demanded.

I found her in a ploughed field three miles away. I parked the car and squelched my way through the mud to meet her. She saw me and waved, all blonde, fluffy hair and sweet smile. 'Rosebud!' she called. 'What are you doing here? I thought you were a city girl!' She strode towards me, cradling a huge potato in her arms. 'I heard about your new temp job. Catherine told me. House-sitting! Well, that's new!'

'Is that what she said?' I asked, cautiously. 'House-sitting?'

'I'm pleased for you! So long as you're not bored. It's important to have an interest. How interesting is he, then? What's it like being kept? What's this about you pinching my books? Feeling better now, are we? About time! I said all along, Rose, all you needed was a good—'

'Is this the Budleigh Beauty?' I asked, quickly. She rubbed some soil off and proudly held up the potato. It was about the size of a brick and almost as cuboid.

'It's incredible,' I said, honestly. 'How do you pull it out of the ground?'

'Easy. They're planted in special trenches, like this, and the topsoil is like this and they just lift out like this.' She demonstrated, pulling on tough green leaves to raise another potato brick. 'The soil here is excellent. This is the most successful trial we've ever done. Isn't the soil lovely?' She crumbled it between her fingers, her pretty face full of smiles.

When we were growing up, we had both been encouraged in our respective interests. Helen had collected soil samples and I had collected words. Mum would draw a big, blobby outline of any word I asked for and I would colour it in. Aside from her carefully wrought flashcards – *precocious* and *inspiration* – I also had *bum* in pink and *poo* in brown. (My mother was broad-minded.) However, if I showed Granny my *bum* word, I also had to show her a very neat *sensible* to make up for it. Granny still kept my first ever lexicographical work, a specially commissioned *Big Book of Nice Words*. Helen, however, had received a copy of my privately circulated, secret underground publication: *We Don't Say That*. It had taken a helluva fucking lot of research and she had been impressed. In exchange, Helen had given me her collection of corked test-tubes containing different kinds of soil: red soil, clay soil, sandy soil . . . Helen and I had always been able to talk about the things that really mattered to us.

'I hear you know Jamie Cameron,' I said, conversationally.

'I do and I blame him for the biggest fucking disaster of my career!'

A worrying start.

'How's that?' I asked.

'He read about the results of our last trial and he came up for that big presentation I did. Do you remember I spent ages preparing for it? I drove Gordon mad! But it did attract a lot of potential investors. Jamie told me it was the most surprising presentation he had ever attended. I was flattered. It made me glad I had gone to the trouble of getting all that dry ice and strobe lighting. The potatoes looked amazing!

'He said he wanted to introduce another interested party. It turned out to be Scot Burger. We all went out to lunch and our marketing department came too. Everything was going well. We were celebrating! Champagne! And then Jamie cracked a joke. He said why not call it the Braveheart Potato and it can compete with the King Edward? We laughed! A joke! But the marketing department – I saw that look in their eyes, full of catchy soundbites and clever headlines, and I knew there would be trouble. Next day, back in Banff, we had all sorts of meetings and briefings, but they got what they wanted. All anyone ever talks about now is the Braveheart Potato. And Scot Burger love the new name. They say it's perfect for a product launch in Scotland. They're spending millions! And Rose, it's so hard to find investment capital! You've got to take it where you find it. I ought to be ecstatic about the new name, but I'm not. I'm having to go along with it. The Budleigh Beauty is dead.' She hugged the potato to her bosom. 'It's as though I never created her.'

'That's not true, Helen,' I said, feeling sympathetic. 'It's still going to be your potato out there.'

'I will never forgive him for the Braveheart joke.'

'He didn't do it on purpose.'

'Too late, damage done.'

I stared at my muddy shoes. Beige suede. Bad footwear decision. 'Were you and Jamie getting on well?' I asked. 'Before he made the Braveheart joke?'

'Very well. I liked him a lot.'

'Really?' I asked, unhappily.

'In a very professional way,' added Helen Verity. 'In a purely business context.'

That night, I asked Jamie if he knew Helen's middle name.

'Verity,' he said, from behind the *FT*.

'Did she tell you herself?'

He put down the paper. 'I found out before I went. That's

what I do, Rose – gather information, read things, speed-skimming. It's on the Bio-Caledonian website. Dr Helen Verity Budleigh, Chief Scientist.'

'She's upset about the Braveheart Potato.'

'I know. She's going to make a lot of money though. Don't worry about Helen. She'll be a lot happier when Bio-Cal announce their deal with Scot Burger. The share price will be a great comfort. I've done her a favour, Rose. They could have paid a marketing consultant for the new name, but I came up with it over lunch, for free – although Scot Burger are giving me a little credit, which is nice of them. Don't feel too sorry for her.' He noticed my muddy shoes drying out on a pile of newspaper. 'Did she make you tramp around a field? She made me – said she wanted to see me ruin a suit. What made her get into potatoes, by the way?'

'She's interested in genetics. Genetics was her father's subject.'

'I thought your Dad was a historian.'

'Helen was born the year our mother enjoyed an experimental open marriage – not her own.'

'Ah, I see.'

'We were still in Edinburgh then. I was four. Dad has always been stoical about Mum's various adulteries. He turned a blind eye to this one, too, until our Aunt Muriel drove all the way from Guildford to point out to him that Mum was pregnant. I can remember her shouting: "I'm telling you, George, she's pregnant! She's not a woman who would wear support tights unless she absolutely had to!"'

'How did he take it?'

'He walked into the garden and stared at his roses – he has a collection of prize-winning hybrids – and he missed an episode of *The Archers*, which was how Catherine and I knew that something very serious was happening. We always got to interrupt his work to tell him *The Archers* was on. He also missed *I'm Sorry I Haven't A Clue*. Catherine and I watched from the window while he escorted Aunt Muriel to her car and pointed out the

124

direction of Surrey. He told her she should put a few hundred miles between them before it got dark. We don't know what happened when he talked to Mum, but we did a hypothetical reconstruction in the garden.'

'A what?'

'Children of pushy parents play games with longer names,' I explained. 'We made reconstructions in the garden – let's pretend-type games. We used to reconstruct our parents' rows quite a lot, and we gave them titles, like little plays. This particular one got refined over the next seven years or so, but in brief: Dad confronts Mum and asks if it's true that she's wearing support tights. Mum says that she is, and sorry, George, sorry. Heart-breaking, difficult. But only human. Still a young woman. Got a bit desperate. Tried to be discreet. Accident. But love you. Love you. If only, if only, if only. But. But. But.'

'Didn't anyone think it was odd, you children acting this out in the garden?'

'No one ever commented on it. We made up reconstructions all the time. The most dramatic one was Helen's father telling Mum he was leaving for good. Helen was just an impressionable foetus at the time. He said he was going to South Africa and he wasn't coming back and what's more he wanted no further contact. Mum was very shocked and there was a big row and I remember him shouting: 'All my research has pointed to the hypothesis that nurture is irrelevant! It's nature that counts! Even if I'm not here, the child will have my stamp on it.'

'You can remember that?'

'Yes, I was hiding in the dirty laundry basket on the landing; Catherine hadn't found me because she was counting up to a million in prime numbers. Mum shouted that he had got it all wrong – that time would show nurture was far more important and he had no evidence for his argument and how could he abandon his responsibilities like that? And he said: 'Don't worry, Fiona. Good ol' Professor Budleigh will look after you, won't he? He's the devoted type!'

Jamie gave a rueful little smile. 'And does Helen ever see her father?'

'Never. He's very absent and Helen's heart has only grown harder towards him. We three sisters have one real Dad. Helen wants to believe that more than anything. All her early work in genetics was guided by her belief that it's nurture that matters most, and that her father's genetic role isn't nearly as important.'

'You could call her father's role important because she decided to call it irrelevant.'

'She calls him a lot of things. Helen wants to prove, empirically, that she is more her Dad's daughter than her father's – if you see what I mean. That's why she got into genetics. The potato venture is simply her day job. There's not a lot of money in the nurture versus nature debate, just a lot of very interesting, very long-term study. Her father's theories are now largely dismissed as inaccurate; Mum says Helen is the only good piece of work he ever produced. We were brought up to believe that truth is the most important thing and that the truth will out. Mum is a philosopher, remember. *Amicus Plato, sed magis amica veritas.*'

'What?'

'"Plato is dear to me, but dearer still is truth."'

'Veritas,' he repeated. 'Helen Verity Budleigh.' Then he picked up a pen and started on the crossword. 'I hated Latin at school. It was compulsory, like Sir Walter Scott. We had to learn verses of *Marmion* off by heart: "Oh, what a tangled web we weave when first we practise to deceive."'

'I quite like *Marmion*.'

'But you're a hopeless romantic.'

'Scott played chess, you know. One of the reasons I like the game is because everything is visible. No secrets, no hidden cards, no deception. There is nothing but the truth of the position.'

'How do you explain a discovered check, then?'

126

'Check is the truth of the position. It's only a discovered check if you didn't see it coming.'

Jamie touched my cheek, pushed a curl of hair away from my face. 'If you're a dreamy romantic, for example.'

Chapter 11

It was very difficult persuading Catherine not to offer me any further advice on how I should conduct myself. 'I don't want your opinion,' I told her over coffee. 'I don't want your coaching tips. I'm playing this my own way. Please keep out of it.'

'But you're playing it all wrong,' she insisted, sipping her short, sharp espresso. 'You've lost your objectivity. You're too involved. He's just drawn you in. Absolutely classic strategy: trap, control, exploit. Helen agrees with me, don't you, Helen?'

'I'm staying out of it,' said Helen. 'And so should you. Interference is against the Rules.' (This was very true. Chess etiquette dictates that spectators should not pass audible comment on a game in progress, even if they believe a breach of the rules has been committed.)

'But Rose,' said Catherine. 'When Jamie offered you this kept woman arrangement, it was just like a Poisoned Pawn Variation. You accepted the gift and now you're trapped. It's going to take you a while to work your way back to a competitive position. It's about time you made a more intelligent move. It's been three months now.'

'Three lazy, wonderful, blissed-out months.'

'This can't go on, Rose.'

'I think it can. I think it will.'

'Do you love him?' asked Helen.

I opened my mouth to speak but Catherine interrupted. 'She doesn't know whether she loves him or not, do you, Rose?'

'I'm smitten.'

'Have you told him that?' she asked, appalled.

'Not in so many words.'

'Say nothing,' she urged. 'Rose, you're in trouble. In deep trouble.'

'In deep smit.'

'If only you would let me tell you what I know!'

'. . . we'd be here all night.'

'I like him,' said Helen. 'Despite his Braveheart Potato joke. I like him because he's made Rose happy and that's enough, isn't it?'

I nodded.

Catherine was unconvinced. 'How much money has he given you now?'

'Don't be vulgar, Catherine. And anyway, I won it.'

She shook her head. 'You are so naive. And what about your real work? Have you done anything else about getting a job on the Dictionary? What about your sense of vocation – or are you deaf to your calling now?'

'I haven't forgotten it. I'm still working on my thesis – now and then.'

'When will it be finished?'

'Oh, I don't know . . .' I said, languidly. 'Some time.'

The very next evening, in defiance of the Rules, Catherine arrived on a surprise visit. 'I'm on my way to a party round the corner,' she announced, 'and so I thought I might as well drop by and meet him.' She was wearing velvet trousers and a black silk shirt undone to *there*. This was Catherine in night-time mode: sleek as a cat and dressed to kill. Slowly, cruelly, ruthlessly.

'All right, Rose,' she said, seeing my face. 'I'll make it quick.' She walked straight past me and stalked off to the living room where she caught Jamie completely unawares, supine on the sofa with a novel and a bowl of cherries.

'This is my sister, Catherine,' I said, hurrying in after her. 'She's on her way to a party and won't be staying long. Catherine, this is Jamie.'

Jamie abandoned the novel and got to his feet. I was surprised to see recognition on his face. Catherine was smiling with a kind of malicious delight. 'Do you two know each other?' I asked.

'We know *of* each other,' purred Catherine.

'You've not met before?'

'Once,' said Jamie, warily. 'At an airport. We played cards.'

They shook hands, exchanged curt little nods and a single word of acknowledgement: 'Jamie,' said my sister, with look-him-in-the-eye contact.

'Catherine.'

Adversarial mutual respect. I stood to one side. She and Jamie behaved like snipers in a ceasefire: both armed to the teeth and ready to shoot. Catherine asked, casually, just how much of his own money he was putting in to Bio-Caledonian and wasn't that insider-dealing? Jamie deflected her question by saying how much he admired her skilful acquisition of Cybersecurity's main competitor and it must have been useful having access to their accounts, but wasn't that just plain old hacking?

And so it went on. I felt a dreadful sense of helplessness. Eventually Catherine stepped over the line. 'Don't think for a minute Rose will stay with you,' she hissed. 'But you won't care, will you? You'll have some other consolation . . .'

I stared at her, outraged at this trespass on to my private territory. I was about to speak when I heard Jamie's voice, very tense: 'Rose has said she will stay with me until the end of July.'

'Did you, Rose?' She turned to me in surprise. 'Set an expiry date?'

'Er, yes. The thirty-first of July.'

'And after that it's all over?'

I didn't reply. I was watching all the colour drain from Jamie's face. It took a few seconds. 'After that it's all over,' he said, quietly. 'And I will miss Rose more than I can say.' Concerned, I took his hand and gave it a squeeze. He squeezed back.

Catherine seemed mollified. 'Then it's not as bad as I thought.'

'It's only two weeks away,' said Jamie, gripping my hand.

'Fine.' Catherine kissed me on the cheek. 'Sorry,' she whispered. 'You should have told me you knew! I didn't realise you knew and had it all under control. Have fun! A bit immoral of you, but have fun.'

She swept past Jamie, ignoring him completely. I remained rooted to the spot, still holding his hand, uncertain what exactly had just happened, but certain we'd had a close escape.

Catherine's brief visit left us feeling fragile. As soon as she had gone, we retreated to the corner of the sofa. I laid my head on his chest and he stroked my hair and we stayed like that, very quietly, for a while. Neither of us said anything. I listened to his heart-rate slowing down. When it got back to about normal, he told me Catherine scared him shitless. 'Like being stuck on a ledge in a blizzard.'

'She's not normally that bad. She just wanted to make sure I was all right. It's a big sister thing. She thinks she's looking out for me, that's all.'

'Do you think she'll be dropping by more often?'

'Only if she's got the time.'

'Can you think of a way to keep her occupied?'

'I think Catherine would like Robert,' I said, determined to get her out of the way. 'He's just her type.'

'Maybe,' said Jamie. 'Robert is the cleverest man I know. It's worth a try.'

'Yes,' I said, warming to the idea. 'He could be just the challenge she's been looking for.'

'I'd better warn him.'

'Don't worry about Catherine,' I said. 'She's probably just jealous. It's none of her business where I live.'

'As you say – she's just looking out for you.'

He sank lower on the sofa as if wanting to take cover. I wondered whether I should spoil everything by voicing the anxiety I felt. Eventually I knew I had to speak. 'Jamie, when you told her it would all be over by the end of July, you sounded like you really meant it.' I lowered my voice: 'Do you?'

'I'd rather not think about it.' The words were almost inaudible. Not the fervent denial I'd hoped for.

'What if I want to stay with you after July?' His heart-rate speeded up again. 'What if I want to . . .'

'You don't know yet,' he whispered.

'What if I want to stay?'

'You won't,' he said. 'I know you won't.'

'How do you know?'

'Because I know you.'

I could have denied it, but I didn't. Instead, I took his hand and held it fast. And there we were, stuck on the ledge in the blizzard together.

As soon as I told Catherine about Robert, she put two and two together, divided it by the square root of infinity and guessed how he made his living, even though so few people knew. She was interested enough to want to meet him. And so it was that she bumped into him, by calculated accident, very early one morning as he came out of a house on Great King Street. She told him she was waiting for a cab. Robert, who had been briefed, asked her about the probability of it actually turning up. It was a loaded question.

When the cab failed to appear (proving him right) he suggested they have breakfast, promising her a bacon roll and a discussion on quantum cryptography. It wasn't long before he was writing her phone number in his Poker Player's Diary. When he casually proved Fermat's Theorem on the corner of a napkin, my sister was done for. They spent the rest of the day together, tossing about arguments on tantalising algorithms (a very esoteric area of physics), and as night drew on they ventured into entanglement.

Jamie and I congratulated ourselves on matching Catherine to Mr QED Right. How long it would last was anybody's quantum guess, but so long as it did, we felt less under surveillance.

Everything should have been perfect for us in those last two weeks. Sunday should have been lovely. A hazy mutual reality. Coffee and croissants and crumbs on the sheets, hours and hours of private illicitness. Hedonising. I had sort of been counting on it, but I was disappointed.

At least the chess didn't fail me, and there's an exquisite satis- faction in inflicting a defeat on an opponent who's proved a carnal disappointment. I didn't know why everything had changed so suddenly, but it was very frustrating. He was fretful and uncommunicative. Something had got to him, I didn't know what it was and he wouldn't tell me. There were times over the past few months when I had seen Jamie emotionally over- wrought (vodka and champagne cocktail), and intensely serious (when I turned down his offer of a draw), but he had always been charming, disarming and very good company.

'Jamie, what's wrong?'

'Nothing.'

'Is it me?'

'No.'

'What's the matter?'

'Nothing.'

So that was it. He read the papers in bed, looking miserable, and then fell asleep sprawled across *Scotland on Sunday*. When he woke up, I asked if he felt any better. He buried his face in the pillow. 'No,' came the muffled reply.

'Can you tell me what's wrong yet?'

'Not yet.'

'When can you tell me?'

'It's more a matter of how.'

'How?'

'I don't know how to tell you.'

'You *did* sleep with Helen!' I cried, bitterly.

'God, no!' He put his arm around me. 'No!' I wilted with relief. 'Not since St Tropez.' I must have looked very shocked. 'Not really, Rose,' he laughed. 'Oh, you always believe me. It's terrible.'

It was good to see him laughing again, although I was mortified that the joke, once more, was me. Back to normal, then. He wasn't feeling all that bad. Despite the sad look returning now, there was nothing much to worry about. He was simply indulging his occasional habit of guilty introspection – probably a healthy thing for the Idle Rich but inconvenient for the Idle Rich's girlfriend. Especially on a Sunday afternoon. However, given the right incentive, Jamie could probably push his conscience to the back of his mind, which was where it stayed most of the time, along with unchecked bank statements and abandoned Penguin Classics.

I passed him the Travel section. 'Before you tell me about whatever it is, can we still go on holiday together?' I smiled at him encouragingly. 'This bad news you've got – is it something that can be fixed? Is it curable?'

'No, it's just inevitable.'

He was staring at an article on shark fishing in the Caribbean. Picture of a big shark thrashing about on a line.

'What is it, then? You're a criminal?'

'I'm wanted by Interpol. I've had plastic surgery on my fingertips – look.'

'My God!'

'Rose, you're so gullible!'

'All right then! What is it?'

'I'll tell you, but not yet.'

'When?'

'Next week.'

'Next week! What are we going to do until then?'

'Carry on as normal. It'll be all right. You know how much I think of you.'

'What do you think of me, then?'

The frown deepened; it made him look years older. I didn't like to dwell on how contemplation of his affection for me could have such a negative effect.

'You mean everything to me,' he said, gravely. 'Everything. I love you. I would do anything for you. The thought of being without you is intolerable. When you leave me, my life will be a wilderness. I love you more than I can express. I would die for you.'

If I hesitated for one, ecstatic moment, I don't think he noticed, because I knew not to be caught out again; I laughed more or less immediately – although I was hurt by the joke. And I knew I had judged it right because he breathed out very fast – a rapid exhalation, like someone involved in a near-miss. We found safety in our jokes. A well-timed joke could stop us skidding dangerously off course in the slalom of our conversations.

He got up and stumbled towards the wardrobe, where he started groping through his jacket pockets. 'What's the matter?' I called. 'Are you all right?' A noise a bit like throttled laughter. He was unscrewing the lid on a hipflask; clumsily, too – spilt some. Downing the contents in one swift action, he found a kind of bracing bravado. 'I'm fine,' he choked. 'It just went down the wrong way.'

I fetched him a glass of water.

'Right,' he said, flushed. 'I think you're a very enjoyable, totally absorbing and very expensive hobby.'

'I'm a hobby?'

Another pensive silence while he stroked my fingers. 'Spot the lie,' he added.

I sighed, tired of the game. I am, it appears, amusingly unable to spot lies, even at close quarters. But practise makes perfect, as

135

they say, and he liked to make me practise by telling me stories – 'Spot the Lie'. He was beguilingly good at this game, so the stories tended towards the outrageous and there usually came a point at which I would blurt out: 'You didn't!'

'I did!'

'Really? Honestly? What was it like?'

Much hilarity: 'I'm making it up, Rose!'

It was in this same vein that he sent me letters – beautiful, passionate love letters, the envelope clearly stating: 'Darling Rose, Lie Enclosed'. That way, he said, we always knew exactly where we were.

'Spot the Lie' was a very one-sided game because I had nothing to contribute but my credulity. Before I met him – before I indulged myself in him – I didn't have an outrageous story of my own.

I do, now.

The rest of that day was very quiet. We treated each other with the care reserved for fragile objects in a storm. We battened down the hatches and stayed inside. We hardly left the bedroom – in fact, we hardly did anything but read. I think we even finished a chapter at the very same time. He was reading a novel by Emile Zola. (Manipulative, over-sexed women luring poor, infatuated men to their death.) 'Which bit are you up to?' I asked.

'His blood's all over the carpet in her boudoir. Which bit are you up to?'

'The bit where Jane is woken by screams in the night.'

He shifted his position to look over my shoulder. 'Rose, how many times have you read *Jane Eyre*?'

'I don't know. It's comfort reading. I wouldn't bother with that *Nana* book. Not much comfort there.'

'No,' he admitted, putting it aside. 'And anyway, I'd rather read something that addresses the really important questions.'

'What are they then?'

'The "What's the point?" questions.'

I shut my eyes. Tight shut. 'Go for something light and pointless.'

'No, I want something heavy and pertinent,' he insisted. 'Give me your well-read academic opinion.'

He looked deeply miserable. 'Are you Very Despairing, Slightly Despairing or Don't Know?' I asked. It was like doing market research for the Samaritans.

'I've not got any hope for my future happiness but I have to keep going.'

Try Albert Camus. Try *The Myth of Sisyphus*. That'll stretch you a bit.'

'Okay,' he said. 'I'll go to Waterstone's first thing tomorrow morning.'

He curled up around me, held me close. I nestled in beside him. I could ignore anything in order to preserve this loving comfort. Look after me, protect me, take the bad things away. I don't want to know, I don't want to think. 'Put the light off,' I mumbled.

'*Jane Eyre* is a very pertinent book,' he said, loud and clear. 'If I read *Jane Eyre*, I'd be so scared I'd have to stay up all night with the light on.'

'Well, you're not reading it, are you?' I said, quickly. 'So put the light off. I want to go to sleep.'

Next morning, I woke feeling surprisingly optimistic. Maybe I had processed my worst anxieties in my sleep. My subconscious must have convinced my ego not to trouble my pretty little id about it.

It was raining and overcast – another one of those dismal days that cheat you out of summer. Pity, because Jamie had taken the day off. I lay on the floor in front of the drawing room fireplace, making notes for the Dictionary. I thought and scribbled and sucked the end of the pen and scrawled a bit more and drew cartoons, and after a few hours I had finished quite a good piece on 'eedle-doddle', a Victorian Scots adjective connected to the English 'idle'. *The Concise Scots Dictionary* defined it as 'easy-going and muddle-headed', but I reckoned from my research that I had found a link between 'doddle' and 'dawdle' and 'doodle'.

'Do you want to go out when I'm finished?' I asked. 'Have a drink somewhere?'

'Maybe. Dunno.'

He was sitting in the armchair beside me, hidden behind a wall of a book. 'Where's the *FT* today?' I asked.

'Lit the fire with it.'

'Where are the other newspapers?'

'Still on the doormat.'

I moved nearer, put my hand on his knee and he didn't move at all, didn't put his hand over mine. I wondered what he was reading. He had got up early that morning and gone out in the rain to Waterstone's. Unfortunately, they had sold out of *The Myth of Sisyphus*. The bookseller told Jamie they could hardly meet the demand for post-existentialist anti-nihilism, but he could reserve a copy from their next delivery. Jamie had bought something else to tide him over. I took a look at the cover of his second choice. Oh no! Chekhov short stories! Couldn't be worse! All those flighty heroines leading empty lives! All those tormented heroes plagued by self-doubt! Russians striding around crying: 'But what's the point, Volodya Mikhaylovich?'

'Jamie, time to go out.'

'I thought you were working.'

'I'm finished and I'm a bit bored now.'

'Oh, sorry. Can't have you being bored.'

'Good, let's go to the pub.'

'It's raining, I can't be bothered.'

I waited a few minutes, then asked, 'Are you enjoying reading that?'

'Not really.'

'Why don't you watch some football instead?' I asked, desperately. 'I'll get out one of your sad videos, if you like.'

'Okay,' he said, all forlorn. 'Pass me the remote, would you? And the other one. Thank you.'

After ten minutes of tragic own-goals and Barber's 'Adagio for Strings' (which even I found quite affecting), we made our way to the St Vincent's, which is a winter pub, really. It's dark and cosy with a pot-bellied stove and a chess table. We opted for some unthreatening analysis of *giuoco piano* – a quiet game. But as we entered the thick of it, we were soon on dangerous ground.

'Rose,' he asked, 'why do you think people get married?'

'Because they love each other.'

'The romantic point of view, of course,' he said and moved his king to a more protected square. 'Think of it more pragmatically. People get married for all sorts of different reasons,' he said. 'They don't have to love each other.'

'I think they should.'

'Well,' he went on, lighting a cigarette. 'I remember, about five years ago, I looked up "love" in a dictionary and it said "warm affection, attachment, liking for, fondness", which isn't much of a tall order, is it?'

'No,' I said, surprised. 'Was that all it said?'

'It went on for a few more columns, but I'd read enough.'

'What else was there?'

'Oh, just some stuff about tennis scores.' He raised his glass to his lips, shut his eyes and drank.

'So apart from the tennis scores, what else did it tell you? It didn't mention anything about overwhelmingly selfless emotions, loyalty and life-long devotion?'

'Definitely not.'

'It might have included a few words from that bit of Corinthians they always read at weddings.'

'Which bit? You've read more dictionaries than me.'

'The bit that goes: "If I am without love, I am nothing but a sounding gong or a clanging cymbal."' I knew it off by heart.

'I don't think it mentioned that, no.' I started shredding a beer

139

mat. 'Let's not get too hung up on esoteric definitions of love,' he said. 'In French there isn't even a verb to love.'

'There's a noun, though. There's *amour*.'

'But you'd think they'd have a verb, too, wouldn't you? I mean, the French have a reputation for sex and philosophy – existentialists do it for no reason at all – and yet a Frenchman can't tell a woman he loves her. He just doesn't have the vocabulary. He can only like her or adore her. It makes it so much simpler for him. It's easy to say: "Rose, you're adorable; I've always liked you."'

'I think,' I said carefully, 'that in all conscience you ought to be in love if you marry.'

'Or you could just like each other a lot.' He leaned earnestly across the table towards me. 'Since people get married for all sorts of different reasons, don't you think that it might be all right for a person to say marriage vows knowing that he meant "fondness" and on a good day "warm affection"?'

He waited for my answer. My heart was in my mouth. 'You're always saying how very fond you are of me,' I said, uncertainly. 'Does that mean you love me?'

He bit his lip. 'I'm not explaining this very well, am I?'

'Explaining what?'

'Proof enough.' He was frowning more and more.

'I might hope for a bit more than "fondness" in marriage, but nevertheless . . .' I stopped. He had his head in his hands. I'd never seen him do that before. It was just for a few seconds, but while it lasted he seemed fairly despairing. 'Jamie,' I gathered my courage, 'do you not want to see me any more?'

'That's not it at all!' he said quickly. 'Of course I want to see you! You mean so much to me. I think of you all the time. I've never felt like this about anyone before.' And on and on he went, like a clanging cymbal. 'I only want you to be happy . . .'

I stared at my empty glass, and then saw my fingers reach out for it and start turning it, twisting and fidgeting. Agitated fingers. As I watched, he moved to touch them, his warm hand holding them still. 'Sh-sh,' he said, gently, although I hadn't said anything.

I looked up and his expression was pained. 'Give me your other hand as well,' he said, almost whispering. 'You like things to be very clear and precise, don't you?' he said. 'No grey areas.'

'It's my academic training. I like a bit of definition.'

'Rose,' he said urgently, 'there's going to be a very big grey area coming up. I'm not sure how things will work out, but they'll just have to.'

'What big grey area?'

'I'm not telling you yet,' he said resolutely.

'Just lie to me, then!' I said, beginning to feel hysterical.

'I can't any more,' he choked. Spoilt his resolute expression.

I felt frightened and I probably looked it. To my absolute horror, so did he. 'Jamie,' I pleaded, 'please talk to me. Please.'

He stared at the last remaining pieces on the board – odds were he'd already lost and he knew it.

'Cuba is a wonderful place,' he began. 'The Caribbean. Very nice.'

'Nice people?'

'Yes, very nice people, very friendly.'

'Who did you go to Cuba with?'

'Robert.'

'What did you do there? On holiday?'

'Yes, pretty much. Havana's very interesting.'

'You've told me so before.'

'Not many restaurants, though.'

'No?'

'No, not proper ones. You eat in people's houses – people who've got a licence to do it.'

'And did you find a nice restaurant in somebody's house?'

'Yes. We had lobster at this place just off the Plaza Catedral. It was very good. Only hotels are allowed to serve lobster, so I suppose it was illegal lobster. There are some very strange laws in Cuba.' He was speaking more clearly now. 'But there's also excellent diving.'

'You went diving there?'

'Yes. Superb diving. Unspoilt, like the Cayman Islands used to be ten years ago. There's Spanish galleons, huge black coral stacks and . . . and there's this massive underwater cliff where the continental shelf just stops and you fall straight off the edge into the ocean on the Gulf of Mexico.' He stopped, blue eyes very bright. 'Anyone who climbs mountains should try stepping off an underwater cliff.'

'What's it like?'

'Free-fall at the deep end.' He went very quiet. 'Feels like surrender.'

'Surrender?'

'Yes.'

We walked home, hand in hand, and neither of us spoke. When we got to the house there was a blackbird sitting on the railings, singing its heart out. It made me happy. We opened the door, and in the hall he put his arms around me. 'I love you,' he said. 'I want to marry you.' It wasn't a question; it didn't require an answer. I kissed him, joyfully.

The phone rang. 'Ignore it,' he said. The answerphone clicked in and the caller was a woman, speaking very fast in Spanish. He held me closer as he listened. A short, exuberant message. 'Did you get any of that?' he asked.

'I heard "compañero".'

'Is that all?'

'I can't be sure. Something about the sea?'

'The sea?'

'Mar . . . something. I don't know. If you replay it a couple of times, I'll probably get it.' He deleted it immediately. 'What was she saying?'

'Hello, how are you and a bit about the weather.'

'Hot in Spain at the moment, I should think.'

'Havana.'

'Someone you met on holiday?'

'Yes.'

142

'And you've stayed in touch.'

'Yes.'

'Did you see her on your last trip?'

'Yes.' He folded me in his arms and held me very, very tightly. 'Promise me you'll not ask any more just yet.'

'Why?'

'Promise you won't ask,' he insisted.

'I promise,' I said, rashly. 'Why did I have to promise?'

'Because you always keep your promises,' he said. 'Like you never tell a lie. Major weakness in your game.'

I wasn't thinking clearly.

He took the rest of the week off. Great! I thought, we'll be lazy, we'll stay in, do nothing. But no, we had to get up very early and drive north for five hours to Assynt. Then we walked for three hours, just to get to the foot of the right mountain. On the climb I thought I wasn't going to make it, but he lured me to the top with squares of bitter chocolate. He said I was actually doing better than he had thought I would. When we reached the summit, I was so proud of myself and so physically decrepit I felt like I'd become my own Granny.

I thought one mountain was probably about as much joy as I could take, but Suilven was just the first. I sat beside him at the summit, wondering at the miraculous view, and he pointed out the other one he wanted us to do. It was a steep, razor-like ridge called Stac Pollaidh. And at that point I started to whimper, very quietly, to myself. It was all just a bit too much.

We stayed at a small hotel in Baddidarach where we had a very comfortable bed and a deep, cast-iron bath. He promised me excellent dinners there, too. I ate the best dinner of my life at that place and as I discovered, the smug climber has the best appetite. We went further north, along the coast, walked for miles over the moors until we came to a long, white deserted beach where a massive sea stack stood sentinel on the shore. I couldn't believe the place was as extraordinary as it was.

143

At the end of the week we did climb Stac Pollaidh – for hours and hours, all of the needle pinnacles, one after the other, and I even did the last bit, where if you want to you can edge your way round the rock with a rope. It's only for a few feet, but it's a long way down. He said: 'I don't think you should do this bit,' and I remember how white his face was when I did do it.

Assynt was glory. I couldn't believe Assynt had been there all the time and I hadn't heard, hadn't read about it, hadn't known. I must have been reading the wrong books. When we got back to Edinburgh, the memory of it sustained me.

Jamie told me he had wanted us to spend that week together in the north. He said walking helped you think more clearly about things and I shouldn't do all my thinking from a supine position indoors. He reckoned I was missing something that ought to have been pretty obvious to me by then and I needed to get a bit more oxygen to my brain. And the other reason we were doing it was because he had read in *The Myth of Sisyphus* that time spent outdoors, surrounded by spectacular scenery, was one of the things that could make you happy – and something he had always suspected. Jamie could now only agree with Albert Camus, French post-existentialist novelist and (now I knew) pre-War goalkeeper for Algiers F.C., that when life seemed absurd beyond belief, you had better just head for the hills.

Chapter 12

In chess, you can't change your mind about playing a piece you have touched. You touch it, you play it. You're committed. It's a fundamental rule and very strictly enforced. If, like Jamie, you play so fast and loose that you make a mess of the board and all your pieces are out of place, escaping from their proper squares, you might want to tidy things up. In which case you say 'j'adoube', which means, literally, 'I adjust', and it lets your opponent know that you would like to clear up any confusion and put things in order.

The international language of chess is not English, but French. There are various French terms – taking a pawn 'en passant', for example. (Sounds so casual, doesn't it? 'I'll just take you in passing!') Then there is 'en prise', which means that a piece which could have been taken earlier hasn't been – for whatever reason. Having a piece lurking about 'en prise' can be mentally very taxing; it can lead to all sorts of complications. The phrase 'j'adoube' requires a response from your opponent – a nod, some sign of agreement. Attempting to straighten out a messy situation without consulting her in advance is against the rules. It's just not on. You need her full knowledge and consent. Otherwise, automatic disqualification.

I knew I was doing badly, no proper development, the king wide open down the central files, no pieces defending. I had wasted too much time early on – ill-advised queen sorties – basic error. Pawns were gobbled up. 'Can we stop?' I asked. So we opted for a soothing sexual interlude, except that it wasn't because I couldn't help thinking all the time. I was very unhappy that I didn't feel soothed. All my worries sprang up and seized me. Fairly paralysed me. 'Let's stop,' I said sadly. No use him being nice about it. 'Can we finish off the chess?' I asked. We resumed the game. He got a pawn to the seventh rank; he'd promote it to a queen. 'I want to resign,' I said.

'Okay, let's put it all away.'

We lay down together in the dark. He put his arms around me, kissed me gently. I must think clearly, I worried. I must worry clearly. I felt his fingers smoothing over my brow. He knew I was worrying. 'I love you. Don't leave me.' There was a long, dark silence. I could hear his breathing; there were some difficult, irregular breaths. I was aware of some imminent cruel awakening; blazing mega-watt bulbs popping on when I was still blinking in cosy obscurity.

I felt the warm covers being thrown back and the cold air rushing in. 'I'm not telling you in bed,' he said. 'Come on.' He helped me into my bathrobe, tied the knot carefully at the waist and then led me towards the kitchen. I pulled out a chair and he sat down beside me, taking both my hands in his. 'Right,' he said. 'No more secrets.' Ah, yes, I thought. Those.

'I've gone over and over in my mind how I should tell you this . . .'

'Just tell me. I'm feeling brave.'

He looked down at our hands clasped together.

'I don't want you to be upset.'

'Then tell me as briefly as possible.'

146

'I'm married.'

For a few seconds I couldn't move or think or speak and then the storm broke around me.

He started speaking very fast. 'I married in Cuba, five years ago. I wanted to tell you, I tried to tell you, but I couldn't. I have to tell you now because she's coming next week. She'll be staying with me, but honestly, it's not a normal kind of marriage. I've told hardly anyone about it. A few people in New York know because that's where I was living at the time, and people in Cuba know, obviously, but shortly everyone will know. It's going to be difficult. I should have told you sooner about Consuela – that's her name.'

'Your consolation . . .'

'But I couldn't tell you, Rose. I knew you wouldn't stay.'

'And she's going to live in your house, with you?'

'It's a big house, Rose – you're always telling me that. And it's not really an ordinary sort of marriage; that's partly why I never told anyone about her.'

'Your wife.'

'Rose, I . . . listen, let me explain. She's staying here and I'm her guarantor.'

'Her what?'

'That's what it says on her visa. It's just a legalistic term. It means I'm responsible for her physical and financial well-being – that's the phrase they use on the visa. Please let me explain. I'm just her—'

'Her husband.'

'Technically speaking, yes.'

'What do you mean, technically?'

'It's complicated. But it doesn't change the way I feel about you, Rose. It doesn't have to change anything between us. But I made a promise to Consuela. We had an understanding that—'

'So your wife understands you!'

'—that if she was ever granted an exit permit to leave Cuba, then she could come here and . . .'

I leapt to my feet and rushed out of the room. I had no idea where I thought I was going, just the primitive 'fight or flight' panic, I suppose. As I flung open the front door, I heard rapid footsteps behind me. 'You can't go out without your shoes,' he said. 'And it's raining. Look.' He stood behind me, wrapped his arms around my waist. 'Don't leave me. Please, please don't leave me.'

'I don't know what else to do!'

'I'd stay in.'

We stood on the threshold together, in the cold, watching the rain pouring down out of the night sky.

I walked numbly into the living room and lowered myself on to the sofa. He sat down in the armchair opposite and waited. Distractedly, I picked up the nearest book. It fell open at the bit where Rochester takes Jane up to the attic to show her his domestic problem.

'Rose, please listen.' He took the book out of my hands. 'I was in Cuba on holiday . . .'

'A holiday romance?'

'In a way. I met her in hospital.'

'And what were you doing there? Fell down another ravine?'

'I got pushed out of a window – defenestrated. Robert says he blames himself. He says he should never have asked me to play. I twisted my shoulder hanging on to this balustrade – a kind of Spanish baroque stonework – and, well, everything in Havana is crumbling and so . . .'

'Jamie, just tell me about Consuela.'

'She fixed my shoulder. I met her at the Clinica Garcia. Physiotherapy.'

'So while she manipulated your shoulder, you fell in love and asked her to marry you?'

'Well, not quite like that, no. I thought she was pretty. And she was very funny too and we just hit it off straightaway, got on really well. She thought I was some kind of genius because I could speak Spanish.'

'How flattering for you!'

'She said that although she liked me a lot, she wouldn't dream of going to bed with me because she had a lot of very pure, shiny morals about certain things. Very virginal and so on.'

'Good for her!'

'But she changed her mind before the end of my trip.'

'So you deflowered your physiotherapist and flew home.'

'That sounds terrible.'

'Oh, don't torment yourself! I'm sure you did it beautifully!'

'She was only teasing me, Rose. Definitely no deflowering involved. After she fixed my shoulder, I met her again diving off the Isla Juvendad. We just ended up seeing a lot of each other.' He searched for his cigarettes, playing for time. I watched him light one; he was fumbling. Nervous. 'Right,' he said, inhaling, 'this is what happened. Now this is five years ago, remember. We were in this bar and we were talking. In Spanish. She was telling me about her sister who was getting married. She said she wished she were getting married, too. Now, Rose, listen, because this is crucial: Cuban Spanish is the fastest in America. All the sounds just blur together. They've got no time for a diphthong in Havana! They don't pronounce all the letters, end syllables just get dropped. Very lazy diction and . . .'

'And the point, Jamie?'

'I had a go at Cuban Spanish and she misunderstood me.'

'You? Misunderstood?'

'I said something like: "Don't worry, Consuela, you'll get married to some very lucky man and I'll wish it was me." And she took it as a proposal. She jumped up and screamed and kissed me and started speaking faster than ever and immediately the place was overwhelmed by all these excited people. All of her family arrived within seconds. It turned out they all lived upstairs. And everybody's dancing and singing. Instant party. Unbelievable! And for the rest of the holiday, I had an amazing time. They were so friendly, so kind, and there was no way I

149

could tell Consuela that I hadn't meant to propose to her. How could I tell her? Instead, we began the whole lengthy process of getting married. I knew it would take ages because I was a foreigner, and it was even more lengthy because I was British but living in the States. I wasn't worried. I knew I had Cuban bureaucracy on my side.'

'So you told her it was a mistake later on, did you?'

'Well . . .' He lit another cigarette. 'I didn't, no. Not straightaway. I didn't like to. You see, I'd decided to go back in February for the Havana Book Fair.'

'You bookworm!'

'Well, that wasn't the only reason, obviously. There was also the Havana Jazz Festival, plus the carnival.'

'So you had a lovely time, did you? And you still didn't tell her?'

'No. I didn't think I needed to by then. You see, she had found out that a report she had written on some medical statistics counted as official government work, and in Cuba that means you won't be granted an exit permit – at least, the odds are stacked against it. But she was still hopeful that being married to me would eventually get her a passport.'

'You mean she was going to marry you to get a British passport?'

'No, to get a Cuban passport. And she was fond of me as well.'

'Why couldn't she get her own Cuban passport?'

'No automatic freedom for Cubans to leave Cuba. You know that. She needed an exit permit first.'

'And for that she had to marry a foreigner?'

'It's the most popular way of getting an exit permit, yes. The rule is: you have to have a reason for leaving. Marriage is a good one; holiday in Miami isn't.'

'I see.'

'So, even though she couldn't leave right away, she was still hopeful she could leave eventually. She still wanted to get married. All the bureaucracy was sorted out by then and there was no reason why we should have waited any longer to get married, but I told her that I thought we should.'

'So you played for time.'

'I told her I was going back to New York and when I was away she would probably meet someone else who deserved her better. She was a bit upset at first but she was good about it; she understood. We had two very nice weeks together and then I flew home. Not long after that, she phoned me up and pleaded with me to go back.' He stopped, sank back in his chair and groaned. 'It was terrible. She made me feel like some kind of deserting seducer.'

'How could she be so inconsiderate?'

'And then she told me that . . . that . . . things were much more complicated than I thought and my conscience got to me. I booked a seat on the next plane to Mexico and went back to Cuba to see her. I behaved better than you think, Rose. I wanted to help her and if anything I was too old-fashioned about it. You've got to remember that it was very difficult for people in Cuba back then. There were shortages of everything – real austerity – and I had just acted like the worst kind of tourist. After she rang me, I realised I really cared what happened to her. I wanted to marry her. I thought it was the right thing to do because . . . because . . . Look, Rose, for a lot of Cubans, it's really useful to have a relative abroad.'

'A husband!'

'If we're being really honest, I was a very welcome source of dollars. And I was happy to send her money. I helped her. What I sent made a difference.'

'Sponsor a poor person! Makes you feel all generous and noble, doesn't it?'

'No,' he said, from the armchair. 'It makes me feel guilty.'

I gripped my hands together; kept quiet.

'Look, it's all worked out very well for Consuela. She's considerably better off for having met me. Don't look like that,

151

Rose, it's not as bad as it sounds. I came home and I didn't tell anybody that I was married. That was wrong of me, I suppose, but it was simpler that way. I made sure she had money and so on, but most of all I promised her that if she ever got her exit permit she could come and live with me. She's got it and she's coming. I found out a few months ago.'

'Before we met?'

'Yes.'

'I would never have agreed to this kept woman thing if I'd known you were married!'

'That's why I didn't tell you. I wanted to spend as much time as possible with you before she came. And I've had to admit to Consuela that no one knows I'm married to her. Only Robert knows. But I've always liked Consuela and we've stayed in touch . . . less so when I moved to London, but she always wrote to me and I rang her up and I sent her things.'

'Little presents?'

'In a way.' He sat forward on the chair, very earnest now. 'Rose, this all happened ages before I met you.'

I folded my arms. 'What did you send her?'

'I transferred money to a bank in Havana. I sent her things – just things.'

'What things?'

'You want to know exactly? I don't think I can remember. I know five years ago I used to send her loads of soap.'

'Soap?'

'They like their toiletries in Cuba. There used to be a shortage back then. What else did I send her? For her last birthday I sent a gold bangle, but it didn't get there. I transferred some dollars so she could buy her own.'

'Not a pearl, then?'

'No,' he said, softly. 'Not a pearl.'

'When did you last see her?' My voice taut.

'The week before I met you. She phoned to say she was definitely going to get this exit permit and I flew out to see her.

The pathos of it kind of got to me. There was some documentation to sort out at this end, but it's done now.'

'What documentation at this end?'

'Immigration.' Another cigarette. Chain-smoking now. 'Now you know everything,' he said. 'You know everything about me.'

I felt light-headed. 'Listen,' he repeated. 'It's really important you understand she's only coming on a visit. The immigration thing is just a formality. I had to provide details of my income; I had to prove I could support her. It doesn't mean she's staying for good.'

'But she's your wife!'

'My estranged wife. It doesn't affect the way I feel about you.'

'It affects the way I feel about you!' I started walking up and down the room. He watched me anxiously. 'You visit her, you send her presents, you're still married.'

'It's a very platonic, long-distance sort of marriage.'

'Just good friends?' He nodded, vigorously.

'Does she say she loves you?'

'What do you mean?'

'Does she say she loves you?'

He hesitated. 'Yes – for what it's worth. Yes.'

'For what it's worth!'

He came towards me, stopped me pacing. 'What she said – what she says – is simply for her the appropriate thing to say. It's not some big, philosophical issue, it's just the right words for the occasion. She's not a romantic heroine, Rose, she's a pragmatist. She doesn't think like you; different things are important to her.'

'Did you sleep with her that week before you met me?'

'What?'

'I bet you did. Keep her as a hobby!' I cried. 'Keep her for holidays! And why shouldn't you have sex with her? You're married, aren't you? When did you start being purely platonic?'

He looked stricken. 'Rose, please . . .'

'Tell me the truth!' I shouted. 'Tell me the truth!'

His face was ashen. There was a very long, very loaded pause. It was the kind of pause you get in gangster movies before everyone starts shooting.

'She stayed with me at my hotel. There's not a lot of privacy where she lives and we needed to talk.'

'And?'

'And nothing,' he said tightly. 'It was a strange situation. It was sad. I said I meant it about her coming to stay with me. I said everything would be all right . . . It was all . . . it was . . .' He looked at me beseechingly. 'Have you ever . . .? You know how . . .?' he floundered. 'You know how something can seem like a good idea at the time?'

'So you slept with her. You're married; it's allowed. Anything else you want to tell me?'

'No,' he said, miserably. 'That's it.'

'Got any children?'

'No.'

'Are you sure?'

'I would have noticed.'

'Maybe you'll get round to it now.'

He looked at me, deeply unhappy. 'She was pregnant when we got married. That's why I went back, really. I thought it would be easier to help her if we were married, easier to get round the embargo and the austerity laws. But after the wedding I left more or less straightaway, and she sent me a letter saying it hadn't been much of a honeymoon. She told me she wasn't pregnant any more. She said it was the wrong time to have a baby. Things were just too difficult.'

I said nothing.

'Rose, don't you have any secrets from me?'

'No. I wish I did.'

'Don't cry,' he said, touching my cheek. 'I can't bear to see you cry.'

'I'm not crying,' I choked, and put my hands over my eyes.

'I thought you didn't do lies,' he whispered. I felt his arms

154

reach round me. 'I won't lie to you again. I promise. No more secrets; I promise.'

'What can you possibly promise me?' I asked, pushing him aside.

I felt strangely detached from everything. There is something about the way I was brought up that demands I have to put the kettle on when I hit an acute crisis. It's like an involuntary muscle spasm.

'I'm putting the kettle on,' I said, surprised at hearing myself sounding brisk. 'I'm getting out the big teapot. Do you want some shortbread? It's in fingers too, so you'd like that.'

He followed me through to the kitchen.

I busied myself with the tea. 'Well, I certainly can't carry on living at the bottom of the garden now, can I?'

'Of course you can.'

'Are you completely stupid?'

He sat down at the table looking defeated and I bustled around him with tea cups. 'I realise now,' he said, 'that I fell in love with you the first moment I saw you. Twelve years ago. I didn't think I'd ever see you again and when I did, I couldn't believe it. It was like a blinding light. I loved you. Fate sealed.'

I knew I was very upset at that point because I started polishing the kettle. Polish, polish, shine, shine, gleam, gleam. Warm teapot. Spoon in the tea. Darjeeling. Add boiling water, stir.

'I was just walking round in a daze. I wanted to be with you, but I didn't know how to tell you about Consuela. It was on my mind; I didn't know what to do. I thought you probably didn't feel the same way about me as I felt about you.'

'Darjeeling takes longer to brew than Assam, doesn't it?'

'What? Oh, no, no it doesn't, it just looks weaker, that's all, but it isn't. Just pour it now, Rose. She's arriving next week. I'm going to meet her off the plane. I knew you'd leave me. I don't blame you. When she gets here, Consuela thought she'd quite like to have a little party. Meet my friends. Oh God! You're going to leave me! Just pour it, Rose.'

I lifted the teapot lid, gave it a stir. 'It's not brewed properly yet,' I said. 'I have standards about some things. Bright, shiny principles!' He started eating the shortbread. I waited another minute, then filled the teacups. He watched me, misty-eyed. 'I can't bear the thought of being without you.'

'You'll live.'

'All she wants is a different passport. She's going to get a Spanish one, not a British one. She can do that because her father was born in Spain. She's going to Madrid for it and it's best I go with her. It means I'll be away for a few days – maybe longer. It all depends on whether the process turns out to be simple or complicated.'

'Belated honeymoon?'

'It'll be the most chaste in history. Honestly. Oh, what's the point? You don't believe a word I say any more, do you?'

'No. Drink your tea. I'd like you to leave soon. I've got lots to do.'

'What are you going to do?'

'Pack.'

'But Rose, we've got to talk about where you're going to live.'

'What do you mean?'

'I can understand you don't want to live here any more, it's too close, but what about a flat around the corner on Royal Terrace?'

'I'm not going to be your mistress! I'm not staying with you after this!'

'But Rose, it's not a romantic kind of marriage, only a very pragmatic one. I've tried to explain that.'

'You've left it a bit late.'

'I just wanted to be with you as long as possible.'

'You've used me.'

'I haven't. I love you. I would do anything for you.'

'Is that all you have to say?'

156

'All right!' He put his hands up in surrender. 'You've had no time to think.'

'You've made things much worse by even suggesting you install me somewhere else around the corner!'

He went very quiet. Stared at the table for ages. I got up from my place opposite and sat down beside him. I hugged him; we held on to each other tightly. Probably only one more of these hugs left to go now, I thought. Probably one at the door when he leaves and that will be it. 'I thought that when I had explained . . .' He started again. 'I hoped that when I had explained, you'd stay with me.'

'I can't.'

'But I love you.'

'Don't spoil all that bad truth with another good lie.'

'I'm not lying.'

'The best liar ever! They're just sweet words to say,' I swallowed hard, 'and I don't want to hear them any more. I don't want to see you any more.'

He turned away from me, hid his face, couldn't meet my eyes and that's when I knew he was lying, because that's what people do when they lie, isn't it? They can't look at you.

'I've lost you, haven't I?' he whispered.

'Not quite yet. Got a few minutes left.'

We sat side by side, very close. We were often companionably close, we didn't always take opposite sides of the table. It's only in retrospect that it seems like we spent all our time improving our chess and sex. Our companionship was always of the touching kind; we always had to have some physical contact. We were needy of each other. I leaned against him, he kissed my forehead and I felt a tightness in my throat, that sensation of the muscles contracting hard to prevent sobbing. It's one of those useful evolutionary things humans have developed, along with walking upright and civilisation.

'Why did you say you wanted to marry me?' I asked.

'Because it's true.'

157

'Flexible, pragmatic bigamy?'

'I only want you.'

The need to cry was becoming unbearable. 'I'd like you to go now, Jamie.'

Very reluctantly, he got to his feet. He put my hand to his cheek, kissed the palm – little kiss, closed my fingers around it. A kiss for me to keep.

'Please,' he said, 'we have to talk again.'

'No.'

'I'm begging you.'

'Don't beg, it's too awful.'

He waited. The most desperate and well-dressed beggar I'd ever seen in Edinburgh. I wished I could just give him some change and walk past feeling better about it. 'All right, we'll talk again.' Relief on his face. 'After I've moved out.'

'Goodbye, Rose.' I clung to him, allowing myself one last embrace. He held me very close and then the awfulness of parting, of seeing him walk away. The deprivation when my hands could only seek each other to hold. I went back into the house and moved about the empty rooms, restlessly, not knowing what to do. All finished. All ended.

He had been my romantic investment and anyone with half my intelligence could have predicted that I would lose everything.

I couldn't hold back the tears any longer. The tightness in my throat was suffocating me. I went back into the living room and sat weeping, with *Jane Eyre*.

'You know I am a scoundrel, Jane?' ere long he inquired wistfully . . .
    'Yes, sir.'

I wiped my tears and turned the page.

'And now you consider my arms filled and my embraces appropriated?'

158

'At any rate there is neither room nor claim for me, sir.'

I sniffed and blew my nose.

'If you think so, you must have a strange opinion of me; you must regard me as a plotting profligate – a base and low rake who has been simulating disinterested love in order to draw you into a snare deliberately laid and strip you of all honour and rob you of self-respect! What say you to that?'

Unable to cope with another word of fiction, I shut the book. Reality overwhelmed me and I cried and cried and cried.

Chapter 13

I knew I had played like a beginner, bumbling aimlessly along, telling myself it was all just a game. Jamie, however, had known exactly what he was doing and had executed his strategy perfectly. His had been a very polished performance. He had developed his advantage quickly, exploited all my mistakes and his timing had been immaculate. And here I was – staring defeat in the face.

I felt exhausted, I couldn't think straight. I went to bed. I took all my problems back to bed with me – seemed a good idea since that's where they had come from. For the first time in months, I set the alarm. Jamie, I thought as I curled up alone, how could you do this to me? I loved you! I shouldn't have told you that! Oh, how I wished I hadn't! Why was I so hopeless – romantic, deluded? Too many stupid books I'd read, too many Victorian romances reprinted by Virago. All those swooning heroines. I fell for the lush Pre-Raphaelite covers. I wished I could forget *Lady Audley's Secret*.

I did sleep, an uncomfortable, restless sleep, and woke early with thoughts crowding my brain. I felt confused and miserable.

Before I could pack I needed to get out, get some fresh air and try to recover that panoramic sense of perspective.

From the top of Calton Hill I could see everything for fifty miles around. The whole of the city was spread out before me; towers, domes and office blocks, hotels, shops and concert halls. Flags were flying importantly. I had visited only one other city that flew more flags than Edinburgh: it was in Africa and my holiday had been curtailed by a military coup. Along with other British nationals I had been air-lifted out for my own safety. I loved Edinburgh; I really didn't want to be air-lifted out. From my place on the hill top I could see the length of Princes Street and the crowds. So much is down to chance and accident. Opposite the castle was the place where we had met.

How much I wanted to be with him! It's hard to wipe out infatuation, even after twelve hours of shock. And all the things he could give me, the luxurious little pleasures, the fabulous big pleasures, the sweet life – *la dolce vita*. And he had taught me a phrase I didn't know: *dolce far niente* – sweet doing nothing. Sounds better in Italian.

When I had first agreed to the whole kept woman arrangement, what had made the relationship workable in my eyes was that I thought he was wonderful and he definitely wasn't involved with anyone else – or so I had believed. 'I do not love him,' I told myself, over and over again. 'I do not love him.' I had only persuaded myself I was in love. Starry-eyed and gullible. I realised that in pursuing my original strategy (the 'Reader, I married him' strategy), I had failed to make any contingency plan for him being married to somebody else.

I gave up, walked home, had a bath, cried again. I didn't have any better ideas.

Packing was more difficult than I had thought. There was never any question that I was going to leave with just the books I had brought with me. I wasn't that sort of selfless heroine. I was going to take all recently acquired valuable editions with me. Shame about the piano.

When I got to the pearl, I didn't know what to do with it. I was rolling it around the table, thinking, when the doorbell rang. I looked out of the window and standing in the lane below was a man with a mass of pink roses. He saw me. 'Cheer up, hen!' called the florist. 'Somebody loves you!' I went downstairs and opened the door. 'I think he's sorry,' said the man, kindly, when he saw my red eyes.

I wanted to throw the flowers away but I couldn't. They were my namesake and it wasn't really their fault we'd found ourselves in this situation. I laid them out on the table, a last floral tribute. There was a card. '*Amamo*,' it said, and it's not an apology, it's a command: love me; I love you. A nice bit of elliptical Latin and a genuine fifth-century term of endearment. He'd have had to spell it out, along with his credit card details. He shouldn't have bothered.

I stood the roses in a vase of lemonade; it would rush straight to their heads and keep them upright for a week – sugared to death. For roses, it's the only way to go. Better than wilt by water. The pearl I dropped in with the roses. It sank, magnified and distorted.

I rang Catherine. 'His Consolation,' I said, 'is arriving next week. I've only just found out about her.'

'I thought you knew.'

'He wants to carry on seeing me, but it's all over. I was only ever infatuated; I've stopped being foolish. The fug of infatuation is lifting.'

'Rose,' she said, sounding concerned, 'you do know you mustn't stay with him now, don't you?'

'Yes.' (How very cool and collected I am!)

'Time to leave. Keep your incorrectness for a better man. Do you want me to come and get you?'

'Please, Catherine.'

'I'm coming now.'

I sat in the kitchen surrounded by bags and waited. All I felt was an insulating numbness. I opened the newspaper and turned the pages mechanically, not really paying attention to anything.

Then, near the back, beside the chess and bridge and crossword, was a name I recognised. It leapt out from the Marriages column: James Cameron and Consuela Casanovas, in Havana, Cuba, July 31st 1993. *Hasta la vista, Jamie.*

The same announcement in every single newspaper.

She was outing him as her husband.

'Entirely understandable,' said Catherine, bundling my belongings into the back of the car. 'She wants everyone to know he lied about her, how he kept her a secret. It's been very convenient for him, hasn't it? Pretending he wasn't married.'

'Robert knew.'

'That doesn't surprise me,' said Catherine. 'Robert knows everything. He's cleverer than Jamie. Now, are you sure you don't want to take the espresso machine?'

Sitting on the white sofa in Catherine's flat, the scene felt depressingly familiar. All my bags on the floor, books and knickers spilling out of them. Catherine's books were kept on concealed shelving. Huge, archive shelves that could be rolled out into the room on tramlines. I found her Travel & Geography section and searched for Cuba. There wasn't much – just a tiny Berlitz guide. I read: 'Cubans are generally fun-loving, sensuous people, and friendship with Cubans will for many visitors constitute the highlight of their stay.'

'You can have Helen's room,' called Catherine from the kitchen. 'She's never here these days.' I put the guidebook away and wandered into Helen's room. There were a lot of mirrors. Wherever I turned, I couldn't avoid seeing myself and I looked awful. My face was blotchy with crying. On the wall opposite the bed was Botticelli's *Birth of Venus*. Catherine appeared at my side. 'Can I take that down?' I asked. 'Can we go out right now and buy something else? Can I have the "Death of Venus"?'

Shopping wasn't really Catherine's thing, but she knew it was mine and I appreciated her making the effort. She cleared a whole three hours in her schedule for it. We went to poster shops and galleries and found dozens of pictures of Venus taking a bath, romping with Mars or toying with Cupid, but none of her dead. 'We're not going to find a "Death of Venus",' said Catherine. 'She's immortal, isn't she?'

'There are quite a few of her lying down with her eyes shut.'

'But she is not dead, she's only sleeping.'

'There must be something I can have!'

'What about this print of a coffin on a chaise longue?' asked Catherine. 'Magritte. Will that do?'

'Yes. Poor Madame Récamier!'

'Are you sure you wouldn't like something less melodramatic?'

'No, I like that one.'

Once the picture was bought, Catherine said she really had to get back to work. 'I'll see you at the flat this afternoon,' she said. 'And try not to buy anything else.'

'I won't,' I said, determinedly. 'I know what I have to do.'

I hadn't been inside a bank for a while, only outside at the cash machine, but glancing at the leaflets on display it seemed incredibly easy to get a loan. There were pictures of proud debtors in shiny new cars, happy debtor couples at glossy front doors, suntanned debtors lying on beaches.

'My account is in credit,' I told the loans manager, 'but it won't be for long. I owe fifteen thousand pounds to a private sponsor and I want to pay him back. I'm going to write a cheque and I'd like it not to bounce.'

We discussed my situation and, after checking my banking history, she pronounced me Very High Risk. I did not qualify for a fifteen thousand pound prearranged overdraft. 'But,' she suggested, 'you might be able to borrow against your Nat West Scottish Widowed No Worries Insurance Plan.'

'Do you really think so? I only put in twenty pounds.'

'It's a Flexi-Finance package. If you sell those books you told me about and raise five thousand, you can top up the Flexi-

Premium. Then you can buy Hardened Debt Protection Insurance for two hundred pounds a month and that will entitle you to a Draw-Down Loan of fifteen thousand at twenty-six per cent APR. In the meantime, I strongly advise you to destroy your Premium Black and Gold credit card.'

'Any other strong advice?'

'Go and get your pearl.'

'You don't look great, Rose,' said my sister when I got back.

'Thanks, Catherine.'

'You haven't been at Nat West all this time, have you?'

'No.'

'What's that in your hand? Good God! Is it real?'

'Of course it's real.'

'So you went back for it, did you? Was he there?'

'No. Has he rung?'

'I told him you didn't want to speak to him. I'll find out how much that's worth for you.' She leapt to her computer. Keywords: pearl prices.

'I don't want to sell it.'

'Why not?'

'Because I'm feckless.' I walked slowly into Helen's room, sat down on the bed and stared at the new picture on the wall. Catherine appeared in the doorway. 'You're only allowed to have that up for a day. Mum says. I phoned and told her what's happened. She says you have to get a job right away. Start being busy.'

'She's very practical for a professor of philosophy, isn't she? Did you tell Helen what's happened, too?'

'She says she sympathises.' Catherine sat down beside me, put a comforting arm around my shoulders. 'Mum said Mungo Mackenzie told her he still hasn't seen your new thesis and when are you going to finish it?'

'I don't know,' I said, guiltily. 'I haven't looked at it for a while – not seriously.'

165

'Now's your chance. Mackenzie has recommended you for a part-time job.'

'At the Dictionary?'

'Not yet,' she said quickly, 'but nearly. He's recommended you to a very influential Member of the Scottish Parliament. A controversial and famously dyslexic member – the one who drove through the funding for the Dictionary.'

'Magnus McTavish?'

'The very same. McTavish is launching his big new project – he wants Edinburgh to be twinned with Las Vegas – and he needs extra secretarial support. His department phoned while you were out. They want you to start tomorrow. Afternoons only, five days a week. It would be ideal, Rose, and in the mornings you could work on your thesis.'

Chapter 14

For my first day in my new job, I tried very hard to put Jamie out of my mind. I had to keep going, I had to concentrate on the here and now. I had to forget my lazy, hazy days of self-delusion. So with this in mind, I wore my sensibly efficient navy blue suit and I borrowed Catherine's smart leather briefcase. However, when I walked up the Royal Mile, I found myself remembering how we had stood on this very street together on that first night and immediately I found myself trying not to cry. I had to make myself forget him. I had to discipline myself not to think of him at all. I clutched Catherine's briefcase and walked on.

Apart from his brave championing of the New Scots Dictionary, Magnus McTavish was known for his explosive temper, restless energy and complete disregard for parliamentary propriety. But what impressed people the most was his expansive hospitality on expenses. He was jovially corrupt.

McTavish's office was the largest and busiest of the many parliamentary offices around Edinburgh Castle. I was met by a nervous-looking woman who introduced herself as Maggie, Magnus McTavish's personal assistant.

'I should warn you,' she twitched, 'he's just come out of a very tense breakfast meeting. An early start is bad for his temper and the coffee didn't agree with him.'

'Nor did anyone,' said a voice from the corner. I turned to see a tall, thin-faced man of about my own age. He nodded politely. 'Alastair Lennox,' he said, introducing himself. 'I run the Proof-Reading Department.'

'I don't suppose proof-readers and dyslexics have an easy relationship.'

'Alastair, this is Dr Rose Budleigh,' said Maggie, loftily. 'Dr Budleigh is a highly qualified expert on lexicography.'

'Is that so?' asked Alastair.

'And she's working for us now. This way, please, Dr Budleigh.'

Maggie ushered me along dusty corridors. The place was labyrinthine. Like many buildings in the Old Town, its rooms and halls had been extended and divided so many times it was impossible to see what the original plan might have been. We passed a dozen tiny rooms, each inhabited by three or four people stuffing envelopes. 'Party workers,' said Maggie. 'Helping out in their holidays.'

At the next corner, we stopped by a mullioned window and she pointed to the building across the street. 'That's Proof-Reading and Political Correctness,' she said, contempt in her voice. 'Foisted on us at the tax-payer's expense! I'm afraid you'll be seeing a lot of Alastair Lennox. Everything Mr McTavish says or writes for public consumption has to be checked by him. The bureaucracy!'

'It must be very time-consuming.'

We walked on, round another corner, down a flight of stairs.

'This is my office,' she said, entering a cupboard. 'We'll be sharing a desk and through that door over there is Mr McTavish's private office.'

She knocked, timidly. There was a distant roar. Phonetic analysis would have seen it pass through a whole spectrum of violent vowel sounds. Maggie flinched. Heavy footsteps and the door was flung open. 'What the fuck is it now?'

'This is Dr Budleigh,' said Maggie, pushing me in front of her. 'Dr Rose Budleigh. She's come to help with the new project. Afternoons only, but she's come in early today to learn the ropes.'

Magnus McTavish had a short, corpulent body and a bristly, bearded face. Bright eyes glared at me. 'She?' he repeated. 'I thought Dr Budleigh was a man.'

'She isn't,' I said.

'Mungo didn't say you were a girl.' He raised his eyes to the ceiling, as if beseeching God for mercy. 'At least it should keep Lennox happy that we've got more women in the department. Has she met him yet, Maggie?'

Maggie nodded.

'You'll be seeing more of him at twelve o'clock. I'm having another bloody meeting with him. I can't get out of it.' Maggie tutted sympathetically. 'Well, Rosie, can you type?'

'Yes.'

'Can you run?'

'I think running is probably on my CV somewhere.'

'Good! Then you'll fit in. I'd like you to record the meeting for me. Keep the bastards taped, that's what I say. Maggie, show Rosie my tapes library, will you?'

'What's the meeting about?' I asked.

'The final draft of a statement on the need for . . .' he assumed an expression of disgust, '. . . political correctness.'

'I see.'

'Do you? It's all a load of crap if you ask me. Utter waste of time.'

'So we won't be staying long, then?'

'Too bloody right. I've got a lunch appointment at half past twelve. The Sauna Licensing Committee. We're interviewing a new vice chairman.'

Maggie scurried to her desk and checked the diary. 'What about your meeting with Mungo Mackenzie at one o'clock?'

'Phone Mungo, ask him if he'll join us. He's normally a good judge of character.' McTavish gave me a scrutinising stare. 'What's happening after lunch, Maggie?'

'You have a three o'clock with the Las Vegas Liaison Team.'

'I'll need you for that, Rosie. I'm going to submit my draft proposal. I finished it last night. Working title: *The Old Grey Lady Meets The Whore of Babylon*. They're gonna love it at Political Correctness.'

'I'm sure they can't wait.'

'I'll need you to check my syntax. Can you join me in half an hour? I'm in the middle of some vital constituency work – got a few favours to call in. Now, Maggie will show you the ropes and then you can join me for a mid-morning apéritif. Do you like a wee dram?'

'Oh, yes,' I said.

'Good! Take some money out of petty cash and go and buy us a new bottle. Now, if you ladies will excuse me, I must get on.' He rubbed his hands. 'Scotland needs governing!'

'He's under a lot of stress,' said Maggie, loyally. 'It's only because he pushes himself so hard. Magnus has a vision. The rest of us try to fit in with his plans and support him. He is the rocket and we are the power-packs. You're not seeing him on a good day. He's really a very generous man and very . . .' she searched for the right word, 'driven. Now, this way to the tapes library.' She opened another door and I realised that her office was simply a cupboard off this, the original room. 'He's a great dictator!' she laughed. 'He does everything by dictation. You'll soon get the hang of it.'

'What exactly is my job, Maggie?'

'You are his lexicographical consultant. You make sure everything he passes to the Proof-Reading Department is absolutely, flawlessly perfect. I never quite managed it; I kept getting things sent back. It was difficult. I have this problem with the "apostrophe s".'

'It's a very common problem.'

'And sometimes I couldn't phrase things in the appropriate

parliamentary language, but it wasn't always my fault. Alastair Lennox and I do not get on. Clash of personalities. We're hoping that he won't dare criticise your work. Not with all your qualifications! Magnus was so pleased when Mungo Mackenzie mentioned you might be available. Now, do you think you can manage on your own this afternoon? I'll collect his dry-cleaning before I go. Oh, and I'll buy a new bottle, too.' Maggie opened a small safe in the wall. It contained thick wads of cash, an almost empty bottle of whisky and a photograph of Frank Sinatra and President Kennedy, doubly autographed. 'Very valuable,' whispered Maggie. 'It was taken at The Sands, Las Vegas.'

At the appointed time, I knocked on McTavish's office door, whisky in one hand, shorthand notebook in the other. 'Come!' he called, imperiously.

His office was a grand Jacobean hall. There was oak panelling on the walls, an impressive stone fireplace and an ornamental plaster ceiling. He sat at the far end of the room, behind a vast desk. 'Sit down, Rosie,' he said. 'We're very pleased you're joining the team. We need as much support as we can get to push this Las Vegas thing through.' He rubbed his eyes. 'It's been a tough morning. I never get a moment's peace.' He shuffled papers on his desk. 'Don't worry about me, though. Wait till we get in that meeting this afternoon – the old adrenalin will start coursing through the veins and you'll see a McTavish revival!

'Here's my dictaphone. I've recorded my opinions on the Minister for Culture. She wants to put the brakes on our Las Vegas reconnoitre expedition. But we need that reccy! And you'll have to come too, Rosie! A pretty girl is always an asset when it comes to press relations. Maggie won't come, but she'll be no loss on this occasion. She's a very capable administrator, Maggie, but she's no spring chicken. That Alastair Lennox will be there because I can't move without the bastard trailing me. I think it's essential that you come to Vegas, Rosie. Have you ever been before?'

'No. Is it good?'

McTavish leaned back in his chair, rested his pudgy hands on his belly and smiled. 'As Mae West once said: "Goodness had nothing to do with it, dearie!"' He chortled to himself, like a happy pig. 'Las Vegas is the antidote to Edinburgh. It's time the Old Grey Lady threw off her corsets and danced naked in the desert!'

'Well, there's a photocall.'

'I can see this twinning project working out, I really can.' He stared at the plaster laurel wreaths on the ceiling. 'People say I'm a dreamer, but . . .' he unscrewed the bottle of whisky, '. . . so many of my dreams have come true.'

'There's the Dictionary,' I reminded him. 'Now that was an achievement.'

'Aye, the Dictionary! An achievement, but also a personal triumph. I was determined to see that through. Can you imagine how frustrating it can be to have so many brilliant ideas in your head and not be able to write them down without people laughing? But all my life I have refused to let my dyslexia hold me back. When I first stood for high office, I surrounded myself with good spellers and grammarians. I have the ideas, the inspiration; you and the others are my weapons in the political war of words. Maggie is my spade of research, my hammer on the word processor. But you, Rose, are of a more intellectual use to me. You,' he said, dramatically, 'are my dictionary.'

'I'll take that as a compliment, Mr McTavish.'

'Call me Magnus, sweetheart.' He smiled and held up his glass in a toast. 'Here's to you, on your first day working for me! We're going to get on very well. I know from my own success what a great communicator I am. The people listen to me, they like my ideas, they know where I'm coming from. I am in tune with the Common Scotsman. Here's to him!' He held his glass aloft: 'The Common Scotsman! Now,' he said, wiping his beard, 'about the project. Twinning Edinburgh with Las Vegas is going to put this city on the map. It'll be a big story for the tabloids –

172

and they love me already.' He poured himself another drink. 'It's going to be a lot of hard work, but I can see the carrot at the end of the tunnel.'

'The carrot?'

'Aye. So, off you go with that tape for me, Rosie. It's for the attention of the Minister for Culture. I want you to translate and rephrase my rantings, type it up and fax it to the old cow. Thank you very much.' I rose to go. 'Oh, and Rosie, one important thing: I don't like to be disturbed. No one comes to see me without an appointment. No one gets to catch me off-guard, sleeping, emotional or pissed. Leave the bottle, would you? Knock on the door at twelve o'clock and don't let anybody past you.'

'I won't.'

'Good girl! Don't let the bastards find you down – that's my motto.'

I closed the door quietly behind me, sat down at my tiny desk and listened to his tape. It seemed that all I was required to do was express McTavish's words through a medium of tact and courtesy. In this way, 'The Minister is an interfering old wifie meddling in things that have nowt to do with her and what the fuck would she know about lap-dancing' was transformed into: 'The Minister is operating outwith her proper remit.'

Piece of cake.

I typed some letters, tidied my desk and did some filing. I tried not to remember that this time last week I had been standing at the top of Suilven, holding Jamie's hand, overcome with joyful emotion. I wondered what he was doing now. He would have had to admit to everyone that he was married. Everyone would know now about Consuela. He had probably been kept very busy. It wouldn't be long before she would be living with him at his big house with its grand views over the park. Perhaps he would rent out the mews house. Whoever ended up there would probably enjoy it. Of all the places I had ever called home, it was my favourite. I missed its warmth and comfort and its enfolding privacy, tucked away at the end of the lane. But what I missed most of all was Jamie living there with me. Jamie sleeping there with me.

I was annoyed at myself for all my self-indulgent nostalgia. Unless I made a real effort to concentrate on what I was doing, I found I day-dreamed about him constantly. It was a bad habit I couldn't give up, but then I didn't really want to give it up. Not yet. I wallowed in memories of the time we'd had together. I wanted to remember what it felt like to love and be loved. I had to keep reminding myself that it had all been a lie. His lie and my infatuation. Not really a good foundation for a lasting relationship.

I was brought back to present reality when McTavish flung open his office door, choleric with rage. 'Rose!' he bellowed. I leapt to my feet. 'Fax this to that poxy Proof-Reader and tell him he knows where he can put his fucking farcical Statement on Scotland!'

'Whom shall I fax, exactly?'

'It's programmed in. It's the "Sod Off" button!'

'Is that Alastair Lennox?'

'Who else?'

And there, on the fax machine, was a neatly typed label: 'Sod Off'. It came after the 'Bastards' button and before 'Blue Skies Chinese Takeaway'.

'And ring him up as well!' he fumed. 'We're not going to that meeting until I know he's got that fax! Ring him up and tell him to wait for it!'

'If Alastair Lennox is the "Sod Off" button, who are the "Bastards"?' I asked, picking up the phone.

'They have a central switchboard,' said McTavish, darkly.

'Hello? This is Mr McTavish's office. We've just sent you an important fax . . .'

'Hello, Dr Budleigh,' said Alastair's voice. He sounded very cheerful. 'Enjoying your first day? Pleasant, friendly working atmosphere?'

'It's lovely, thank you. Call me Rose. We're due to attend your meeting in five minutes, but I'm afraid we're not coming unless you tell me you've received our fax on your Statement on Scotland. It should be appearing about now.'

'Ah yes! Something's coming through. It says: "Re: your far cycle statement . . ." Well, Rose, I do deal with policy on bicycle paths, traffic wardens, that kind of thing – could Magnus be referring to the Integrated Transport Policy?'

McTavish looked at me uncertainly. 'He's got it,' I said.

My first visit to the Department of Proof-Reading and Political Correctness was an informative experience. McTavish was bullish. In no uncertain terms, he defied their insistence on the use of non-sexist language in parliamentary press releases. 'Look, man!' he shouted at Alastair Lennox. 'If I want to say I speak for the man on the street, I will bloody well say that! To hell with you!'

Alastair listened to this, thin lips pressed into a firm line. He waited patiently for McTavish to pause for breath, then interrupted his monologue. 'Magnus, it is policy to address both man and woman. You have to say: The man and the woman on the street, the person on the street. If you say you speak for the man on the street, you are referring to only forty-eight per cent of the population.'

'Bollocks!'

For twenty minutes I listened to their debate, and despite my dislike of my new boss's communication style I was fascinated by the vitality of his argument. The question of 'man' was something we had discussed in my last tutorial class at Cambridge and I was waiting for the chance to let Alastair Lennox know the conclusions we had drawn.

'If I may say something, here . . .'

'Is it time for lunch, Rosie?' asked McTavish, hopefully.

'If I could perhaps provide some etymological basis for Mr McTavish's argument. The word "man" until the fourteenth century was a neuter noun and stood for both man and woman. In modern German the word "man" is translated as "one" – again a neuter pronoun. Even until the late Medieval period it was common to use "man" for "wife". The word is still used colloquially in Scotland and the north of England – Magnus used it before when referring to Alastair and he could just as easily have used it when referring to me. In northern English dialect – around Newcastle for instance – women will happily use "man" in the same colloquial sense when addressing each other. I met up with a really good crowd last time I had a night out in Newcastle and they said things to me like "divvunt be stupid, man", but they were being very friendly when they said it. To suppress the use of a centuries-old colloquial expression just to satisfy the short-lived fashions of political correctness is, I would suggest, a mistake.'

No one spoke. Alastair Lennox appeared to have no rebuttal argument, which was a shame because I was ready to counter it had he been at all prepared. A slow, delighted smile was expanding across McTavish's ruddy features.

'And as I was saying,' he beamed, 'before my assistant, Dr Rose Budleigh, gave us her learned academic opinion – time for lunch.'

The meeting broke up. 'You're a star!' he exclaimed, squeezing my shoulders. For one horrible moment I thought he was going to kiss me. 'Wait till I tell Mungo. It's a pity, Rose, you can't come to lunch. I would have asked you, but given the sensitive nature of sauna licensing we'd better not have you there with the wee tape recorder. You take a long lunch, sweetheart. See you back at McTavish HQ at three o'clock. Las Vegas, here we come.'

He strolled off, giving an airy wave to the political correctors.

Alastair Lennox, Chief Corrector, appeared at my shoulder. 'Rose Budleigh,' he said. 'I hope you're on a short-term contract because I can see you're going to cause me trouble.'

'I'm not being deliberately troublesome. It's just that it was an interesting question and I haven't had a good academic argument for ages and . . .'

'You have to realise, Rose, that here it's not a just an academic argument. Here it's a policy decision. McTavish is a dinosaur and he's on the way out. I can't imagine why you're working for him.'

'Maggie doesn't think he's a dinosaur. Maggie says he's a rocket and we're his power-packs.'

'Does she now? Well, the less said about Maggie the better.'

'I quite like Maggie.'

'McTavish bullies her. Here, I brought this for you.' He produced the department's policy on bullying in the workplace.

'Thank you, but I'm sure I'll be fine.'

Alastair looked at me and smiled. 'I think you probably will.' The smile made him look so much less dour, I smiled back. 'You're very different to Maggie,' he said. 'What are you doing working for McTavish?'

'Earning some money. And I only have to put up with him in the afternoons. In the mornings I'll be working on my own project. I want a job at Dictionary House.'

'So being McTavish's secretary just pays the rent, does it?'

'That's the idea, and to be perfectly honest I don't think the afternoons are going to be hard work. Look how long he takes for lunch! And he wants me to go to Las Vegas too.'

'So you've got the spare place, have you? I was wondering who would be favoured with that. I didn't think it would be Maggie. We're going to be working together quite a lot, Rose, and while I can be good-humoured about the occasional academic argument, I'd be grateful if you didn't make a habit of it.'

'I thought I was just doing my job.'

'What is he calling this new job of yours?'

'I'm his lexicographical consultant.'

'Are you? That's a new one. Officially, you're his temporary private secretary.'

'Am I?'

'You are according to his departmental budget. He's not paying you the correct rate, though. You should be on a temping rate and that's higher. I'll sort it out for you.'

'Can you do that?'

'Yes. Why don't we go for a coffee and I'll explain all about it?'

We went to the clean, bright, non-smoking canteen of the PC Department. It was very smart, all black and white – no grey areas. Chairs and tables were grouped in neat rows, and there was a corner where children could play. A sign read: The parent/guardian/carer must remain with his/her child at all times. The department reserves the right to confiscate any toy/book/game/recreational learning aid it deems inappropriate.'

Alastair told me that the question of 'appropriateness' was the central issue of his department's work. It had become something of a nightmare in the recently introduced Casual Dress Policy. This new policy applied to everyone, with the exception of those in McTavish's department (or 'petty fiefdom' as Alastair called it). To wear a suit or not to wear a suit? It troubled Alastair every morning. 'It's important to look business-like in the work-place,' he said. 'That's why I insisted on the "No Jeans" rule. The Casual Dress Policy works if everyone respects its basic rules and dresses appropriately.'

'You look very appropriate,' I assured him. He fingered the cuffs of his shirt.

'It's hard to strike the right balance.'

He confessed he had ducked out of wearing black cords that morning – too casual for a combative meeting. In the end he had compromised on black cotton chinos.

I teased him gently. 'What are you going to wear in Vegas? You'll have to look casual while at the same time being very official. It's a business trip, not a holiday, but it's still going to be very hot in the desert.'

'I don't want to send out the wrong messages. I don't want people to think it's a holiday at the tax-payer's expense.'

'Heavens, no!'

'It will be very hot, won't it? Maybe a lightweight suit?'

'In Bermuda, they wear executive shorts.'

'I don't think I could carry that off,' he said, uneasily.

'And there's the civic reception to think about. Could you wear a kilt?'

'We won't be going to the civic reception. It's just McTavish and a few dozen close personal friends. That will be our night off.'

'Great! What shall we do? See a show? Gamble away the Council Tax?'

'God help us if this thing comes off! It won't. I'm not even thinking about it. It won't happen. But it's too late to block the Liaison Team's visit. I know Maggie's booked the flights. He's going First Class; we're in Economy. Plus, the Las Vegans have already been here and McTavish has a reciprocal arrangement with the Nevada state legislature. It's our turn. It's like having people round for dinner – you've got to go to their place next time. When they were here, they caused me nothing but grief. They packed out the Members' Bar and drank sixty-year-old Macallan with ice – shocked the bar staff. I don't want to go to Vegas,' he said, 'but I have to. It's my civic duty.'

'If this twinning thing comes off, will it be your civic duty to go very often?'

'It won't happen.'

'McTavish thinks it will. He's got other things through.'

'Don't remind me,' admitted Alastair. 'There's the multiplex cinema on Greenside Place and the Subsidised Saunas Scheme, for starters. But we managed to halt his plan for the shopping mall underneath Princes Street Gardens and we put the brakes on Feels on Wheels.'

'He gave Mungo Mackenzie a lot of support for the Dictionary. Don't you think it's a good idea to have a Voice-Activated Spell Check on the Dictionary software? McTavish takes full credit for that.'

179

'Do you know how much it cost?' Alastair's brow furrowed at the thought.

'Dictionaries are always expensive to produce. So much work goes into them.'

'Lexicography,' he said, enunciating every syllable. 'A laboriously fascinating subject.'

'Isn't it?' I was glad to meet someone who shared my enthusiasm. 'I suppose you use dictionaries a lot in your work – being a Proof-Reader.'

'We can't just limit ourselves to dictionaries. There are numerous sources of reference on correct English usage.'

'Of course.'

'I saw your draft of his memo to the Minister for Culture. A nice bit of euphemism. Very good précis, too, I should think.'

'Thank you. How did you see that? I didn't send it to you.'

'I see everything that comes out of his office. Faxes, letters, e-mails – everything is re-routed through us before it reaches its destination. We filter and refine and check everything. We like to know what's going on.'

I got back to my little desk in the cupboard to find McTavish had rather surprisingly finished lunch early and left me a note attached to the dictaphone. 'Play this.' I pressed play. 'Rosie, we have appointed a new vice chairman and I have written a summary of our cogitations over lunch. You will find it in a sealed envelope on my desk. This envelope must go to the addressee as soon as possible. Do not send it to the post room, or the PC bastards will intercept it. Send it by Sprint-Cycle Couriers. I've got an account under the name of Rob Roy. Oh, and I've left for the day. Mind the phone till five and see you tomorrow, sweetheart.' I phoned Sprint-Cycle and sorted out Rob Roy's special delivery. The courier arrived in a flash, jogged on the spot while I signed his record card and shot off again.

They're very good, Sprint-Cycle. Everyone uses them in Edinburgh these days – the traffic is so terrible. You see Sprint-

Cyclers in their blue kit all over the place. There seemed to be more of them about than ever, over-taking motorbikes at traffic lights, short-cutting through Princes Street Gardens and dashing through the narrow closes in the Old Town where the new Members of the Scottish Parliament had their busy, busy offices.

And so I began a new daily routine: I spent my mornings at the library writing my thesis, my afternoons at the office drafting correspondence and my evenings at my sisters' flat, crying over Jamie's letters and drinking whisky in the bath. I refused to speak to him on the phone so he wrote to me instead. Letters which did not carry the warning: 'Darling Rose, Lie Enclosed'. They were beguiling letters full of love and longing and pleading and apology. I wept over them, threw them away, retrieved them, read and re-read them, and at last destroyed them in Catherine's desktop paper shredder.

I knew when Consuela was due to arrive. I knew he would go and meet her off the plane. I could imagine it, their reunion. A kiss, a hug, the protective arm around the shoulders. And then he would take her home.

Helen decided that the night of Consuela's arrival would be a good night to take me out. We went to noisy bars packed with people determined to enjoy themselves and we went dancing at some subterranean place where the walls were streaming wet and the floor was a mass of writhing colours. We came home at six in the morning but I felt like death and couldn't sleep. I lay, wide awake, and waited for the post to be delivered but there was no letter from Jamie that day. He was with his wife now. I told myself the absence of a letter meant he had got his priorities right.

In an effort to keep my mind occupied, I worked hard for McTavish. I made sure that his dictaphone messages were rephrased in the most flawlessly diplomatic prose and I insisted that his off-the-cuff remarks were always practised in advance. After a few weeks, some of the people he had alienated started speaking to him again. I don't know if it were coincidence or not, but his plans began to progress rather more rapidly than they had before.

Alastair started dropping in at the cupboard office. 'Just spying on you!' he would call cheerfully to McTavish. And: 'Rose, do you think you could try to be a little less efficient? A few tactless press statements wouldn't go amiss.'

In a fit of generosity, McTavish gave me a bonus of a hundred pounds and an extra long job title: Lexicographical, Semantics and Political Correctness Liaison Consultant. He would stand at the desk I shared with Maggie and talk about how pleased he was with my work and how it was a hell of a lot better than anything Maggie had ever produced. It didn't make for good relations in the cupboard office. Poor Maggie continued to make excuses for McTavish's bad temper and also made her own excuses to me for having worked for him for fourteen years.

I sought refuge in the PC canteen, which Maggie regarded as fraternising with the enemy. The enemy, however, had real coffee (produced by a workers' co-operative on an organic plantation). Usually I sat by myself, reading. Sometimes I left an incorrect book lying about, just to put up a token resistance. I even brought in the original *Noddy and Big Ears* for the children's box.

Whenever Alastair found me sitting there, he always stopped to say hello and ask how I was getting on. He would often solicit my opinion on the tricky semantics he was labouring over in some government document. One day he told me he had looked up a piece I'd written for an academic journal, all about the usage of slang. 'I completely disagree with your argument,' he said, 'but the grammar is perfect.' He thought slang was simply an abuse of the English language, not a subversive enrichment of it. He disapproved of swearing under any circumstances. When pressed, he admitted that he allowed himself a few words when watching football, but he argued that football could also move him to expressions of joy, which he reckoned balanced things out a bit. Alastair had the theory that in a civilised society football was the only appropriate medium for passion. When I laughed at this, he got very earnest and said: 'Passion is a loss of self-control, and although it might be appropriate under certain circumstances it's still a liability. It's like trusting to your intuition and all that rubbish. It undermines your judgement. If you want to make a sensible decision, you've got to be rational about it. If you don't, your delusions will be shattered soon enough.'

Privately, I considered my own shattered delusions and couldn't help thinking he had a point.

Talk to Alastair about anything and you would find he had fixed opinions, confident beliefs. There was a kind of moral certainty about him which I found reassuring. I could talk to Alastair like a fellow academic: we would disagree, but we would be very civilised about it. I think he liked having someone he could share a bit of pedantry with – or perhaps with whom he could share a bit of pedantry. He agreed I had a right to my opinions and he was always careful to recover my incorrect books from the confiscation area and return them to me at the end of the day.

I received a last postcard from Jamie. Our correspondence game. I had been wondering if he would make the final move. His postcard showed one of Duchamp's chess pictures, the pieces distorted as if blown by a high wind, a storm tearing across the board. No words any more, just the inevitable move followed by a double question mark. In notation, a question mark means a bad move. A double question mark means a very bad move. This last move of his, he knew, meant the game was up. I carried the postcard around with me all day, promising myself I'd throw it away before I went home. And at seven o'clock I was alone at my desk, the postcard in my hand, unable to bring myself to tear it up and put an end to everything.

Alastair put his head around the door. 'I saw the light on,' he said. 'You're working late.' I put the postcard in my bag. 'What's the matter?' His voice was sympathetic. 'You look upset.'

It is possible to be stoical about your private misery, to be brave and resolute, but then somebody says a few kind words and you just dissolve.

'What has McTavish said now?'

'Nothing. It doesn't matter.'

'Come on,' said Alastair, putting a very un-PC arm around my shoulders. 'It's time you went home.'

'I don't want to go home yet.'

'Neither do I. I'm going for a drink. Coming?'

Chapter 15

It had taken a little time to sort out my draw-down payment from Nat West Scottish Widowed No Worries, but at last I had fifteen thousand pounds ready and waiting to be returned to Jamie. I had arranged to get all the money in cash because I thought it looked more real that way.

For half an hour I rehearsed a normal, even tone of voice and then I rang him. 'I'd like to meet you,' I said.

'When? Now?'

'I'll come round tonight. Seven o'clock. I'll meet you at the mews house.'

I tried to prepare myself for seeing him again. I stood in front of the biggest mirror in Helen's room and told myself over and over again that I did not want him. I knew there was a danger that in the heat-haze of the moment I might want him very much indeed. Before I left the flat, I practised saying no. 'No,' I said in the mirror. 'No, no, no, stop. No. Stop. No, no, no. Stop.' I felt like a bad news telegram.

It was a twenty-minute walk to my old home. I set out with my mind full of misgivings and my handbag full of cash. Turning the corner to the cobbled lane, everything leafy and quiet, my heart thudded with every step. At the door, I fumbled with the keys – the last time I would ever use them – and let myself in. There he was, waiting for me. He stood quietly for a moment and looked at me. Melting tenderness. Made me catch my breath. 'Rose,' he said, his arms open for me.

'How's Consuela?'

He took a step back. 'She's fine.'

'What about that little party she wanted to have to meet your friends?'

'It's next Saturday.'

'That'll be nice for you.'

'Terrific.' He stood, tensely, his arms folded. 'I heard about your new job. How's it going? It can't be easy working for McTavish.'

'It's all right. I spend a lot of time working in a different department. I liaise with Political Correctness.'

'You're joking!' The tension left his face and he started to laugh. 'How wonderful for you!'

'It's not a laughing matter,' I said, sounding prim.

'Sorry,' he said, a hand over his mouth.

I knew I had to keep things as brief and business-like as possible. 'I'm returning the money I owe you.' He looked surprised. I walked past him into the kitchen and he followed me. 'Fifteen thousand, remember? The loan you gave me. I'm paying it back.' I opened the bag and tipped the money on to the table.

'Where did you get all that?'

'I borrowed it. It's an advance on my Nat West Scottish Widowed No Worries Insurance Plan.'

'Has it come to this? I don't want the money back. I couldn't care less about the money.'

'You said it was a loan.'

'I said it was a golden hello. Prize money – whatever. We laughed about it, remember? I *gave* you the money. I don't want it back. They didn't make you take out one of those terrible Flexi-Finance things, did they?'

'You lent me this money,' I insisted. 'It was a loan and I'm paying it back.'

'You can call it whatever you like – a loan, a gift, bribery . . . '

'There are huge areas of difference.'

'Only in the mind of a lexicographer.' He gave me his infuriatingly superior look. 'Money is a universal language, Rose.'

I pushed the cash towards him. 'I have to pay the debt I owe you.'

'Keep it, Rose.'

'Take it!'

'You and I owe each other nothing.'

'You must accept the payment of my debt.'

We confronted each other across the table. 'All right,' he said, evenly. 'Then watch how I'll spend it.' He reached for a fifty-pound note, flicked open his lighter and set fire to it. I watched, fascinated, until the last little corner was a burnt fragment of confetti. He let it float down on to the table.

'I tell you what, Rose,' he said, all amiable again, 'why not let me put all this money into your Fantasy Finances portfolio? It's been doing well, hasn't it? You could turn it into a proper investment. I might even track it myself. How about that for a negotiated compromise?'

'Don't patronise me.'

'I thought you quite enjoyed the patronage thing.'

'Taking money from you is the stupidest thing I've ever done.'

'Only if you try to pay it back. Only if you take out a loan with a stupid interest rate of twenty-six per cent.' He shook his head. 'This is all so unnecessary, Rose. I never dreamt you'd do something like this. You must pay that flexi-loan off. I'll do it for you tomorrow morning. Don't look annoyed, I'm giving you very sound financial advice here – as well as the cash to go with it.' He pushed the money across the table.

All my carefully rehearsed self-control deserted me. 'It's so typical of you to be this arrogant!' I cried. 'You think the rules don't apply to you, don't you? Why didn't you tell me you were married? Because you wanted to spend as much time as possible with me before your wife arrived. You actually said that to me!'

'I regret the way it all happened.'

'No, you don't! You had it all worked out. Everything has happened just as you planned.'

'I didn't set out to hurt you. That's the last thing I wanted. Didn't you read my letters? I kept trying to explain. I want to explain. I wish you would listen.'

'I've spent months listening while you lied to me.'

'Rose, please . . .'

He reached out for me, but I was too angry to be touched. 'You just sail through life with plenty of money and no conscience!'

'Can you remember saying you loved me?'

'I don't want to remember.'

'I can remember. It's all I think about.'

'You only think of yourself.'

'That's not true. I love you.'

'You don't know what love is! You had to look it up, remember? Do you mean "liking and warm affection"? What about your wife's love – *for what it's worth!* You asked me to trust you. And I did! I must have been mad! It was just infatuation – a delusion. I can't trust you any more, Jamie. I wouldn't have any self-respect if I did. There are people I've met in my new job that I trust more than you – and I've only known them a few weeks. People who believe in playing by the rules and doing the right thing.'

'Working for McTavish?' he asked, incredulously.

'No. I've made friends in Political Correctness.'

'Not your natural soul-mates, I should think.'

'*Good* friends,' I said, indignantly.

'Anyone in particular?'

I was a bit taken aback at this, and instead of saying, 'Yes, Alastair Lennox is a good friend,' I stared at the floor and felt uncomfortable. My silence seemed to hang very heavy in the air.

'I wouldn't have thought he'd be your type,' he said, quietly.

'I've only shared a drink with him. I'm not going out with him.'

'I bet he'd like to, though.'

Then he looked at the money on the table and laughed. The kind of forced laugh people make when it's not funny. 'A few weeks ago, you wanted to marry me.'

'I can't believe I ever wanted to marry you. You're not the sort of man a woman ought to marry.'

'What d'you mean by that?'

'You'd only make me miserable. There would be lots of misery and tears and jealousy and the occasional sexual high and basically it just wouldn't be worth it.'

'What do you mean, "occasional"? And I'm sure it would be worth it. You thought I was very much worth it.'

'You're the sort of man a woman should only ever dally with. Dalliance is your forte.'

'What a wonderfully quaint way of putting it.'

'It's the perfect word for you. It means to amuse oneself; to sport, flirt or trifle with. It means to consume time and opportunity to no purpose. The word appears in a very valuable twelfth-century Anglo-Norman manuscript. The first ever use of the verb "dalier". I wrote a whole thesis about it for my Ph.D.'

'So you've got a Ph.D. in dalliance. I might have bloody known!'

At that, I heard my voice say – so cold and hard I barely recognised it – 'I made a mistake with you. You've been a waste of my time.'

And that was the point at which he began to lose his touch. After having given me at least a memorable ending – burning the fifty-pound note and so on – he started playing it all wrong, losing with very ill-grace indeed. Very unlike him. All sorts of utterly crass, prattish moves that only an idiot would make.

'What do you mean, I wasted your time?'

'You've treated me like some kind of expensive toy.'

'You were the one who was playing! You were more than happy to take my money. Don't pretend you didn't enjoy it.'

'It was never just about money.'

'But you did like that bit, didn't you?'

'No, I just felt guilty and . . . and . . .'

'And then you got over it.'

'The money meant absolutely nothing to me.'

'You can't claim that moral high ground, Rose.'

'Don't talk to me about morals!'

'Think what I spent on you! What does that make you?'

There was a horrible silence. 'Compromised,' I said, grimly.

He leafed through the bank notes. 'This is all yours. You won it; you deserve it. It was well earned.'

I turned angrily away from him and headed for the door. 'Oh, Rose,' he groaned. 'Don't go.'

'What do you expect me to do?' I shouted. 'Here's the keys to your bloody mews house. Catch!' I lobbed them across the room and he caught them, easily, in his left hand. (A brilliant reflex action and he wasn't even left-handed.) 'I'm going now,' I said, furiously.

'Not yet.'

'Give me one good reason.'

I wondered what he would come up with. Pressure on. He was good at clever, short-order lies – thinking on his feet, shifting the blame and all those other executive skills for which he was so highly paid.

'Will one last good suggestion do?' he asked, smiling his wicked smile. But it was a serious miscalculation of risk. I was livid.

'I wish to God I'd never met you! I wish I'd never taken your money.'

'You wanted to.'

'Anyone can be tempted – especially if she's poor!'

Oh, did I really say that? Yes, I did. My memory of that night is still excruciatingly clear.

'Oh, I love the melodrama!' he exclaimed. 'You agreed to it all, Rose! There isn't a single thing you didn't agree to.' He pulled me fiercely towards him. He laughed, kissing my neck. And I still wanted him. Nothing complicated about it. Just a simple want. Like flicking a switch. He knew it, and he probably expected something much more exciting than my pulling away from him and stumbling in the direction of the door. 'Oh, are you leaving now, after all? So you're not going to tempt me right away, then? Shall I just take that as advance warning?'

I stood outside, keeping the door open, still. He picked up the keys and started throwing them in the air and catching them. Throw, catch, throw, catch. I watched, mesmerised. 'Let me know when you want to come back!' he called. He was playing it all badly now. No coherent strategy whatsoever. 'Don't you want me any more? Not even to waste your time?' The keys clattered on to the floor. He lit a cigarette. 'What are you doing now? Are you staying or going? Make your mind up!' He sat down under a halo of smoke and I waited in the shadows. Make me stay, I thought. Say something tender and loving and easily make me stay. 'You're going to see him now, aren't you?' he said, bitterly. 'Well, tell him he fucking owes me!' He put his head in his hands.

I left him like that.

Chapter 16

I ran all the way down Royal Terrace. I felt terribly hurt and angry. I wanted to hurt him as much as he had hurt me.

Catherine didn't approve of revenge. She said thoughts of vengeance could put a poker player off her game. Keep a cool head, that was always her advice. With this in mind, she had suggested that after my final goodbyes to Jamie I should come straight home. She said she hoped I had learnt my lesson – the lesson never to be passive, never to play the lazy passivist in any relationship. She had promised me a shoulder to cry on, a cup of tea and a stark, white room where I could vent my impotent fury. But running down the street, I knew I didn't want her tea and superiority.

I stopped running when I got to a club called Shout Out. Voices and laughter drifted from the open door. Here, the staff from Proof-Reading and Political Correctness were having their party. It was actually their Christmas party but they always held it in the summer so they didn't have to use the word Christmas.

Shout Out had three vast gold mirrors framing the purple entrance. I straightened my dress, dragged my fingers through my hair and generally tried to look less like a desperate woman. While I peered at my very pink face in the mirror, Alastair's cool, calm features appeared just over my shoulder. 'Hello, Rose,' he said. 'I'm glad you could make it. No need to run, though.'

'I'm sorry to be late.'

'It's okay, you're not last.'

'I've been really looking forward to this party,' I babbled, 'and I'm not normally ever late for anything.'

'Not one woman has arrived on time tonight,' he complained, before correcting himself: 'Not that I meant that as a sexist comment.'

'I'm sure you didn't.'

'And you're the only person from McTavish's department to turn up, although I made a point of extending an open invitation to everyone. I'm glad you're here, Rose,' he said, firmly. 'It's good to know I can count on you. Thank you for your support.' He made to shake my hand.

I laughed. 'No need to be so very formal, Alastair.'

A blush enlivened his phlegmatic face. 'Sorry,' he said. 'Sometimes I take myself too seriously.' He forced an awkward smile, then bent forward and kissed me on the cheek. 'There!' he said. 'That was less formal, wasn't it?'

'You could even call it frivolous.'

'I'll have to be frivolous more often.'

'You'll have to draw up a new policy document for it, won't you? Sorry, that was rude of me. Sorry, Alastair.'

'It's okay, I'm not offended.'

'I've just . . . It's been very . . .'

'Nice dress, Rose.'

'Thank you.'

'You look . . .' he hesitated, '. . . very pretty in it – if you don't mind my saying so.'

'I don't mind at all.'

'Just practising for the new frivolity policy.'

'You're doing very well. Shall we go in now, get a drink?'

We squeezed through the crowds to the bar. The queue was three-deep. Some people wore fancy dress and we got stuck behind three nuns with the obligatory dirty habits and a very tall chocolate Santa. Beside us, a group of friendly girls compared belly-button piercings and a beautiful boy checked his profile in a mirrored compact. On the dance floor, I saw my hairdresser. I waved to him but he didn't see me. He was burning up the floor to an old Abba hit and everyone was singing along.

'Do you think I'm wearing the right clothes for an office party?' asked Alastair. He was wearing his deliberately casual black trousers and an almost fashionable black sweater. 'It's a party, but I'm at work, really.'

'The whole outfit – it's very you.'

'Is that good?' he asked, uncertainly.

'You're good through and through, Alastair.'

He seemed reassured. 'I'm glad we came here – solidarity with the gay community.'

We waited for ages at the bar. Flaming cocktails flashed by us and kisses were blown over our heads. When one of the friendly girls gave me some cheesy Wotsits, I realised I was hungry. I hadn't eaten all day – too nervous about seeing Jamie again. 'Alastair, when do we eat?'

He checked his watch. 'Not for a few hours yet. We're due to leave for a pizza at ten o'clock – that's what the committee decided.'

'Ten o'clock!'

'I voted to eat earlier but I was over-ruled. I must admit, I'm already feeling a bit peckish.'

'I'm starving. Why don't you and I go and eat now?'

'I don't think it would be right for me to go on ahead,' said Alastair. 'I'm supposed to be the team leader on this project.'

'Then lead the way.'

He dithered. 'Seriously, though, Rose. I think I should stay until the others are ready to go at ten o'clock, as arranged.'

'Frivolously, though, Alastair, I think you should come with me.'

★

A few days later, I checked my bank balance and found I was richer by £14,950. Jamie had returned the money – less the fifty pounds he burnt. It was all sitting in my bank account again, still highly combustible.

'I'll take it off your hands,' said Catherine, charitably.

'No, I have to think what I'm going to do with it.'

'Why don't you just write him a cheque?'

'Because he'll return it again, minus another fifty quid! Can't you see his game, Catherine? I'm going to have to keep it until I get some kind of inspiration as to what to do next. I'm going to give it back to him somehow. In the meantime, I'm not going to touch it.'

'You'll have to move it somewhere else, then. If you keep it in your current account, you'll spend it.'

'No, I won't. I've thought of a way to avoid that. I'm going to add up what I spend and take it away from what I earn and I'll be careful not to spend any more than my income.'

'It's called budgeting,' said Catherine.

Over the next few difficult weeks, my sisters were kind to me. At weekends, when Gordon was away testing single bedrooms in Spanish paradors, Helen came home. She tried to get me to talk about my weeks with Jamie but I wouldn't. Instead, we spent comforting evenings in the kitchen making chocolate fairy cakes and then ate them in front of the telly.

'Do you think of him much?' she asked on one such evening, licking the icing off her cake.

'A bit.'

'What about Alastair?'

'What about him?'

'Catherine says you've been seeing him quite often, but he's not your type.'

'We see each other every day at work and he's very nice – very chivalrous in a politically correct sort of way.'

'And you've met him in the evenings too.'

'We go to the pictures together. We have a mutual interest in foreign art house films, in black and white, with subtitles. They're the sort of films Jamie would never go to see. They rated high on his list of The Most Boring Things A Man Can Suffer, along with terminal illness and drinking the house wine. I like going to the pictures with Alastair but we're very proper, very decorous. We don't hold hands or anything. We pay attention to the film and have a cup of coffee afterwards. He likes to deconstruct the plot and analyse the subliminal messages. It's all very academic.'

'It sounds like The Most Boring Thing A Woman Can Suffer.'

'It's just what I need right now. I've had enough shocks and surprises. I want a dependable, honest man who can talk to me about Hungarian cinema.'

'No sex then.'

'None.'

'Not even a little bit?'

'I get a polite kiss on the cheek when we say goodbye.'

'Catherine says you didn't come home at all the first time you went out with Alastair. The night of that party at Shout Out.' Helen's round blue eyes looked questioningly at me. 'She thinks you stayed with him. Did you?'

Keen to clear up any misunderstanding, I put my fairy cake down and gave Helen my full attention. 'We went for a pizza together and then to a club. Along with about twenty other people from his office. The party then moved on to my hairdresser's flat on Broughton Street and that's where we stayed. It was a very nice party. At four in the morning we were sitting on John's four-poster futon watching *Breakfast at Tiffany's*.'

'Is that all?' asked Helen, disappointed.

'Alastair is the most morally correct person I've ever met. Before our first trip to the Filmhouse, he consulted the guidelines on *Managing a Close Personal Relationship with a Colleague*. He told me about the split infinitives on the first page and left a copy lying around where I would find it. I read that the department does not encourage close personal relationships between colleagues. Such relationships are incompatible with Rational Working Practices. So, I think it's safe to say Alastair isn't going to do anything. He'd have to work himself up to it for months. Maybe he is working himself up to it. What the hell – maybe I'll say yes.'

'Not one of your brighter ideas,' said Catherine, coming out of her study to join in the conversation. 'He's not your type at all and you're not his.'

'I like him. He's been very good to me at work. He knows McTavish is a difficult man to work for and he always tries to smooth things over and make life a bit easier for me. I can rely on Alastair to help me out.'

Catherine perched on the arm of the sofa beside me. 'What do you think he sees in you?' she asked, bluntly.

'Obviously, he thinks Rose is very attractive,' said Helen.

'He notices what I'm wearing and he always compliments me on my clothes or my hair or my earrings. He's asked me to a dinner party so I can meet his friends. They're all couples and I get the impression he's tired of them making jokes about him being single. He doesn't like being the odd one out.'

'Have you said yes?'

'It's not until we get back from Las Vegas.'

Catherine laughed. 'What will you do with him in Vegas? Last time I went, I didn't notice a single art house cinema.'

'I'm looking forward to going.' I bit into the chocolate topping on my cake. 'I like Alastair. He's very nice.'

'Nice is boring,' said Helen. 'I've told you before, you don't want nice.'

Catherine was silent for a few moments. 'I've met Consuela,' she said abruptly. 'She's got her head screwed on. She knows exactly what she's doing.'

'You've met her?' I asked, worried. 'When?'

'Last night at the Edinburgh Chess Club.'

'She plays?' I said, in despair.

'Chess is very popular in Cuba – all that Russian influence.'

'Does she play well?'

'Well-ish.'

'Well-ish! What does that mean?' I demanded. 'Be specific.'

'Sensible strategy, combinations unsurprising, always accepts a sacrifice. No novelties, but a couple of startling moves to put you off your stride. She plays like an old-fashioned computer. Average, but still competitive.'

'Opening?'

'Queen's Gambit or Ruy Lopez.'

I digested this information. 'You've met her,' I repeated.

'I'd just finished a match. I hadn't played him before, but he was quite good and it took a while to pin him down. Most of the tables were busy. We were talking through the game and then I noticed he wasn't listening to me any more, he was staring at this young woman standing beside the door. She was very pretty – strikingly so – and when she walked past the tables everyone's eyes followed her. She had this sexy wiggle – quite comical, really. I heard her introduce herself as Consuela Casanovas. She was very popular. Everyone said she was the most sensational Cuban to visit the Edinburgh Chess Club since Capablanca in 1919.'

'I don't want to know anything else about her.'

'You should. She knows all about you.'

'Does she?' I asked, horrified.

'She joked that her husband's girlfriend had left him. She seemed to find it all very amusing.'

I felt weak. 'How do you think she knew?'

'Jamie probably told her.'

'But why would he tell her?' I sank miserably in my seat. 'Maybe they had one of those agonising "Let's confess everything" type of conversations and now they're trying to make a new start together.'

'But she was laughing about it,' said Catherine, pointedly. 'She found it funny.'

'Maybe she's got a very pragmatic sense of humour. It doesn't mean to say she wasn't hurt by his infidelity.'

I stared hopelessly at the blank white walls. 'She's his wife and they're together again. I was only his way of passing the time. I was only ever a fling.'

The next night Helen went back to Banff, loaded down with fairy cakes, and Catherine brought Robert home. They sat up late, drinking and plotting and trying to out-do each other at card tricks. I went to bed, but couldn't sleep. There were too many thoughts running round my head, too many thoughts of Jamie with the very striking, very pretty, very popular Consuela. After an hour or so I put the bedside light on and reached for my Dictionary notes – they were always close to hand these days. Mungo Mackenzie had been more positive about the last piece I had sent him and I was getting a few hours of work from Dictionary House. My thesis was very important to me. I spent all my evenings writing and researching. It kept my mind from wandering to lazier, more thoughtless times. I leafed through the pages of *Ambiguity and Misunderstanding*, chewed the end of my pen and started making notes. Now and then, I heard Catherine's laughter from the living room and her cries of 'Cheat!' I hoped Robert loved her as much as she loved him, but it was always difficult to tell what he was thinking. He could sit for hours, his face as motionless and inscrutable as an Easter Island statue, and for this reason it could be very startling when he laughed. It made you listen.

'I shouldn't laugh,' said Robert, and his voice travelled loudly through the open door of the living room, 'but I've never known Jamie work so hard in his life.'

What's so funny about that? I thought. I put my pen down, climbed out of bed. I must find out. I crept down the hall and peered round the door. The living room was in darkness, just some candles glowing in pools of light on the floor. I could make out Robert sitting on the sofa, shuffling cards. Catherine had her back to me. 'He's made a deal with Bio–Caledonian,' said Robert, speaking more quietly now. 'He's putting his own money in – professional suicide – but he says he doesn't care. If she doesn't want him back, he's lost the will to win.'

Catherine leaned towards him and said something I couldn't catch.

'But he's always loved her,' said Robert, loudly. 'He loves her so much it's embarrassing! The problem is she doesn't believe him any more and he's racked by guilt about it. He blames himself. That's why he's throwing himself into his work. He's just trying to keep his poor, anguished mind occupied.'

I retreated to my room, pulled the bedcovers around me and picked up my pen. 'It is possible,' I wrote, 'to live very happily under a misunderstanding. Ignorance can truly be bliss. But when one learns the truth, when one becomes aware of one's misunderstanding . . .' My handwriting deteriorated badly.

So he had always loved Consuela. It was hardly surprising that she didn't believe him any more. Not after he had told her about me. It must be difficult trying to build your marriage when you're used to living eight thousand miles apart.

I sat up writing until dawn.

Chapter 17

From my cramped seat in Economy, I saw the lights of Las Vegas illuminate the desert like a distant explosion. It astonished the eyes after so many hundreds of miles of darkness. When we left the plane, the first thing I noticed was the slot machine. It sat, squatly, at the door of the aircraft, just inside the Arrivals building. I fed it a dollar.

'What did you do that for?' asked Alastair.

'I've got money to burn.'

We found our luggage and hailed a cab. McTavish and a few dozen of his close personal friends had gone on ahead to the hotel. Not being in First Class, Alastair and I had missed the VIP welcome party with its fleet of limousines. Instead, we got into a cab and asked the driver to take us down the Strip. It was fabulously brash. A glorious, vulgar, comic triumph. I fell in love with the place immediately. We reached downtown Las Vegas, turned round and came all the way back again. We passed Treasure Island as the on-the-hour sea battle was reaching its fiery crescendo. A British warship was sunk by a deafening volley of cannon as we waited in a traffic jam. We passed the sugar pink Venezia, with its canals and gondolas and replica St Mark's campanile. Sky-scrapers and the Empire State at New York, New York. Fountains and waterfalls at the Mirage. And on, and on, and on. So much water in the desert! Alastair was as open-mouthed as I was.

Our own hotel was modelled on the Great Pyramid of Cheops (actual size), with its own Sphinx guarding the entrance to the car park. At the apex of the pyramid was a vertical beam of light I had seen from the plane. It shone miles into the sky and I could see swallows soaring there, illuminated like glitter.

The lobby was as vast and extravagant as one might expect, full of massive pharoaic statues and palm trees. There was a strange, ethereal sound, like incidental music for a performance of *The Dream*. I left my bags with Alastair and followed the sound. It got louder as I got nearer the casino. It was just like a C major arpeggio, played very fast, repeatedly, insistently. Two octaves apart and you have the first notes of *Somewhere Over the Rainbow*. It's the same sound in every casino in Las Vegas. It's the sound of thousands of slot machines, pinging and ringing away. Now and then, you hear a soft shower of coins.

I wandered back to reception where Alastair was waiting for me. 'Here's your key,' he said and handed me a mock stone tablet and a plastic card. 'We've got to take the inclinator. It's a special lift designed for pyramids. You haven't been spending your money on those slot machines, have you?'

'Only a little bit.'

He tutted. 'Come on. We've got an hour before the cocktail reception in the Nefertiti Lounge. I'm going to unpack, send a few e-mails and write up a progress report on the Integrated Transport Policy. What are you going to do?'

'I might have a little sleep.'

'This is work, Rose. We're not here to have a little sleep. Have you rung McTavish on his mobile? He wouldn't tell me which suite he was in.'

'He told me.'

'What did he say?'

'Four-six-zero-two, sweetheart.'

Alastair grimaced. 'Okay, here we are. This is your room. I must be . . . over there – on the north face.'

'In two-zero-seven-one, sweetheart.'

'I'll see you at Nefertiti's,' said Alastair, briskly.

Stepping into my room, I felt light-hearted for the first time in months. I had left a chill Scottish autumn and arrived in a hot Nevadan fall. In my hieroglyphed bedroom, I lay on my queen-size bed and gazed out of the window to the mountains of the Sierra Nevada. A whole new panoramic sense of perspective. When I slept, my dreams were full of luck and magic. The blue eyes were still there, but I'd learned to look away.

McTavish was losing at keno when I found him. Nile-maiden keno waitresses had taken a hundred dollars, but he was still in ebullient mood.

'You pick my numbers, Rosie,' he said. 'I'm having no luck.'

'How do you play?'

He passed me a Nefertiti Cocktail List. 'The rules are on the back.' He waved his arm towards the casino. 'Amazing place, this, isn't it? Fantastic!'

'Fantastic in the true sense of the word.'

'Want a drink?' He beckoned a waitress over. 'A Nefertiti Special for me and my companion will have her Just Deserts. Thank you, sweetheart.'

He sat back and grinned. 'I'm glad you're enjoying yourself. Make sure you don't let that Lennox spoil your fun! And speak of the devil . . . Lennox! Lennox! Over here!' Alastair was making his way across the room, carefully avoiding the tooth-some, winsome, silicone-breasted waitresses. 'Good evening, old pal,' said McTavish, magnanimously. 'Want a Deadly Asp Bite? Here's the list.'

'I'm fine, thanks.'

'Go on, have a cocktail.'

'Well . . .'

'I'm having one,' I told him. 'Nice shirt, Alastair.'

'Do you think so? Thought I'd keep the tie on, though.'

'Hurry up, man! Here's the girl with Rose's Just Deserts.'

Alastair, suddenly eye-level with a cleavage he could park his bicycle in, lost his concentration. 'I'll have a . . . I'll have a . . .'

'Deadly Asp Bite,' said McTavish. 'A double.'

As midnight approached, Edinburgh's representatives on the Twinning Liaison Committee had become so relaxed that they didn't raise a murmur when their whisky arrived with ice. The warmth of the Las Vegan welcome was such that by the end of our first evening any ice had well and truly melted.

For the whole week of our visit, Alastair and I found we had very little work to do. Magnus McTavish and his friends were wined, dined and entertained at the most exclusive venues in the city. These places provided all that a politician might ever want, so the services of Private Office and Proof-Reading were very rarely required.

For six days and nights we were at leisure, and although Alastair felt guilty about it at first, and spent a lot of time analysing traffic congestion on The Strip, there is no doubt that he loosened up quite a lot. Relaxed would be too strong a word, but there was a definite loosening of the shirt collar and disappearance of the tie. After a while, the clothes got more daringly casual. To test how far he would go, I bought him a Hawaiian shirt and he was endearingly pleased with it. Strolling round Las Vegas in his new shirt and dark shades, he seemed a much happier man than the serious soul who worked in Political Correctness.

I enjoyed myself. I did whatever I felt like and Alastair often decided he felt like doing the same as me. This meant that every morning we went swimming in the pool beside the pyramid and then sat in the shade of the palm trees, drinking iced tea. I read Edith Wharton novels and he read the sports pages of every British newspaper he could find. We spent the afternoons doing funfair rides and in the evenings we cruised through the different hotels, playing on the fruit machines and drinking free cocktails. I enjoyed the sunshine; it made me feel much better. I bought little cotton dresses in neon colours and plastic flower earrings to match. Alastair went so far as to buy a pair of shorts. By the end of the week, he was actually wearing them with the Hawaiian shirt. I think all the cocktails helped.

On our last evening, we had a double Deadly Asp Bite for auld lang's syne, then set off down The Strip. And Alastair didn't count the limos – not even the ones parked with their engines idling. He bought himself an extra-huge ice cream and a bag of popcorn for me and together we wandered along the dazzling sidewalk. Alastair seemed quite wistful. 'It's the end of our week,' he said. 'The very last night.'

'Yes, all the glitter's come off my "I love Las Vegas" tee-shirt. Never mind. It's not the sort of thing I could wear in the office, is it?'

'No,' he said, sadly. 'It's not.'

Walking in Las Vegas was a surreal experience – the flowers talk, for example. Concealed in the herbaceous borders are tiny speakers and when you pause to admire a bed of roses, you hear something like: 'Hey! Why not visit the Pirate Pizza Parlour by Treasure Island!' In fact, you don't have to walk at all in Las Vegas, because there are miles and miles of air-conditioned moving walkways, where huge-bottomed Americans glide effortlessly along to their next ice-cream sundae. It's all about revelling in excess. For someone who has been accustomed to moderation and self-discipline the Las Vegas experience can be gluttonishly liberating, and Alastair ate enough chocolate ice cream to make even a PC Proof-Reader chill out.

And so, via the talking flowers and the ice cream stops and the walk-free walkways, we arrived at a brand new hotel, built like a vast Roman villa. It was called The Dissipare Diem.

'I'm going to the Bar of Capri,' said Alastair. 'I'm going to check out the Tiberius Triples and the Pompeii Pop. Where are you going to be?'

'It'll have to be the casino. I'll be over there, by the wall fresco of the Three Fates.'

'Okay, but be sensible on the fruit machines. Stick to nickels and dimes. Don't do dollars. Now is not the time for high-stakes fruit.'

'I promise I won't go near the dollar fruit machines.'

Off he went, and I was alone with my credit card and fourteen thousand, nine hundred and fifty pounds' worth of kept money. I would surrender it all up to Fate.

People who aren't very good at maths, who claim they can't count past ten, might be interested to know that to play baccarat you only need to add up to nine. I had to look around for a baccarat table where the stakes were high enough. People who can only count up to nine obviously prefer to keep their risk to a minimum. I played baccarat for an hour. Alastair appeared now and then, each time with a different-coloured cocktail. For an hour, I added up to nine so brilliantly and so consistently it got boring. I found myself apologising to the croupier: 'Sorry, I just can't seem to lose.'

I left the table to move on to blackjack (counting up to twenty-one) and still managed a spectacular run. Twenty-one over and over again. When I abandoned the blackjack, a fat man followed me. He was wearing a very smart suit. No one but casino employees wears suits in Las Vegas. 'You're on a winning streak,' he said. 'I'm following you for luck.'

'Actually, I'm trying to lose,' I told him.

'Are you, *actually*?' he said, laughing at my accent. 'Well, if you wanna burn money, try roulette.'

'Thank you.'

'Don't mention it.'

However, roulette seemed to be a low-stakes game. It was never like this in the movies. People were playing with a few dollars, just for the sake of enjoying the fun. It took a bit of time before the fat man could arrange a bet for me of eight thousand dollars on number five. This took place in a special part of the casino, in a corner, sheltered by a glass wall. 'But Alastair will never find me here,' I said.

'I'll locate him for you.'

When you're playing the tables, all your drinks are free. Even Pompeii Pop and Tiberius Triples. I asked for champagne. It arrived, closely followed by Alastair. 'How much have you won?' he asked, swaying slightly.

'I'm not sure.'

'I'd better stick around and count it for you. How much are you putting on?'

'Eight of these.' (It's easy to see chips as pretty bits of plastic rather than colour-coded dollars. Each one was a thousand-dollar chip, but to Alastair they might as well have been tiddlywinks.) 'On number five.'

Five, I remembered, was Jamie's lucky number.

The ball clattered round the roulette wheel. I lost.

'So you actually lost at last,' said the fat man.

'Can I try again?'

'Sure.'

Burning, burning, getting rid of it.

The croupier looked at me questioningly. 'Sixteen thousand,' I said and put my chips on number thirteen. 'Friday the thirteenth and a full moon, too,' I whispered to myself. 'That's when I met him.'

'What?' asked Alastair.

Sixteen thousand on number thirteen. Spin, spin, spin. The odds for roulette are thirty-five to one. If number thirteen came up, I would win thirty-five dollars for every dollar I'd put on, because that's the way they work it out. Spin, spin, spin, clickety, clickety, clack. Equals: five hundred and sixty thousand dollars.

The fat man grinned and nodded to the people standing next to him. Instant celebrity. Toga-clad flunkeys appeared from all directions. Alastair was astonished. 'How much have you won?' he kept asking. 'How much did you bet?' When someone told him, he got very excited. (And according to everyone who knew

207

him at work, Alastair never got excited.) 'You're sensational, Rose!' he raved. 'I can't believe you did that!' He squeezed all the breath out of me.

'It happens,' I said, numbly. 'Better odds than the Lottery. It's just luck.'

Thereafter, he stuck to my side like semtex.

I got 'comped' as it is known. Suddenly a whole lot of things became complimentary. A case of champagne appeared. A suite of rooms was put at my disposal.

'Great!' shouted Alastair. 'I'll tell them where to get our bags!'

I rested my spinning head on the satin pillow and stared at the silken drapes of the king-size bed in the Vestal Virgin Suite. It was probably about ten o'clock in the evening. We had been overwhelmed by room service, who'd brought us a selection of high-roller cocktails so we could pick our favourite. This was then made up by the gallon and kept on chill. Alastair was watching us on TV (they give you a video of you winning). 'What do you want to do now?' he asked, smiling broadly.

'I don't know,' I said, stupidly. 'I'll phone my sister and ask her.'

'Bank it! Bank it!' Catherine shouted down the phone.

'I might try playing craps. I like the silly name.'

'Don't, Rose, craps is complicated. You wouldn't be able to calculate the payoffs. You wouldn't like it.'

'But it's mesmerising to watch. High stakes, very fast and . . .'

'It's played by people who understand it. Don't do it, Rose. It's all about number combinations. You'd lose. It's maths! Mean maths with knobs on!'

Alastair and I circled an unused craps table in the special High Roller Lounge. It had a glass cover and the rakes, sticks and dice were laid out in readiness for the next game. There was a slip of paper, handwritten, totalling the chips. The starting float for a craps table was three-quarters of a million dollars. I know; I counted it.

The table nearby was busy, with large amounts of money changing hands. I watched for ages, absorbed in the rhythm of the game. 'When are you going to start?'

'Not yet.'

'When?'

'I don't know. Go and watch Vesuvius, it's due to erupt.'

He disappeared and I began to play. I lost four hundred and ninety-six thousand dollars. It's just amazing how fast you can lose. When Alastair returned from the ruins of Pompeii, he was dismayed at my change in fortune. 'Just stop now,' he said. I kept playing and won back forty thousand. Alastair hugged me. I felt sick and exhausted.

'I think I'll stop for a rest,' I told the fat man.

'We'll show you to your suite.'

We got upgraded to a palatial penthouse, like a set from the Ziegfeld Follies. I half expected a line of chorus girls to dance down the white marble staircase. If we had put in a request to room service, they probably could have arranged it. There was also a white stretch limo now at our disposal. 'You're wonnerful, Rose!' slurred Alastair. 'Isn't this incredible?'

I wallowed in the jacuzzi and analysed the epic video of my win, move by move. Ratio of luck to skill probably 4:1. 'Do you want some more champagne?' called Alastair, just outside the door. 'Shall I get you some more vodka to put in it?'

'Okay. I'll be out in a minute.'

I got changed into the white satin nightdress I had bought just the day before at a specialist white satin shop. It came with a free white satin evening purse. I felt like I was in my own movie. Nothing felt real. 'You look really lurvely, Rose,' said Alastair, sounding nothing like his usual phlegmatic self. I lay down on the bed, closed my eyes and the room started to spin. When I opened them, he was there, blurrily, beside me.

'I think I need some fresh air,' I heard my voice say. 'Let's try out the limo.'

And so, at three in the morning, we called it up and out we

went. Cruising through our own patch of surreality. Me in my long white satin nightdress and Alastair in his baggy shorts and designer vest. (He had rung room service and simply asked for 'casual clothes, please'.) We sat in the back of our white limo and held hands. 'Heartbreak Hotel' was playing on the radio and I sang along. The driver seemed to know where we were going, although we hadn't said. We knew we had arrived when he parked the car (engine running) and opened the door to let us out.

'County Courthouse,' he announced. We fell out of the limo. I clutched Alastair's hand and tried to stay upright. 'Just up those few little steps,' our driver said, pointing out the way. 'I'll be right here waiting for you.' Alastair supported me and we made it up the steps. I told him he was my bestest friend in all the world.

There was a sign saying 'No Firearms'. Inside, it was 'Traffic Citations' on the left and 'Marriage Licenses' on the right. 'Only thirty-five dollars,' read Alastair. 'That's very reasonable.'

It's dead easy to get married in Las Vegas. All you have to do is prove you're eligible. You just turn up at the County Courthouse with ID. A credit card will do. You're supposed to be sober. The Marriage License Bureau is small, but it's open twenty-four hours a day at weekends and very nearly that on weekdays. You won't have to queue for long – five minutes at the most. We stood in line between a young couple speaking Spanish and an elderly couple speaking German. When your turn arrives, you go to one of the barred cashier windows and hand over the simple name and address form you have completed in the queue. There were some balloons tied to the bars when I was there. And there was a pink plastic sign saying 'Congratulations!'.

Our driver waited for us, just as he said he would. If you get a marriage license in Las Vegas, your driver might contact your hotel to let them know what you're up to, so that when you return the Wedding Consultant will be fully briefed and ready to offer you a number of attractive options for this, your special day – whatever time of night it is. At the Dissipare Diem, you can say your vows in the hotel swimming pool. In at the deep end, right next to the Bar of Capri, in a Roman Wedding Grotto complete with water nymphs and mermaids.

'This is incredible,' said Alastair to the Wedding Consultant. 'Let's do it, Rose.'

'All right, then.' Giggle, giggle.

You can wear whatever you like to get married. It doesn't have to be a long white nightie. You can wear a string bikini if that's what you want. Yes, you can be attended by mermaids. And when your husband-to-be suddenly declares: 'I want to be married by Elvis!', this too can be arranged. There are many Elvises in Las Vegas – ministers with a special vocation.

We bobbed about in the grotto in matching inflatable armchairs. Elvis sang 'Love Me Tender' and we just about cried with emotion. My attendants in their flippered tails and sequinned brassières joined in. 'I can hear the mermaids singing,' I wept. 'Give me a peach! I dare to eat a peach!' Someone threw me one.

I reeled off my vows without prompting: 'To have and to hold, and tell the truth, the whole truth and forsaking all others. Nothing but the truth, so help me God. Reader, I married him.'

Nobody minded this coming out wrong, because, as the mermaid told me, they're pretty cool about people making up their own vows round here; lots of people do. I threw my bouquet over my shoulder and the inflatable armchair capsized. After that, I can only assume the mermaids rescued me because I don't remember anything else.

I cannot describe the awfulness of my hangover the next day. In the bleariness of waking I wished for Jamie's oxygen canister and his soothing hand on my fevered brow and all his tender ministrations. My head throbbed painfully as I swam up to consciousness. Even when I opened my eyes and saw the vast, heart-shaped bed, it didn't really occur to me that this was the Honeymoon Suite. I turned to look at my watch and saw it was three in the afternoon. I checked my watch again and that's when I noticed the wedding ring.

In the room, I could hear Alastair moving about. I twisted the wedding ring round and round my finger. Painful, neon memories flashed back to me. 'Alastair,' I croaked. He appeared at my side, bleary-eyed and anxious. 'I dreamt it, didn't I? There were mermaids and . . . I thought I saw Elvis.'

'It was the Reverend Elvis Presley.' Alastair's voice was hoarse too. 'Can you remember now?'

'Did . . . did we get married?'

'Yes. We were married by an Elvis impersonator in the swimming pool of the Dissipare Diem hotel.'

'I didn't know you liked me as much as that,' I said, weakly.

'I like you very much indeed.' He went bright red. 'Rose, this is terrible. We were only just getting to know each other and this is all very sudden and I didn't want it to happen like this.'

'But it's not real, though, is it? It's not legal?'

'It's definitely legal.' He showed me a piece of paper, but I found it hard to focus. 'Look,' he said. 'Our signatures, and here it says Elvis Presley – he must have been practising the autograph – and the ones at the bottom are the names of the mermaids.'

It was ludicrous, but it was legal. We were married. Married in the eyes of God, Elvis, the Siren Sisters and the State of Nevada.

'It's not how I wanted it to be,' said Alastair. 'Rose, I never told you before but you must have guessed how I feel about you and even though this is all very sudden and I know you're probably as shocked as I am and I don't know how we're going to explain this when we get home, I still . . . I . . .' He bent down and put his arms around me, lifted me up from the pillows. My head throbbed, nauseatingly. 'Oh, Rose, I haven't even told you that I love you.' He hugged me and I felt so wretched that hot tears started to trickle down my cheeks. He kissed them away and I wanted to die.

'We've got to leave straightaway,' he said, rocking me gently. 'We mustn't miss the plane. I've paid the bills. The wedding rings were charged to room service, along with Elvis's fee and all the other things. It wasn't cheap. At least you've still got some of your roulette money. I've done your packing for you. I didn't want to look through all your private stuff, but I thought I'd better get your things together. I've packed all your clothes, all your new little dresses and tee-shirts and I found your daisy earrings and your wedding nightie out on the balcony – don't worry, Rose, I don't remember anything about it either. I got all your souvenirs together and I see you got one of those Treasure Island Pearls from the Pirate Pizza Parlour. Complete with its own velvet box. It's huge, isn't it? How many pirate pizzas did you have to eat for that?'

Freeing myself from his arms, I rushed to the bathroom and threw up. When I didn't think I could be sick any more, I sat down on the cold tiled floor and wept. Alastair knocked on the door. 'Rose, we have to leave in five minutes.' There was a pause, and then he said softly, 'Rose, please don't cry. It'll be all right.'

'I'm fine,' I lied. 'Just give me a minute.'

Looking up, I noticed there was a telephone just above the washbasin. Slowly, I dialled Catherine's number. 'Hello? Catherine? It's me, Rose.'

'Did you lose it?' she demanded.

'What?'

'The money! Did you lose it?'

'I can't remember.' There was an exasperated tutting. 'I think I've got some left. Yes, I have. I have.'

'Good. Now, come straight home.'

'Catherine, I've been thinking. Chess isn't a game of chance, it's a game of skill, and if you gamble at it, you're heading for disaster. You know how I never finished that game with Jamie – the one we started that first night with the antique set I told you about . . .?'

'Can we fast-forward this conversation, please?'

'Well . . . the question is: do you think a queen sacrifice is a good idea or not? I mean, the queen is the most valuable piece on the board, but you know how sometimes we all make mistakes and . . .'

'Look, Rose, it's late. I want to go to bed. Can we analyse your funny little foible on another occasion?'

'Catherine, something's happened.' I crawled to my feet and stood up.

'What?'

'Something's happened.' I forced the words out. 'I'm married. I got married last night to Alastair.'

'You've done WHAT?'

'I got married.'

There was a few seconds' delay, then: 'How could you be so BLOODY STUPID? I can't believe this! I just don't believe this!' I heard her call for Helen, heard Helen's squeal of shock.

'Rose! Is it legal?' cried Helen, grabbing the phone. 'What are you going to do?'

'She'll just have to come home and get a divorce,' said Catherine in the background.

'Oh Rose!' wailed Helen.

Catherine seized the phone again. 'You can't stay married to a prat like Alastair Lennox. What the hell did you think you were doing? I only hope you were pissed at the time! And now you want me to get you out of trouble again, don't you? When are you going to grow up? You live in a dream world.'

'Please, Catherine . . . I . . .'

And she chanted: 'Please, Catherine, I've done another silly thing. Would you mind finding out for me the cheapest way to get divorced? You're a stupid idiot, Rose! It would have been better if you'd just stayed being Jamie's mistress!'

I clung to the washbasin. 'You're such a bitch to me, Catherine! How dare you speak to me like that!'

'I dare speak to you like that because you always come running to me. You expect me to sort out the mess you make of your life. All you ever do is fuck-up and now you want me to help you get a divorce!'

And then the words came, furious and defiant: 'What makes you think I want a divorce? Alastair is a good man. A good, kind, honest man. I'm glad I married Alastair! I'm married, I'm married and that's final!' I threw the receiver down and stood, trembling, before the bathroom mirror.

I saw red eyes staring from a pale, angry face; wild, dishevelled hair. A ghastly, gothic apparition shrouded in a white bath towel.

Not myself at all.

The End Game

The subtleties that exist in this branch of the game are prodigious, and seemingly hopeless positions may be redeemed by witch-like manoeuvres. It demands imagination, patience and accurate calculation

The Right Way to Play Chess by D. B. Pritchard

Chapter 18

On the plane, Alastair immediately began work on a news management strategy to tell everyone about our surprise marriage. His usual phlegmatic pallor had gone and he was bright-eyed and pink-cheeked. 'All we have to do,' he said, speaking very fast, 'is tell people in the right way. It's a good news story. No one will believe it at first, but it's true.' He patted my hand. 'Don't worry. It'll be fine.'

I sipped my Bloody Mary and felt shaky. 'So we're definitely going to tell them?'

'If we don't go public about it, it'll come out anyway. We can't go home and act like nothing's happened. You can't ignore the fact you're married, can you?'

'I've only told my sisters. I could always ask them to keep it a secret.'

'I don't think that would be a good idea, Rose. We'll just explain that people get married like that in Las Vegas all the time. Every single hour of every single day. You heard what the Wedding Consultant said.'

'I can hardly remember anything.'

'He said Las Vegas can have a very catalytic effect on personal relationships.'

'But is it wise to speed up your relationship as much as this?'

'Rose, I understand how you feel,' said Alastair, patting my hand reassuringly. 'I've never acted on impulse either – not until now – and we both know that if we'd stayed in Edinburgh it would have taken us ages to get round to doing anything.' He looked bashful. 'This has saved us a whole year of working up the courage. You know, when I met you I thought: here is someone who – someone with whom I could share . . . the important things in life.' He stared yearningly at his Special News Announcement, then snapped the notebook shut. 'You have to think this over,' he said, firmly. 'You have to be sure.'

I looked out the window at the darkening horizon and the inky-black clouds; I pulled my cardigan round me and shivered. 'Cold?' asked Alastair. He got one of the thin airline blankets and tucked it round my knees. 'There,' he said. 'Just take some time to think about things.'

I took the time to think about things. For a few thousand miles, I thought about Jamie. Helen reckoned that what I had felt for Jamie was not love but a general buzz caused by increased serotonin in the bloodstream. 'He just made you happy,' she said.

'Was that all it was?'

'That's enough, isn't it?'

I had believed in the whole romantic dream and my definition of love was hopelessly out of step with reality. What was it Jamie had said about marriage? I spoke the words out loud: 'People get married for all sorts of different reasons.'

'And they stay together for the best ones,' said Alastair. 'Do you want a cup of coffee, Rose? It doesn't taste very nice but it'll warm you up.' He passed me a plastic cup.

'Thanks.'

'Your hands are freezing.'

I turned away and stared out at the darkness again. Two weeks ago, Catherine had told me how happy she and Robert were together. They had talked about marriage but had decided to leave it all up to Chance: heads we marry, tails we don't. It was heads. The lucky coin was now encased in perspex and displayed on the wall of Catherine's bedroom. Friends had given them engagement presents. But when it had come to deciding the date of the wedding, the happy couple had gone for a gamble with much longer odds. They would marry if I ever came across a copy of *The Expert at the Card Table*, signed and verified by the real author. For almost a century, this book has been the card sharp's bible, but the author's true identity is unproven. 'It might turn up,' she had said, cheerfully, 'in one of those boxes you buy at sales.' It was like leaving their wedding in the hands of Fate. 'Why don't you just get married?' I asked.

She had given me a look that said: You wouldn't understand, Rose.

My mother (who had given the question of marriage serious philosophical and practical consideration) believed that if you were going to marry anyone, you should marry a fair-minded, kind and rational individual. A loyal companion who valued your work, shared your interests and tolerated your foibles. Alternatively, you might find someone who tolerated your work, valued your interests and shared your foibles. All permutations were possible in 'a marriage of true minds'. This was my father's favourite sonnet. When they had married thirty years ago, my mother had written it out for him, in gold letters, on the inside of his garden shed. I wondered, sometimes, how he felt about it when he retreated there after one of their rows.

Alastair met all my mother's criteria for a marriage partner in that he was fair-minded, kind, rational, loyal and companionable. We valued each other's work and shared many interests. As for foibles – well, that was a grey area.

I wasn't sure how to define love any more. I had allowed my academic argument to become dominated by romantic literary references. It was time I started using the long-neglected perception of reality part of my brain. Arranged marriages often worked, didn't they? Love grows. I had certainly made a mess of every relationship I had tried to arrange myself. Too gullibly romantic. I thought about the casino at the Dissipare Diem and the fresco of the Three Fates. It seemed the Fates had conspired with Chance to arrange my marriage, too. They had stepped in while I was incapacitated and taken charge.

The romantic dream was, after all, only a dream. In my heart, I put away all my futile desire for Jamie. I buried my feelings very deep. I buried them tenderly and irrevocably.

The sky was pitch black. No moon, no stars. Beside me, Alastair was reading a book about the use of the subjunctive tense. 'You're already an expert on this, aren't you?' he asked, smiling. 'I read your article: "The Small Tragedy of the Subjunctive: the Role of the 'If Only' Tense in Romantic Fiction". It was excellent, Rose. Brilliantly argued. Of course, romantic fiction is not my usual reading. We'd have to agree to respect our different preferences on that one.'

Hours passed, the lights were dimmed and we sat side by side, cramped and cold, in the dark together. Finally, somewhere above the Arctic Circle, I told my husband my opinion of what a sound and successful partnership should be. It took me a while to explain, but the language of realism was a new one for me. 'Love is about friendship and respect,' I finished. 'And trying to be happy. People get married for all sorts of different reasons. The Fates have thrown us together. Maybe we should take that as a sign we should try to make it work.'

'I don't believe in Fate,' he said. 'Or signs. But I would like to try to make it work.'

We agreed to try.

We were met off the plane at Edinburgh Airport by my sisters. Catherine was tight-lipped, Helen wide-eyed with disbelief. It had been a long, arduous journey and when Helen asked me to describe our wedding I couldn't. Alastair explained that I was exhausted and needed to get some sleep.

'Mum and Dad are on their way up from Cambridge,' said

Catherine, flatly. 'They're bringing your books and all that junk they've been storing for you. Dad wants his garage back.'

We got in Catherine's car and drove to Alastair's flat in Marchmont, which is Victorian, rather than Georgian, Edinburgh. I hauled my bags out of the car.

'Are you really staying here now?' asked Catherine.

'Yes.'

Without another word, she got in the car and drove off. Helen waved apologetically from the window.

Exactly five minutes after my first ever visit to Alastair's flat my parents arrived at my new home. My father clumping up the stairs in his heavy brogues, my mother trailing scarves and rattling bangles. Dad looked worried; Mum was all airy insouciance.

'And you must be Alastair!' she beamed. 'Now, I want to tell you both right now that if it doesn't seem to be working, you have to be honest with each other and admit it!'

Alastair managed to laugh, despite the jet-lag. 'I know it was sudden and rather bizarre,' he admitted. 'But I assure you, the commitment is a very genuine one.' He took my hand. 'Isn't it, Rose?'

I nodded, mutely.

My mother asked to see the flat. I couldn't remember my way around so I told her to make herself at home. She floated off down the hall and I hovered around while Dad tried to engage Alastair in conversation. 'I see you have a piano,' he said.

'Do we?' I asked.

'That looks like a piano to me,' said my father.

'It was here when I moved in,' said Alastair. 'The people who used to live here couldn't face getting it down the stairs – and neither can I,' he added.

'Rose has always wanted to learn the piano, haven't you, Rose?'

'Have you?' asked Alastair, worried.

'I'm not very good. Just a beginner.'

223

'Make sure you practise, Rose,' said my father. He walked over to where the piano stood in a corner and looked out of the window. 'It's the ground floor flat that has the garden here, isn't it?'

'Yes,' said Alastair.

'Pity you're on the fourth floor. You could have had some lovely roses on that wall. Compassion would have been good, or maybe even Albertina. Prone to mildew is Albertina, but a vigorous rambler with stupendous blooms. You could always move house, I suppose.'

'No, I like it here.'

'Ah, well. They say gardening comes with age. Play golf?'

'No.'

'Good Heavens! You're in Scotland!'

'I don't play golf.'

'Hiking? Rambling? Long walks?'

'Not my thing.'

'Chess?'

'No.'

With all his topics of conversation now exhausted, Dad took his glasses off, polished them and frowned. Was there anything else he could try? Any other subject on which he could talk with confidence? There was only one. He blinked, stuck his hands in his pockets and said casually: 'Know anything about tenth-century Byzantium?'

Poor Dad. He did his best, but when he failed to arouse Alastair's interest in the mapping of Constantinople's underground canal network, he gave up on him altogether. 'Any chance of a cup of tea, Rose?'

'I'll go and put the kettle on.'

'I'll come with you.'

In the kitchen, Dad hauled himself precariously on to a tall stool and leaned against the bench. 'Alastair seems a nice chap.'

'He is. He's very nice.'

'Quiet though – had to draw him out.' Dad put a hand to his

224

wrinkled brow and tried to compose his worries into a sentence. 'Rose,' he said urgently, 'he's very nice, but what on earth are you going to talk about?'

'We have lots of things in common.'

Dad shook his head.

'There are similarities in our work.'

'I can't believe you're working for McTavish,' he grumbled.

'Needs must, Dad. I've never lost sight of the fact that my real work is the study of vernacular English.'

My father nodded, reassured. 'Has Mackenzie been in touch?'

'Yes. He's starting to put some research work my way.'

'Good.' He shifted his position on the bar stool. 'Tell me what Alastair does.'

'He's a Proof-Reader for Political Correctness.' Dad stifled his contempt. 'In a branch of the civil service . . .'

'Hrumph!'

'. . . with responsibility for correct English usage – I mean . . .' I added, correcting myself, 'English and Scots usage. Historically, Scots has enjoyed the freedom of a spoken language, unencumbered by standard spelling, but Alastair sees this as a failing and he's keen to enforce standardisation. He also drafts speeches for ministers and . . .'

'I know about his paid job,' growled my father, 'but what does he really do? You know – interests, hobbies, that kind of thing.'

'He likes football.'

'Does he play?'

'He refereed once, but they were nasty to him so he hasn't done it again.'

'Football . . .' repeated my father. 'Is that all?'

'It's more important than life or death, Dad.'

At that point my mother entered the kitchen, smiling serenely. She kissed me, patted my father's balding pate and then sat down cross-legged on the floor. 'I have found out something very interesting about our new son-in-law,' she teased. 'It turns out he's a bit of a dark horse.'

225

At these words, I was lifted up by hope.

'We've been talking politics,' she went on. 'And Alastair told me he once stood for election to the ward of Inveresk as an SNP councillor. He didn't get in, of course, but how wonderful that he tried.' (My mother was Cambridge's most active member of the Scottish National Party. Her whisky and shortbread fund-raising nights were famous.)

'Oh, God!' groaned my father.

'Now, George, don't be like that,' she said. 'I'm proud of Alastair for taking a stand. If only there were more like him. Fighting for his country's freedom is the most vital role a man can play. If only more people knew the facts, if only they could be bothered to take an interest. Alastair is in a position of influence.'

I interrupted her. 'Alastair's only active service has been to referee in a five-a-side match against the Conservatives.'

My father chuckled and slid off his stool. 'It's important, George,' insisted my mother. 'At least he's involved. What's the greatest obstacle to Scottish independence – ignorance or apathy?'

'I don't know, Fiona,' he grunted. 'And I don't care.'

'I think I'll start bringing the books in from the car,' I said, hurrying off. My husband offered to help. While Alastair strained under the weight of all my fiction, I carried up my reference books, volume by massive volume.

When this was finished, there was a polite half-hour of stilted conversation before my parents prepared to leave. 'We're staying at Catherine's' said my father. 'We didn't want to get in the way here. You're on your honeymoon, you know.'

'Our honeymoon?'

'We'll go somewhere nice,' whispered Alastair, in my ear. 'When I can take some time off.'

'I expect you'll be quite happy sorting out all your books,' said my father. 'Putting your library in order and so on. It's a good job Alastair's got a lot of empty shelf space.' He nodded towards the wall of shelves in the sitting room.

'Most of my books are at the office. Reference materials and so on. The shelves were there when I came,' said Alastair. 'I kept meaning to take them down – just as well I didn't now, isn't it?'

My mother kissed me goodbye. 'Here,' she said, 'take this.' She pushed into my hand a beautifully bound edition of Kipling's *Just So* stories.

'Oh, Mum, thank you!'

'Read *The Cat that Walked by Himself*,' she advised.

'Kipling?' said Alastair, with disdain.

My mother ignored him. 'Now, Rose – Best Beloved – remember the story of the cat.' She recited: "I am the cat who walks by himself and all places are alike to me."'

I clung to my book. 'Come on now, George,' she said. 'The traffic will be terrible, we've got to make a start.' Her voice was shaking a little. I watched my parents go. 'Hurry up, George!' called my mother.

'All right, all right!'

I stood on the top landing and watched my father's bald patch as he went round and round the stairwell, his voice echoing, '"If you can keep your head when all about you are losing theirs and blaming it on you . . ."'

We bought a Habitat dinner service and started being married.

There was a dinner party rota in operation in Marchmont and the next weekend I met all his closest friends. Everyone was pleased for us. 'There won't be an odd number round the table any more now,' Alastair joked.

He was asked to tell and retell the story of my spectacular gambling success and our limo trip to the Marriage License Bureau. We both admitted it felt as though we had seen it at the cinema rather than experienced it in real life. We tried to explain how quickly and easily one can get married in Las Vegas, how potent is the atmosphere of recklessness, how strong the cocktails. And how exciting it is to win so much money.

I suppose marriage is the biggest gamble of all,' said one.

'What if she'd said no?' another asked.

'You wouldn't have said no, would you, Rose?'

'I never gave it a moment's thought.'

Alastair believed very firmly that even though our marriage had been sudden, that didn't stop it being right. Certitude was Alastair's defining characteristic. He had unclouded opinions, a crystal clear sense of right and wrong. Fuzzy logic could not beguile him. I had a lot of respect for Alastair and so did all of his friends. I heard many reports of his sensible behaviour, many accounts of his responsible actions saving the day.

As the last of his circle to get married, Alastair had been to everyone else's stag party but had always remained sober. He saw it as his duty to make sure the bridegroom got home fully dressed, relatively conscious and without the requisite Saltire tattoo on the left buttock. In the direst of circumstances, in the coldest of weather, Alastair could be relied upon to carry his comrade home should he be unable to hail a taxi.

'That's why we call him the Stretcher-Bearer.'

'Who held the other end of the stretcher?'

'There wasn't really a stretcher. It's just a—'

'A figure of speech,' I said, quickly. 'I knew that.'

'But I suppose Gary could have held the other end. Gary's a recovering alcoholic.'

That night, I asked my husband if he were a recovering alcoholic.

He looked astonished. 'I am not and have never been an alcoholic, but while we're on the subject, I can't believe you asked me for wine as a wedding present.'

'I know.' (He had told me about his incredulity several times now.)

'I wanted to buy you something nice. I can't believe you spent all that money on three bottles of wine. You could have bought enough Vin de Table to last until our first anniversary – and that's a lot of dinner parties, Rose.'

'But you asked me what I wanted and I wanted the burgundy.'

'How did you get a taste for such expensive wine?'

'Practice.'

'And Rose, those receipts from your last trip to John Lewis . . . I thought you were just buying a roller blind for the bathroom window.'

'I was. I did.'

'Then why did you buy . . .' he pulled out a neatly folded wadge of receipts from his pocketbook, 'Hosiery, Hats, Handbags and Cosmetics?'

'I was just shopping.'

'I don't go off and spend money on whatever I want, do I? That would be selfish of me. It's just a shame you paid all your winnings into your Nat West Scottish Widowed No Worries Account.'

'I told you, the interest on the draw-down loan was astronomical, and you agreed with me.'

'But you did more than pay off the loan. You put an extra sixty thousand in. All we had left from your winnings in Vegas. We could have used that to pay off the mortgage as I suggested on the plane on the way home.' He tucked the receipts tidily into his pocket. 'We could have paid off the mortgage, bought another flat and rented this one out.' Alastair shook his head with regret at the lost opportunity. 'But we're together for richer or poorer. Where are you going, Rose?'

'I thought I'd run a bath.'

'Leave the whisky. You don't need it.'

'Can I still have my candles?'

'Don't play with the matches.'

I lay in the bath, pondering the fact that despite the irksomeness of sharing everything there was something very reassuring about being married. It was like choosing the right travelling companion in Bunyan's *Pilgrim's Progress* – Prudence instead of Profligacy, Love instead of Lust. I felt I had seen the light. I was now as enlightened as the sensible heroine who ditches the sexy cad in favour of the nice young curate. I was ruined no longer. And marriage to Alastair was so very *grounding*. We complemented each other: I liked long, lazy baths in the evening, he liked a quick cold shower in the morning when he got back from his jog around the park. There was his Zingy Grapefruit Shower Gel next to my Patchouli Bath Melt.

Helen had been quick to point out to me that Alastair had no gift for sensuality – not by any stretch of the imagination. He was proud of his rather spartan, sober way of living and I started to feel guilty about what he called my 'indulgences'. He was faintly shocked that I stayed in bed till midday on Sundays, reading all the newspapers. He liked to get up early and do a hundred lengths of back crawl at the local swimming pool. It was only under these rigorous conditions that he could immerse himself in water; hot baths he regarded as decadent.

As I gazed at the candlelight on the ceiling, I realised that it was now far too late to confess to Alastair about my shameful past as a rich man's expensive hobby. How I regretted those four months of madness! Four months of mutually selfish indulgence in a passionate chess-sex-cash tryst. It all seemed impossible to explain now. Especially to Alastair. Best not to tell him at all.

Alastair's belated stag night had been arranged for the following weekend at a wine bar in Morningside. I spent the evening at home, batch-cooking for the freezer and listening to an interesting psychology programme on Radio 4, *Delusion and Denial*. Dr Antony Cluney explained how it was possible for a perfectly normal person to be in complete denial about their true feelings. 'How extraordinary!' I said to myself. 'Surely if you've reasoned things through and made a sensible decision, you can't be in denial, can you?' Dr Cluney pointed out that the state of denial could be so profound as to last many years.

I had just cleared away and sat down with a cup of cocoa to

watch *The Ten O'Clock News* when Alastair returned. 'You're back early!'

He slammed the door behind him. 'Had enough.'

'Why? What happened?'

'Gary arranged a Strip-o-Gram. Some kind of sick joke. He said he thought I'd see the funny side.'

It did seem a wicked thing to do to a man who spent his working hours drafting reports on political correctness. 'What was she dressed as?'

'I don't want to talk about it.' He picked up the remote control, flicked through the channels.

'But I'm watching the news.'

'Oh Rose! I've had a bad day! Can't you go and do something else?'

'Only if you tell me what she was dressed as,' I replied, crossly.

'Oh for God's sake!' he shouted. This was the first time I'd ever heard him shout and it made me leap out of the armchair. 'Go and . . . do something else!'

'I'm going.'

'And I'm sorry for shouting,' he finished, lamely.

A few days later, Catherine and Robert came to see us and brought a wedding present: Monopoly.

I loathe Monopoly. It goes on for ever and it's always the same. I could have six hotels on Park Lane and it still wouldn't give me a thrill. Catherine saw my disappointment. 'Alastair likes Monopoly,' she explained. 'He told me so himself. You'll soon get used to it, Rose. If you're going to have a monopolous relationship, you'll have to learn to adapt.'

Alastair was happily unpacking the box. He was shuffling the Community Chest cards and lining up the pieces at Go.

'Let's have a drink,' I suggested. 'And we can play another day.'

Catherine took a good look at her surroundings and kept perfect control of her facial expression. I suppose it was still very much Alastair's flat. There was a bit of football memorabilia about the place. He supported Arsenal, which was unusual in Scotland, but he explained to me that a true supporter doesn't choose who to support – it's more of a *calling*. My own possessions had not made much of an impact on the living room. A lot of books, to be sure, and I had set up my desk beside the window, but that was it.

'Shall we tell Rose about that pal of mine?' asked Robert. 'Jamie Cameron and his scandalous behaviour.'

'I think we should,' said Catherine.

'Oh, I don't think we want to hear about that!' I said, horrified. 'That . . . that gossip!'

'I have come to give you the truth,' said Robert, undeterred. 'It's not gossip, it's the T-R-U-T-H.'

'I know how to spell it. I just don't think we should be discussing it.'

'Don't panic,' said Catherine. 'We just want to tell you what happened when Jamie's house-sitter left him.'

'His house-sitter?' asked Alastair.

'After she left,' said Catherine, looking at me meaningfully, 'Jamie sank into a Slough of Despond.'

'A what?' asked Alastair, abandoning the Monopoly.

'It's a kind of depression,' said Catherine. 'Bunyan writes about it in *Pilgrim's Progress*. It comes before Vanity Fair. Rose will show you the valuable rare edition she's just bought, won't you, Rose?' I nodded, uneasily. (I had yet to break the news of this purchase to Alastair.)

'You never told me you collected rare books,' he said. 'Is that an expensive hobby?'

'I usually manage to sell them at a profit.'

'This is the first time Rose has invested in a book about moral and spiritual guidance,' said Catherine. 'Normally she specialises in Victorian romantic fiction and eighteenth-century French episolatory erotica.'

'But I've sold all that now,' I mumbled.

'Okay,' said Robert. 'Let's just say Jamie was not his usual

232

optimistic self. I took him out for a few quiet drinks to try to talk him round, but it didn't work. He tried ringing her up, he sent her begging letters, but he got nowhere. He couldn't persuade her to speak to him for love nor money.'

'And he tried both!' I said, indignantly. 'You could have told me in private,' I blurted out. 'I don't think this is the time or the place for this conversation.'

'But Alastair is quite interested,' said Catherine, maliciously. 'Aren't you, Alastair?'

My husband smiled at me, kindly. 'We don't need to have any secrets from each other, do we?' he said. I stared at him, feeling the panic rise in my throat.

'Of course not,' said Catherine, sweetly. 'Isn't that right, Robert?'

'Definitely.'

'I have nothing to hide from Rose and Rose has nothing to hide from me,' said Alastair.

'Confidently said.'

'So there's no need, Rose,' he added, 'no need at all for you to be told anything in private. What could there possibly be that you don't want me to hear?'

He trusts me, I realised. He trusts me implicitly. He trusts that I am the serious academic he thought he married. A sensible soul-mate who reads all the time and goes to the office in a neat navy blue suit. He doesn't know about my fondness for extravagant lingerie because I've hidden it all away. He doesn't know about my collection of cask-strength whisky because I drank it when I parted from my lover. He can almost tolerate my taste for interesting burgundy and my long, lazy bath-times, but he has *no idea* of the true extent of my sense of indulgence.

Catherine patted Alastair on the knee. 'Don't worry, Alastair,' she laughed. 'We're just catching up on all the gossip – who's going out with who, who's sleeping with who . . .'

'Whom,' corrected Alastair.

'. . . and who's sleeping alone, broken-hearted, in the mews house at the bottom of his garden.'

'So, about Jamie's house-sitter,' said Robert, continuing. 'At first, Jamie reacted to her resignation by burying himself in his work. Buried alive in Bio-Caledonian's share flotation. His Consolation was travelling round the world on a brand new Spanish passport – which was always the intention, Rose. Did you know, Alastair, that if you're Cuban but you have a parent born in Spain, you can claim dual nationality?'

'I didn't know that,' said Alastair, politely.

'It's true, but it's one of those Catch-twenty-two situations: you can apply for your Spanish passport in Cuba, but it's effectively worthless because you still need a Cuban passport to get out of Cuba. And they won't give you one.'

'That's very bad,' said Alastair.

'If you can get to Spain, you can get your Spanish passport straightaway. Some people will go to enormous lengths to get out of Cuba. One way is to marry a foreigner, preferably a feckless one with plenty of cash.'

'Got her head screwed on,' said Catherine, giving me a nod.

'What's a house-sitter?' asked Alastair. 'Like a housekeeper?'

'Actually, Irina has left him, too,' said Catherine.

'Irina,' said Robert. 'Irina, the retired Russian spy and former concert pianist – or at least that's what Jamie told Rose. Isn't it, Rose?'

'But she's known him for years. She taught his mother the piano.'

'And Irina was hurt that he'd never told her about Consuela.'

'Irina resigned,' said Robert, 'because she felt pushed beyond the limits of her considerable phlegmatic endurance.'

I had bumped into Irina once as I came out of the drawing room. I was wearing red stockings, ridiculously high heels and Jamie's shirt.

Anyone seeing Irina and I standing together on the landing would have noticed immediately that I was taller. 'Good afternoon,' she had said from the moral high ground of her sensible shoes. Her steel-grey cardigan had shuddered at the sight of me but her face had given nothing away.

'Good afternoon,' I had replied. 'The weather's turned chilly for this time of year.'

'It has,' she'd responded. 'You should never have taken off your vest.'

'I must have left it somewhere.'

The corners of her mouth had twitched a little. 'If you mean your beribboned scarlet confection,' (you need to tell this story with Irina's refined Edinburgh accent to appreciate the witty nuance she gave to the words 'beribboned scarlet confection'), 'then that particular item is draped over the candelabrum in the dining room.' More twitching. 'Never cast a clout till May's out.' And off she went, solidly, down the hall. There was no doubt that in order to resign Irina must have felt very seriously aggrieved.

'The thing is, Rose,' said Catherine, 'Jamie was feeling very low and then when you came back from Las Vegas—'

'—I thought I'd better pay him a visit,' said Robert. 'And tell him the happy news.'

I started fidgeting with my wedding ring.

'Jamie is Rose's ex-boyfriend,' said Alastair, slowly.

'Oh, Robert, please!' I begged. 'Do we have to go into this?' I looked angrily at my sister. 'I think you should go now.'

'No, let's hear the rest,' said Alastair, frowning. 'So how did he react?'

'We had a chat, shared a drink and I left him to his private grief. Next day, I called in to see how he was coping and to collect my winnings.'

'Your winnings?'

'He had finally accepted the fact that Rose wasn't coming back.'

'You made a bet with him about that?' asked Alastair, shocked.

'And I won – obviously. I rang the doorbell for ages but there was no answer. I went round the back, climbed over the garden wall and squinted through the window.'

'Was he all right?' I asked.

'He was in a distressed state,' said Robert.

'How distressed?'

'Very distressed. Destroyed. Wrecked, racked and ruined.'

'Defeated then?'

'On the floor. Out for the count. Full of self-recrimination and,' he confided, 'excellent malt. Scandalous waste. Unconscious. I had to break a window to get in.'

'The key's under the flowerpot.'

'Frequent visitor, were you?' asked Alastair. I glanced up, guiltily.

'So there he was, in shock,' said Robert, hurrying on. 'I've seen Jamie in shock on many previous occasions, but there was no doubt about it, this beat the lot. Fortunately, he began to come round. And when he could speak – the things he said . . .'

'What did he say?' I asked.

'He was delirious. He said that her loss was the single greatest disaster ever to befall him. He quoted Shakespeare, Burns, Catullus, Virgil and *Chess Monthly* – a cherished twelve-year-old copy.'

'I didn't know he had that.'

'I tried making him walk up and down the garden, but he just kept asking me if I knew Madame Grégoire was an old-fashioned rose.'

'Rambling.'

'Exactly. I said, "Who's this Madame Grégoire?" And he kept saying, "Compassion". "Compassion, compassion, got no compassion."'

'I told him that,' I said. 'It's evergreen. A pinky-peach colour. I told him to put it at the bottom of the garden.'

'I said to him, "What are you on about, Jamie?" And he just lay down in the middle of the lawn and started raving in a foreign language. It wasn't Gaelic, it wasn't Spanish. He kept talking about a girl called Pearl. Know anyone called Pearl?'

'"Pearl, pleasaunt to prince's pay",' I quoted. '"To clothe in gold."'

'That's very like it.'

'It's from an elegiac medieval poem,' I said, moved.

'He'd lost it,' Robert muttered. 'Lost it completely.'

'The grief-stricken poet is lying in a garden, breaking his heart about this flawless, matchless pearl he's lost. He's pining away, mortally wounded by love. It's very poignant because his Pearl has left him for ever – she's dead to him and he can only dream about her.'

'See what I mean? Not himself at all. And after the roses and pearls, he sat up, put his head in his hands and said: "Nemesis".'

'Nemesis?'

'Yes,' said Robert, drily. 'Just "Nemesis" – nothing else.'

Phew! I thought.

'Even when he was sober, he ranted on about how no one could replace her. Ever. And that he might as well just go and look for an interesting way to die.'

'So what did you suggest?'

'I said, "Why not have another go at rash, unbridled, suicidal hedonism?" I asked him why he hadn't got me round before he opened the Port Ellen. I said I couldn't stand any more of his embarrassing lovesick torment. His . . . his . . . Byronic posturing!'

'Byronic posturing?'

'I blame myself,' said Robert, 'for what happened next.'

Despite Robert's efforts to remind him to be sensible, Jamie couldn't manage it. Instead, he did all sorts of rash, unbridled things. Fortunately, Robert was always at his side, just to keep an eye on him.

'I said, "Why not have a party? That'd cheer you up." I said, "Jamie, it's about time you pulled yourself together." Then he picked up a flowerpot, smashed it against the wall – just being melodramatic – and said, "What the hell, let's have a party and let's invite everyone I've ever known and all their friends."'

'I was looking forward to it,' said Robert. 'Last time Jamie threw a big party, it made the papers. It was during the Festival and it got reviewed by a critic who thought it was Art. Haven't you seen the cutting? He's got it framed in the downstairs toilet. Anyway, the party last weekend was better. It's just a pity the host wasn't fully aware of his surroundings.'

I couldn't blame Jamie for throwing a party. Self-pity tends to concentrate the hedonistic mind on the need for compensation. It provides an incentive for drunkenness, a motivation for the consumption of things narcotic.

'I'm pleased to hear he's feeling better.'

'He's not feeling better at all,' said Robert. 'He can't sleep, he can't eat, he just works all the time or sits alone reading books of French philosophy about the pointlessness of life. On his better days, he listens to music – requiems and so on. He's planted some roses at the bottom of the garden and he . . .'

Tears pricked my eyes.

'Thank you, Robert,' said Alastair. 'I think we've heard enough.'

Alastair folded his arms awkwardly, as if trying to protect himself from a blow to the stomach. 'No doubt Rose will fill me in on the background later.' My sister and Robert took the cue and stood to go. My legs felt weak. 'Rose will see you out. I expect she'd like to say goodbye.' Alastair turned and left the room.

My sister smoothed her unruffled hair and made for the door. 'What was the point of all that?' I asked, angrily, following her out.

'This marriage is never going to work. I'm only trying to speed things up a little.'

'You always think you're right, don't you? Whatever you do – however tactless, crass and insensitive you are!'

'Rose,' said my sister, urgently. 'I know you married when you were drunk, but why the hell are you staying with him?'

'Because I want to! I want to stay with him. I want to make it work.'

'That's the most ridiculous thing I've ever heard!' Catherine's eyes were bright. She didn't seem so composed any more. 'It's just a matter of time before you split up. It won't last. I give it—'

'Don't,' said Robert, but it was too late.

'Three months at the most.'

'Alastair and I want to be together. And we're certainly planning on being together for longer than three months!'

Robert put a hand to his forehead and closed his eyes – the gesture of a man with a plan gone wrong. It was surprising coming from Robert; he didn't normally go in for gestures or failures.

'I'm sorry,' said Catherine, tensely. 'But I know I'm right.'

'Don't come here again, Catherine. I don't want you to come here.' I could feel the awful tightness in my throat again. 'Robert, did Jamie ask about me?'

Robert looked very unhappy. 'He always asks about you.'

'Tell him I'm very well. Tell him I'm working hard and getting on well.'

'He misses you very much.'

'Is there anything else you have to say before you go?'

'No, but he especially asked me to notice your hands.'

'Did he? Well, here they are.' I held my hands out, remembering how Jamie used to kiss them. 'You can tell him that you've seen them.'

'He was wondering if you'd reverted to the finger-twisting, hand-wringing habit.' I felt my fingers squirming with the effort of stillness. I twisted my wedding ring round and round my finger and then decided that folding my arms was probably safer. 'Oh, well, have I? Have I been fidgeting?'

'Yes,' said Robert. 'All the time. The whole time.'

'Why did he ask that?'

'He must have his own peculiar reason, I suppose,' said Robert. 'What could that tell him?'

It's the chess, I realised, wringing my hands. I was missing the chess with him desperately. Missing it, missing him. All of it, all of him. There are times in a game when neither side has the advantage; when every move is a bad one.

I watched Catherine and Robert leave. They didn't speak to each other. The front door shut quietly behind them.

Back in the house, I could hear football commentary coming from the bedroom. Alastair was lying on the bed, watching his television. I sat down beside him. 'Alastair?' He kept his eyes on the screen and said nothing. 'You mustn't take any notice of my sister – or Robert.'

'I'm not thinking about it,' he said.

'I want to explain.'

'I don't want to know.' He stared straight ahead.

I waited a few moments, then raced on: 'I left Jamie when I found out he was married. He didn't tell me he was married. I didn't know.'

Alastair's face wore its closed, tight expression. 'When did you leave him?'

'A few months ago. It's finished, it's all over. It's all in the past.'

'Is it?'

I considered my position. I was very concerned that I should say and do the right thing. I knew that there had to be more to a lasting relationship than a mutual interest in chess. (Although it had seemed very satisfying at the time.) There was absolutely no chance of Alastair impressing me with an interesting combination, a surprising pin or a daring fork. I walked over to the window and stared out at the garden below.

'Rose?'

Alastair was good in other ways. He was a good man. I knew he would always tell me the truth. He was loyal to his friends and to his principles and he would always be loyal to me. I felt safe with him. And if I were being really sensible about it, I knew that that was a sound basis for a marriage. A realistic definition of love. Jamie belonged to a part of my life I knew was over. I turned to see Alastair watching me, waiting for my answer. 'It's definitely over,' I said, firmly.

He got up and came to stand beside me at the window. He

didn't take me in his arms or kiss me; he just stood at my side, a solid, dependable presence. A stoical husband as good as any stoical wife could wish for. 'We'll go out, shall we?' he said. 'When the match has finished. We could go out for a walk or something.'

'All right, that would be nice. I'll make a cup of tea first.'

I made tea, brought it to him and then took mine into the living room. Here the view was of the street outside. We would go out for a walk. Good idea. I could walk off some of my rest-lessness. I paced up and down in front of the book shelves. All my books. Floor to ceiling of print. Travel guides, biographies, dictionaries, reference books. I saw *Hall's Dictionary of Subjects and Symbols in Art*. Feeling nostalgic, I looked up Nemesis. What a goddess! The things she did! The fun she used to have!

In Greek mythology, Nemesis was one of the daughters of Night, who brought retribution upon those whose natures were hardened by pride, or *hubris*. The figure of Nemesis resembles that of the goddess Fortune, with whom she has some affinities, since both can bring about a man's undoing. Nemesis is represented as a naked woman, blindfold, with a globe of the earth at her feet. In one hand, she holds a rope with which to bind man's pride and in the other, riches and honour to reward the just. Her victims may crouch at her feet.

My God but Jamie knew how to use a metaphor when he wanted to! That was better than a metaphor, that was an allegory! Drank my tea, thinking about Nemesis.

A few days later I was alone in the flat, working at my desk, when a parcel arrived for me. A box wrapped in wedding paper, with a big silver bow. Inside was an antique chess set. I recog-nised it immediately. The smooth, polished board; oak and mahogany pieces. I didn't dare touch it again. It would mean reaching out for my old life. There was a gift card: 'Now you can enjoy playing with someone else. Felicidades from Consuela and Jamie.'

I placed the card between the pages of *Jane Eyre*. It would help discipline the mind should I have any more stupid moments of nostalgia. Then I wrapped everything carefully, called up Sprint-Cycle and sent the box back.

After a few more weeks of marriage, we had a weekend's honeymoon in Venice. While my husband watched Serie A football in the hotel room, I deliberately lost myself, wandering by the canals and thinking about all that glorious decadence sinking slowly into the sea.

When we returned to Edinburgh, it was as though I had brought some of that sadness with me. It was probably made worse by my tendency to play a few minor chords on the piano whenever I passed by it. Sometimes I just held them down too long. My married life settled into a sedate, melancholic rhythm. If it were a piece of music, it would have been like Albinoni's 'Adagio', only not as poignantly beautiful.

I developed a passion for puddings and stodgy pastry. It was nice to be able to potter around the kitchen without someone's arms around my waist. I was able to cook without someone standing behind me and kissing my neck at the same time. And the way he had always wanted to hold my hands! So annoying. It was great not being bothered by that sort of thing any more.

'Give me your hands,' he used to say.

'No, I'm using them.'

'One hand then. Thank you.'

My husband was not particularly demonstrative in his affection, but he told me he loved me, he needed me and he wanted to be with me all the time. Sometimes, I found this irksome.

'Why do you always check up on me?'

'I don't check up on you.'

'You phoned the office yesterday to check what time I'd left, you rang Helen to ask if I'd arrived yet, and if I go out anywhere at night you phone me every half-hour on my mobile.'

'You might get mugged or something. I need to know where you are.'

'I don't like having to give such a minutely detailed itinerary, Alastair.'

'I just feel protective towards you, that's all.'

Alastair got so protective, he sometimes felt bad about it afterwards and said sorry. I knew it was all because he had been upset by Catherine's tactlessness. I begged her never to mention Jamie's name again. I told her she had only succeeded in making life difficult for me and she reluctantly agreed.

I tried to reassure Alastair. I never went anywhere alone without leaving him notes about where I was going. I promised him that the only time I would switch my mobile off was at the cinema or at a concert. I told him which cinema and which concert. He often turned up to surprise me. In this way, he sat through a lot of politically incorrect movies ('How can you watch this rubbish, Rose?') and heard a lot of chamber music which bored him to tears ('They must be nearly finished now, surely?'). I gave up my luxury of solitary walks in the north at weekends. I only went up hills that were within an hour's drive of Edinburgh and where I could maintain telephone contact. Sometimes I found this very trying, but I told myself this phase would pass, Alastair would recover from his unpleasant bout of jealousy and we would be good companions once more.

What else was trying? Difficult to say, really – and that was the problem. I didn't want to talk about it and he felt you should just do it. And keep it simple, please. Keep it simple, in bed, in the dark, and don't make a noise.

I spent more hours reading than at any other time of my life. I re-read Nancy Mitford's *Love in a Cold Climate* and all of P.G. Wodehouse's Jeeves books. There are times when a spot of humorous comfort reading is essential to one's emotional survival. And yet, I refused to name my sorrow, even to myself. Lots of old insecurities returned to haunt me. It was probably a secret wish for celibacy that prompted me to interrupt Alastair in the middle of *Sportscene*. Timing is everything.

Example:

'Shall we go to bed now?'

'I'll just see the score.'

After the score:

'I'll just see this goal.'

After the goal:

'I'll just see the replay.'

After the replay:

'I'll just get the post-match chat.'

After the post-match chat:

'Alastair, I'm going to bed. See you in the morning. Put the lights off, will you? Night-night.'

He would nod, absent-mindedly, and I would go to bed alone.

This all made me wonder if, perhaps, that was why Jamie had sometimes had this thing about sex before dinner, because then, when he got to the TV bit later on, he could sit there with his perfectly contented and satiated girlfriend snuggled at his side. All sorted by ten-thirty! I wondered if he had actually planned it that way, if he had, at some time in his life, worked it all out. Perhaps he had had a *eureka* moment in the bath ('I know, I'll just roger her before dessert! Watch *Sportscene* unimpeded') and that moment of insight had stood him in good stead for years. I tried to remember watching *Sportscene* with Jamie. It must have happened. *Sportscene* was inevitable, like death. But I honestly couldn't remember having seen it. Too sleepy, dreamy and full of dessert by then. I remembered watching Barcelona beat Madrid because we had been sitting in the Neucamp stadium at the time. But *Sportscene* – must have missed it. My secret admiration for him only grew.

Alastair loved football so much, he needed it to go on for hours.

Example:

'We could still score in Extra Time.'

'How long is that?'

'And then there'll be Injury Time.'

'How long is that altogether?'

'Time Added On.'

He was very wound-up about it. I had never seen him so tensely excited. 'Penalties,' he said, shivering. He couldn't sit still, he was actually hugging a cushion. Somebody scored and he was overwhelmed. Jubilant. Like a seven-year-old who's had his dream fulfilled. Like he'd woken up on Christmas morning to find a Ferrari under the tree.

'Can I drive it now, Dad?'

'Yes, son. Make sure you keep it clean.'

Sportscene, Spot the Sport, Sports Quiz, Sport Report, Sport Extra.

I waited for him. It was like ringing someone up and being kept on hold while an awful tune plays over and over in your ear: 'Oh!-that-was-offside!-Oh-yes!-That-was-offside!' Football could take Alastair to heaven and hell and back in ninety minutes, plus Time Added On, and I, his wife, could not compete.

I gave up. There were times when I found myself sinking to his level and using a football metaphor in a bedroom context. Like: I just want it to be all over and it is now. Then I was left with nothing but his snoring and my own post-match analysis.

I found myself thinking: call that a goal? Amateur!

And then my mind would start to wander as I drifted off to sleep: I know we've got a contract, but his form is very disappointing. What about replacing him with that brilliant talent I spotted last March? A radical move, sure to cause controversy, but it's more important than life or death, isn't it?

Chapter 19

It was very cold in the cupboard-office I shared with Maggie. There was an electric bar-fire standing in the corner, but we were only allowed to use it for an hour a day as the departmental budget had been heavily cut since the Las Vegas trip. McTavish had railed furiously against the imposed savings measures. I had accompanied him to meetings where he had table-thumped till the crockery rattled with his indignation, but it was all to no avail. My husband was, as ever, his chief antagonist.

'They're trying to freeze us out,' said Maggie. 'But Magnus won't give in.'

'But do you think it was a good idea to turn the heating off?'

'I told you to take your work home if it got too cold for you.'

'I'm glad I did. His report on Las Vegas took me hours to translate into politically correct prose. Can we have our hour with the fire on, Maggie?'

'Not yet. I know it's chilly, Rose, but there are hard choices to be made. Magnus feels we have to maintain the entertainment budget. He can't be expected to take visiting dignitaries out for a fish supper.'

'They might enjoy it.'

Maggie regarded me suspiciously. 'I fully support Magnus's decision to turn off the heating and so should you. Hasn't he seen to it that every single party worker has a hot-water bottle?'

'Can I have five minutes with it, Maggie? My hands are freezing.'

'You're not a party member,' she retorted. 'Anyway, you've got your thermal gloves on. You've had too many years in Englandshire. It's made you soft.'

I shrugged and picked up the dictaphone. 'I've got work to do.'

'I bet that husband of yours keeps the heating on at home – what with all the money you've got to burn. You probably leave the windows open and go round in tee-shirts like it's summer.'

'Where are the headphones, Maggie?'

'In the top drawer. What have you done with all that money you won in Vegas? None of us have seen anything of it.'

'I used it to pay off my debts.'

'Pay off the mortgage, you mean.'

'And the rest has gone into a savings account – not that it's any business of yours, Maggie.'

'I think Magnus has already explained to you that that money was won at the taxpayer's expense and therefore a little of it would be appreciated by others in the department. We're all in the Lottery Syndicate. If one of us wins, we all share it.'

'It wasn't won on the Lottery.'

'The principle is the same.'

'I did supply a case of whisky, if you remember.' I fumbled with the dictaphone, unable to press the buttons with gloved fingers, and had to resort to removing the gloves. 'And for some reason I got one of the bottles back as a wedding present.'

'That was simply a misunderstanding. Your husband rejected our original gift and he was less than polite about it.'

'I've already apologised for that. I have to get on with this

247

work, Maggie. Magnus had a long meeting this morning and I have to type it up.'

'Anyone would have loved that hamper! We went to a lot of trouble over it.'

'I know and I'm sorry, but Alastair doesn't eat shortbread or cake because it's fattening and he doesn't like whisky and he's allergic to smoked salmon and he won't have politically incorrect jams in the house and he didn't approve of the other things because of . . . one reason or another. There are quite a lot of things we don't keep in the house. I've got the headphones on, now, Maggie.'

She shook her head. 'You poor, oppressed fool.'

'I can't hear you.'

I sat with my bare fingers poised over the keyboard, ready to type up McTavish's latest verbal fight in Alastair's central-heated office. An embittered voice in my ear recorded the date of the meeting: 'December fourth. Budget Meeting, fifth round. McTavish versus Lennox.' Numbly, my fingers hit the keys.

'After making many sacrifices, my department has now met your unreasonable, petty-minded demands.'

'I have to inform you,' I recognised Alastair's measured tones, 'that by turning off the heating you are contravening Health and Safety regulations. Your staff cannot be expected to work under such conditions.'

'Every single one of my staff has a hot-water bottle.'

'Every single one?'

At this point, the recording had been switched off. Click, click. When it resumed there was the unmistakable sound of a table being thumped.

'For the record!' shouted McTavish. 'The temperature in Mrs Lennox's room has not dropped below fifty-four degrees Fahrenheit which is above the legal minimum requirement.'

'Her name is still Rose Budleigh.'

'Aye, whatever . . .'

'Rose's assistance has been invaluable to you in drafting your Las Vegas report, Magnus, especially when one considers that she was never at any of the business meetings you claim to have attended.'

'She doesn't have to attend all my meetings. I put everything on tape and give the tapes to Rose. She knows what to do with them.'

'She filters your words through a veil of euphemism.'

'She's a good PA!'

'Euphemia is her middle name. But I have heard the tapes, Magnus. I know what you and your cronies were getting up to in Las Vegas – and at the taxpayer's expense, too.'

I stopped typing, my fingers frozen stiff. 'It's too cold to type in her office, so she brought her work home. I played the tapes when she was in the bath listening to *The Financial World Tonight*. You've been economical with the truth, Magnus, if not the budget. From now on, every meeting you attend will be minuted by a member of the Department for Political Correctness. The reports will be submitted directly to me. The Las Vegas project is over. I have all the evidence I need.'

I switched off the tape and my hands clutched each other for support. I looked up to see Maggie knitting by the electric fire. 'When you've finished listening,' she said, casually, 'Magnus will see you in his office.'

I had to hear the rest. Rapid clicks. On, off, on, off. 'What the fuck . . .?' On, off. 'You sanctimonious bastard!'

'I don't think you fully understand the consequences, Magnus.'

'I'll tell you what I've never been able to understand . . .'

'The difference between the letters "d" and "b"?'

'Why the fuck did she marry you?'

Click, click. Silence.

Maggie, the tricoteuse, held up her red scarf to check the length. She only needed a few more rows of knit-one, purl-one and it would be finished. I took off my fleece jacket, a sweater and one of my cardigans. 'Ready?' she smiled.

In my black lambswool twin-set, I stood to meet my fate. Maggie knocked on the door. 'Send her in!'

The vast room was glowing with warmth and light. Just before the central heating ban, McTavish had applied for and received a conservation grant to restore the Jacobean fireplace in his office. He sat in his shirt-sleeves, back to the open grate, sacks of smoke-less coal lined up beside the hearth. His face was ruddier than ever.

'Rosie,' he said, gravely. 'Sit down.'

I sat.

'Have you heard the tape of this morning's meeting?'

'I have.'

'And so you'll understand that a conflict of interest has arisen between us.'

'I hope it can be resolved.'

He waved this aside. 'Alastair Lennox has appointed a new secretary to work in this department. Maggie doesn't know this yet, but your husband has forced upon us a homosexual favourite of his to take minutes and do my typing.' McTavish wiped his brow. 'There is absolutely nothing I can do about it. They've got me over a barrel. I'm buggered.'

'I had no idea he would listen to those tapes. I really didn't.'

'Those tapes are government property and should never have left the building. Haven't you signed the Departmental Secrets Act?'

'No.'

'You must have done.'

'I haven't.'

He stroked his beard and growled to himself. 'They watch me all the time! Why do you think I have to send my correspon-dence by Sprint-Cycle? I expected a little more discretion from you, Rose. Look, you've been lovely to have about the place and a great asset to this department, but now, I'm afraid, I have to ask you to clear your desk and . . .'

'Clear my desk!'

'You are being sacked,' he explained. 'I am no longer permitted to appoint my own private secretary. Your husband appoints my private secretary. He has made his appointment and, well . . . it isn't you.'

'But—'

'Your husband wants you out of this office. He has made his decision and we have no choice but to abide by it. He's replacing you with his own man. Don't count on him finding you a new job in his own department – he doesn't go in for that kind of helpful gesture. I'm sorry, Rose, I truly am. You're the best speller we've ever had and your euphemisms are second to none.'

I was speechless. McTavish walked round his desk to where I sat, stunned. 'It's time to leave, now.'

He escorted me to the door where Maggie was waiting for us. 'I've put all your things together,' she said, smugly. 'They're in this carrier bag. Shall I see Rose off the premises, Magnus?'

'No,' he said, darkly. 'Rosie can see herself out. I want a word with you, Maggie, about the Departmental Secrets Act.'

I took my carrier bag and walked. I walked straight across the road to confront Alastair about my sacking, but the Chief Corrector was not available; he was visiting schools all afternoon. I went home, angry and frustrated.

Shortly before midnight, I heard Alastair's key in the door and his footsteps in the hall. I was sitting at my desk, working. 'You're still up,' he said, surprised. 'I thought you would have gone to bed by now.'

'I've been updating my CV.'

'Ah, yes, good idea.'

'Because of you, Alastair, I have lost my job.'

'But, surely you see, Rose, it's in a good cause. It's for the greater good. We've got our own person in that office now. You never really wanted to work for McTavish, did you?'

'I didn't want to be sacked! Why didn't you tell me?' I demanded. 'Why didn't you tell me you had listened to those tapes?'

'I made copies of them, too,' he said, proudly.

'Why didn't you warn me what was going to happen!'

'It was better that you didn't know. I'm sorry it had to be this way.' He put an arm around my shoulders. I pushed him away. 'Look, Rose,' he said, impatiently, 'I know you're upset, but we needed our own Proof-Reader in that key position and I couldn't run the risk of letting you in on our plans.'

'Why not? What do you think I would have done?'

'I wasn't sure. I haven't known you very long.'

As soon as Professor Mackenzie knew I was out of a job, he asked me to write a lexicographer's view of Scottish political administration. He explained that what he *didn't* want was a study of official language as expressed by Alastair and his department. He was tired of those; he got one by e-mail every single day. Instead, he wanted an unflinching account of the language of politics *as it is spoken* in all its subversive vitality.

I was flattered that Professor Mackenzie trusted me with such a big commission and I threw myself into the task. It involved a lot of late nights in bars, listening to politicians and journalists, but I was determined to do my work thoroughly. This time, I would not fall short of his rigorous standards of research.

It soon emerged that Alastair had his own plans for my career. At breakfast one morning, I was poring over a fax forwarded to me by a journalist. It had been sent to him by the Member for the Isle of Muck, and it was full of the most interesting slang. 'Don't worry, Rose,' said Alastair, 'you won't have to read that kind of thing for much longer. I've enrolled you on the Civil Service Fast-Track Training Scheme for Proof-Readers.'

'You've done what?'

'You'll be specialising in punctuation. The first year focuses on the use and abuse of the "apostrophe s" – which, as you know, is at the very front line of proof-reading. In your second year you'll be tackling comma splices and your final year will be taken up with a report into the harmonisation of European punctuation.'

I stared at him, open-mouthed.

'I know it's a little radical, but there's no reason why we shouldn't embrace the Spanish inverted question mark or the French double-arrowed speech mark. I've always believed, Rose, that your language skills could be best applied to the proof-reading of government documents. Think of the number of mistakes that occur in the civil service every single day. You could make a real difference to the grammar of government.'

'I don't want to.'

Alastair was affronted. 'I told the course co-ordinator that I was sure you would be very keen on the idea.'

'Tell him you were wrong. Tell him you ought to have asked me first.'

The weeks before Christmas were tense and difficult. I finished my piece for Mungo Mackenzie and delivered it by hand. To my disappointment, the great man had already left for his annual holiday at his home in Shetland. I knew I would have to wait at least a month before he returned and gave me his verdict on my work. I had heard rumours of a new permanent research post at Dictionary House. It was the job I had dreamed about.

Alastair worked hard at dismantling McTavish's department. The staff were dispersed throughout Proof-Reading and Political Correctness for a period of rehabilitation, but Maggie chose resignation rather than compromise. An old pal of McTavish's eventually offered her a job at a distillery near Inverness. McTavish himself took early retirement in Tenerife, although he threatened to stage a comeback in the spring.

I stayed at home, feeling redundant in every sense of the word. Alastair always got up early, bright as a cornflake, keen to get to the office. He hummed happily to himself while I made bleary-eyed attempts to do those simple breakfast things like find a mug.

'So, what are you going to do today?' he would ask.

'Oh, breathe in and out, grow my hair – that kind of thing.'

When Alastair was out at work, I practised the piano; I got very good at minor scales. The bleak midwinter had arrived. It reminded me of the misery of the year before, when I had spent many of my waking hours trudging up and down with a clipboard, and most of my free time shivering in flannelette pyjamas in a damp basement. But now, staring out of the fourth floor window of Alastair's flat, I couldn't help thinking that celibacy in a box room was looking quite attractive. I spent a lot of time staring out of the window. For two weeks, I didn't see the sun at all. When it did appear for one whole surprising day, it made a low arc over the horizon and then sank quickly, as if it found the experience depressing.

One of my former colleagues from McTavish's department offered me a few hours a week at the Council Offices, shelving plans. I told Alastair I thought I might as well accept it.

'I thought you only breathed for a living,' he said.

'I have a whole portfolio of skills, although respiration is obviously the most important.'

He made the effort to smile and managed to look less sad.

'Alastair's a good man,' said my mother on the phone.

'I know.'

'What are you reading these days, Rose?'

'I've just finished *Madame Bovary*. It made me think I should get out more.'

'Is reading *Madame Bovary* a good idea at this stage? Marriage is beset by the challenge of finding some kind of *modus vivendi* with one's spouse. The first year is always difficult. It's a time of adjustment. Compromise is what makes a marriage work.'

That's a relief. I thought you were going to say it was sacrifice.'

'Sacrifice is what makes it last,' said my mother, sagely. 'But compromise is the first step and, of course, love helps in a marriage.'

'Love helps,' I repeated to myself.

'You have another question, Rose,' stated my mother.

I hesitated, then went for it. 'What helps sex in a marriage?'

'Good red wine and marijuana,' pronounced my mother, coolly. 'Anything else you want to ask me?'

'And when does a compromise become a sacrifice?'

'I'm a philosopher, darling, and this is peak rate, long distance. I haven't got time for dreary Stoics any more. Ask your father.'

'Is he there?'

'He's just plodding his way along the hall. Hurry up, George.'

I heard Dad's smiling voice down the phone: 'Rose, how are you, blossom?'

'Fine thanks, Dad. How are you getting on with Byzantium?'

'Complicated as ever.'

'Have you two had a row again?'

'You know your mother and I love each other really. How's the chess?'

'Dad, when does a compromise become a sacrifice?'

'When you don't get something of equal value in return. Think of exchanges. You match your opponent move for move, piece for piece. When you surrender a piece, you might well be compromised. Obviously, you've made a sacrifice, but if it turns out you win you can call it a gambit. Pity Alastair doesn't play. By the way, what happened to your old boyfriend – the one who did?'

'He's just bought half of Bio-Caledonian. Helen says they're going to float the company soon.'

'What was his opening?'

'King's Gambit.'

'Really? Pure bravado!' I knew Dad would be shaking his head. 'Feckless, reckless bravado. You'll have won, then,' he added.

'I don't think so,' I said, sadly.

In an effort to get out more, I arranged to meet Helen at the Gallery of Modern Art. Good pictures, nice café. When I found

255

her she was sitting alone in a corner of the hall, looking beautiful and sad. We embraced and she told me that Gordon had left her.

'What happened?' I asked, astonished. No one had ever left Helen before – not willingly, anyway.

'It's for the best.' She shifted uncomfortably in her chair. Wriggle wriggle. Then she squeezed her eyes shut and set her lips into a line that pressed the pout out of existence. The blonde bombshell looked about to explode. 'He said he disapproved of my work.'

'He left because of that?'

'Gordon isn't only a travel writer. He's an eco-warrior, too.'

'I thought that was just at weekends.'

'He told me he only went out with me because he wanted to find out where the test sites were. It was later that he fell in love with me – or so he says. When I wouldn't tell him the exact locations in Banffshire, he was offended.' She tossed her blonde curls, indignantly. 'I told him how I had developed the Budleigh Beauty and we discussed some of our experiments and what amazing results we'd had. I thought I could win him over, but I was wasting my time. Last night he told me he could never reconcile himself to my work.' Helen's beautiful eyes were wet with tears. 'He's left me, Rose.'

'He doesn't deserve you!'

'I'm probably as upset as Jamie was when you left him.'

I felt an ache in the pit of my stomach. 'Do you see Jamie much?' I asked.

'He's been up to Banff a few times. I know he's been putting in some long hours on the share flotation. Things have been pretty hectic.'

'What about Consuela?'

'She's got a lovely boyfriend in Madrid called Ernesto. She's in Spain most of the time now.'

'Doesn't Jamie mind?'

'Of course not. Why should he mind?'

'Because she's his wife.'

Helen looked at me as if I were stupid. 'Consuela's going to marry Ernesto as soon as her divorce is through. What's the matter, Rose? You've gone very white.'

'I haven't eaten since breakfast.'

'We'd better go to the café before we look at the Art.'

'I'll be fine, give me a minute.'

Spots appeared before my eyes and faded away again. My mind was a complete blank. A self-induced, brainwashed blank.

'Jamie's taking a risk buying half of Bio-Cal, you know,' said Helen, by way of conversation. 'I only have five per cent. He wanted to buy in before we float. I don't think he's supposed to, but he has. Next Wednesday we're announcing a deal with Scot Burger. All their chips are going to be made from my potato. Didn't Catherine tell you? The day after that, we float the company. Please come to the launch, Rose. It's going to be a big day for me – the culmination of all my work. I've asked Catherine but she can't come. Say you can come. And Alastair, too, of course. Will you come?'

I nodded, tried to smile.

'Promise?'

'Promise.'

'Jamie will be there, too. Oh, and Consuela. She really is good fun, you know. Ernesto won't be there because he's giving a lecture on "Pragmatic Cuban Capitalism" at a conference in Barcelona. How are you feeling now, Rose?'

'Kind of strange.'

'Do you want to see the Art?'

'Why not?'

We set off around the first gallery. 'You know, Rose, I realise now how little I knew about Gordon and yet we were together for almost a year. When you married Alastair, it was all very sudden, wasn't it?'

'Spontaneous, almost.' I stopped, appalled by the stark emptiness of one vast canvas. It took up a whole wall. It was so well lit, I couldn't bear it.

'Do you ever find yourself thinking of Jamie?' asked Helen.

A great tide of emotion rose and fell inside me. 'Who?'

'Jamie,' she repeated. 'Do you miss him?'

'I don't think about him.' I marched stoically on, but at the corner of Surrealism, I stopped. 'Oh, the chess!' I cried. 'Oh, God, how I miss the chess!' Helen didn't know what to say. She patted me on the arm and decided it was best to leave me alone for a few moments. I sat down on a bench and stared at the painting in front of me. It was entirely grey but for a horizontal black line across the middle.

My sister returned to drag me away. We wandered on through the other galleries. The Gabrielle Keillor Collection. Dada and Surrealism. Picasso, Magritte, Duchamp, Dali, Man Ray, Miró.

'If Gordon had asked me to marry him,' said Helen, 'I would probably have said yes. It just goes to show how wrong you can be about a person. If we're being objective about it, marriage is simply a marketing exercise for the packaging of love.'

'That's a bit cynical, isn't it?'

'I know all about marketing now,' said Helen. 'I can't believe what the marketing department has done with my potato. Everything has changed at Bio-Caledonian. It's not about scientific discovery any more, it's about creating a brand. I tell you something, Rose, if the institution of marriage were to be launched today as a new product, it would be marketed with great fanfare as "exclusive rights to a lifetime of sex with the unique partner of your dreams" – none of this consumer-scaring stuff about fidelity until death. Because that's what marriage is about, isn't it? Rose, you're really not looking well. I think it's about time we went to the café.'

We found a table by the windows, ate our lunch and looked out at the sculpture garden. A wintry drizzle hung over everything like a pall and the sculptures stood on the lawn like tombstones.

'In summer,' I said, closing my eyes and trying to remember it, 'there are beautiful rambling roses here. All along the building

258

and up to the first floor windows. You can sit out on the terrace and the scent is gorgeous.'

Helen wasn't listening. She had noticed a very good-looking man sitting at the next table, drawing. He glanced up at her and then went back to his sketch-pad, but my sister continued to stare. When he looked up again, she quickly dropped her gaze; it was his turn to stare. Then their eyes met. One, two, three slow seconds – quite a lengthy oeillade for Edinburgh, although I've heard they do it for much longer in Cuba where it's more of a whole body sweep. The man lost his nerve first and looked away, but it had happened. The shared conspiracy. Deeply instinctive and yet, without doubt, the most artful thing I'd seen all afternoon.

Back at the flat, I sat quiet and alone on the sofa and allowed myself to remember a time I had gone to an art gallery with Jamie. He had rung me up from work and suggested we met at the National Gallery at one o'clock. I had found him exactly where he'd said he would be: standing in front of the Canova sculpture (or rather, behind it).

'Rose.' He kissed me. 'You look lovely. Tell me what you think of *The Three Graces*.' I walked around the three marble girls. There was a delicate tenderness about the way they draped their arms over each other.

'Very graceful,' I said.

'The middle one is definitely the prettiest.'

'Do you think so?' I smiled.

'She's probably the cleverest, too. You can tell the other two Graces look up to her.'

'That's because she's taller.'

'She's got your bottom and your legs.'

'Shsh!'

'She has your legs down to the ankles, but only from the back, not from the front. Now that's interesting, isn't it? Not your feet, though, not from either angle.'

I read the plaque and discovered that *The Three Graces* had spent years being ornamental at the bottom of somebody's garden. 'It's just a bit of Victorian erotica,' I said. 'He probably wandered down the garden now and then – gave them a pat.'

'Sounds ideal.' He patted my bottom in a proprietorial sort of way. 'See you tonight.'

When he arrived, I was reading my latest acquisition: a copy of *Les Liaisons Dangereuses*. It had once belonged to the Comtesse de Grégoire and was probably liberated from her private library at the time of the French Revolution.

If you're reading in the nude, you can't just fling yourself on the silk rug and get engrossed in the story. Oh no! Some advance planning is necessary. As any Grace will tell you, a bit of artful drapery might be good, and if you're wearing your hair up because you've just got out the bath you'll need a few pins to keep it in place as well. You might also be wearing your favourite necklace, the one he gave you for your birthday. The chief aim when reading in the nude is to look completely absorbed in your book, entirely at ease, as if you've been reading naked all your life. The way to achieve this is to pretend you're on your own. This is the difference between 'naked' and 'nude' (as an artist once explained to me: naked means you're on your own; nude means you're being watched). Artistically speaking, I was being a nude, but I was *pretending* to be naked – just a small point, but an important one.

'Which bit are you up to?' he asked, nonchalantly.

In anticipation of this, I was ready to turn to Letter 81, where the Marquise de Merteuil tells her lover, the Vicomte de Valmont, exactly what she thinks of him – which, in English, is as follows:

Do you have anything that you've actually earned on merit? You're handsome but that's just a matter of luck. You're charming company but then you've spent a lot of time idling in charmed circles. You've got a quick wit, but one can hardly overlook your terrible weakness for silly jokes. Your bold self-confidence is most commendable – but then everything's always come easily to you, hasn't it? That, if I'm not mistaken, is the sum total of your assets.

'Not that bit,' said Jamie, between kisses, 'read the bit where he seduces the convent girl, whatsername.'

'Not the bit when he pursues a happily married woman until she succumbs to his charms and he ravishes her on the tapestried ottoman, despite her protests?'

'I haven't got a tapestried ottoman.'

'There's the sofa.'

'Read the bit I said.'

'Oh, all right. About Cécile.'

'You just read, Rose. Ignore me.'

That exciting, insides-flipping-over feeling. 'I just happen to know,' I said faintly, 'that the relevant letter is number 96.' Quite a long letter too, so I just read the good bits and did my best to concentrate.

Poor Cécile! Never stood a chance! Valmont knew what he was doing – all that stuff about not applying any more force than could be resisted. I tried to find Cécile's own account of the experience, flicked uselessly through the pages, missed it, backtracked, gave up.

'Why have you stopped?' he asked.

'I've lost my place,' I panted.

'Talk to me, then.'

I made a real effort to speak: 'Not long after this novel was written . . .' gasp . . . 'there was the French Revolution.'

He laughed. 'You are lovely, you know.'

'And lots of French aristocrats . . .'

'What about them?'

'French aristocrat refugees came to Edinburgh and they lived around Holyrood Park.'

'A whole sentence!'

'One of them may even have brought this book – maybe even my copy and . . .' moan, sigh, 'and . . . it was very scandalous at the time, banned everywhere and . . . Oh!'

My ex-boyfriends had bored me frigid – which at the time I had found quite acceptable. I used to ask myself: what is lust anyway? It was one of those words I had been meaning to research. I even went to the library to look it up. Could lust have its origins in a past tense irregular form of the fourteenth-century verb 'luse', conjugated like the modern 'lose' and 'lost'? What about 'list'? Cross-reference with 'list' in Thomas Wyatt sonnet, 'Whoso list to hunt?' NB: does he use it in that other love poem – the one about 'with naked foot stalking in my chamber . . .'?

He didn't have a tapestried ottoman but there was still the sofa. Some mutually reassuring kisses. Some urgent mutual desire. Passionate and breathless wriggling from me and passionate and breathless manoeuvring from him. He trailed my necklace across my mouth, gathering the beads up in his hand.

'But,' I panted, 'what if it snaps and I swallow the beads?'

'It won't,' he said, thickly.

'How do you know? How do you know it won't snap? All my necklaces snap.' (You can speak very clearly when you've got a string of beads between your teeth. Try it. Perfect elocution.) He groaned a bit and clutched me. 'Jamie, it's lasted through six volumes of *Fortunes of War*. It could easily go now.'

'It won't snap.'

'But . . .'

'It won't bloody snap!'

'It could! I could choke and die!'

He stopped, exasperated, and we both lay still, breathing heavily. 'Look, Rose, it just won't snap, okay? I got it strung on top-quality sea-fishing nylon.'

'What?'

'The kind you could use to haul in a shark.'

'Honestly?'

'So it just won't snap. Happy?'

'Did you really get it strung on top-quality sea-fishing nylon?'

'Yes.'

'Really?'

'Yes!'

'But what did the jeweller say when you produced a reel of fishing line?'

'Rose! Do you expect me to ravish you if you keep asking me questions like this? Do you? Say "No"! Say it!'

'No!'

'Say it again!'

'No, no, no!'

Note for the curious: top-quality sea-fishing nylon, available at £5.80 a spool from John Dickson & Son Ltd., Frederick Street, Edinburgh. Technically it has a breaking strength of thirty pounds, but because of the reduced force of gravity in water you could land a much bigger shark than that.

On land, you could recommend a jeweller use it to string a special necklace. Make sure you ask the jeweller to string the beads on the fishing line, tie a proper reef knot and then take a match to it, melting the nylon, so that it is securely sealed. The only disadvantage of nylon is that after years and years of exposure to sunlight, it will start to deteriorate. So keep it for the dark.

Chapter 20

I prepared very carefully for Bio-Caledonian's launch party. I made a special appointment with John, my hairdresser. I told him I wanted him to sweep my hair up very firmly and anchor down the corkscrew curls. He wanted to allow a few to escape, but I refused. I told him I was going to a very tense social function and I had to look poised and elegant, refined and serene. No one must suspect that I was the ex-mistress of the corporate sponsor. John was unfazed. He asked about my outfit and suggested that if I added a cream silk stole to cover my bare arms I could easily do demure. In the end, I looked so above suspicion I could have done lunch with Caesar's wife.

I had secretly hoped Alastair would not want to go to Bio-Caledonian's launch party. He had an important statement to check for errors; it was called 'Rebranding Scotland' and it was keeping him very busy. When I mentioned that Helen had invited us to Bio-Caledonian's launch party he said he might as well come because it counted as relevant work. He asked who else would be there: 'What about that ex-boyfriend of yours?' I admitted that, yes, Jamie Cameron was a major shareholder and he was going to be there too. Armed with this information, Alastair treated the whole thing with deadly seriousness. It became less like a party and more like a raid behind enemy lines.

We arrived at the Caledonian Hotel rather late. 'Now, listen,' said Alastair, taking charge. 'Are you listening, Rose? This is the plan: we go up the steps, straight ahead, main reception room, duck the flower arrangements. Stick by me. We're out of here in half an hour.'

I smoothed my favourite pink silk dress and felt guilty. 'I should have worn something else,' I said.

'You look fine. Okay, this is it, this is the room . . . What the hell is that?'

'It's the Braveheart Potato.'

There was a fifteen-foot-high model standing centre-stage. It wore a kilt and a tartan bonnet. There was a carefully drawn expression of pride in its potato eyes and a giant spear-like chip stood at its side. 'They're not really that big,' I told Alastair. 'The ones on the tables are actual size.' Each place setting was adorned with a mini Braveheart Potato, complete with kilt and bonnet.

'This is terrible,' he muttered. 'We desperately need that rebranding statement.'

'What rebranding statement?' said a voice. We turned to find an attractive young woman holding a glass of champagne. She introduced herself: 'I'm Emma Smith, marketing consultant.'

'You're not responsible for this, are you?' asked Alastair, rudely.

'No, but Helen Budleigh has asked for my opinion on the launch.'

Alastair seized his chance to talk about work. 'What do you think this tells people about Scotland's image? This is sending out some very regressive messages.'

'Scot Burger are delighted with the branding. Personally, I wouldn't have chosen to have a giant potato as the centrepiece of a launch, but Scot Burger's vice president for Europe was very keen on the idea.'

'I don't think you understand what's being promoted here!' blustered Alastair.

'Shall I explain it to you?' she said sweetly, and Alastair was temporarily silenced.

I excused myself. 'There's Helen, I'll go and tell her we're here.' (It was easy to follow her progress by all the heads turning as she sashayed through the crowd.)

'Rose!' she said, hugging me. 'I'm so pleased you're here! What do you think? Do you think it's going well? People seem to be enjoying themselves, don't they?'

'It's going very well.'

'There will be dancing later on. Can you stay?'

'I don't think so – I'll see.'

'You'll be wanting to see Jamie, won't you?'

'No, no, not particularly,' I said, pretending I hadn't been looking out for him from the moment I arrived. I was worried I might find myself being cornered and checkmated and finished off completely.

'He's over there.' She pointed to the far side of the room, where Jamie stood surrounded by a crowd of people drinking champagne and eating chips. 'Have you met Consuela yet?'

'No.'

'Don't be surprised that she looks a bit like you,' said Helen, guiding me along. 'He must go for a particular type. But you're the original, aren't you, Rose?'

'I don't want to meet her.'

But it was too late; before I knew it, I was face to face with Jamie's wife.

She didn't look anything like me. She didn't look anything like me apart from the eyes, but then brown's a pretty common colour and we were at eye-level so I couldn't help noticing. Her hair tumbled in dark curls about her face, and at her throat was an expensively demure diamond cross. 'Holà,' she said. I turned, panic-stricken, to Helen but she had gone.

'Holà,' I replied.

'Hamey, who is this?' she asked. I realised, shocked, that Hamey was standing right behind me.

'This is Rose,' he said, tightly, like a man trying to keep a grip. 'Rose, this is Consuela.'

Consuela smiled a row of pearly teeth and leaned forward to kiss me on each cheek. Her skin was petal-soft and her scent a waft of something sensuous and delicious. 'So pleased to meet you, Rose.' She was smiling at me in an oddly conspiratorial sort of way and then she started to laugh. For one so apparently demure, she had quite a dirty laugh. 'We must talk,' she said. 'You and I.'

Alastair came hurrying up to us. 'Sorry, everyone, we have to go.' He took my arm and pulled me away. 'I've had an urgent call, Rose. We've got to get back. Right now. Come on.'

I just had time to say, 'Sorry,' and that was all.

'We have to get back,' he said, hurrying me down the steps to the hotel lobby. 'There's an urgent press release I have to attend to.'

Helen came running after us. 'Rose doesn't have to go too, does she, Alastair? Can't you stay for dinner, Rose? You're sitting beside me. That lovely Emma Smith is on our table. You've met her, haven't you?'

'Who else is going to be there?' asked Alastair. 'Anyone else Rose has met before?'

Helen reeled off a list of names, none of which I recognised. 'Rose doesn't have to go home with you right now, does she, Alastair?'

'What do you want to do, Rose?' he sulked.

'At least stay for dinner, Rose. Please.'

I looked at Alastair's jealous face and felt resentful. 'I'll stay for dinner.'

'All right,' he snapped. 'I'll come back and pick you up at nine-thirty.'

All through dinner, I kept looking over to the other side of the room where Jamie was sitting with Consuela. Sometimes she patted his arm in a consolatory kind of way. Once, she kissed his cheek.

'Don't you want your chocolate mousse?' asked Helen, tucking in. 'I thought it was your favourite. Can I have it, then?'

'Help yourself.' I suppose the food was good, but my jealousy felt like chronic indigestion and I couldn't eat a thing. I think Helen realised I wasn't good company for her guests because when the coffee was served she suggested I take it to that quiet little sitting room down the hall where I could read my book and wait for Alastair. She promised she would come and tell me when he arrived.

Gratefully, I picked up my coffee and escaped. The sitting room was empty. I hid myself away in a corner and got the book out of my bag. Around me was the muffled noise of the hotel; doors opening and closing, crockery rattling on its way back to the kitchens.

I was reading when Jamie appeared.

He sat two feet away on the sofa and waited for me to notice he was there. 'How are you, Rose?' he said. I opened my mouth to reply, but he rushed on: 'She's got her Spanish passport and she's buying a flat in Barcelona with her money from the divorce.'

'I see.'

'It all went through very quickly – something to do with living separate lives for five years.'

'Where is she staying tonight?'

'Tonight?' He shut his eyes with something like despair. 'Tonight, she will be staying at my house.'

'In the spare room?'

'I've got more than one. She likes the top floor best. There's a whole flat up there.'

'Is there a fire extinguisher?'

'A what?'

'A fire extinguisher. I think you should get one. What if there was a fire? What if there was a big fire and you rushed into the burning building and out on to the roof where she was standing behind the parapet with her black hair streaming against the flames?' He stared at me. 'You could get hurt. You could be crushed under the staircase as it collapsed when you tried to escape after she'd jumped and you could lose an eye and be blinded in the other one and have your left hand so mutilated it has to be amputated.'

He reached across and turned my book over. 'Rose, why not take a rest from Charlotte Brontë?'

He said he was selling up and going away. Irina had returned, only to opt for a high-risk personal pension plan.

'Where will you go?'

'I don't know. I'll travel about for a while. I'd like to go somewhere fairly remote, somewhere without many people.'

'It was quite busy in the Nevada Desert.'

'Just before you left,' he said, 'I tried to speak to you. I went round to your sisters' flat but you weren't there. I left you something, with a letter. Helen returned it; she said you never looked at it.'

'I didn't need to. I knew what it would say: "Improved job offer: bigger mews house, grand piano, bathroom with minibar, credit card with double air miles." Am I close?'

'It said something along the lines of: "Can't live without you, please come back, any terms acceptable."'

'Was there a Welcome Back Reward too?'

'There was, as a matter of fact.'

'What was it? Expensive earrings? Cheap sweets? I miss the soor plums.'

'It wasn't as big as a soor plum.'

'Was it as big as a pineapple cube? If it was smaller than a midget gem, I'm not interested.'

'Kind of in-between.'

'What flavour?'

'Turkish delight. Rose-pink diamond flavour.'

'Oh!'

'It's okay, they took it back.'

For a minute, we were both quiet. 'You didn't take the fifteen thousand back, though, did you?' I said in a low voice.

'At casino exchange rates, I suppose that must have been worth about twenty-four thousand dollars. Tell me the story – I've only heard rumours. How much did you bet at roulette?'

'Eight thousand – on one throw.'

'Honestly?'

'Yes, and I lost, so I bet sixteen thousand on the next throw.'

'Did you really, truly do that?' I nodded. 'So you won five hundred and sixty thousand dollars on one throw of the dice?'

'How do you know your thirty-five times table?'

'And then you lost it all at craps. Is that right?'

'Do you want to know – really, honestly, truly?'

'Yes.'

'I lost four hundred and ninety-six thousand, then won back forty – I was beginning to get the hang of it and then I started thinking how every chip was really money and I stopped playing. But I did come home with enough to pay off my flexi-loan and I've got the change in my Nat West Scottish Widowed No Worries Account. I'm saving for a special occasion.'

'So you'll have about sixty-five thousand pounds.'

'You're very quick at converting from dollars. What's my overall percentage increase on fifteen thousand?'

'Four hundred and thirty-three per cent. How many hours did it take you?'

'Nine till midnight. How much did I make an hour?'

'Getting on for twenty-seven thousand dollars.'

'Incredible, isn't it? But it was just luck.'

'Well done, Rose. Better than Scot Burger rates.' He picked up my book. 'So Jane comes into money.'

'I'm a few chapters further on from that bit now. She's about to live happily ever after.'

'Well, good for her.' He put the book down. 'It's not really a happy ending, though, is it? Not for him, anyway. He doesn't make much of a recovery.' Then he said quietly, 'Are you happily married, Rose?'

'Yes. Marriage is very different from a short affair. Marriage is a serious thing.' I tapped my coffee spoon on the rim of the china cup. Rap, tap, tap.

'Good,' he said, taking the cup and saucer and putting them on the table. 'So he's the perfect husband.'

'I can trust him absolutely.'

'That's important.'

I started on a bit of linen napkin-folding. Fold, crease, fold, crease. 'We trust each other. I can count on him.'

'Husband material, then. Very reliable.'

'Yes.'

'Not for dallying with.'

'Not at all. Fidelity is very important.' I turned the fanned, fluted napkin inside out. 'And love.'

'Good, because I'd hate to think of you as being cynical.'

'I'm not cynical!'

'Love and cynicism don't mix. And when the person you love goes and marries somebody else, you feel all hope is gone, and I suppose that's the point at which cynicism sets in.'

He stood up for a well-calculated exit.

'I'm not cynical,' I said, desperately. 'I'm not. I wouldn't do a cynical thing like you did – sending me a chess set as a wedding present!'

'What chess set?'

'The one you keep in the drawing room.'

'It's still there, Rose.'

'I sent it back.'

'What are you talking about?'

'Here's the card – look,' and I pulled the card from the pages of *Jane Eyre*. 'Keep it. I don't need it any more.'

He looked at it for a long time, and when he spoke his voice was sad. 'When she heard you'd got married, Consuela was pleased for you. She said it was a very pragmatic choice and you could be sisters under-the-skin. I think the chess set was supposed to be a joke. She probably thought it would make you laugh.' He put the card in his pocket. 'I sent you nothing.'

He gave me one last, searching look, and left me alone with my book and my linen napkin origami.

When I got back to the party, the dancing was well underway. Helen had forgotten to let me know Alastair had returned and I had been too busy reading the end of *Jane Eyre* to notice the time. I felt guilty when I saw him stride impatiently across the dance floor to reach me. When he was almost upon me, a breathless woman stopped him and declared, 'I claim you for the Duke of Atholl!' This turned out to be a dance rather than some archaic feudal due (in Scotland, both might have been possible). She bore him off and so delayed his interrogation of me.

Near me, Consuela was holding a small audience rapt with an account of her experience of Cuban physiotherapy. 'I just had to be a patient,' she said. 'It take years. But is good now because I have a freedom of movement. It take a few squeezes and some arm-twisting, but I go everywhere now without a problem.'

Her broken English belied the subtlety of her argument. She was obviously good at the art of manipulation. It was easy to see where the attraction lay. I don't suppose it was her grasp of the English language that had interested him. Jamie joined her, whispered something in her ear, drew her away from the crowd. She listened, with a show of coquettish protestation. '*Lo siento*,' she pouted. 'I'm sorry.' She shrugged her shoulders. I concentrated on maintaining an expression of serene composure. There is an art to this kind of thing and I was now almost as cool as the Marquise de Merteuil. (In Letter 81, she explains how to get the hang of it.) It's just practice. I had been practising for weeks, digging my nails into the palms of my hands while still engaging my husband in conversation about Arsenal's mid-season form.

It was clear Jamie wasn't going to meet my eyes for any longer than the socially acceptable half-second. He must have deliberately decided against it because there was the opportunity for an electrifying oeillade. I wanted to look into the blue eyes I had turned away from in my dreams. My heart ached for my old love. I took a step towards him, but retreated when my husband walked through the crowd to claim me.

The Bio-Caledonian share flotation was spectacularly successful. Over the space of a week, the share price soared. Scot Burger's chip production time was halved because of the potato's cuboid shape and the company announced plans to expand the use of Bio-Caledonian's product in their outlets all over the world. *The Scotsman* and *The Herald* carried articles on the booming bio-science industry in Scotland. There had already been Dolly the Sheep and the trans-species cloning of Brian the Hedge-Hamster, but the Braveheart Potato was the first vegetable to capture the public imagination.

The industry itself hailed the marketing of the potato as a breakthrough in customer relations. In the past, bio-technology companies had foundered when presenting their product to the public. It was the image of 'Frankenstein food' that put people off. The market researchers at Bio-Caledonian, however, had planned their campaign very carefully.

It was interesting to read in the newspaper the results of a survey I had worked on last summer. It began with the question: 'Have you ever met anyone who didn't like chips?' I remembered that nobody had. The Bio-Caledonian researchers had worked on the theory that chips were all about satisfying the need for a cheap feed, with associations of pleasure, comfort and familiarity. No one could imagine the cheerful chip clutched in the hand of Dr Frankenstein.

Helen's five per cent Bio-Cal share-holding was soon worth a great deal more than she had ever thought possible. Jamie's fifty per cent was probably not worth more than he ever thought possible, but it was still enough to impress him. He told Helen he thought the share price still had some way to go before it peaked. He had heard that Scot Burger was about to announce the acquisition of a huge chain of fast-food restaurants in the United States, so he waited, on tenterhooks, for the right moment to sell.

Bio-technology share prices are among the most volatile on the market. It is possible to make a fortune and it's even easier to lose it. When the chip hits the pan, anyone can get burnt.

Chapter 21

Christmas came and went. Hogmanay, too. I hated January – all those resolutions and long nights and the freezing weather. I sat at my desk, stared out of the window and did nothing, overwhelmed by apathy. There is a golden rule for endgames which is simply: 'Don't give up'. Even the most appalling situations can be turned to your advantage. I tried to remember this golden rule but it was hard. I seemed to have lost hope.

'How are you, Rose?' asked my mother. 'Not still on Flaubert, I hope.'

'No.'

'Re-reading *Jane Eyre*?'

'I'm taking a rest from Charlotte Brontë. It's existentialism that interests me at the moment, and the Absurdists.'

'I'm coming to see you.'

'There's no reason why you should. I'm all right.'

'I'll be on twenty-four-hour stand-by. I expect you to ring me every night.'

'Mum . . . ' I hesitated. 'Mum, does love make cynicism impossible?'

'No.'

'Does cynicism make love impossible?'

'No.'

'I thought you didn't do short answers.'

'I'm late for bridge.'

'If you feel that all hope is gone, is that the point at which cynicism sets in?'

Irritated sigh. 'I think you're having difficulty making the leap from Romanticism to Post-Modernism, darling.'

'What if it's all hopeless, Mum? What about the really important questions? I mean, is it all pointless or is there a Great Big Point out there?'

My mother tapped her fingernails against the phone. 'I'm partnering a theoretical physicist this evening. He's working on a Theory of Everything, so I'll let you know.'

'Mum, what should I do?'

'Have you heard from Mackenzie yet?'

'No, he's still in Shetland. Don't tell me to work hard at my research and write up another piece for him. I can't face it.'

'Then eat, drink, sleep and go for brisk walks in Holyrood Park.'

'Is that all?'

'Mozart can have a balancing effect, but don't play the "Requiem" and avoid *Don Giovanni*. Take care, Rose.'

Through the haze of smoke, I saw my face looking pale in the mirrors at the Café Royal. It was the only place I had wanted to go. 'Fidelity, love, friendship,' Alastair said, kindly. 'Just being together – all more important, so don't worry about it.' (Fidelity is always top of his list.) 'I'm not worried if you don't want to do it any more. You'll get over it.'

I ate my ready-opened safety oysters without that much enthusiasm.

'What are you thinking about?' he asked.

'Nothing.' I looked at the tablecloth. It was spotlessly white.

'Tell me the truth, Rose. You owe me that much.'

And he was right, I did feel indebted. Would he release me from my debt?

'You have to tell me the truth,' he repeated, anxiously.

'I don't know what you mean.'

And there was only his silence and my desperation.

My sister, Catherine, knew that I was not at all myself. She rang me up, made a rude joke about power showers and I didn't laugh. Instead I said primly: 'That's a bit vulgar, Catherine,' so she got Helen to ring me up as well (double test). Helen's joke about vacuum cleaner attachments was truly ribald and I told her so (prudishly): 'Actually, I find that rather offensive, Helen.'

My sisters arrived to cheer me up. They announced that we were going out. Alastair was very good about it. 'Have a nice evening,' he said. 'Have you got your mobile with you, Rose? Make sure you ring me. I'll wait up for you. What time will you be back?'

'She doesn't know!' chimed my sisters.

'Can you be back by ten?'

Eventually, Alastair decided to stay at a friend's place so he wouldn't be disturbed when we came home late. I promised to ring him at ten o'clock to say good night.

My sisters took me out, got me drunk and told me about their boyfriends. They didn't mind when I kept crying for no apparent reason. Helen was taking a sabbatical from Bio-Caledonian and was now freelancing at the Soil Association. She said there were some lovely male bio-scientists there and she was spoilt for choice. 'How's marriage?' she asked.

'It's great,' I said on autopilot, wiping my eyes.

'How's your latest experiment, Helen?' asked Catherine.

'Better than my control.'

'Rose, you used to have an opponent, didn't you – or was he just a player?' I stared at the floor, thinking of Jamie. 'And as far as I can gather,' Catherine breezed on, 'Rose and her opponent had some sort of a game going on . . . which, though quite bizarre to me, was very agreeable to both of them. It's all right, Rose, we all have our different preferences.'

'How's Robert, the accomplice?' I asked.

'Accomplished.'

'Why not have a lover?' I said out loud.

Catherine and Helen spent quite a lot of time in quite a lot of bars trying to get me to say why I was feeling so sad, especially when I claimed to be happy. I managed to hold them off until ten o'clock when I made my call to Alastair. After that I drank too much too fast and they decided we had better go home early after all.

Back at the flat, surrounded by dreary domestic familiarity, I broke down and cried. 'I don't understand it,' I wept. 'I suppose it's a kind of depression brought on by achieving your dream, like an Olympic athlete who finally wins the gold medal. Just wants to go home and weep. What else is there left to live for?'

Catherine, however, remembered the lingerie at my old home and was crafty enough and curious enough to ask to borrow a pair of tights, saying hers were laddered. She rifled through my new collection of winceyette winter warmers and saw immediately how psychologically revealing it was. My underwear spoke volumes. She kept quiet about it and accepted a pair of ninety denier, but she knew. She knew. Lingerie is such an interesting word. I had thought its origins were from the Latin, 'lingere', but I found out when I got married that it comes from the French word, 'linge', meaning linen. Rather boringly domestic.

'I had the most wonderful, romantic summer last year,' said Helen. 'And I don't regret any of my field experiments.'

'But what about the midges?' asked Catherine.

'They don't come anywhere near a field of my potatoes.' Helen looked thoughtful – the finger in the mouth, head on one side, gazing into the middle distance, dumb-blonde look. Then: 'Perhaps the cellular modification that resists aphid attack also repels the Scottish midge. How interesting!'

278

'You'll have to do a few more field experiments to make sure.'

'At the first ray of sunshine, I'll be out there. Don't you get tired of staring at a computer screen all day, Catherine?'

'Not if there's something interesting on it, like Rose's bank account last year. Rose, do you have any idea how much you spent on lingerie? I'll give you a clue: the handmade couture bra you bought on a trip to Paris cost more than you earned in a whole month of tele-sales.'

'Did it?' I said, not looking up.

'Yes. It's the one I tried on when I called in to see you. That's why I came round.'

'How much did he actually give you, Rose?' asked Helen. 'What was it a month?'

'I don't know,' I said, trying to sound casual. 'I never worked it out.'

'I did,' said Catherine.

'Don't tell me!' I cried, sitting up. 'I don't want to know.'

'Then tell us about him instead,' said Catherine, archly.

Despite my whisky, Catherine was suddenly sober. How did she manage that sobriety thing? She could always out-do me. So crafty! I suppose bluffing a winning hand at the end of seven hours of illegal poker must demand a certain *froideur*. It was always hard to tell with her whether she ever meant anything she said, or if she was just trying to get you to disclose something interesting. 'Have you always had this thing about sex and chess?' she asked.

'Only in my dreams.'

'Rather limits one's choice of future partner.'

'You must have been very compatible,' said Helen, kindly. 'Very lucky to find someone kinky in the same way as you.'

'It's not at all kinky!'

'Yes, it is.'

'No, it isn't,' I said, indignantly. 'Any normal, healthy adult chess player will experience some sort of sexual interlude in their chess life. It can take weeks to finish a game. Especially if it's

279

a correspondence one. There can be very long gaps between moves and . . .'

'Do you miss him?' she asked. 'Only, I keep asking you and you won't say.'

My sisters waited. That exciting hiatus in a conversation when everyone takes a collective sip of anticipation.

'I can't explain the way I feel,' I said sadly.

'Can you explain the way you fellate?' giggled Helen. 'I believe the word comes from the Latin verb to suck. Fellatio is a classical reference, isn't it, Rose?'

'It's slang. The Romans didn't do fellatio.'

'They must have done. All those orgies.'

'They just didn't call it that.'

'What about it, then?'

I took my chance to retreat into etymology. 'There's a line in Virgil that I can loosely misquote as "Euphoria led me into error". The verb is "fallit", a past participle of "fallere", which means to lie or betray. It sounds very much like "fellat", which *is* what the Romans did. The line in Virgil is a double entendre. Anyway, the Victorians invented the word "fellatio".'

'I'm not really interested in the etymology,' said Helen. 'I was kind of hoping you might tell us something about—'

'The pronunciation?' I began, in an academic tone of voice, 'Traditionally, in Latin, letters are enunciated: "tio" with a hard "t", as in "Tio Pepe", and not a soft "sho" as in "Alas, Horatio, I knew him". But in sung Latin softer pronunciations are preferred: "dulce" is "dul-chay" rather then "dul-kay". So if you did Latin but also sang in a choir then your pronunciation may vary.'

'That's not what I meant,' said Helen, disappointed.

'Tell us about the lying part, Rose,' said Catherine, pouring herself another whisky. 'The betrayal bit.'

'It may have originated in the Greek word for "deceiver".'

'Deceiver?' said Catherine.

'Deceiver. Ah yes, deceiver!' I got to my feet, agitated. I think

I was experiencing a form of etymological La Tourette Syndrome – the urge to shout out the *origins* of sexual slang. 'It's from the Greek. It's in Virgil! He deceived me! He lied to me!'

'Never mind, Rose,' said Catherine smoothly. 'You've got Alastair now, haven't you? Lucky old you.'

'Yes,' I said, on autopilot again. 'It's a marriage based on friendship and respect. We're loyal companions, the best of friends and I'm very happy.'

'Liar,' said Catherine, quietly.

'You're not happy at all,' said Helen. 'Are you?'

I couldn't speak.

Catherine got up from her chair and put her arms around me. 'Oh Rose,' she said, sounding surprisingly emotional. 'You're still in love with Jamie, and it isn't fair to Alastair to pretend that you're not.'

'You miss Jamie, don't you?' said Helen.

'You still love him, don't you?'

'Yes,' I whispered. 'Yes.'

Terrible collapse into sobbing.

Imagine *The Three Graces* in their going-out clothes, with The Middle One in despair, clinging to her sisters, all holding handkerchiefs instead of roses.

'I'm different from Alastair,' I sobbed, 'and he's different from me.' Tears and wails. 'We're married! Oh God, how can we ever work it out?'

Catherine dried my tears. 'I don't know,' said the cleverest girl in the world. 'Ask me a different question.'

'What should I do?'

'Leave him.'

Chapter 22

'When are you going to call Jamie?' asked Helen as soon as I had stopped crying.

'I don't know,' I sniffed.

'Call him now,' she urged.

'It can wait,' said Catherine, sensibly. 'Let Rose take her time. She's got to talk to Alastair first.' She turned to me. 'I'm going to have to go home. I've got work to do for a conference call first thing in the morning.'

'But it's the weekend.'

'This is important. They're phoning me from Sydney.' She hugged me. 'I wish I hadn't been so horrible to you when you rang to say you were married. It's been on my conscience. Sometimes I wonder how things might have turned out if I'd only been a little more sympathetic.' Her voice had a faint tremble in it, but when she stepped away from me a second later she had recovered her perfect self-control. 'Don't do anything hasty,' she warned. 'Give yourself time. Think about what you want to say and the best way to say it.'

When Catherine had left, Helen and I looked at each other with complicit understanding. We had a whole history of not doing what our big sister had told us. 'Ring him now,' said Helen.

Chess players tend to make impulsive moves when victory is just within grasp. It's all too easy to make a serious misjudgement which can cost you the match. It often happens at the end of a demanding game when you're desperate to checkmate your opponent so you can get on with playing something else instead. This tendency towards impulsiveness in the endgame was a weakness I knew I shared with Jamie. Our games had often ended chaotically. I knew that, and so I tried to be cautious, despite my anxious excitement.

'But what should I say to him?'

'Just tell him you'd like to see him again.'

'What if he says no?'

'He won't say no.'

'What if he does?'

'He won't,' she said confidently. 'I bet he won't say no.'

'But what about Alastair?'

'He's not here. Don't worry about him.'

'But I feel so guilty.'

'Why? It's Jamie you love, isn't it? Not Alastair.'

My stomach twisted in a terrible pang of guilt. 'Alastair hasn't done anything wrong, has he? What has he done to deserve this?'

'Let's not go through all that again,' said Helen, impatiently.

'I'm not sure about this, Helen.'

'You're only going to ring him up.'

'It's half past midnight.'

'He won't mind. He'll be up working; he's always working. And I'm sure he'd love to hear from you. He was saying to me just the other day how he'd love to hear your voice again.'

Was he?'

'Yes. Tell him you'd like to meet him,' she urged. 'Say you have to talk to him. If you wait until tomorrow, you might lose your nerve. Ring him up now.'

I felt panicked. 'I'm not ringing him up while you're here listening.'

'I'll go in the other room.'

'No.'

'What then?'

'I can't do it.'

'You have to,' said Helen. 'He loves you.'

'How do you know?' I asked, anxiously. 'How do you know?'

'Because,' said Helen, getting desperate. 'Because he told me.'

'Did he?'

'Yes. Tell him you want to meet him as soon as possible. He may be surprised at first – after all, you're the love of his life and you left him. How do you think he felt when you went off and married Alastair?'

I folded my arms and tried to hold myself together. 'Oh, Helen, what a mess!'

'You married somebody else but Jamie can't help being in love with you – any more than you can help being in love with him.' Helen started walking me over to the telephone in the hall. 'It's not too late to put things right, but you have to call him now.' I looked at her imploringly. 'Will you do it if I leave?' she asked.

'Yes.'

Instantly, she picked up the phone and dialled his number. 'Just say: "It's Rose, can I see you?"' Helen pressed the receiver into my hand, walked swiftly down the hall and the door clicked shut behind her. I heard her quiet, retreating steps down the stone stair.

'Hello?' said Jamie's voice.

'It's Rose.'

'Rose,' he asked, concerned. 'Are you all right?'

'Can I see you? Can I come and see you now?'

'All right. I'll be waiting for you.'

By three o'clock in the morning, I was shivering in a call box on

Marchmont Road, ringing the Samaritans. I apologised for being a bother and said I wouldn't keep them long.

'It's no bother,' said the Samaritan, 'take your time.'

'I expect there's a lot of people phoning in at the moment, what with the awful weather and the long, dark nights and everything.'

'Do you want to tell me your name?'

'Do I have to?'

'No, but . . .'

'Rose, it's Rose.'

'Would you like to talk, Rose?'

The tears were pouring down my face; the handset in the call box on Marchmont Road was wet with them. 'I married my husband and I shouldn't have done. I'm in love with someone else.' The tears ran all the way down my arm and soaked my sleeve.

'You can talk to me,' said the voice.

'I rang him up and said I had to speak to him. And when we met . . . I'm so embarrassed now . . . I went round to his house and when he opened the door I was so pleased to see him and just threw my arms around him and said how much I had missed him and how I wanted to be with him again and I just wanted to kiss him and . . .' My tears choked me. 'But he moved my arms away and he said: "Why did you marry Alastair?"'

Minutes of me trying to speak, and failing.

'I'm still here. Just talk when you can.'

'And I told him I wasn't really responsible for my actions when I got married. I tried to explain that it had been a strange situation, that I had had too much to drink and I'd got carried away by the complimentary cocktails and the hotel's wedding package. I was married by an Elvis Presley impersonator. In a swimming pool. And Jamie said he could forgive me just about anything – even a drunken, spontaneous Las Vegas marriage – but what he couldn't forgive was . . . was . . . He said, "Rose, you live with him! You are living with him as his wife!"'

My breath came in great, drowning gulps and I clung to the handset.

'And he said, "Did you honestly think we could just pick up from where we left off? Did you think that all you had to do was ask? Did you think I'd say yes?" He said he had tried to come to terms with the fact that I'd left him, that I didn't love him, didn't want him, didn't need him any more. He said he wished things had been different and he knew he should have done things differently himself. He should have told me about Consuela much sooner. He said he hadn't handled that very well – very badly, in fact. But he said, "Rose, what am I supposed to do? Here you are, you just turn up on the doorstep in the middle of the night, with no apologies, no explanation – just some grand romantic gesture like, 'Take me back!'".'

And I couldn't breathe for crying.

'I'm here. Talk when you can.'

'When I left him . . . he was devastated . . . and now . . .'

'I'm listening. I'm here.'

'And now, he said, "The truth is, Rose, you're married to somebody else!" And, "Oh God, Rose! What can I do? What can I say to you?"'

Minutes passed.

'He doesn't want me back. He doesn't want me back.'

The Samaritan listened to me breaking my heart for the next twenty minutes. 'I could never do your job,' I wept, 'and it's voluntary, isn't it? You're so good to do your job. How do you stand it?'

'Oh, it's not a matter of having to stand it.'

'I could never do what you do.'

'I'm here if you want to talk some more.'

'I think I'll stop now. Exhausted. I'll get off the line. There must be a lot of other people trying to get through. I'll make a donation. Maybe I should set up a direct debit. Thank you, thank you.'

'Ring back if you like. There'll always be someone here.'

Chapter 23

For the serious player, chess is about mental stamina and psychological endurance. The implacable relentlessness of the game means it's not unusual, sometimes, to think you're going a bit mad.

I walked through my days in a trance. Ordinary tasks seemed impossibly difficult. I couldn't sleep for thinking of different scenarios, different possibilities – maybe I should do this, if only I hadn't done that. There was a lot of self-accusation and guilt and anxiety. I was in love with Jamie, but Jamie didn't want me; Alastair did, but I didn't want him. And that, I recognised, was the whole guilty truth.

When I told my sisters about my disastrous meeting with Jamie, they reacted by arguing with each other. Catherine said it was all Helen's fault. Helen defended herself by saying Jamie had overreacted and it would all have been fine if only I had made it clear to him that I was leaving Alastair. But I hadn't told Jamie that. I felt I owed Alastair at least the courtesy of telling him first. So far, I had failed to summon up the courage to tell him anything at all. I didn't know how to tell him and I didn't know what my move ought to be after that. Where would I go? What would I do?

Alastair watched while I turned into an agitated wreck of a woman who couldn't hold a conversation for more than five minutes and whose bad fidgeting habit had become a worrying obsession. He was alternately concerned and exasperated. 'What's the matter with you?' he asked for the umpteenth time.

'Nothing,' I said, appalled again at the way I lied to him.

'Tell me what's wrong.'

I had to tell him the truth. I had to. 'There's nothing wrong.'

'Please stop clutching your hands like that.'

'Sorry.' I started clearing the breakfast plates away and one dropped from my clumsy fingers. Another piece of our Habitat dinner service gone.

He watched me pick up the pieces. 'Are you not feeling well?' he asked.

'I'm fine, don't worry about me.'

He started putting piles of corrected documents into his brief-case. 'I have to leave for the office now or I'll be late.'

'Off you go, then. I'll see you tonight.'

'What are you doing today?' he asked.

'I'm going to wash the dishes, then go out for a walk.'

'Let me know when you get back. Ring me at the office. When do you think that'll be? Lunchtime?'

'Not sure.'

'Where are you walking to?'

'Just around town.'

'How long do you think you'll be?'

'Three hours, forty-five minutes.'

The best way to end an interrogation is always to give precise answers.

Off I went, shopping. But I didn't know where I was any more. I practically sleep-walked my way round Jenner's, up and down the escalators, wringing my hands. I felt like Lady Macbeth having a different kind of dream: 'Oh, will these hands ne'er be kissed again?' It was better to be outside. Fresh air. On George Street, I passed Phillips the auctioneer's and there in the window was a very nice Hepplewhite four-poster bed and all I could think of was . . .

A cup of tea might do me good, I thought, so I went round the corner to Henderson's. Oh, I don't know what it is, but when you've decided on celibacy and the single life, you become obsessed with your libidinous memories. Not just gentle, soothing love-making either, but torrid, intoxicated, hot, sticky sex! I stood by the till with my pot of Darjeeling, only I was miles away, lying on the floor of a steamy bathroom, getting hotter and stickier. I heard myself say: 'I'll have a sticky bun, please – the one with the squidgy filling.' Why was it so difficult to be normal? I sat down at a quiet table for one, picked up the newspaper and those chess columns just set me off again.

The depths I plumbed.

When I got back to the flat, I was surprised to find Alastair's briefcase standing in the hall. He was there, waiting for me. 'Alastair?' I called. 'Haven't you been to the office?'

'Yes. I opened the mail and came straight back.'

I saw his tense, grey face and felt afraid.

'There's a letter here for you,' he said, holding out a sheet of paper. 'It was sent to McTavish's private office but got redirected to me, probably because it said Mrs Lennox on the envelope. I saw my surname and opened it by mistake. Here, read it.'

I took it from him. A single sheet of thick, white paper. I recognised the handwriting and the letter began to tremble with my hands. 'Dear Rose,' he had written. 'I said some hurtful things to you last night and I want you to know that I'm sorry. I've spent so many nights hoping you might just turn up on my doorstep, and so when you actually did – and asked if you could stay – I couldn't really believe it and . . .'

The words blurred before my eyes and I couldn't read the rest.

'Is this the *nothing* that you told me about earlier?' demanded

Alastair, snatching the letter back. I had never seen him so palely angry. 'You went to see your old boyfriend and he turned you down?'

'I'm sorry, I'm sorry,' I stammered. 'I wanted to tell you, but I didn't know how. I feel guilty about it. We married only a few months after I had broken up with Jamie and I should have explained certain things to you, but I didn't. When we married, I hadn't really got over that relationship. I thought I would be able to put it behind me and our marriage would have a chance to work but . . . but . . .'

'But what?' Alastair took one more look at the letter, then tore it up

'But I haven't been able to forget him. It's been on my conscience and . . .'

'Do you have a conscience, Rose?' he said, acidly. 'I don't think you do. I think you're a compulsive liar. I don't think you know the difference between right and wrong.'

All my words deserted me. All I could say, over and over again, was 'sorry'. 'I'm sorry, Alastair, I'm sorry. I wanted to make it work. I tried, I really did.'

'I thought you wanted to be with me,' he said, sounding anguished now. 'I thought you wanted to be married to me, but you don't. You probably never did.'

'I'm sorry,' I said, hopelessly.

'I've heard rumours about you and him,' he said, bitterly. 'But I ignored them. I tried to put them out of my mind.'

'What rumours?'

'At that stupid launch party. Consuela was talking about how her husband used to keep some girl. She said she knew who it was but she wasn't going to say because the girl had got married and her husband didn't know. You were the girl, weren't you, Rose? He gave you money, he set you up somewhere, visited you when he felt like it. He kept you like some kind of toy. It's true, isn't it?'

'I should have explained . . .'

'Is it true?' he asked, angrily.

'When we met, I was still upset about leaving him and . . .'

'Just tell me if it's fucking true, Rose! Did he keep you? Did he pay you money?'

'He didn't pay me exactly. I won it, playing chess. We were quite well-matched, but I just had the edge on him, you see. We played for money and I won so much that when he won it was easy to pay him back. And he gave me money to pay off my debts. The fifteen thousand I had in Las Vegas was actually his. It was a loan, only when I left him he wouldn't take it back. He said we owed each other nothing and . . . ' Alastair's expression darkened. 'I know you're upset, but . . . '

'Jesus Christ!' he shouted, and the shrapnel of his anger went flying through the air. 'It's not just you I'm angry at, Rose, it's the whole fucking thing!' He kicked a pile of my books across the floor, then crumpled into the armchair.

'I'll get my things and go,' I said, quietly.

'Yes. Go. Just go.'

I put some clothes in a bag and left my Las Vegas wedding ring by the side of the bed. When I let myself out, I felt a guilty mixture of grief and liberation.

Our marriage was never going to work. Helen, blue-eyed girl, said it wasn't all my fault. I had married on the rebound. While under the influence of the drug, I had married the placebo. Love is a blind trial.

Chapter 24

I went to see a flat advertised to let on St Stephen's Place. The owner showed me around. It was on the top floor and it was very small, just two rooms and a galley kitchen in the hallway that connected them. The bathroom was once a cupboard by the front door. If you got out a ladder and climbed up through a hatch in the kitchen ceiling there was a whole extra room up there, which you could use very comfortably as long as you were five foot two like the owner. The loft was lined with shelving; it would be perfect for all my books.

The north-facing room was damp, gloomy and empty, and I was advised to keep the door shut. The south-facing room had an open fire and was warm, bright and comfortable with a sofa, a table and a new brass bed. I offered her a month's deposit.

My sisters helped me move house. We carried all my books down the four flights of stairs from Alastair's flat and up the four flights of stairs to mine. The surge of energy I felt on leaving him subsided into exhaustion and I spent the next three days in bed, sleeping, reading and feeling fragile. I started *All Passion Spent*; I never actually got it finished though.

One of the first phone calls I had at my new home was from Professor Mackenzie. 'Your husband gave me your number,' he said, 'and your new address. I want to send you our offer of a permanent post at Dictionary House.' His words spoke volumes. I accepted his offer with gratitude.

The next day, I began working again. *The Mutability of Definition: Truth and the Challenge of True Meaning.* It was more philosophical in tone than anything I had written before – although 'rueful' might be a better word. And on my first day in my proper job, Mungo Mackenzie welcomed me warmly and congratulated me on my in-depth study of the Scottish political vernacular. He said it showed meticulous research, erudition and stylistic vigour. I was too relieved to be thrilled.

My parents were ecstatic. 'I knew you could do it!' said my mother.

'Well done, blossom,' said my Dad, proudly.

They arrived next day to visit me, to celebrate my new job and to see my new home. My mother brought a tiny bronze statue of a Hindu domestic goddess. 'Keep her near the fireplace,' she advised. 'It's auspicious.' My father brought his golf clubs so he could fit in a few rounds before he went home, and a miniature rose for my window box. The family party was complete when my sisters arrived. Helen brought me a soft red cover to throw over the bed and Catherine's house-warming present was a very generous case of wine. 'It was a present from a grateful client,' she explained. 'I organised a special kind of encryption for all his international banking transactions. It was a very tricky commission.'

It was only after we had drunk two bottles of burgundy that Alastair's name was finally mentioned. It was as if there existed a collective family guilt about him.

'He'll be all right,' said my Dad, examining the bottle label closely. 'He's a stoical type. He'll be upset, of course, but he'll survive.'

'Do you think I should have stayed with him?'

293

'Not if you were sure it wasn't going to work.'

'I did the wrong thing in marrying him, though, didn't I? So it's my fault, isn't it?'

'He married in haste, too, Rose. You're not solely to blame.'

'Rose feels bad because she thinks Alastair really did love her,' said Helen.

I winced.

'Are you going to get divorced?' asked my mother.

'He's divorcing me,' I said, bracing myself for the next question.

No one said anything.

After a few weeks, I got into a comforting kind of routine – spending my days at Dictionary House engrossed in my work and my evenings at home, propped up in bed with the fire on, reading. But the comforting routine didn't last long because my sisters took it upon themselves to resuscitate my social life. I met up with people I hadn't seen for ages. I went for pizzas with friends, tried new drinks in new bars and generally made an effort, but always there was this heavy heart whenever I thought of Jamie, which was often. You can get used to missing someone; the pain becomes part of your life, like emotional toothache. Sometimes it's acute and you have to take something to numb it (whisky is an old remedy), and at other times there's a little respite. You hope that, eventually, the periods of respite will last longer.

I started going to night classes on Intermediate Gaelic and took up aqua-aerobics. I recovered from that dreadful time when I had found a cup of tea, a sticky bun and a copy of *The Scotsman* the height of eroticism. When I walked past Phillips, I saw a chaise longue in the window and thought, 'What a nice piece of furniture!' I stood at the counter in Henderson's without my pupils dilating (and it's dark in Henderson's). I sat down at a neat little table for one and noticed that someone had left a copy of *The Scotsman*. It was folded open at the second-from-back page and I tried, tried, tried to resist the chess column. I buttoned up my cardigan and ate my oatbran biscuit. But, furtively, my eyes strayed to the moves, and before I knew it I was playing out the whole game in my head, feeling exhilarated when Black threw down a triumphant little gauntlet of a move. White picked it up. Bit of a tussle. Black won.

Why am I so heavily defeated? I thought sadly and turned to the business pages.

BIO-CAL CRISIS.

The organic oats stuck in my throat.

Scot Burger today moved quickly to disassociate themselves from Bio-Caledonian plc following revelations by investigative journalist Gordon Covert that the laboratory mice fed on Braveheart Potatoes suffered from acute nausea.

A spokesman for Bio-Caledonian was quoted as saying that the mice had been made to consume enormous quantities of chips before any ill-effects were observed. No one had foreseen that these extreme experimental conditions would actually be replicated by members of the chip-eating public.

Dr Helen Budleigh, Chief Scientist at Bio-Caledonian, today attempted to reassure consumers by saying it was perfectly safe to carry on eating Braveheart Potatoes.

I ran out of Henderson's and into the newsagent's. Headlines in the *Scottish Sun*: SPEW WHAT A SHOCKER.

Blonde, curvaceous super-scientist Dr Helen Budleigh, 24, has denied creating a Frankenstein monster chip. Her former lover, eco-warrior travel writer Gordon Covert, 26, says, 'People have a right to know the truth!' Mr Covert refuses to confirm or deny that he cavorted naked in a Banffshire tattie field in order to pursue his investigations of the nubile Dr Helen.

And so it went on.

Helen was upset by the public reaction to what she termed 'nothing but a bit of indigestion' and very upset at Gordon's betrayal of her confidence. Three days later, *The Scotsman* reported: 'Cataclysmic deflation in Bio-Cal share price'. The company was soon declared bankrupt.

Helen told me that the whole Bio-Cal crisis was unnerving her more than she cared to admit. It wasn't simply a matter of the potato-nausea issue, nor the question of professional credibility, nor even the embarrassment of Gordon's revelations about their relationship. Just before the story broke, Catherine had retreated to her study saying she had a very big job on and didn't want to be disturbed. That was a week ago, and since then she had left her study only for minutes at a time to go to the kitchen or the bathroom. All she said to Helen was: 'Don't speak to me. You'll break my concentration.' We both knew that Catherine would be sitting at her desk, two computers humming busily, surrounded by what she called 'state-of-the-art science' and 'elegant equations'. Helen had dared to enquire what she might be working on and had got the impatient reply: 'You wouldn't understand.'

'Have you heard from Jamie?' I asked Helen.

'Not for a bit.'

'Has he lost a lot of money? He must have done.'

'He didn't have that much control of the situation,' was Helen's careful reply. 'Things escalated faster than he thought they would. Catherine will probably be able to tell you more when she finally shuts down her computers.'

Next morning, Catherine arrived at my flat clutching a laptop and looking dazed with exhaustion. The linen trouser suit was creased and the smooth, bobbed hair was now a curly chaos. 'I haven't slept,' she said, huskily. 'Not since this Bio-Cal thing happened.' I prised the laptop from her hand and made her sit down. 'I'd rather lie down,' she said, looking at the bed.

'Have you heard from Jamie?' I asked.

'Robert's with him. They've gone up north somewhere. He's sold his house in Regent Row. Liquidating his assets. He was out to lunch when the story broke. Lost a fortune, as far as I can tell.' She lay down and pulled the bedcovers up. 'You would not believe what I've been through this week. He owes me such a favour! He's not as clever as Robert, you know.' Catherine let out a deep, slow breath and shut her eyes.

'How is he? Is he . . .?' But she was asleep.

She slept for ten hours – right through the day – and I crept about the place, worrying about Jamie and about Catherine herself. When she woke up, she announced she didn't feel like going home. Instead, she decided to catch up on the workaholic's workload by doing a night shift. She had a lucrative contract with a French insurance company who were venturing into on-line banking. I said I'd stay up too – mainly because I wanted to try and find out more about Jamie.

'Was he upset about having to sell his house?' I asked.

'Not as much as you might think. He said it was only bricks and mortar – that kind of attitude. Most of the contents have gone for auction, but he's moved a few things into the mews house – that's where he's staying all the time now. How's your work coming on, Rose?'

Mungo Mackenzie had sent me a huge batch of words to define. 'Very well. I love it. I'm doing what I always wanted to do.'

'Good,' she smiled.

'What things did Jamie take with him when he moved?'

'Why don't you drop by one day and find out?'

'He wouldn't want to see me.'

'Don't be so sure.'

'I couldn't bear it, Catherine.' I looked down at my notes and she let the subject drop.

By six a.m. my sister had worn herself out with excitement at the inadequate security precautions she had discovered at Crédit

Follie. 'I really want to fit this project into next week's schedule.' She opened her diary pages.

'You won't have time.'

'Rose, you're so limited. In a curved universe, time is not a linear entity. We're talking about the fourth dimension here, and all sorts of things are possible. Time will bend over backwards for me.'

During the next few weeks, I continued to read about the bankruptcy of Bio-Caledonian. Helen had recovered well from the disaster and was taking a greater interest in the work of her new employers at the Soil Association, but I was increasingly worried about Jamie. I knew he had hired a very expensive lawyer from Wransack & Warbuck to advise him during the investigation.

It was reported by the Bio-Caledonian receptionist that Dr Helen Budleigh had received a peculiar message on her voice-mail before the share price began to fall. The call took the form of a series of taps and a Morse Code expert translated the message SELL, SELL, SELL, but Helen told the investigators that she thought the noise was merely digital interference.

The Investment Management Regulatory Organisation then discovered that Helen Budleigh's five per cent share-holding had been bought by an anonymous private client, and what was more, this anonymous private client already owned fifty per cent of the company. The client was found to be Patatas Serento, operating from Madrid. Serento had sold the shares on again (at a profit) to the Free Havana Hamburger Company – which in turn was revealed to be the trading name for Scot Burger's new chain of restaurants in Florida. It was Scot Burger who was left with a loss of several million dollars.

IMRO called in Cybersecurity to investigate the matter further and Cybersecurity, for the first time in their corporate history, drew a blank. They declared that the encryption system used for all the international banking transactions had mutated into a data-destroying virus which had wiped out the whole audit trail, down to the last genetically modified silicone chip. This discovery caused a sensation in the world of cryptography, especially when Cybersecurity claimed the right to patent it. And as for the accusations of insider dealing – no one was able to prove a thing.

In financial circles, the gossip was that Jamie considered himself lucky to escape with dismissal and ten penalty points on his dealer's licence. The prospect of a golden handshake never arose.

Chapter 25

The mews house was up for sale.

I read the description on the display board in the Edinburgh Solicitors' Property Centre: 'This charming mews property is quietly located in a most sought-after district of Edinburgh. While enjoying a tranquil setting, the house is only a stone's throw from the bustle of Princes Street.'

Open viewing was seven till nine o'clock on Thursday evening.

The cobbled lane was just as I remembered it and at the far end was a 'For Sale' sign flagging up the doorway. As I got nearer, a couple left. 'We could split it into two flats,' the man said, 'and rent them both out . . .'

I rang the doorbell and walked in, along the flagstoned hall and up the stairs. The bedroom door stood open and I heard voices. A man and woman talked in a loud whisper about another place they had seen that afternoon. 'I liked the last one better,' he said.

'But I like this furniture,' said the woman.

'I don't think it's for sale.'

'Can't we put in an offer anyway?'

'I don't think we should bother. I preferred the flat in Dublin Street.'

'I didn't. If we leave here now we've just got time to make it across to Marchmont to look at Sylvan Place.'

It's odd finding strangers in your bedroom. I went back along the hall and downstairs again to the kitchen.

'I like the big, shiny fridge,' another woman said.

'It's included in the sale,' said Jamie's voice, listlessly. He was sitting on the deep windowsill, arms folded. Seeing him again was overwhelming. He turned to look at me. 'Come to view?' he asked.

'What about the dishwasher?' asked the woman.

'That, too.'

'Included in the price?'

'Yes.'

'Can I buy the espresso machine?'

'Okay, why not?'

'But the fridge is included. Good.' The woman wrote something down on her schedule and left.

I walked towards him. 'Of all the places I've lived,' I told him, 'this one means the most to me.'

'Catherine said you've got a flat in Stockbridge.'

'Yes, you'd like it – it's characterful.' I held back from saying: 'Please come back with me now.'

'She says it's a freezing garret.'

'Not with the fire on. I love it, it's romantic – like *La Bohème*.'

The smile I knew returned and he laughed. He put his arm out towards me and for a moment I thought he was going to touch me, but he didn't. He just picked up a schedule from the pile on the piano. 'Want one?' he asked. 'You can read about the luxury bathroom and the residents' parking.'

'Is this where you've been staying since you sold your house?'

'Yes, but I'm selling this too, now.'

'Is that because you need the money?'

'It's not that, Rose. I just can't stand the nostalgia.' He looked out of the window. 'Maybe it won't bother you, though.'

'My flat's on a very short lease. I'm looking for somewhere more permanent. Jamie, where will you go?'

'I haven't decided yet.'

'But are you leaving for good?'

'Why should I stay?'

I reached out and touched his hand.

The fridge admirer returned. 'When is the closing date for bids?' she asked.

'Saturday lunchtime.'

'Can I ask you a couple of questions?'

'Yes, I'll be with you in a minute.'

She stood and waited. 'I'm sorry, but I have a train to catch and . . .'

I turned to Jamie. 'I'd better go now.'

He looked at me for a full three seconds and I read his eyes.

I went to Blether's WS on Atholl Crescent and explained that I wanted to make an offer on a house. I had it all worked out. I had done my sums. Mrs Blether wasn't so sure. 'I don't think the vendor will part with his house for that price!'

'I'd like him to stay.'

'Are you saying you want to buy the property with the vendor in residence?'

'Yes.'

'You want to bid half the value of the property? This is very irregular. I don't think the vendor's solicitors would contemplate such an offer. On the contrary, I'm sure they would advise him against it.'

After a prolonged discussion on the inadvisability of my offer, Mrs Blether agreed to submit it to Wransack & Warbuck for their client's consideration.

The deadline was midday on 13th March. I had done every-thing necessary – apart from talk to Jamie. It was now ten to twelve and I was very, very nervous. What would I do if he said no? What if he took it the wrong way and felt insulted? I told myself I should have talked to him about it, not made him an offer in this peculiar way. I could at least have written a letter and explained myself. And then I remembered Sprint-Cycle's silver bullet service. I phoned them up. There was just enough time.

Only thirty seconds after my call, the courier sounded the buzzer at my door. I scribbled the last frantic line – 'If the answer is no, please don't reply' – and then waited at the top floor landing while he ran up the stairs at a high-velocity three-at-a-time. 'Rose Budleigh?' he demanded. 'Letter to James Cameron by twelve o'clock?'

'Yes,' I said, impressed.

'Arrived at sender,' he said into his radio. 'Six minutes to target destination. Where's the letter?'

I ran back to the desk, but in all the confusion of paper and books and dictionaries I couldn't find the safe place where I'd put my letter.

'Five minutes, fifty seconds.'

'I can't find it! I can't find it!'

'Five minutes, forty seconds.' I found it, stuffed it in an envelope, wrote the name and address on the outside and thrust it into the courier's silver backpack. 'Sign this,' he commanded. I scrawled my name. 'Bullet loaded,' he called into his radio and ran for the stairs. 'Five minutes, twenty seconds to target.'

I had asked for Hand-to-Hand delivery. As soon as the letter had been signed for, Sprint-Cycle would telephone and let me know. Sure enough, I got a breathless phone call confirming that James Cameron had received my silver bullet at precisely 12:00 on 13th March.

The king is the only piece on the chess board that can never actually be captured. The game is over when capture is inevitable. I waited for his declaration.

Nothing. I lay down on the bed, clutching the pearl he had given me, and it seemed like a fat, round zero.

An hour passed.

I phoned Sprint-Cycle and checked. Yes, he had signed for it. He had even printed his name underneath. For a modest fee,

303

they could send someone to show me the Response Record.

'No, thank you.'

The customer service man was very good at his job. He immediately sensed the absence of customer delight in my voice and checked whether or not I had requested the Wait For A Reply option.

'No.'

It would only be another twenty-five pounds for a courier to return to Mr Cameron and request a reply. And I wouldn't have to pay for it straightaway, I could wait sixty days if I opened an Off-Peak Sprint-Cycle account. And if I signed up now I could get a free Walk & Talk delivery.

'No, thank you.'

'So you're not waiting for a response from Mr Cameron?'

'Not any more.'

I already had my answer. It was No.

This is the end of the endgame, I thought. I've lost.

I've lost.

Finality can be a hard thing and defeat can be shattering. You've played your best game and you've lost. 'I wasn't good enough,' I said, under my breath.

When you know you're beaten, you have to resign in good grace. I felt a sense of abandonment at the ending of my own love story. What makes an ending so difficult is that one questions the reality of it. It seemed so sudden. I couldn't help wondering if there might yet be something else. I knew Jamie would be familiar with that concept because he had studied Cosmology and Astrophysics at university, but my degree in English Literature had taught me to believe in the existence of a dénouement. And here it was. I tried to accept it. My overwrought brain could see that the game was finished, but my heart rebelled. I just couldn't believe that this tangled knot was

The End

So I went out, and walked for hours in a state of limbo. Eventually, I sat down, tired and hopeless, on a bench in Princes Street Gardens. I read the plaque on the bench and it told me that it was dedicated to the memory of someone 'Who Loved This City'. I might love the city, but for me Edinburgh had been a disaster. If I died now of a broken heart, my bench could say, 'In Memory of Rose Budleigh Who Failed in this City'. I got up and my whole body ached. Is this what a broken heart feels like? I wondered. It's a physical thing, like nausea and bruising.

I wanted to get as far away from Edinburgh as possible.

But what about my job? I thought, walking painfully towards Waverley Station. I couldn't resign from my job. Not when I had tried so hard to get it. Perhaps Mungo Mackenzie wouldn't mind where I lived so long as I did my research and got my work in on time. I could live anywhere. It didn't make any difference. I still had to learn to live with my loss and my guilt. I would try to take comfort in the good things I had, like my work and my books and the companionship of my sisters.

Maybe I would get a dog.

At Waverley Station, I checked the destinations board. The Penzance train was waiting at the platform. Penzance looked promising. I bought a ticket and got on board. A few minutes later, the guard blew his whistle and the train pulled out of the station. I looked out of the window and it wasn't long before I saw the curved façade of Carlton Terrace. Round the corner was the house where I had lived. We passed Salisbury Crags and Arthur's Seat – the places where we had walked together. I didn't mind going for walks there on my own, I told myself. I might even see him, by chance.

Soon we were speeding through East Lothian. Green fields, big blue-grey skies and long, low-lying houses with red pantile roofs. A few defeated, abandoned castles in ruins.

I've lost. I've lost. I kept repeating it under my breath to force myself to accept it. I've lost and I'm never going to play again. I couldn't bear to go through this again. I don't think I could survive it.

The train travelled on and I shut my eyes, feeling nothing but a terrible sadness. I thought of Alastair and my guilt. Alastair, who was now going out with a very nice translator he had met on a course on The Use of the Imperfect Subjunctive. Alastair, a good man, who said he now forgave me, adding: 'If I were you, Rose, I would put the past behind me.'

The train rushed through the Borders, towards England. Perhaps I should go back to Cambridge for a few days. I hadn't been there for eighteen months. It seemed like a world away. And for a whole year it felt as though Jamie had been my entire life. He had been in my waking thoughts and in all my dreams.

It was ridiculous to allow someone to become so important, so necessary. It was asking for trouble. But then, I reasoned, he had become necessary to my life because I had fallen in love with him.

I loved him very much indeed.

I love him.

The train slowed for Berwick-upon-Tweed and came to a stop. And something strange happened there. At Berwick Station I experienced some kind of magical phenomenon and it made me realise the ending was still being worked out.

I was at my window seat, watching people come and go. There were a few men in suits, carrying briefcases. A couple with camping gear climbed on board, a man with a bike got off. A young mother with a baby hugged a grandmother, an old man waved goodbye to a friend. They all came and went.

Still waiting was a man in his fifties with a strong, handsome face. He was wearing a dark overcoat and carrying a bunch of roses. He kept looking down the platform. At his feet was a dog, a spaniel, watching and waiting. I wondered who they were waiting for. Everyone had left the train or boarded it; the platform was empty except for them. The little dog sat down, disheartened. The man checked his watch. I wanted him to have his reunion; I wanted to see her with the flowers in her hands.

It was very quiet and still, as if time and sound had been suspended. Again the man looked down the platform and then he saw someone and a sudden smile came over his face – gladness and pleasure. The little dog leapt to its feet, barking with delight, and sped off, pulling the man along. He laughed and I recognised the laughter.

A woman was walking towards him. She wore a red mackintosh and slung over her shoulder was a bag full of books. Her face was animated with smiles. Good bone structure, I thought. The face has aged well, just like my mother's. The curly hair was shorter than mine, but I'd always said I'd not wear it long for ever. Around her neck was a beautiful silver necklace with one very large pearl.

They met, and when I saw their happiness at being together again I put my hands over my eyes because I was crying. I recognised them. *I knew who they were.*

I ran for the door of the train, pushed it open and jumped down on to the platform. I must find a telephone, I thought. I must speak to Jamie.

I rang and there was only the answerphone: 'It's me, Rose,' I said. 'I'm at Berwick Station but I'm coming back. The next train leaves in an hour and it's an inter-city and it takes fifty minutes to get to Waverley, so . . . um . . . what distance is it from Berwick to Edinburgh?' I hung up, tried again. 'It's Rose. Did you get my letter? I'll be in Edinburgh at whatever time that train gets in. Are you going to be there?'

There is no sight more joyful than seeing your beloved walking swiftly towards you, his face full of love, his arms open to embrace you. We stood there in stillness together while the noise of Waverley Station passed us by. 'When did you get my letter?' I asked, holding his hand tightly.

'What letter? I got something called *The Mutability of Definition: Truth and the Challenge of True Meaning*. It had to be you, Rose. Never use a courier. Has all that romantic fiction taught you nothing?'

We walked, hand in hand, up the steps and out on to Princes Street. 'I saw us meet at Berwick Station,' I told him. 'You were meeting me off the train and I was coming home. But it was you and me in twenty years' time.'

'I wasn't fat and bald, was I?'

'No, you looked very handsome, and you had brought me roses.'

'That was nice of me.'

'And you had a dog.'

'The spaniel was yours.'

I stood still. 'You saw it, too?'

'Dreamed it, maybe.'

It's serendipity, it's just coincidence.

Along Waterloo Place, past St Andrew's House. The view opened up of the cliffs in the sunset and I felt elated. 'Tell me how much you love me.'

'That'll take ages, Rose,' he said, indulgently.

At the end of the lane I could see our house. 'Then say you've loved me from the first moment you saw me.'

'I've loved you from the first moment I saw you. You say something.'

'What sort of something?' (He was usually more specific, like: 'Say something you don't mean' or 'Say something you'll regret'.)

'Something real.'

'Something real?'

We had come home. As we crossed the threshold I said something undeniably real, and once I'd started I couldn't stop. I rambled on about how much I loved him. And how desperately I had longed to be with him since our parting. So much regret! So much anguished, guilty regret. I kissed the bits of him that were easily accessible. 'The thing is . . .' I said, in tears, 'the thing is . . . if you love someone, it makes you vulnerable – you've had it, really. You can't win, you can only surrender, and all you can do is hope against hope that the person you love . . . that the person you love . . .'

'Loves you,' he said. 'And I do – I do love you. You know I do.'

And then the whole thing just slipped deliciously out of my conscious control – that sweet moment when you forget yourself. Some part of my mind was still working but it was the uncomplicated part that sends simple messages like 'breathe' and 'feel'. It was like knowing something off by heart – everything is in the memory and the fingertips, the notation discarded.

All my strategies ceased.

We ran up the stairs. I remember sweeping round the corner of the landing in a big arc spun from his hand, running into the bedroom, breathless and laughing.

And all those things we had to say to each other – he was right, it took ages. Days! Nights! Definitely more than three dots at the end of the line . . .

We wanted to be together, always. And yet, human beings are too frail for little immortalities like vows of everlasting love. Marriage vows are poetry – beautiful words to live up to in a prosaic world. You can't mortgage your soul, all you can really know is what you feel in your heart, and hope is the only honest promise you can make.

'Being human never stopped anyone hoping for a little immortality,' he said. 'I'll share with you a hopeful, frail, human promise.'

Aside from all the neediness I felt for him, I had good academic reasons for being in love. The word has an interesting etymology. Its meaning falls somewhere between wishing for something and believing in it. Its origins are in the word 'lief', which implies a willing choice, as in 'I'd lief as be with him . . .', and also in the word 'belief' – faith. Wanting something and believing in it. It's the only way to play it when you've met your match.

THE END.
REALLY, TRULY.

310

WHSmith

SAVE £2

Usual price £6.99
now £4.99 with voucher

A NICE GIRL LIKE ME

By Abigail Bosanko

Subject to availability

To the customer: Present this voucher at participating WHSmith High Street stores and redeem it for £2 off *A Nice Girl Like Me* by Abigail Bosanko. **Terms & conditions:** 1. This voucher entitles you to £2 off one paperback copy of *A Nice Girl Like Me*, from participating WHSmith High Street stores. (Offer is not valid in station, airport, hospital, workplace stores or any outlet centres). Subject to availability. While Stocks last. 2. Voucher valid from 16 September until 16 December 2004 inclusive. 3.Cannot be exchanged for any other merchandise. 4. Only one voucher per transaction. 5. May not be combined with any other offer. 6. Only original, unaltered vouchers will be accepted. WHSmith reserves the right to reject any voucher it deems, in its sole discretion, to have been forged, defaced or otherwise tampered with. 7. Cash redemption value 0.001p. Promoter: WH Smith Retail Limited, Greenbridge Road, Swindon, Wiltshire SN3 3RX. **To the Store:** Please scan voucher and product. Do not 'mint return'. Destroy voucher.

3074 2659